DANCING WITH DEMONS

Dancing
with Demons

A Mystery of Ancient Ireland

PETER TREMAYNE

MINOTAUR BOOKS

NEW YORK

This is a work of fiction. All of the characters, organizations, and events portrayed in
this novel are either products of the author's imagination or are used fictitiously.

www.minotaurbooks.com

The Library of Congress has catalogued the hardcover edition as follows:

Tremayne, Peter.
    Dancing with demons : a mystery of ancient Ireland / Peter Tremayne. — 1st
U.S. ed.
        p. cm.
    ISBN 978-0-312-37564-5
    1. Ireland—History—To 1172—Fiction. I. Title.
PR6070.R366D33 2008
823'.914—dc22

                                                                    2008025760

ISBN 978-0-312-58741-3 (trade paperback)

First published in Great Britain by Headline Publishing Group,
a division of Hachette Livre UK Ltd

First Minotaur Books Paperback Edition: November 2009

For those intrepid enthusiasts from ten countries
who gathered in Cashel, 8–10 September 2006,
to attend the first *Féile Fidelma: Sister Fidelma's World at Cashel*,
and to the organisers and citizens of Cashel
in appreciation and thanks.

AD669: Iar mbeith cúicc bliadhna ós Érinn h-i righe do Sechnussach mac Blaithmaic, do-cear la Dubh Duin, flaith Ceneoil Coibre. As for Sechnussach do-athadh an teistimen-si:

> *Ba srianach, ba h-eachlascach*
> *In teach h-i mbidh Sechnussach*
> *Ba h-imdha fuigheall for slaitt*
> *h-istaigh i mbidh mac Blathmaic*

Annála Ríoghachta Éireann

AD669: After Sechnussach, son of Blathmac, had been five years in sovereignty over Ireland, he was slain by Dubh Duin, chief of Cinél Cairpre. It was of Sechnussach that this testimony was given:

> Full of bridles and horsewhips
> Was the house in which dwelt Sechnussach.
> Many were the results of his tributes
> In the house in which dwelt the son of Blathmac.

Annals of the Kings of Ireland

pRINCIpaL ChARACTERS

Sister Fidelma of Cashel, a *dálaigh* or advocate of the law courts of seventh-century Ireland
Brother Eadulf of Seaxmund's Ham in the land of the South Folk, her companion

At Rath na Drinne

Ferloga, the innkeeper
Lassar, his wife

At Cashel

Colgú, King of Muman and brother of Fidelma
Brother Conchobhar, the apothecary
Caol, commander of the Nasc Niadh, bodyguards to the Kings of Muman
Gormán of the Nasc Niadh

At Tara

Cenn Faelad, the new High King
Barrán, Chief Brehon
Sedna, deputy Chief Brehon
Abbot Colmán, spiritual adviser and *rechtaire* or chief steward to the High King
Brother Rogallach, *bollscari* or factotum to the High King
Gormflaith, widow of the High King Sechnussach
Muirgel, eldest daughter of Sechnussach and Gormflaith

Irél, commander of the Fianna, bodyguards to the High King
Erc the Speckled, a warrior of the Fianna
Cuan, a warrior of the Fianna
Lugna, a warrior of the Fianna

Mer the Demented
Iceadh the Healer, physician to the High King

Brónach, chief female servant
Báine, a maid
Cnucha, a maid
Torpach, a cook
Maoláin, his assistant
Duirnín, a servant

Assíd, a slave
Verbas of Peqini, his master and a merchant

Bishop Luachan of Delbna Mór
Brother Céin, his steward
Brother Diomasach, a scribe
Brother Manchán of Baile Fobhair
Ardgal, chief of the Cinél Cairpre
Beorhtric, a Saxon warrior

ḣISTORICaL NOTE

The events in this story commence at the beginning of the winter of AD669, which places it a year after the events told in the story *A Prayer for the Damned*. I have deliberately made the choice to follow the dating of Sechnussach's assassination as given by the *Annála Tighernach* and *Annála Ríoghachta Éireann* although I am aware that some other annals, such as the *Annála Ulaidh* and the *Chronicum Scotorum* place the event much later, at the beginning of the winter of AD671. Some scholars argue for the first date while others for the second.

The *Ban Shenchus* (History of Women), which was compiled by Gilla Mo Dutu Ua Casaide, in Daimh Inis (modern Devenish, Co Fermanagh) in AD1147, gives, in different references, both AD669 and AD670 as the dates of the High King's murder. The *Ban Shenchus* mentions Sechnussach's three daughters and says that the youngest, Bé Bhail, died seventy years after this event, which would place her at a very young age at the time.

All chroniclers agree that the High King Sechnussach was murdered by the chieftain of the Cenél Cairpre, whose clan lands are placed in modern northern Co Sligo and north-east Co Leitrim. Moreover, the *Annála Tighernach* states that Sechnussach was killed by having his throat cut (*jugulatio*). So the murder of the High King in this story is not so much a 'whodunit' as a 'whydunit' – or is it?

With the majority of place-names, as in previous stories in this series, I have sought to eliminate the anachronistic. Hence I refer to Muman instead of Munster – the *ster* or *stadr* being a Viking suffix (*stadr* meaning 'place'). However, I have decided, for the sake of more easy identification, to break the rule by using the Anglicisation of Tara, as I have also used the Anglicisation of Cashel instead of *Caiseal Mumhan*. Tara is the form more readily known throughout the world as the seat of the High Kings of Ireland. The name is an Anglicised form of the genitive *Teamhrach*, from Téa who was wife to Eremon, son of Mile Easpain or Milesius, who led the Gaels to Ireland. However, there is still some debate as to the meaning and origin of the name.

PROLOGUE

Erc the Speckled, the guard at the entrance of Ráth na Ríogh, the royal enclosure of the great Palace of Tara, knew the man whom he had challenged in the darkness. He knew him and therefore he let him pass inside without any suspicion; pass freely into the fortified sanctuary of the High Kings of Éireann. Erc, while an imperturbable warrior in a crisis, was also unimaginative. It did not occur to him that even people who were known to the palace guards should be asked what had brought them hither when they sought to gain entrance to the royal enclosure in the early hours of the morning. That he recognised the man, who presented himself in the light of the burning torches that lit the main portals to the enclosure, was enough for Erc. He allowed him entrance without further thought and question as to his purpose. After all, this chieftain had often been admitted to the High King's presence during daylight hours. At least, that's what he would eventually tell the examining Brehon – but by then it was too late.

In his defence, one could argue that there was good reason to believe all was secure. It was well-known that no enemy could penetrate the large complex that made up the buildings of Tara. It was too large and well-defended, both in the number of guards and in the physical structure, to allow any serious threat. The hills over which the royal centre spread had been built upon for countless centuries, dominating the luscious valley whose great river was called after the ancient goddess, Bóinn. It was said that the palace complex itself had been called after Téa, the wife of Eremon who, with his brother Eber, had led the children of the Gael into this land and settled it at the dawn of time. But Erc the Speckled was not interested in ancient legends. He knew only that the royal enclosure was impossible for any enemy to attack and he added complacency to the folly of being unimaginative.

The celebrated High King, Cormac Mac Art, three centuries before, had ordered the construction of the interior royal enclosure with its large rectangular house still called *Tech Cormaic*, Cormac's House, in which the High Kings dwelled. It was opposite the *Forradh* or Royal Seat, to its east, from where the High Kings dispensed the duties of governing the five kingdoms. Even the colossal *Tech Miodhchuarta*, the banqueting hall, owed its existence to Cormac. And he had built fortifications to protect this inner sanctum of the kings. High walls and ditches, great oval earthworks, protected the buildings, with guards at all the entrances.

Tara was impregnable and so Erc the Speckled was not one whit concerned when the noble, whom he recognised, came walking to the gate that he guarded, in the darkness before dawn. He merely raised his spear in salute and went down the wooden stairway to the *immdorus*, the small door set in the now closed and bolted great gate of the fortress, released the lock and swung it open. He then motioned the man to the royal enclosure. The man did so with a smile and brief nod to Erc.

Once beyond the gate, and across the bridge over the defensive ditch, in which three tall men could stand on each other's shoulders from its bottom to its top, the man's attitude seemed to tense. He began to hurry with long loping strides, his head bent forward, his shoulders hunched, keeping to the semi-gloom beyond the pathways. He made his way between the great banqueting hall, towering up in the darkness to his right, and the fortified building known as the Ráth of Synods, where the High Kings summoned their assemblies, to his left. He turned left at the end and moved quickly towards the burial mound, which had been old even before the coming of the children of the Gael to the land. Then he moved past the *Forradh* and turned to face the great building of *Tech Cormaic*, the residence of the High King.

He halted in the shadow of some trees and bushes, designed to give privacy to the building, and stood surveying it for a moment. It was mainly in darkness except for two burning brand torches, stuck out in their iron braziers, which protruded on each side of the central dark oak doors, causing a faint light and countless dancing shadows to obscure the portal.

A movement caught his eye and he drew back further into the shadows, his hand sliding to the hilt of his sword, eyes narrowing as if the action would help him see more clearly in the darkness.

A warrior with drawn sword, whose blade rested easily against his shoulder, moved with an almost lazy gait around the edge of the building and paused before the oak doors. A moment later, a second warrior joined him.

One spoke in a low voice, but on such a still night as this, the watcher could clearly make out what he said.

'The night passes slowly, Cuan, my friend.'

'Too slowly,' the other replied with a yawn. 'How long until dawn, Lugna?'

His companion glanced at the sky. It was almost cloudless but the clouds that were fleeting in the high winds were obscuring the pale gibbous moon. The man quickly assessed the position of the stars.

'A while yet.'

'Perhaps a small libation will keep the early-morning chill at bay until the sun rises? There is a jug in the kitchens.'

The second man seemed to hesitate. 'It is wrong to leave the doors unguarded. What if Irél comes to inspect the guard?'

Cuan chuckled. 'Our good commander has retired to his chamber. He will not come to inspect the guard until it is time to change it at dawn. Come, a drop of *corma* will keep out the night chill.'

The warrior addressed as Lugna made as if to protest. Then, in a tone of resignation, he said: 'I cannot argue. Lead the way.'

The two guards moved off along the side of the High King's house into the darkness towards the *ircha*, or kitchen, which was situated at the back of the building and entered by a separate door.

In the shadows, the waiting man smiled in satisfaction, glanced swiftly around and then, assuring himself that there was no one else in the vicinity, crossed quickly to the heavy doors. His hand did not tremble as he turned the iron handle. One of the double doors opened with ease and he passed into the hallway of the large building. With the two guards in the kitchen, he knew that there were no other guards inside the royal house. He eased the door quietly shut behind him. A few spluttering oil lamps caused shadows to dance over the wood-panelled walls of red yew. Thus far, thus good, he thought.

If his information was correct, the High King slept alone that night. His wife had gone, in the company of her daughters, to Finnian's abbey at Cluain Ioraird to offer prayers for the repose of the soul of her mother, who had but recently succumbed to the Yellow Plague. In any case, the intruder also knew that the High King never slept with his wife, the lady

Gormflaith, these days. So now, unless the High King had invited someone else to his bed, he would be found alone.

The man knew his way to the High King's bedchamber. With a calm deliberation, he moved up the single flight of broad wooden stairs and into the deserted upper corridor, where he halted, head to one side, listening. All was quiet. Now he just had to hope that the others had played their part. A few seconds passed before he heard the slight creak of a door swinging gently open to his right. He pressed back against the panelled wall, as a shadow appeared. It was the dark figure of a woman. He had been expecting her.

No greeting was exchanged between them. Instead, the woman held out a hand and his own closed on the cold bronze *eochuir* or key.

'The lock is well-oiled,' the woman whispered. 'I saw to that.'

'And he is alone?'

'I am fairly certain of it,' came the soft reply. 'The Old One has been watching the steps leading to the privy door at the back and has seen no one go up since he retired for the night.'

'That is good. Return to your chamber and if I am successful I shall call you. You know what it is you must look for?'

The woman's voice was scornful. 'Of course. Have I not waited a lifetime for this? Are you prepared?'

'I know my part as you do your own. We must be away from here before daylight.'

'The Old One knows the way. She will guide us. We must not be caught. If anything happens, you are aware of what must be done?'

'I am,' he replied grimly.

She disappeared whence she had come without a further word.

He trod noiselessly to the dark oak door at the far end of the corridor. Then he stretched out to insert the key . . . and turned it slowly. The lock was indeed well-oiled, and made not the slightest sound. A turn of the handle, a slight push and the door opened a fraction. The man felt a second of relief. He listened: in the darkness beyond, he could hear nothing. Stepping stealthily into the gloom, he slipped the key into the purse that he wore at his belt and stood for a moment, back against the door, waiting for his eyes to adjust.

The room was lit by moonlight. The clouds seemed to have moved on, leaving the pale glow to permeate through the window and spread itself over the bed on which the recumbent figure lay.

The High King appeared to be asleep, stretched on his back.

A look of satisfaction formed on the face of the man. In one quick motion, he drew his knife, its blade sharp like a razor, and moved rapidly across to the side of the bed. Barely pausing, he plunged the knife down towards the High King's exposed throat. The severed jugular spurted a little blood as he moved the knife across the throat like a butcher slaughtering a lamb. It happened so fast that there was not even a movement of the features of his victim. The assassin doubted whether the sleeper even knew what had happened.

The killer stepped back, still holding the knife in his right hand, a thin smile of triumph on his lips.

He was just about to turn away when a high-pitched shriek of terror echoed through the chamber. His head jerked up. On the far side of the room, a door had opened and the figure of a young girl stood there. She was naked and held her hands to her cheeks in a stance of obvious shock and horror. She screamed again and ran out, slamming the door shut behind her.

For a second the assassin stood aghast. Should he pursue her, or turn for the door by which he had come? Almost immediately, he was aware of shouting and the sound of running feet. Her screams had aroused the servants and the guards. There would be no escape. He knew then what he had to do. There could be no surrender. He felt one moment of regret but there was a greater will than his which compelled him to obey his orders. Raising the hand with the dagger . . .

A few moments later, the door flew open and Lugna rushed in, his sword drawn. His companion, Cuan, followed, holding a lantern.

It was too late.

The assassin was slumped against the bed of the High King, blood spurting from his chest. He was still alive and but the light was dying in his eyes. Lugna bent down, restraining the urge to finish him off.

'Why?' he demanded sharply of the man.

The murderer stared at him with a dull gaze for a moment. Then the pale lips moved. A word was whispered which Lugna stretched forward to catch. There was a gasp and the assassin toppled sideways onto the floor, staining it with one last outpouring of blood.

Lugna rose to his feet, his face showing his disgust. He took the lantern from his companion and looked beyond the assassin's body to the figure on the bed to assure himself that the victim was beyond help.

Cuan glanced curiously down at the body on the floor. 'What did he say?'

Lugna shrugged. 'Something about blame. I think he meant that he was accepting the blame for the crime.'

His companion laughed shortly. 'That was stating the obvious.'

There was a continued shouting in the corridor and the noise of people running hither and thither, and some began crowding in. Lugna turned towards the door, telling them to stay back. As he did so, Cuan suddenly noticed a small bracelet by the side of the dead assassin; it was a chain from which silver coins hung. It looked valuable. He picked it up and turned to Lugna, but his comrade had not noticed for he was trying to prevent people entering. One or two of them held oil lamps in their hands. Someone was shouting for the High King's physician. Cuan's hand closed over the trinket.

'Too late for that. The High King is dead,' Lugna informed those at the door, as he sheathed his sword. 'And the assassin is dead also, but not by my hand.'

Then Irél, the commander of the Fianna, the High King's bodyguard, appeared, pushing through the alarmed servants.

Lugna stiffened as his superior's gaze swept the scene with an aghast expression. The man's eyes alighted on the body of the assassin, slumped on the floor by the bed, and he uttered an exclamation of surprise.

'It is Dubh Duin, chief of the Cinél Cairpre!'

Lugna had not recognised the man but now he turned with curiosity, holding the lantern over the dead features. By its flickering light he saw that the assassin had been correctly identified, and he whistled softly in disbelief.

'He was of the Uí Néill, of the same family as the High King,' Lugna said nervously, turning to Irél. 'Can this have been some family blood feud? Or does it signal insurrection?'

The commander of the Fianna was noncommittal but he was clearly worried by the same thoughts.

'We must send for Abbot Colmán, the chief steward, also the High King's brother, Cenn Faelad. He is heir apparent and will now succeed as lawful King. He must be informed. Meanwhile, I shall order the Fianna to stand to arms until we know what this means.'

Lugna glanced once more at the still form lying on the bed.

Sechnussach, son of Blathmac of Síl nÁedo Sláine, direct descent of the immortal Niall of the Nine Hostages, High King of the five kingdoms of Éireann, was dead. If this were a blood feud, then the five kingdoms would soon be threatened with civil war.

chapter one

Ferloga had been an innkeeper most of his adult life and was in the habit of boasting that he had seen all manner of guests – rich and poor, the arrogant and the humble. He had had dealings with kings and chieftains, religious of all descriptions, rich merchants, travelling players, farmers passing on their way to market and even beggars desperate for shelter. Ferloga's proud claim was that no guest had ever tried to cheat him of his fee, for there were few of them that he was unable to judge; after a glance, he could tell what calling in life they followed and whether they were trustworthy or not. But, as the elderly innkeeper sat talking with his wife while she finished cleaning the utensils after the morning meal, he freely confessed to confusion. The guest who had arrived not long after nightfall on the previous evening had been an utter mystery to him.

A tall, thin man, almost skeletal, the pale parchment-like skin had stretched tightly over his bony features. That he was elderly was indisputable, but whether sixty or eighty years of age was impossible to discern. He had curious eyes, the left one made sinister by the white film of a cataract. His unkempt white hair seemed to tumble in all directions, thick and curly, ending around his shoulders. His neck reminded Ferloga of a chicken's scrawny folds with a prominent bobbing Adam's apple. A dark grey woollen cloak, which had probably once been white, covered the man from neck to ankles. He carried a long wooden staff with curious carving on it, and a leather satchel was slung from his shoulder.

At first Ferloga had thought that he was a wandering religious, for he certainly looked like one of the hermits that one infrequently encountered on the road, and it was clear that he had arrived on foot. However, once he loosened his cloak, the stranger displayed none of the usual symbols of the New Faith but wore a curious necklet of gold and semi-precious stones which, Ferloga knew, no religious would ever wear.

The conversation had been unexpectedly short. Ferloga was used to some sociability from his guests but this elderly traveller merely demanded a bed. He even declined a traditional mug of *corma* to protect against the chill of the night. When Ferloga asked whither he had come, the man replied: 'A long journey from the north,' and nothing more. Ferloga took the view that the man was exhausted from his travels and, indeed, he noticed that the newcomer was swaying slightly and the dark skin under his eyes was a trifle puffy. So the innkeeper did not press the late arrival further but conducted him to a small room above the stairs, and withdrew.

Now, in the light of dawn, Ferloga was still wondering about his mysterious guest.

His plump wife sniffed in irritation as she gave the cauldron of porridge, still warming over the fire, a stir to stop it sticking.

'Rather than sit there trying to make guesses, why don't you go and rouse the man. It's long past sun up. All the other guests have risen, broken their fasts and continued on their way. I do not plan to stay here all day making sure the porridge does not burn. I need to go berry picking.'

Ferloga sighed and slowly rose from his comfortable seat by the side of the fire. Lassar, was right, of course. The business of the inn could not wait for ever and it was unusual for guests to delay so long in the morning.

Fidelma of Cashel halted her horse on a rise of the road, which ran from Cluain Meala, the Field of Honey, the settlement on the banks of the broad River Siúr, where she had spent the night, north to her brother's fortress. She had spent a week away from Cashel in attendance at Lios Mhór, the great abbey and settlement south beyond the mountain range of Mhaoldomhnaigh. Although she had slept well the previous night, Fidelma felt exhausted after a week's hard work. She was a *dálaigh*, or advocate, of the law courts of the five kingdoms of Éireann, proficient to the degree of *anruth*, the second highest qualification in the land. Her rank therefore allowed her not only to plead cases before judges but, when nominated, to hear and adjudicate in her own court on a range of applications that did not require the presence of a judge of higher rank. It was a task that Brehon Baithen, the senior judge of the kingdom of Muman, often requested her to perform. It was also a task that she liked least.

She frequently found it tiring to sit in a stifling court and listen to the complaints and arguments of those who appeared before her. Often it was a waste of time and the plaintiffs should have been advised that their claims, more often than not, were born from pettiness and malice and without foundation in law. But it was her task and duty to sit patiently and decide whether there was a case to be answered and whether it should be brought before a more senior Brehon. And, after a week in the law courts at Lios Mhór, she felt drained and irritable and was delighted when she could finally mount her horse and set off across the mountains back towards her brother's royal fortress at Cashel.

Turning in her saddle, she watched her companion trotting up towards her. The youthful warrior who joined her was Caol, the commander of her brother's guard. He had been designated to act as her escort on the trip.

Fidelma smiled as he reined in his mount beside her and gestured with an outstretched arm. 'That's Ráth na Drínne ahead. I could do with refreshment at Ferloga's inn before we continue on to Cashel.'

Caol inclined his head briefly. 'As it pleases you, lady.' Those who knew Fidelma as sister to Colgú, King of Muman, always used the respectful form of address rather than her ecclesiastical one of Sister. Caol added: 'We did leave Cluain Meala without breaking our fast and I could do with something to fill the emptiness in my stomach.'

There was a slight note of rebuke in his voice as he reminded Fidelma of her eagerness to be off even before daylight that morning. However, Caol knew why Fidelma was anxious to return to Cashel. She had been a week away from her little son, Alchú, and Caol appreciated her anxiety as a mother. He knew that she must be feeling an additional anxiety because her husband Eadulf, the Saxon, had left Cashel over a week before on an embassy to the abbey at Ros Ailithir on behalf of Ségdae, Abbot of Imleach and chief bishop of Muman. How long he would be away on his embassy, which involved matters of ecclesiastical importance, was anyone's guess. Perhaps he would be gone several weeks. That being so, Caol had tried not to complain about her general impatience and quickness of temper during this last week.

Fidelma was smiling almost apologetically at him, as if she read his thoughts.

'I know, I know,' she said softly. 'Had I not been in such a hurry to be on the road to Cashel this morning, we could have broken our fasts and had something warming to keep out the chill on the journey. But Ferloga's inn lies ahead of us and we can soon rectify the lack of nourishment caused by my impatience.'

She turned and nudged her horse forward towards the distant rise of Ráth na Drínne.

It was not long before they trotted into the yard before the inn, causing the chickens and geese to start an angry chorus at being disturbed. Before they began to dismount, the door of the inn swung open and Ferloga himself came hurrying out. The first thing that Fidelma noticed was his pale features and concerned expression.

'What ails you, Ferloga?' she asked, frowning down at him.

'Lady . . .' The innkeeper's expression seemed to brighten as he recognised her. 'Thank God that you have come.'

Fidelma raised an eyebrow in query as she dismounted and faced the elderly innkeeper.

'You appear distraught, Ferloga. What is the trouble?'

'One of my guests, lady,' replied the man. 'He was late to rise and so I went up to wake him. I have just found him in bed – dead.'

Caol had dismounted and was taking Fidelma's reins from her. 'Dead?' He suddenly looked interested. 'Murdered?'

Ferloga looked shocked. 'Murdered? I hadn't thought . . .'

'Put the horses in the stable, Caol,' Fidelma instructed before turning to the shocked innkeeper. 'Come, let us examine this body. Who is this guest, anyway?'

As he turned to lead the way back into the inn, Ferloga contrived to shrug. 'I've no idea, lady. He arrived late last night and told me nothing. He was elderly, that is all I know.'

As they entered the inn, Lassar came forward anxiously. 'Ah, it is good that you are here, lady. This could be bad for us if the kin of the guest claim we have been neglectful in our duties towards him and somehow contributed to his death.'

Fidelma knew exactly why the elderly couple were concerned. The laws for innkeepers in the *Bretha Nemed Toisech* were very precise about their responsibilities. A guest, by virtue of the fact, was given legal protection, and anyone killed or injured while under that protection was counted to have been a victim of the crime of *díguin*, the violation of such protection. The responsibility was down to the *fer tige oíget* or the guest-house owner, whether it was a public hostel or a private inn. If responsible, Ferloga might lose his inn and be fined a heavy sum.

Fidelma gave the old woman a smile of reassurance. 'Where is the body?' she asked Ferloga.

He turned to ascend the dark wooden stairs that led to the upper floor. 'This way,' he said.

The body lay on its back in the bed. Ferloga had already opened the shutters to allow light to flood into the room. Fidelma wished that Eadulf was with her. Having studied medical matters for a period in Tuam Brecain, the renowned Irish medical college, his knowledge would have been invaluable. She bent down and allowed her eye to traverse the body of the old man who lay there. There were two things she noticed immediately. The facial muscles seemed twisted into a grimace, as if a last moment of pain had been frozen on the features. That death could not have taken place much before dawn was clear because the flesh was not really cold. The second thing she noticed was that the pale lips were blue, unusually so. Disguising her distaste, she drew back the covers and quickly ascertained that there were no marks of physical violence on the body. Replacing the covers, she stood up, turning to face the anxious Ferloga.

At that moment, Caol came hurrying up the stairs into the room and cast a look at the corpse.

'Can I help, lady?' he asked.

Fidelma shook her head. 'Take a closer look and see if you agree with me. I believe the old man suffered a fit.' She used the word *taem* to indicate the condition.

Caol glanced down, nodding. 'Blue and twisted lips and a convulsion of the muscles. I have observed the like before, lady, on the battlefield. Twice now I have seen men work themselves up into such a rage that, suddenly, they clutch at their chests and their faces become contorted and they fall into a paroxysm. Many have died from it.'

Fidelma agreed. 'There seems no barrier to the condition, old age nor youth. I have even heard that some can survive the fit, and have described it as a terrible, debilitating pain here in the centre of the chest. No, have no fear, Ferloga, yours is not the responsibility for this death.'

There was a deep sigh of relief from the doorway. Lassar had followed Caol up the stairs and stood watching them.

'I'll go below and prepare some refreshment for you, lady,' she said.

'If you have fresh bread and honey, it will more than satisfy me,' Caol added quickly as the old woman turned away.

Fidelma was gazing quizzically down at the corpse again. 'Who was he?' she asked.

Ferloga shrugged. 'I had little chance to find out. He arrived after dark, only said that he was from the north, which was not a matter of surprise for I could hear the northern accents in his speech. He answered no questions, asked only one of his own, ate nothing, drank less and demanded to be shown to his bed.'

Fidelma looked keenly at the innkeeper. 'Asked only one question? What was that?'

'He asked what road he should take this morning to find Cnánmchailli.'

Fidelma shook her head thoughtfully. 'The place beyond Ara's well? But there is nothing there, only an ancient pillar stone.'

'Just what I said,' agreed Ferloga. 'But he wanted to know the road, so I told him.'

'Did you form any opinion of the man? You have a reputation for knowing your guests even when you spend only a few moments with them.'

Ferloga grimaced wryly. 'I was saying only this morning to Lassar that I am perplexed. At first, I thought he was a religious until I examined his clothing and ornaments more closely. Alas, this man puzzles me.'

'And he came here on foot?' asked Caol. When Fidelma shot him a glance of surprise, Caol added, by way of explanation: 'When I dealt with our horses just now, I saw no other horse in the stable that would belong to a guest.'

'You are right,' Ferloga said. 'This man arrived on foot with only that strange staff to help him on his travels.'

Fidelma moved to the ornately carved staff that had been propped in a corner of the room. Taking it in her hands she gazed curiously at the dark oak wood which was mounted and tipped with bronze, both as a spiked ferrule and as an ornate headed piece. In fact, at the top part of the staff, the piece of bronze was shaped as a head wearing a torc; a male head with a long, flowing moustache and some semi-precious glinting red stones for the eyes. From ear to ear was a crescent-shaped head-dress studded with little triskel-style solar symbols.

'It's quite beautiful,' muttered Caol, gazing over her shoulder.

'It's also quite old,' said Ferloga.

'It's certainly very ancient,' agreed Fidelma. 'I seem to have seen those symbols before, but I can't quite recall where . . .'

'There are curious symbols and animals carved all over the staff,' observed Caol, pointing. 'It must be very valuable.'

'What else did he carry that might identify him?' demanded Fidelma, turning to Ferloga.

The innkeeper gestured at a leather satchel, which the man had been carrying the night before. There was also the richly inscribed gorget, which he had worn around his neck and which was now placed on the table by the side of the bed. The old man had obviously removed it from his neck before reposing himself for sleep.

'Apart from his robe and clothing, there is only the satchel and this ornament.'

The satchel revealed no more than a change of clothing, an extra pair of sandals and a knife, and such toilet items as anyone might carry. However, if the staff had been a fascinating object of art then the gorget was even more so. The necklet was made of intricately beaten gold, decorated with all manner of ancient symbols that also seemed disturbingly familiar to Fidelma – but which she could not place at all. She was about to remark on it when Caol gave a grunt of surprise.

She turned to see him removing a small leather bag from under the pillow on which the old man's head lay. He held it up and the bag clinked as if it contained metal. He handed it to Fidelma.

'I think we'll find that this strange old man was rich,' he said.

Fidelma opened the string that tied the leather pouch together. Indeed, it was full of coins, mainly of gold and silver but with a few bronze coins. She glanced at several of them.

'They are mainly old coins of Gaul and Britain, ones the Britons struck before the coming of the Romans. That's curious. I can't see any Roman coins among them either and they are the easiest to come by these days.'

'That may mean the old man intended to travel in Gaul or Brittany?' suggested Caol.

Fidelma returned his smile but shook her head. 'It only means that he was in possession of coins from those countries, but they are centuries old. If someone was going to travel, why would they not be in possession of more modern coins?'

Caol looked a little crestfallen. 'You are right, lady. But the old man must have been some sort of merchant, to have these foreign coins and so many. Only merchants are so rich.'

'I doubt that he was a merchant.' It was Ferloga who uttered the thought.

Fidelma turned to give him a quizzical look. The innkeeper was looking worried.

'Not everyone has converted to the New Faith, lady. You know that already. Some keep to the old ways.'

She suddenly realised what the innkeeper was implying. Picking up the old man's gorget, she examined it carefully and let out a slow breath as she agreed with Ferloga's unspoken thought.

Caol was standing frowning. 'I don't understand,' he said.

'Ferloga is saying that he thinks this old man might have been a Druid priest,' Fidelma explained.

Caol's eyebrows shot up. 'But the old religion has died out. The Druids are no more.'

'I have had several encounters with those who cling to the old religion,' Fidelma said, a little grimly. 'It was only a short time ago that Eadulf and I were sent to the valley of Gleann Geis when Laisre decided that his people should convert from the old ways to the New Faith.'

'Gleann Geis is way over to the west,' Caol dismissed airily. 'They are always slow to move with the times.'

Fidelma smiled at the young warrior's arrogance. 'Or perhaps they move in a different direction?' she observed quietly. 'You are wrong, Caol – there are many who still move along the old paths and venerate the old gods and goddesses of this land. Many, even of the New Faith, respect and do reverence to the Druids or see them as they were – as great teachers. Did not Colmcille, the dove of the Church, write in one of his poems that Christ, the son of the One God, was his Druid?'

Caol shrugged indifferently. 'So you are saying that the old man,' he jerked his head towards the corpse, 'might have been a Druid?'

'It would fit in with the way I initially mistook him for a religious,' interrupted Ferloga, 'and yet he is certainly not of the Christian Faith. Look at the symbols he carries. They are found among the carvings on the stones where I have heard that people gathered to worship in the old days. And then there was him asking the way to Cnánmchailli, the place of the ancient pillar stone.'

'You may well be right, Ferloga,' Fidelma said. 'However, there is little we can do now to identify him, unless someone comes in search of him.'

'I do not know what to do, lady,' muttered the innkeeper. 'No one has ever died in my inn.'

Fidelma thought for a moment or two. 'We will take his belongings with us to Cashel. Brother Conchobhar is very learned in many of these old customs and symbols. He might be able to tell us more about what they signify and perhaps we can trace where this man came from.'

'But the body?' Ferloga still looked unhappy. 'What am I to do with it?'

'There is a small chapel beyond the next hill,' Caol pointed out. 'Two brothers of the Faith look after it and there is a burial ground nearby. Send someone to bring them hither to take away the body and give it a decent burial. Whatever the man's beliefs, he deserves that much.'

The old innkeeper's face grew longer but Fidelma, with a smile, reached in her purse and handed a few coins to Ferloga. She knew what he had been thinking.

'Tell them it is my wish that they give the deceased a proper burial,' she said. 'And you will find there is enough there that you will not be wanting for your fee for his night's repose.'

'But I can't accept that,' protested the innkeeper, half-heartedly.

'I am taking the old man's purse,' Fidelma cut off his protests, 'because I believe that the coins may be a means of discovering more about him. I would not have you suffering any loss for this misfortune – and if anyone comes by making enquiries for him, tell them to come to Cashel.'

Ferloga's hand closed over the coins. 'A blessing on you, lady.' He hesitated and then added nervously, 'Do you think anyone *will* come looking for him?'

'Why so uneasy?' asked Fidelma.

Ferloga compressed his lower lip with his top one for a moment. 'If he is a man of the old religion, his comrades might also be of that belief and custom. We are good Christians here, lady. My grandfather was baptised in the Siúr by the Blessed Ailbe himself.'

Fidelma smiled. 'There is nothing to worry about, Ferloga.'

'But if this man were a pagan and knew the ancient arts, the secret arts, and curses . . .'

Fidelma's expression grew sharp. 'We do not have a monopoly on all that is good, Ferloga. The New Faith binds us to have charity towards all and not to fear those who follow different paths.'

She glanced at Caol and, reading the meaning of her expression, Caol picked up the gorget, staff, the satchel and the purse of coins, and then followed her to the lower floor, where Lassar had set out a table with their refreshments on it.

Ferloga went to find the boy who usually helped him with the stables and outside work in order to instruct him to go to the chapel and summon the aid of the religious as Fidelma had advised. Meanwhile, Fidelma and Caol sat down to break their fast with freshly baked bread, honey and mugs of sweet mead. Fidelma took time to reassure Lassar about the situation and then, when Ferloga returned, she asked if he had any news from Cashel. The inns were the one sure way of hearing news and gossip.

'There is little of consequence that has happened in the last few days, lady,' he said. 'Did anything of significance transpire at Lios Mhór? Were there any matters of importance that came before you?'

'Nothing at all that is worth the breath of a storyteller,' she observed. It had been a boring week with only petty crimes to speak of, such as a man failing to support his wife and a woman charging rape against a man who turned out to be innocent. Fidelma's interrogation had discovered that the woman was inspired by vengeance after the man had rejected her. 'Have there been no other travellers with news who have stayed at your inn?'

'Only some religious who passed through a few days ago who were lately returned from the kingdom of Dál Riada beyond the seas,' Ferloga told her.

Fidelma was at once interested for she had once travelled through Dál Riada and stayed at the tiny island of Í, called Iona, where Colmcille had built an abbey. It had been nearly five years ago since she had stayed there when travelling to the Synod at Witebia for the great debate between the Irish clerics and those who supported Roman rule.

'What news did they bring? Does Iona still send missionaries into the Saxon kingdoms?'

'They did not say. They spoke of warfare among the Cruithin and among the Saxons. But there was peace in Dál Riada. The King, whom they named as Domangart, son of Diomhnall Brecc, has succeeded in consolidating affairs and bringing peace to the country. They say that everyone speaks well of this King.'

'So Dál Riada prospers?'

'Yes, but there is some fear and unrest, due to a Saxon King called Wulfhere who rules a kingdom called Mercia, which I understood is situated to the south of Dál Riada. Apparently he is attempting to expand his borders even among the other Saxon kingdoms and beyond. These same travellers brought news that a great abbey of the Britons in Gwynedd has been burned down in one of his raids into that country. Many of the religious have been killed.'

Fidelma sighed sadly. 'The Saxons always seem to be fighting, and when it is not with their neighbours, then they fight among themselves,' she observed. Then she thought of Eadulf and flushed guiltily. Yet, she thought, it was a true comment nonetheless.

'Oh, and they brought word that the abbot of Iona had died.'

Fidelma eyes widened. 'Cumméne the Fair?' she queried.

'That, indeed, was the name they mentioned, lady. You have a great knowledge of such things,' Ferloga added, showing a little awe.

Fidelma shrugged indifferently. 'It is when I travelled through that land that I met the old abbot.' Cumméne was a respected scholar, the seventh abbot of Colmcille's foundation, who had written a life of the holy founder. 'Was the cause of his death a natural one?'

'They said so, lady, for the abbot was apparently very aged and infirm.'

'Who replaces him? Did they say?'

'Failbe of the Cenél Conaill.'

It seemed that Iona was following the custom of many of the Irish abbeys where the abbacy succeeded in the same family, being elected by the *derbfine*, three generations of the family of the first abbot. Failbe, whom she had also met on that trip, was a nephew of another former abbot, Ségene, who was a cousin to Colmcille, founder of the abbey.

'Failbe will have much to contend with,' she observed, thinking aloud. 'Cumméne will be hard to replace, for he was a great thinker and scholar.'

They chatted on for a while over the meal until Fidelma rose unhurriedly and announced that they must continue on to Cashel.

Caol went out to prepare the horses while Fidelma again reassured the innkeeper and his wife that they had no reason to feel responsible about the death of the stranger at their inn. Soon, she and Caol were back on the road out of Ráth na Drínne and trotting along the highway that wound through the woods towards her brother's fortress.

chapter two

The journey to the fortress of Cashel passed swiftly. As soon as they arrived, Fidelma left Caol to take care of the horses while she made her way to the chambers that she and Eadulf shared. Muirgen, the nurse, had been alerted to her arrival and was already waiting to greet her, holding young Alchú by the hand. Fidelma paused on the threshold, her eyes anxiously on the child. A moment's examination to ensure that he was well and then she crouched down with her arms held out. Muirgen let go of the boy's hand and he came stumbling into his mother's embrace. They clung together, making those strange, inarticulate sounds that only a mother and child can exchange.

Finally, Fidelma glanced up at the old nurse with a smile. 'Has all been well, Muirgen?'

'Yes, lady,' the nurse replied. 'Brother Eadulf returned yesterday and he is in good spirits.'

'He has returned already?' Fidelma was surprised. 'Where is he?'

'He is with Bishop Ségdae discussing his findings at Ros Ailithir. Now – shall I prepare a bath or would you prefer refreshments first?'

Fidelma stood up and threw off her badger-fur riding cloak. 'We halted at Ferloga's inn to break our fast this morning, so a bath would not come amiss,' she replied, before turning to her son. 'Come, my little hound. We'll sit for a while until Muirgen has prepared my bath. Your mother is dusty after such a long ride this morning.'

As Muirgen headed for the door, it opened suddenly and Eadulf came hurrying in, his face expectant.

'I heard that—' He stopped when he saw Fidelma and made straight for her. Wisely, Muirgen left them together, closing the door quietly behind her.

After a while, Eadulf was anxiously plying Fidelma with questions.

Little Alchú had wandered to a corner to play with his toys. Fidelma assured Eadulf that her time at Lios Mhór had been a tedious one with nothing exciting about the charges brought by the plaintiffs. Eadulf told her that his trip to Ros Ailithir had been equally boring, the return journey even more so. Then his eyes fell on the staff that Fidelma had brought with her. He picked it up and examined the curious mountings.

'This is a strange object for you to be presented with.'

'I was not presented with it,' said Fidelma. Briefly, she recounted the events at Ferloga's inn. 'I thought that I would show it to old Brother Conchobhar as he knows much about such things. As soon as I have bathed and rested, I'll go and have a word with him.'

She showed Eadulf the other items that she had brought from Ferloga's inn.

'So there is no indication of the old man's identity among his possessions?' asked Eadulf.

Fidelma shook her head. 'It would be sad for him to be buried without a name, for he must have been someone of consequence to have such belongings.'

'And the coins,' added Eadulf, as he inspected them. 'These coins are valuable. I wonder what manner of man he was?'

'It is a waste of time to speculate without facts,' Fidelma admonished, but with a mischievous smile for it was a saying of which she was particularly fond. 'We'll wait to hear what old Conchobhar has to say.'

It was late afternoon before Fidelma made her way down to Brother Conchobhar's apothecary shop, tucked away in the shadow of the chapel within the fortress complex. Eadulf had been summoned back to Bishop Ségdae for further discussions and so she had gone alone.

As she entered the gloomy interior, the musky smell of the dried herbs and potions caused her to halt momentarily and catch her breath. The odours were not unpleasant but merely heavy. At the far end of the shop, bent over a table with pestle and mortar and various bowls and vessels, beneath a hanging oil lamp, was an old man in worn and stained brown robes.

He glanced up and, seeing her there, he rose from his stool, coming forward with a smile and outstretched hands to greet her. Brother Conchobhar had known Fidelma since childhood for he had served her father, the King Failbe Flann, and, indeed, other kings of Cashel before and since. For many it seemed impossible to imagine the great capital of

Muman without the aged figure of Conchobhar, the apothecary, physician and astrologer. He had taught his skills to many, including a young Fidelma who had been anxious to be proficient in as many of the arts as possible. In spite of their long relationship, Brother Conchobhar was always punctilious in addressing her as 'lady', although he had nursed her through childhood ailments, had taught her and advised her. She had only once disagreed with his advice and that had been when he had suggested that she was ill-suited to life as a religieuse at the abbey of Cill Dara. In fact, old Conchobhar knew her character so well that he had disagreed with her entering the religious life at all. That she had left Cill Dara soon after entering it was never mentioned. While she was entitled to be called 'Sister', he reminded her that she was the daughter of a king, the sister of a king and of the line of the Eóghanacht. 'Lady' was the more respectful form of address in old Conchobhar's eyes.

'Is all well, lady?' he asked now. 'You and yours are not ailing and need my potions?'

Fidelma smiled pleasantly. 'Thanks be, no, we stand in no need of cures or restoratives, my old friend. But I do stand in need of your knowledge and advice.'

'How can I be of service, lady?' He suddenly realised she was holding a staff in her hand and peered at it.

'Can you identify this?' she asked, allowing him to take it and move to the better light provided by his lantern.

He stood turning it over, examining it carefully. 'I have not seen anything like this since I was a child,' he observed at last. 'It is very old and beautiful. Where did you get it?'

'So you have seen something like it before?' pressed Fidelma. 'Tell me about it first.'

Brother Conchobhar shrugged. 'It is an old staff that symbolised one of the wise teachers of the times before the New Faith was brought to this land.'

'The Druids?'

Brother Conchobhar nodded absently. 'The Druids – and that should be a term of respect, for the word "vid" means "knowledge" and the prefix "dru" means "an immersion". The Druids were considered as people who were immersed in knowledge. There were none wiser nor better informed.'

Fidelma could not hide her impatience. 'I have heard all about them and, indeed, I have met some who still claim to be so. Yet they are people who cling on to the old beliefs and ideas.'

'This symbol speaks of a teacher of some importance. Where did you get it?' he asked again.

Fidelma told him what had happened at Ferloga's inn.

Brother Conchobhar was thoughtful. 'Did he carry anything else with him? Anything other than the staff?'

Fidelma reached into the bag she carried and brought out the gorget, its polished crescent shape sparkling with its curious designs and symbols beaten onto the panel. Brother Conchobhar took it and, unexpectedly and uncharacteristically, a soft whistle broke from his lips.

'I did not think that anything like this would have survived the zeal of those who spread the New Faith in this land. I have seen something similar only once before in my life, and it was on the body of a dead man. They said he was a great teacher, a mystic but withal a pagan. The object was taken from him by a warrior and, at the direction of a priest, was cast into the sea with the body of the man, with many prayers and cries to Christ to protect the pious.'

'Superstition and fear is no way forward,' Fidelma said.

'Any faith is spread by a certain degree of fear, lady,' the old man replied philosophically. 'Faith is not logic otherwise it would not be Faith. In those times it came down to those whose magic was the more powerful. That is why the stories of the miracles had to be told so that people would know what power the early fathers of the Faith had over their pagan enemies. Hence the Blessed Patrick could walk into fires or the Blessed Ailbe could restore to life the son of Mac Dara after he had drowned in the river. Look how it is told that Patrick smashed the skull of the Druid Lochru on a rock, using, as we are told, his magical powers to do so. This was to demonstrate that his magic was more powerful than their magic. In fear, they turned to the Faith that he brought as being more advantageous to their well-being. This fear spreads the Faith.'

Fidelma was slightly disapproving of the argument but she knew the stories well enough. For herself, she did not believe in miracles of any sort.

'So this is a symbol of the old beliefs?' she said quickly as she saw the old man about to extend his argument.

'It may well be the only surviving symbol of a great Druid.' Brother Conchobhar nodded slowly.

'You think the old man who died in Ferloga's inn was such an important member of the Old Faith?'

'It is impossible to say with certainty, but it is rare to come upon such accoutrements. Do you know anything else about him? Was it known where he came from or where he was going?'

'Apparently, he was from the north. He asked Ferloga the innkeeper, what road he should take for Cnánmhchailli. But there are no dwellings around there. It is an empty and desolate place.'

Brother Conchobhar's eyes had widened. 'Except for the ancient pillar stone,' he pointed out.

'So Ferloga said,' Fidelma grimaced. 'Why go to an old, decaying pillar stone? I have passed it a hundred times. It is of no significance.'

'To you, perhaps. But if this man were truly one of those who clung to the pagan ways, then it might make sense that he would be going there.'

'How so?'

Brother Conchobhar leaned forward, confidentially. 'Have you heard of the legends of Mug Ruith?'

'The sun god of the pagans?'

'Yes. He became known as *mac seanfhesa*, the son of ancient wisdom, chief of all the Druids in the five kingdoms. He rode a great chariot, which at night shone as bright as daylight. In the days before the Blessed Ailbe of Imleach brought the teachings of Christ to this corner of the world, it was said that the pillar stone was a fragment of the wheel of Mug Ruith's great chariot that had become petrified.'

When Fidelma smiled cynically, Brother Conchobhar told her: 'It is not wise to dismiss other beliefs without understanding them. Among those who cling to the Old Faith it is said that Mug Ruith is their great champion against Christianity and that his Roth Fáil, his wheel of light, will one day be an engine of destruction that will sweep the teachings of Christ out of the five kingdoms; that we will once again encompass the old way. I believe that many of the Old Faith still search in the hope of finding the Roth Fáil.'

'An old pillar stone is hardly the Roth Fáil.' Fidelma was dismissive.

'The Druids spoke in symbols. Who knows what they meant? Tell me, did this man carry anything else with him?'

Fidelma brought forth the bag of coins. 'He carried these.'

Brother Conchobhar emptied the coins on his table and peered at them. 'Roman coins?' he asked.

'Look closer. They are ancient coins of the type the Britons and Gauls used to cast before the coming of the Romans, centuries before the birth of Christ. I have seen them before in my journeys. And here are also some marked with the name of Tasciovanus, who ruled in Britain two generations before the Romans invaded. Do you see the letters CAM on this gold stater? That signified his capital of Camulodunum. Not one of these coins is later than the time that Rome moved into these territories. They are the most ancient coins of our western world.'

'Why would this old man be carrying such coins with him?' frowned the apothecary as he sifted through the coins. 'This is proof of wealth indeed.'

'I was hoping that you would have some arcane knowledge that might explain it,' Fidelma told him.

'Alas, lady, I have not.'

'Well, I will leave these items with you, my friend, in case you can discover anything else. If the old man was one of those ancient ones, a man who does not recognise the New Faith, it would be interesting to know what he intended. Do you really think he was searching for the Roth Fáil?'

Brother Conchobhar glanced at her with a worried expression. 'Perhaps. And there might be something else.'

'What do you mean?'

'I have heard that there is a new and growing activity from those who adhere to the Old Faith.'

'Growing activity?' Fidelma was surprised. 'I haven't heard this.'

Brother Conchobhar inclined his head seriously. 'Some travellers from Inis Celtra in the Red Lake told me that they had heard stories.'

'That is the school which the Blessed Caiman set up. I well remember him from when I was a child. A kindly old man who died when I was away at Brehon Moran's school.'

'Indeed. The travellers from Inis Celtra said that they had been hearing stories from some of the remoter regions of Connacht that Christian pilgrims have been attacked by bands who proclaim themselves to be of the Old Faith and who carry a totem with a wolf's head affixed to it.'

'A wolf's head?'

'Yes. In the old days, among Corco Baiscinn, the people who dwell near the Red Lake, there was a band of those who followed the old religion and they called themselves the Fellowship of the Wolf.'

'And these stories, are they just stories or did these travellers know for certain such attacks had taken place?'

The old man shrugged. 'They were repeating stories that they had been told.'

'One can therefore place no reliance on such tales,' Fidelma said briskly. 'You know that. The Faith has only been spread for two centuries in this land and although you will find groups here and there who still believe in the old gods, they are usually elderly folk who cling to the traditions of our ancestors. Violence is not part of their character, nor did the old beliefs teach brutality or violence as a virtue. These people live in perfect amity with their Christian brethren. Indeed, there is something sad about them as they come to accept that the youth have eagerly devoured the New Faith and that the future of this land is inevitably linked with the teachings of Christ.'

Brother Conchobhar's gloomy features did not lighten. 'Even so, the story that the travellers recounted was told with such conviction that the Brehon Baithen has gone with some of your brother's warriors to Inis Celtra to investigate.'

Fidelma was surprised but not concerned. 'Well, there was no wolf's head among the possessions of the old man who died at Ráth na Drínne. There seems no link that I can see and no need to bring the matter to the attention of my brother's Brehon.'

She was about to leave the apothecary shop when Caol burst in. He seemed full of suppressed excitement.

'Lady, your brother has sent me to bring you to him . . . immediately.'

'Is anything wrong?' she asked anxiously.

'Nothing, lady, but he asks you to join him at once.'

'Why does he summon me thus?' she demanded.

Caol made a helpless gesture with his hands. 'Lady, I am not permitted to say.' He glanced at Brother Conchobhar and his eyes, still full of some excitement, came back to her. 'All I can say is that half an hour ago, a messenger arrived from Tara, would not rest, bathe nor refresh himself until he saw the King. He is still with him.'

'Do you know more?'

'Lady, do not press me. I must take you to your brother now.'

A deep furrow of curiosity formed on her brow. Fidelma bade farewell to Brother Conchobhar, before turning to follow the commander of her brother's guard. Caol was moving so quickly that she was forced almost to run to keep up with his strides. They crossed the courtyard in front of the chapel steps and went into the main dwellings. Two warriors, well-known to her, Enda and Gormán, stood outside the doors of her brother's private chambers. They smiled at her and then Enda turned and struck the door twice before opening it so that she and Caol could pass inside. As Fidelma did so, she thought it strange that her brother was meeting a messenger from Tara in his private chamber and not in the official reception hall, as was the custom.

Inside, her brother, Colgú, King of Muman, was standing in front of the fire, hands clasped behind his back. His handsome face wore a haggard expression. Before him stood a dishevelled young man, still with the dust of travel on his clothes and exhaustion chiselling his features. He bowed stiffly as Fidelma entered. She acknowledged him with a nod and then addressed her brother.

'There is bad news from Tara?' she asked.

'Caol has not told you?' demanded Colgú.

'Caol has told me nothing except that this messenger is from Tara. The expression on your face tells me that he does not bring good news.'

Colgú's mouth formed a thin line for a moment as though he was hesitant to tell her. Then he said simply: 'The High King has been murdered.'

There was a pause and, shocked, she looked at the messenger. He seemed to feel the need to confirm Colgú's statement.

'It is true, lady. Sechnussach was murdered in his bed.'

Fidelma blinked slightly. The High King had been at her wedding scarcely a year before. She had met him a few times before that and, indeed, had solved a matter of the theft of the official sword of the High Kings of Éireann, without which he would have been prevented from holding office.* Fidelma had respected Sechnussach for, during the few years he had reigned from Tara over the five kingdoms, he had proved a just and bountiful monarch.

'Is it known who did this?' was her next question.

'It is, lady,' replied the messenger. 'It was Dubh Duin of the Cinél Cairpre. He also killed himself when the High King's guards rushed into the chamber.'

'The Cinél Cairpre?' Fidelma thought for a moment.

'A northern tribe,' Colgú explained. 'They claim descent from Cairbre, one of the sons of Niall of the Nine Hostages. They dwell around Loch Gomhna, the Lake of the Calf, in the High King's own territory of Midhe.'

'They are Uí Néill, then?'

'Distantly related to the High King's own family who descend from another son of Niall. In fact, the Cinél Cairpre once provided a High King themselves – Tuathal Maelgarb. But that was well over a century ago.'

'And what was the motive for the murder? A blood feud?'

The messenger sighed. 'Alas, that is not known, lady.'

---

*'The High King's Sword' in *Hemlock at Vespers* (1999)

'But some reason must be suspected?'

The young man glanced at Colgú as if asking him to respond.

'This messenger has come here from the High King's *tánaiste*, his heir apparent . . .' Colgú paused and shrugged. 'The next High King, Cenn Faelad.'

'Sechnussach's brother? I have met him.'

'Cenn Faelad sends his messenger with a request: that you make the journey to Tara and undertake the enquiry into the causes of the murder of the High King.'

Fidelma looked astonished. 'But what of the Chief Brehon, Barrán? Surely it is he who should conduct this enquiry?'

'That is impossible, sister. You see, Barrán is of the Uí Néill, too. He is cousin of Sechnussach and Cenn Faelad. Apparently the Great Assembly, or those of it who were present in Tara, felt that someone from outside the Uí Néill should undertake this investigation, someone who is not seen as partisan to one branch of the Uí Néill or another. As both victim and assassin were members of different branches of the Uí Néill it is feared that, at best, a blood feud could arise or, at worst, a war that would have devastating effects on the unity of the five kingdoms. The investigation should be seen to be without bias.'

Fidelma thought for a moment. 'And what if such an investigation found that it was an internal Uí Néill quarrel?'

Colgú shrugged eloquently. 'The truth is the truth, Fidelma, and truth is often a bitter fruit.'

'There is another aspect that you might have forgotten, brother,' Fidelma said. 'The motivation of the Eóghanacht for their intervention in this matter might also be questioned.'

Colgú looked perplexed, then replied, 'The motivation is that you have been requested to investigate by the Great Assembly. Neither I, nor my *tánaiste*, Finguine, who have a right to sit in the Great Assembly, were privy to this decision. So what other motivation could be ascribed to the Eóghanacht?'

'If there is strife between the septs of the Uí Néill, then the Eóghanacht might be suspected of taking advantage of the situation to reassert the old tradition of also providing High Kings.'

'One needs a long memory to go back to the old days when the Uí Néill and the Eóghanacht contended with each other to elect one of their number to the role of High King!' Colgú scoffed. 'Why, according to our chroniclers, it is five centuries ago when the last Eóghanacht was High King.'

Fidelma smiled gently. 'You see, brother? Even you can put a date to it when our ancestor Duach Donn was High King. People do not forget.'

But Colgú was adamant. 'No one could seriously bring forward the accusation that I, or any Eóghanacht, want to claim the High Kingship. The Uí Néill have maintained the office for too many centuries now. We are content with our own kingdom of Muman.' He looked his sister in the face. 'Are you saying that you do not want this mission?'

Fidelma grimaced. 'I am saying that I will undertake it for the sake of the memory of Sechnussach. The truth about his assassination deserves to be known. Out of respect and my duty to the next High King, Cenn Faelad and the Great Assembly, I will go to Tara even though it grieves me to desert my son after returning here a short time. But it is fair to be aware of any pitfalls that lie ahead.'

Colgú seemed to relax and he smiled at his sister.

'We are not always in control of our destinies, Fidelma. I will ensure the boy is well looked after. I presume that you will take Eadulf?'

She nodded. 'Of course.'

'Can I suggest that you also take Caol? It will take you several days to ride north to Tara and you do not know what dangers may be in wait. If a High King can be assassinated . . .' He left the sentence unfinished.

'I will be happy to accompany the lady Fidelma and her husband,' Caol suddenly broke in. He had stood in silence during the whole of the exchange and now felt he should say something, since he had been referred to. 'I would suggest one other warrior of the guard accompany me.'

'Who did you have in mind?' queried Colgú.

'All my warriors are fine men but perhaps it would be best to take Gormán. He has accompanied the lady Fidelma before. He is not only adept with his weapons but has a good mind and is able to act on his own initiative.'

'An excellent choice, Caol. Do you agree, Fidelma?'

She inclined her head. 'I am happy with the choice. It is too late to begin the journey today, so I suggest we leave at first light tomorrow. If we make a steady pace and do not overtax the horses, we can be in Tara within five days. I will go and tell Eadulf.' She turned towards the door.

'Much hangs in the balance of this investigation, Fidelma,' Colgú called after her. 'Perhaps the peace of the five kingdoms itself . . .'

Chapter Three

Fidelma was correct in that her party, consisting of four riders, reached the gates of the palace of the High King at Tara in the afternoon of the fifth day after leaving Cashel. The five kingdoms of Éireann were well provided with roads. There were six different types of road and each of them classified by a different name. They ranged from a small track called *lámrota* to the great highways called *slíge*. There were only five *slíge*. These were the main arteries of the five kingdoms, which all converged at Tara. The highway that ran from the kingdom of Muman to Tara was called the Slíge Dalla or the Way of the Blind. It carried its unusual name because it was said that it was such a good and well-kept highway that a blind person would have no problem traversing it. It spanned rivers with bridges of wood and stone called *droichet* and crossed marshes and bogs on causeways called *tóchar*. A *slíge* was constructed so that two large wagons had plenty of space to pass one another without having to slow down.

The laws on the repair and maintenance of the roads were strictly enforced. It was the responsibility of the local chieftain, in whose territory each section of the road lay, to maintain it. This was part of his duties to the provincial King, and part of the provincial King's duty to the High King. The chieftain had to ensure the road was in good condition, clear of brushwood and weeds and drained of water. The laws stipulated that there were three times when the roads had to be inspected: at the beginning of every winter; at the time of horse racing when some roads were turned into racing tracks; and, of course, during time of war when the roads became the arteries along which bands of warriors had to pass. If any person caused damage to a road, they had to pay compensation to the chieftain in whose territory the road ran.

Fidelma and Eadulf, with Caol and Gormán, had set out along the Slíge

Dalla just after first light on the day after they had heard the news of the High King's death at Tara. Fidelma was aware that this was the beginning of winter with the daylight period at its shortest so that they were restricted to travelling only during those hours. She made a mental calculation of the length of time it would take them to reach their destination. Fidelma was as much at home on horseback as on foot but decided on an easy pace, not merely because she knew that Eadulf was not the best of horsemen but because of her care for the horses themselves. They should maintain the horses at a fast walking pace for long periods but now and then allow them to canter. She dismissed trotting, as this was tiring not only to the horse but also to the rider, who had to rise up and down in the saddle on alternate beats.

In this fashion, the party made good progress and as dusk began to fall on the first day they had reached a little fortified church and hostel called Rath Domhnaigh. By the end of the second day, leaving the territory of Muman and entering the kingdom of Laigin, across more hilly country, their pace slowed but they had reached Dun Masc, a fortress rising on a rock nearly fifty metres high and dominating a flat plain in the land of the Uí Chremthainn Áin. The chieftain had heard the news of the High King's death and shrewdly guessed why Fidelma was journeying to Tara. He welcomed the group with courtesy and offered lavish hospitality.

At the end of a third day's easy ride, they came to the great abbey of the Blessed Brigid at Cill Dara, the church of the oaks. It was a *conhospitae*, a mixed religious house, where Fidelma had first entered the religious. Abbess Ita, whose behaviour had caused Fidelma to leave the abbey, was no longer there.* The new abbess was called Luan; she had been a contemporary of Fidelma's and seemed pleased to see her, greeting her like an old friend and making them all welcome. Fortified once more by a good night's sleep and food, and with their horses well cared for and rested, they set out again. On that fourth day, they were moving due north and crossing into the High King's own territory of the 'Middle Kingdom' – Midhe.

Fidelma had made this journey to Tara many times and so she knew they were entering the Magh Nuada, the Plain of Nuada. The highway crossed the plain, passing through areas of woodland that were barely inhabited. There was a small church with its own hostel by the roadside in one stretch of woodland, and Fidelma had decided that they would spend their final night there before moving on to Tara. The plain was named after Nuada Necht, of whom there were many confusing legends.

---

*See 'Hemlock at Vespers' in *Hemlock at Vespers* (1999)

Some claimed he was a powerful god of the ancients and husband to the goddess Bóinn, who gave her name to the great river that ran close by. Others dismissed him as merely a pagan king.

The sun was low in the sky when Caol called from behind them: 'Smoke, lady! There's smoke ahead.'

Fidelma drew rein, as did the rest of the band. Beyond the border of trees that lay ahead of them rose a dark column of smoke.

'That's no hearth fire,' muttered Eadulf. 'It is much larger. Can it be that the trees have caught alight?'

'A winter fire among the forests is no natural phenomenon, Brother Eadulf,' replied Gormán. 'It looks more like—'

'There is a church and a habitation in that direction,' interrupted Fidelma. 'I know it well, for I have stayed there many a time on this road. That is where I meant us to stay this night. Come!' She dug her heels into her mount and sent it speeding down the road, heedless of danger.

Caol's protest was lost but he paused only a second before racing after her, drawing his sword at the same time. Gormán was following and, with a groan, Eadulf also urged his own mount after them.

With Fidelma leading, the band of riders galloped swiftly along the road through the small skirting of woodland. They could smell the acrid stench of the smouldering wood before they came into the clearing, where the blackened remains of a small wooden church still poured smoke and ash into the air. Nearby, other outbuildings that Fidelma recalled as a cowshed and pigpen and a guesthouse were already so much charcoal. Remains of belongings – torn pages of books, clothing and domestic items lay in profusion around the clearing. Two figures lay outstretched on the ground before the buildings. Both wore the woollen habits of religieux; these were stained with blood.

Caol cried: 'Wait, lady!' as Fidelma made to dismount. He looked carefully around, head to one side, listening. Then he slid from his horse, sword still in his hand, explaining: 'Whoever did this thing may still be lingering nearby.'

He walked across to one of the bodies but did not even bother to bend down to check the first, shook his head to indicate that the religieux was beyond hope. Then he moved on to the second. Here he bent down quickly and raised the man's head.

'This one lives!' he called excitedly.

Eadulf, who knew something of medicine, dismounted and went to kneel at the side of the man. A brief glance, and he shook his head. The man might still live, but not for long. Blood was pouring from a deep gash in his chest.

'Pass me the water,' he instructed Caol. 'It will not harm him for he has not long.'

He allowed the dying religieux to swallow a gasping mouthful.

'Who did this thing, my friend?' he demanded.

The man's eyes flickered open and stared up, dilating orbs of pain. He tried to form words but could not find breath to make the sound.

'Who is responsible?' insisted Eadulf, bending so that his ear almost touched the man's lips. He caught a sound and then heard a rattle of breath. The man was dead. He laid him gently back on the ground and stood up.

'Did he answer your question?' Fidelma asked, still seated on horseback with Gormán, sword defensively drawn and on the alert, at her side.

Eadulf shrugged. 'A single word . . . something about blame, I think. Perhaps he meant that he was to blame. I don't understand.'

Caol looked around vigilantly. 'We can do nothing here, lady, and this could be a dangerous place to linger in.'

'This was where I meant us to stay this night.' Fidelma glanced anxiously at the darkening sky. 'It will be dusk before long.'

'I would venture that this would not be the best place to spend a winter's night, lady, for there is no shelter now.' Caol looked at the smoking buildings. 'And whoever did this might well return. I'd rather be in the open country than surrounded by woods.'

'I remember that there is an inn further along the road,' Fidelma said tiredly. 'About half an hour's ride from here. If it still stands, we can seek shelter there.'

Eadulf gestured at the two bodies. 'Should we not bury them?'

'It would be dark before we could do so, my friend,' Caol replied practically. 'It is my duty to protect my King's sister and you, her husband. We must ride together now.'

As if joining in at an appropriate moment to remind them of the dangers, a wolf began to howl in the gathering dusk.

Caol frowned. 'We will inform the innkeeper and ask him to request his chieftain to send men back here when it is daylight.'

'There might not be much left to bury if we leave these poor souls exposed overnight,' Eadulf commented.

'The least we can do is remove the bodies to a more sheltered spot,' Fidelma agreed. 'There was an *uaimha*, as I recall, near that building where they stored food.' She indicated the smouldering ruins that had once been the guesthouse.

'A cave?' asked Eadulf, trying to translate the word *uaimha*.

'An artificially made underground chamber,' explained Fidelma.

Caol walked across and peered among the debris. It took a few moments to locate the entrance into the souterrain, which was a common method of storing food and provisions in a cooler temperature. Eadulf and Gormán lent a hand to carrying the bodies of the slain religieux to the chamber and depositing them inside, securing it against the attentions of preying animals.

Fidelma drew a sigh and glanced apprehensively at the approaching dark. 'At least they will be safe awhile,' she said. 'May God have mercy on their souls. Now, we must try to reach the inn before nightfall.'

They remounted and resumed their journey along the road. Fidelma led them in a canter, for the sooner they reached the warmth and safety of the inn the better. Across the plain, the howling of wolves echoed distantly in the gathering dusk.

By the time they saw the light of the inn, after rounding a bend as the road wound over the shoulder of a hill, night had already fallen. At least the light was welcoming. All inns and hostels had a lantern raised at night on a tall pole set on the *faithche*, the area just outside the entrance to the inn, to guide travellers to it from a distance. It was with some relief that they trotted into the yard, the sound of their arrival disturbing a sleepy cockerel that set up an indignant cry which seemed to agitate the brooding hens. The door opened and a thickset man emerged and surveyed the visitors with an appraising glance before turning and calling to someone inside the inn. Then he took a step forward.

'Welcome, strangers. You are late abroad. Do you seek shelter for the night?'

Fidelma dismounted as two young men appeared at his side. 'We do, indeed,' she replied. 'But first water to bathe after our travel and food to eat.'

'Then enter and be comfortable.'

The others also slid wearily from their mounts and took their saddle-bags, allowing the two young men to lead their horses to the stables.

'Welcome, lady, welcome, my friends,' the man said again. 'I am the *brugh-fer*.'

'Ah, so this is a *brugaid*? A public hostel?' asked Fidelma.

The man nodded. Hospitality was a virtue highly esteemed in the five kingdoms, and each clan made provision for lodging and entertaining travellers and officials. The public hostels ran side by side with private inns, and strict laws applied to both establishments. The keepers of each were restricted in what they could and could not provide for their guests, and as guests were constantly arriving and departing, the furniture and other property in the hostels and inns was carefully protected by law from wanton or malicious damage and, as Fidelma knew, the laws went into detail about the compensation to be paid, and for any injuries sustained.

'Are you travelling to Tara?' the man asked, showing them into the main room where a fire was spreading a comfortable heat. A fire in a public hostel had to be kept constantly alight, according to law.

'We are,' affirmed Fidelma.

'Ah, then you must travel on a sad business. I heard of the High King's death. And you are from the south, if your accent is not false.'

'This is Fidelma of Cashel,' Caol interrupted, indicating Fidelma's social rank with some pride.

The hostel-keeper's eyes widened as he regarded her. 'I have heard stories of Fidelma of Cashel – a famous *dálaigh*.'

'I am Fidelma,' she said simply. 'And a *dálaigh*.'

'You and your companions are most honoured guests, lady,' the man said. 'I will call my wife and there shall be drink and food upon the table shortly. Water will also be heated soon.'

He made to leave but Fidelma stayed him. 'We came across Magh Nuada,' she said.

'Oh yes? Of course, that is the main road from the south-west,' said the hostel-keeper, puzzled by the solemn way she spoke. 'Was something amiss?'

'Some miles back we came upon a church and its buildings destroyed by fire, and the two Brothers of Christ who tend it were dead upon the ground and all their animals driven off.'

'Dead?' echoed the man in bewilderment. 'I know those Brothers of the Faith!'

'They were slain,' explained Caol.

The man's eyes widened and then he shivered. 'These are troubled times. I have heard that there are *dibergach* who are active in the west. The High King's death has come at a difficult time.'

'*Dibergach*?' queried Eadulf.

'Brigands, marauders – tribeless and desperate men, Brother Saxon, who plunder and rob at will.' The man had either identified Eadulf by association with Fidelma or had recognised his accent.

'Are you telling us that there are robbers who would attack a church and kill clerics?' Eadulf was horrified.

'I have heard stories from the west,' the innkeeper repeated. 'There are groups of them who cling to the old religions, so attacking Christians does not worry them. But they have never come this far east before.'

'You say that you have not been troubled by them before?' asked Caol.

'This is a *brugaid* under the protection of my chief, the noble lord Tóla. They would not dare rouse my chief's enmity by destroying any one of his public hostels. He has but to stretch out his hand . . . his reach is long and vengeance swift.'

'Who is your chief?' asked Fidelma.

'This is the land of the Cairpre,' replied the innkeeper.

'But I thought . . .' Eadulf was about to point out that it had been the chief of the Cinél Cairpre who had killed the High King, but a look from Fidelma stopped him.

'It is just that the church is so close to here and we had no time to bury the poor religious who were slain there,' Fidelma said quickly. 'We placed their bodies in the underground food store so that scavengers would not disturb them. But they should be buried properly.'

The hostel-keeper was in agreement.

'In the morning, I shall send my sons to acquaint my chieftain with this news and see that men are sent to give burial to those unfortunates.'

'That is good.' Fidelma smiled briefly in thanks.

'You mentioned that you have heard of similar raids in the west,' Eadulf pressed. 'What is known about these robbers – these *dibergach*, as you call them? Who are they and who is their leader?'

The man shrugged. 'I only hear stories from passing travellers like yourselves. No one knows who they are – perhaps they are escaped hostages, *daer-fuidir* – the unfree ones who have committed great offence to their clans and should rightly be working to restore their rights and freedoms. Perhaps they have banded together to live a life without the law. That is all we know. However, the fact that they are raiding on the Plain of Nuada is worrying news.'

There was not much else to learn from the hosteller and so, after they had eaten and refreshed themselves, they retired to bed so they could be up again at first light. The hosteller and his sons, the young men who worked as stable lads, had their horses already saddled and waiting by the time the small party had broken their fast and were ready to leave. In these public hostels, food and beds were provided free for up to three days, as part of the obligations of hospitality on a local chieftain. After three days, another arrangement had to be reached between guests and host. They left with the further assurance from the hosteller that he would take care of the bodies of the slain religious.

The final day's riding was easy. It was a bright morning with pale blue skies and a pastel sun. However, a chilly wind was blowing from the north almost directly into their faces. They rode north-east along the banks of the great River Bóinn for a while and, while it was still daylight, they came within sight of the distant hills over which spread the great walled complex of the palace of the High Kings at Tara.

The highway had led over several rivers and streams, for the stately Bóinn was fed by a myriad of such watery arteries rising in the surrounding high ground. Now, within a few kilometres of Tara, Fidelma remembered there was one more crossing through a marshy area in which the waters were like a spidery web that finally emerged into the Bóinn, which lay some long distance away on their left. Indeed, it came back to her that the last river was called the Scaine from the word that meant a cleaving or dispersal. But she knew that the bridges and the road to Tara were good and well-kept so the journey should be straightforward.

They moved downward through wooded country and emerged onto the banks of a small stretch of water. A well-constructed wooden bridge led across it into more thickly wooded countryside which consisted of close growing evergreens so that the onset of winter had not dispelled the darkness of the forest behind.

'The hills of Tara rise behind this stretch of trees,' Fidelma informed her companions with some relief. 'We can rest soon.'

As she led the way onto the bridge, Fidelma suddenly noticed a crouching figure who appeared to be washing something in the river on the far bank, close by the end of the bridge. It appeared to be a bent-backed old woman in torn clothing and a wild mess of once-white hair. A poor old country-woman washing some clothes, was the thought that came to mind.

She had almost reached the far bank when the crouching figure straightened a little and gazed at her. A bony white arm protruded from the ragged clothing and a finger pointed directly towards Fidelma.

'Be warned, Fidelma of Cashel,' came a sharp voice, almost like a screech. 'You are not welcome in Midhe.'

Fidelma was so surprised that she jerked the reins of her horse and drew up sharply, causing some consternation among her companions. She gazed at the dishevelled figure, frowning.

'Do you address me, old woman?' she asked.

There was a rasping sound that Fidelma realised was meant as laughter.

'Is there another Fidelma of Cashel, another who is a Sister of the Usurping Faith that blights our land? Be warned, I say, and return from whence you came.'

Caol had clapped a hand to his sword but Fidelma motioned him to be still.

'You know *my* name, old woman. May I know yours?'

There came another cackle from the crone. 'Who would sit at Ath na Foraire, the Ford of Watching, but the watcher herself?' came the reply.

Eadulf noticed that his companion Gormán had shivered slightly but he could not see the features of Fidelma and Caol, whose horses were in front of him and now standing motionless on the bridge. Clearly this meant something to Gormán and he was about to ask for an explanation when Fidelma replied, quietly addressing the old woman: 'And does the watcher have a name?'

'Some have called me Badb,' came the croaking response.

To Eadulf's ear the name sounded like 'bave'. It meant nothing to him, but at his side he heard Gormán groan a little.

Fidelma's voice was light and bantering. 'Are you claiming to be the hooded raven of battles, old one? The goddess Badb who delights in setting one person against the other, incites armies to fight each other so that she may delight in the slaughter and haunt the battlefields for lost souls? I declare, I never thought to meet so distinguished an entity. So you call yourself Badb?'

'Your mind is reputed to be sharp, Fidelma of Muman. You clearly heard me say that some have called me so, therefore it is pointless trying to match your wits with mine in an attempt to irritate me.'

Fidelma's voice was still bantering. 'Well, old one, why am I not welcome in Midhe?'

'You come seeking a solution to the death of Sechnussach. You will not find the truth, I tell you. There will be no peace in this land until all you of the New Faith have given up this heresy and returned to the Old Faith and the gods and goddesses of the time before Time began. You must welcome them back into your hearts and lives. When the great Cauldron of Murias is brought to the Hill of Uisnech, the navel of the world, when the sacred stone of Falias, the mighty sword of Gorias and the great Red

Javelin of Finias are once more together, then shall the Children of Danú, Mother Goddess, reign supreme again over their people. It will be soon, for the Wheel of Destiny is found. The White One has spoken of these things and she speaks the truth.'

Fidelma and her companions sat spellbound by the old woman's chanting tones. As she spoke, the crone seemed to rise up so that her hunched back was almost straight, her voice still rasping but powerful.

'Turn back across the bridge and return to the land which your brother rules and take this message to him: "Return to the Old Faith before it is too late, for the path you are taking leads to the destruction of the peoples of the five kingdoms, and foreign kings will take the place of those who now rule in vanity". *Go back, Fidelma of Cashel!*'

Then, with a wild cry, the old woman turned from the riverbank and scuttled away into the woods.

'Wait!' Fidelma called to her. Even as she spoke, Caol had slapped his horse forward and was off the bridge and trying to follow the woman through the dense undergrowth.

Fidelma, Eadulf and Gormán walked their mounts slowly forward off the bridge and waited for Caol to return.

Eadulf was bewildered. 'What was all *that* about?' he asked.

Fidelma smiled without humour. 'I'd say it was a poor demented old woman who is living in the past. There are still some who believe in the old ways and the old superstitions, and she is certainly one of that number.'

Gormán coughed nervously. 'But, lady, how did she know that you are Fidelma of Cashel and the reason why you have come to Tara?'

The thought had also occurred to Fidelma.

'It is no use speculating when I do not have information,' she replied airily. 'It is not beyond the bounds of possibility that Cenn Faelad's sending for me has been talked about at Tara so that she acquired such knowledge that way.'

'Well, I have no understanding of half the things that were said,' Eadulf commented. 'What or who is a *bave*?'

'*Badb*.' Fidelma corrected his pronunciation slightly. 'She was one of three evil goddesses who presided over death and battles, who loved slaughter and bloodshed, and would often sow baneful thoughts to incite people to commit violence against one another.'

Gormán chimed in: 'And she is often depicted as an old woman washing the skulls of those slain in battle while sitting at a ford – that is why she is also known as the Washer at the Ford.'

'Except the old one called herself a watcher at the ford,' corrected Fidelma, with a smile at the young warrior's nervous features. 'The demented one was as human as you or I, Gormán.'

The young warrior grimaced. 'I fear no human, lady. That you know. But . . .' He shrugged.

'Well, I would like to know what all that meant – the cauldron, sword and spear,' interrupted Eadulf. 'I have never heard the like.'

Fidelma turned to him with a soft smile. 'It is the ancient tales, Eadulf. It was said that in the time before Time, the ancient gods and goddesses of Éireann, who were known as the Children of Danú, the Mother Goddess, came from four great mystic cities. They came to this island bringing with them their greatest treasures, one from each of their lost cities. From Falias they brought with them a sacred stone which was called the Lia Fáil, or the stone of destiny; from Gorias they brought with them a mighty sword called "Retaliator"; from Urias they brought with them the "Red Javelin" which, once cast, would seek out its enemies no matter where they hid; and from Murias, they brought a great cauldron – the Cauldron of Plenty – from which no one went away hungry. Those were the great treasures and symbols of the Old Faith.'

She did not mention the old woman's reference to the Wheel of Destiny, the *Roth Fáil*, for it was the only thing that worried her by the coincidence of the reference after what Brother Conchobhar had told her.

Caol suddenly broke cover along the bank and came riding back, looking crestfallen.

'I lost her,' he confessed. 'Either that old woman knows these woods really well, or . . . or she has the ability to vanish.'

Fidelma chuckled. 'She doubtless knows the secret paths, my friend, but I doubt if she has learned the art of vanishing. Well, a fascinating encounter, Caol, but we cannot delay. We are but a short distance from Tara.'

Eadulf looked around anxiously. 'Shouldn't we take what the old one said more seriously? She did after all threaten us.'

'A threat from someone clearly demented . . .' began Fidelma.

'Is still a threat,' interrupted Eadulf.

Caol was also looking gloomy. 'Eadulf is right, lady. We should be on our guard.'

'I would hope that is exactly what you are about, you and Gormán,' Fidelma said airily. 'As bodyguards and my brother's élite warriors, you should always be attentive to danger. Come, let's not delay further.'

CHAPTER FOUR

When their presence at the gates of the royal enclosure was announced, it was Abbot Colmán, the spiritual adviser to the *Airlechas* or Great Assembly of the High King, who emerged to greet them. He was a thickset, ruddy-faced man in his late fifties. As Fidelma dismounted from her horse, he came forward with both hands outstretched, as if greeting an old friend, but behind his welcoming smile, his features wore an expression of anxiety.

'Sister Fidelma! It is always good to see you here at Tara. But alas, it is sad that such tragedy brings you hither again.'

He gripped her hands warmly and she returned the greeting with the same warmth. It had been some time since their last meeting, when Fidelma had won the respect of the abbot by her abilities, firstly in solving the riddle of the theft of the High King's ceremonial sword, and next by discovering the truth that lay behind a haunted tomb in the graveyard of the High Kings.[*]

'You are looking well, Colmán, and I swear that the passing years have not changed you,' she complimented him.

Colmán assumed a solemn countenance. '*Vanitas vanitatum, omnia vanitas,*' he quoted piously. 'I would like to think so, but alas, my reflection calls me vain if I do.' Then he turned to greet Eadulf. 'You are welcome here, Eadulf of Seaxmund's Ham. We have heard much about you, Brother Saxon. The tales of your deeds with our dear Sister Fidelma are told by the storytellers around many a hearth during these dark winter months.' Then Colmán greeted Caol and Gormán in turn as Fidelma introduced them.

'The hospitality of Tara is yours,' he said with a gesture that encompassed them all, before adding significantly, 'Such hospitality as can be obtained in this troubled time.'

---

[*] See 'The High King's Sword' and 'A Scream from the Sepulchre' in *Hemlock at Vespers* (1999)

'What is the situation here?' asked Fidelma, as Abbot Cólmán signalled to the waiting *gilla scuir*, stable lads, to take their horses and remove their saddlebags.

'It is best that Cenn Faelad tells you directly,' the abbot said. 'He desires to see you. However, the rituals of hospitality must first be observed. Rooms have been prepared in the guests' hostel and orders already given for water to be heated. Come, I will show you to where you may refresh yourselves.'

Fidelma fell in step beside Colmán while Eadulf and the others followed. Caol and Gormán had taken the saddlebags from the stable lads and kept close behind Fidelma and Eadulf.

'Who knew that I had been sent for, aside from the Great Assembly?' asked Fidelma.

Abbot Colmán glanced at her, surprised by her question. 'It was no secret. All the members of the Great Assembly who met to debate the situation after the death of Sechnussach knew it and there has been talk of little else. Why do you ask?'

'I just wondered. It's of no consequence,' she replied. 'I presume that the obsequies have been conducted for Sechnussach?'

'He rests among his predecessors and ancestors in the compound of royal graves,' replied the abbot, a trifle unctuously. 'It was not possible to wait for all the *cóicedach*, the kings of the five kingdoms, and their nobles to attend the ceremonies. However, it is the intention of Cenn Faelad to invite all the kings and nobles to a memorial feast once the investigation into his brother's death has produced its findings.' He added with emphasis, as if it needed explanation, '*Your* investigation, Fidelma, and *your* findings.'

'Sechnussach was a great king and a generous man,' Fidelma observed softly. 'I hope Cenn Faelad stands in likeness to his brother.'

'A wise sentiment and heartily echoed, Fidelma,' agreed the abbot. 'I have known him many years and I think the five kingdoms will notice little change, for he and his brother agreed on most things.'

'And when will be Cenn Faelad's inauguration as High King? That will certainly need the presence of the *cóicedach*.'

The worried look on the abbot's face deepened.

'It has been decided, on the advice of the Great Assembly, that there must be a delay before Cenn Faelad can take the sword of the High Kings in his hand and place his foot on the *Lia Fail* to proclaim his accession.'

'The *Lia Fail*?' queried Eadulf, remembering what the old woman had said at the river crossing.

Abbot Colmán smiled indulgently. 'It is part of our inauguration custom here, Brother Saxon. You probably do not know of it, but those about to be installed in the office take the ancient sword of the High Kings in their hand and place their foot on an ancient stone, which we call the *Lia Fail*, the Stone of Destiny. It was said in pagan times that when the sacred stone feels the foot of a just ruler it responds with a shout of joy. You may see the stone in the royal enclosure, beyond those buildings . . .' he indicated with his hand '. . . for it stands here still.' For a moment, the abbot looked embarrassed. 'Do not think it is merely a pagan custom, Brother. Our ecclesiastical scholars have concluded that the stone was used by Jacob as his blessed pillow, and was brought out of Ancient Egypt by Goidel, son of Scota, daughter of the Pharaoh Cingris, after whom we Gaels take our name. And it was the descendants of Goidel, the worthy sons of Míle Easpain, who brought it hither to this land so that all our rightful rulers can rest their foot upon it and receive the blessing of the one true god.'

Fidelma sniffed impatiently. 'It is an old legend . . .' she saw Abbot Colmán frown and corrected herself. 'An old *story*. The stone is supposed to be of great antiquity – but remember that there is another story about the stone. Four or five generations ago, the brother of the High King Murtagh mac Erc became king of the Dál Riada across the sea in Alba. Fergus mac Erc sent to his brother Murtagh and requested that the stone be shipped to Alba so that he could be crowned upon it. Murtagh obliged his brother and after the inauguration Fergus refused to return the stone and the true *Lia Fail* now rests in Dál Riada.'

Abbot Colmán appeared irritated. 'I have heard that story, Fidelma, and the answer is that Murtagh mac Erc sent another stone to his brother Fergus. The true *Lia Fail* remains here in Tara and always will.' He turned and glanced at Eadulf. 'Why are you so interested in the *Lia Fail*, Brother Eadulf?'

'Eadulf is always delighted to learn new things about our lands and its legends,' Fidelma answered for him. 'Now, Colmán, you were saying that there will be a delay before the inauguration ceremonies for the new High King?'

Eadulf sighed, wondering why Fidelma was apparently unwilling to mention the encounter with the old woman.

They came to a large wooden building at the far end of the royal enclosure. Abbot Colmán indicated that this was the *bruden* or special guest-houses for the High King's visitors. He halted outside the doors and turned to Fidelma.

'With the murder of the High King, even though we know who did the deed, your enquiry into the motives and whether anyone else was involved, is essential before any ceremonies can begin. We have to know all the details. So nothing can be done before you have concluded your investigations. We await your findings.'

'Surely Cenn Faelad is not suspected of involvement?' Eadulf asked. 'After all, Sechnussach was his brother.'

'Brother Saxon, family feuds are not uncommon,' Abbot Colmán said. 'The killer, Dubh Duin, was a member of the southern Uí Néill. Sechnussach was of the same Uí Néill ancestry as Dubh Duin. So, of course, is his brother Cenn Faelad. Some might suspect that there is an internal family quarrel here. A grasping for power. No one is above suspicion here. You can see why it was thought proper that Cenn Faelad should not be named as High King until this matter is resolved.'

Fidelma had already appreciated the point.

'Where is Sechnussach's sister, Ornait?' she asked suddenly.

When Sechnussach was about to be inaugurated as High King, the sacred sword of office, the sword said to have been fashioned by Gobhain, the smith god for the ancestors of the Uí Néill, had been stolen. For a High King not to be inaugurated with the sword and with his foot placed in the *Lia Fail*, the sacred Stone of Destiny, could have brought chaos and dissension in the five kingdoms. It had been Fidelma who had discovered that the culprits had been Ornait, the sister of Sechnussach, and her lover, Ailill Esa Flann, who had then been the *tánaiste* or heir apparent.

Abbot Colmán's eyes sparkled in amusement. 'I was awaiting your question about Ornait. Her name did cross my mind at the time of the murder,' he admitted. 'But, as you know, the Chief Brehon exiled Ornait and her lover Ailill and they went to the kingdom of Rheged on the island of Britain. To my knowledge they have remained there ever since.'

Eadulf was looking bewildered at this exchange and Fidelma relented.

'I will tell you the story later, Eadulf,' she promised before turning back to the abbot. 'The shore of Rheged is only a day's fair sailing from these shores,' she said. 'Ornait and Ailill were ambitious for power five years ago. They could be equally ambitious today and might have a hand in this matter. They would not be the first to be driven into exile and then return to be acclaimed in triumph.' Fidelma was actually thinking of her own ancestor, Conall Corc, who returned to Muman after his exile not only to become King but also to establish Cashel as his great capital.

'We would surely have heard some rumour of Ornait's return if return she has,' Abbot Colmán argued.

'Anyway, these are just speculations,' Fidelma summed up impatiently. 'There is much to be talked of, but later with Cenn Faelad. Once we are refreshed, and start to gather all the facts, we can put our minds to this problem.'

The abbot nodded and, turning to the *bruden* doors, he clapped his hands to attract attention.

At once, they were opened and a tall, slim, dark-haired girl came forward to greet them. Her dark eyes seemed to have an angelic quality to them, or so Eadulf thought, and she had a ready smile. 'Pretty' was a word that came to his mind. She carried herself with a certain grace.

'This is Báine,' Abbot Colmán announced. 'She will attend to your wants while you are staying in the guesthouse. There is no one else here at the moment and so I have presumed that you will want your escort,' he nodded at Caol and Gormán, 'to be on hand. There is room enough for all.'

The girl Báine made a deferential move of her head towards Fidelma. 'Water is heated, lady, and the *dabach* is filled ready.'

The *dabach* was the wooden vat in which one bathed.

'Good,' Fidelma said. 'Then I will seize the opportunity to bathe first.'

Abbot Colmán made his excuses. 'After you have refreshed yourselves,' he said, 'I will come for you and Brother Eadulf to escort you to see Cenn Faelad. He is staying in my house on the other side of the royal enclosure. It was thought better not to move into the royal residence until after things have been settled. The *tánaiste* has arranged a private meal for you so that we may discuss the matter that brings you hither. Báine will see to it that your warriors are fed.'

He turned with a wave of his hand and moved away towards the central buildings of the royal enclosure.

They followed the young girl into the guests' hostel. She was thorough and efficient, showing Fidelma and Eadulf to the chamber they would share and then conducting Caol and Gormán to rooms close by. Like most of the buildings, the guests' hostel was a rectangular structure of wood, mainly oak beams and yew panels, with a thatched roof. It was fairly dark in the interior without *seinester* or windows to admit light, so the place reeked of the heavy fumes of tallow candles and oil lamps, even though it was still light outside.

It seemed that Fidelma and Eadulf had hardly had time to look round the chamber assigned to them and unpack their few belongings from their saddlebags before the girl, Báine, returned.

'I will take you to your bath, lady,' she announced. 'I have laid out all the toiletries you may need; even a comb is provided so you have no need to bring anything else. We have fragrances and items for all your needs.' Fidelma glanced at Eadulf with an amused expression. 'Hospitality indeed,' she murmured, as she left the room to follow the girl.

Hardly any time passed before the girl was back again, knocking gently at the door of the chamber.

'Excuse me, Brother, but I wonder if you would like a beaker of the juice of crushed apples to slake your thirst while you are waiting for your bath to be prepared?'

'Indeed, that I would.' Eadulf smiled gravely.

The girl went to pour the drink and Eadulf followed her into the side room where she was preparing it.

'Have you served in the guests' hostel long, Báine?' he asked.

The girl looked anxious. 'I hope nothing is amiss, Brother?'

'No, no.' He shook his head reassuringly. 'Nothing at all is wrong. You are very efficient in your work, that is all.'

Báine looked relieved. 'This is my first time attending to the needs of the guests here. You are my first guests.'

Eadulf raised his eyebrows a little. 'I would not have realised it. I thought that you had been born to the task.'

The girl handed him the drink and grimaced prettily. 'I *was* raised to service – but not in a guests' hostel. I usually serve in the High King's household.'

'Ah?' Eadulf said, putting a question into the soft breath.

'I was sent here today by Brother Rogallach especially to look after the lady Fidelma and yourself.'

'Brother Rogallach?'

'He is in charge of all those who serve in the High King's household. He is the *bollscari* – the High King's factotum.'

'And you have served in the royal household long?'

'Since the age of choice.'

Eadulf knew that girls reached the *aimsir togú* or age of choice when they came to their fourteenth birthday.

'That cannot be long ago,' he mused.

'Five years ago,' the girl replied in seriousness, not recognising that Eadulf was paying a clumsy compliment.

44

'A lifetime,' he smiled indulgently.

'It seems so . . . now,' Báine replied with a curious pause.

'Were you serving in the household when the High King was slain?'
She blinked and nodded dumbly.

'It must have been a shock for you?'

Báine swallowed and said, 'A great shock. Sechnussach was a . . . a kind
man to serve. He was gracious and generous to those who attended him.'

'Then it is a great sadness. You were actually in the house when the
assassin broke in?'

'I was in my bed, asleep.'

'Quite so. I had heard it was not long before dawn that it occurred. So
undoubtedly you were woken by the sounds of that awesome discovery.'

To his surprise the girl shook her head. 'I was roused from my bed by
Brónach who told me what had happened. I slept through the noise of the
discovery.'

'Who is Brónach?'

'She is the senior female attendant in the High King's household. There
are only three of us in the immediate household. She is older than us and
so takes charge of us.'

Eadulf was about to press the girl for further information when Fidelma's
voice hailed her from the bathing room.

With a muttered apology, Báine turned to answer the call. Eadulf
remained, thoughtfully sipping at his apple juice. A few moments later
the door of the guests' hostel opened and another girl entered. She was
slightly built, wearing dowdy clothes, with unremarkable brown hair and
almost plain features. It made her seem younger than she actually was
which, in Eadulf's estimation, was not more than eighteen. Her whole
stance seemed that of someone who wished they were anywhere else but
here. She regarded Eadulf with one quick frightened glance before dropping her gaze to the floor.

'Forgive me,' she muttered, clasping her hands before her, her shoulders slightly bent as if to make herself as small as possible.

'*Absolvo te a peccatis tuis*,' responded Eadulf jocularly. 'I forgive you
all your sins.'

For a moment the girl was startled, raising her gaze to his before quickly
looking down again.

'You are making a joke, Brother,' she said, then added: 'I am looking
for Báine. I was told to ask if she needed help.'

Eadulf smiled kindly. 'She is attending in the bathhouse at the moment. And who are you?'

'I am Cnucha.'

Eadulf reflected for a moment. 'I thought that meant a small hill? I have heard a legend of how the great warrior Cumal, the father of Fionn of the Fianna, was killed at the Battle of Cnucha.'

The girl, eyes still focused on the floor, added to this: 'It is also the name of the wife of Geanann, one of the five great kings of the Fir Bolg who first divided this island into the five kingdoms.'

Eadulf felt guilty at his amusement in reaction to the slight note of pride that entered into this drab servant's voice.

'And who were these . . . what did you call them – Fir Bolg? Who were they who divided this land into five kingdoms? I have heard only that your people were descended from the children of Milesius and are called Gaels.'

The girl raised her chin a little. Eadulf heard a note of pride again.

'The children of Milesius were the last people to arrive in this land. The Fir Bolg had conquered this island back in the mists of time, many generations before the coming of the children of the Gael. The five kings met at Uisnech, the sacred centre of the land, and it was from there that they divided it so that each one would rule a fifth.'

Uisnech again. Fidelma had explained its significance to him after the old woman had mentioned it at the bridge. Even the coming of Christianity had not displaced it as a great sacred ceremonial site, for it was thought to be the 'omphalos' or navel of the five kingdoms of Éireann, the point where the five kingdoms met. It was the spot where the goddess Éire, whose name had been given to the entire island, was venerated in ancient times. And it was the place where the Druids of the Old Faith gathered to light the ritual fires at the time of Beltane, the fires of Bél, marking the end of the dark half of the year.

'So you are proud of your name?' he observed.

Once again the girl's eyes flickered to his and this time he saw some tiny sparks of emotion.

'My name is all I have,' she said simply. 'I am a servant in this place. And, if you will forgive me, I will now go to Báine and see if she needs my help.'

She left as Caol and Gormán entered. Eadulf motioned to the jugs of drinks and suggested they help themselves.

Caol sprawled on a chair and stared moodily at his drink while Gormán leaned against the wall.

'You two do not look happy,' observed Eadulf.

Gormán shrugged indifferently. 'I can't say that I am happy to be here,' he acknowledged.

Caol smiled thinly. 'I think he is worried by the old woman at the ford.'

Gormán did not seem offended. 'You have to admit it was an unusual welcome to Tara. We have received better ones. I was raised on the old legends of the goddess of death and battles waiting at a ford and warning people of their death.'

Eadulf was not going to confess that he, too, had felt an apprehension about the old woman. He merely said: 'Well, she did not foretell our deaths. She merely told us to return to Cashel, which I am sure we will do as soon as possible. After all, this affair cannot keep us here long. Sechnussach is dead, we know who killed him and we know that the assassin took his own life. There is little enough to investigate.'

'Then why did the Great Assembly send for the lady Fidelma?' demanded Gormán.

'Merely to have someone unconnected with the events pronounce the findings,' replied Eadulf calmly. 'It seems a logical enough request.'

'There is a feeling of gloom in the place,' Gormán sighed, not assuaged.

'Why wouldn't there be? Is it often that a High King is murdered?' countered Eadulf.

'True. Neither is it so often that religious are slain in an attack for no good reason.'

'You are thinking of the deaths on the Plain of Nuada?' mused Eadulf. 'There does seem some atmosphere of restlessness in this kingdom of Midhe.'

Caol drained his beaker with a decisive motion. 'Well, there are robbers and outlaws in every kingdom. Even in Muman. Mind you, things have become very quiet now since the Uí Fidgente have decided to pay their respects to Cashel.' He grinned wryly and added, 'In fact, I quite miss the conflict.'

Eadulf shot him a look of disapproval. 'You miss conflict? That is not a good thing to—' he began, but Caol held up a hand, stopping him.

'I should be specific in that I miss the *excitement* that is attendant on the conflict. Of course it is not right to be addicted to death and battle. So, when will you and the lady Fidelma start to consider this matter?'

'Probably not until tomorrow. My guess is that we will be here a few days at the most. We shall know better after we have seen the heir to the High Kingship, Cenn Faelad, this evening.'

At that moment, Báine returned and announced that the water had now been heated for Eadulf's bath. He rose with an inward groan. The one thing he had never grown used to among the people of Éireann was this custom of having an evening bath before the main meal. He would never grow used to it, not if he lived to be a hundred. Then he summoned a smile for the girl and adopted an enthusiastic tone. 'Lead the way.'

CHAPTER FIVE

There was no mistaking Cenn Faelad as anyone other than the brother of Sechnussach, the late High King. He was only a year or so younger but they might have been twins. He was of the same height – tall, above six feet – with hair as dark as a raven's wing and eyes as grey as the restless seas of winter. He was handsome and his features would cause many a maiden to simper and swoon at his smile. But beyond that superficial exterior, so Fidelma had heard, he spoke several languages, excelled in many arts, and knew the law.

When Abbot Colmán showed Fidelma and Eadulf into chambers that Cenn Faelad was using, later that evening, the High King elect actually rose from his chair and came forward to greet them both with outstretched hands. His face, albeit composed, showed the marks of grief. There was one other person in the chamber and that was the Chief Brehon of the five kingdoms, Barrán. Fidelma and Eadulf knew him of old. He also greeted them without ceremony. He was a tall man, still handsome in spite of his age and greying hair, exuding an air of quiet authority. There were no servants in Abbot Colmán's house; indeed, they had all been dismissed to their quarters for the evening, and Cenn Faelad offered the visitors drinks from his own hands as he gestured to chairs already set out for them to be seated.

'I thought that we should gather in private at first,' the young heir to the kingship explained. 'Abbot Colmán has provided us with a meal in the next room but first let us speak of why you are here. We can conduct ourselves without ceremony and without protocol.'

Fidelma inclined her head in approval of the idea while Eadulf remained silent, his expression grave.

When Cenn Faelad had seated himself and they had all taken the first dutiful sip of their drinks, the *tánaiste* glanced at his Chief Brehon.

'Perhaps you should explain, Barrán.'

The elderly man cleared his throat before addressing them in his crisp, legal voice: 'The situation is simple and I believe it was outlined by the messenger whom we sent to Cashel. The High King Sechnussach, being alone in his chamber, was murdered in his bed by the chief of the Cinél Cairpre, a distant relative and descendant of Niall of the Nine Hostages, and therefore a member of the Uí Néill, Sechnussach's own family. You follow?'

The last question was directed more to Eadulf than to Fidelma. Eadulf indicated that he did.

'I am also of this same family,' Barrán admitted. 'This being so, and because of the implications which might arise, the *Airlechas*, the Great Assembly, decided that it would be inappropriate for me to investigate this matter, nor would it be appropriate for any of the Uí Néill to be involved. Justice must not only be done but must also be seen to be done . . .'

'*Fiat justitia, ruat caelum,*' muttered Eadulf. Let justice be done even though the heavens fall.

Cenn Faelad smiled thinly. 'Even so,' he agreed. 'Abbot Colmán reminded the Great Assembly of the services that Fidelma has rendered to Tara in the past. He suggested that they send for her, an Eóghanacht, someone who is not involved in the internal politics of the Uí Néill. So, Fidelma of Cashel, it falls to you to resolve the mystery of why Dubh Duin killed my poor brother and whether anyone else was involved. Only when all is known can we mourn his passing and prepare for my succession.'

Fidelma looked thoughtfully at him. 'I am to have a free hand?'

'Of course.'

'And there is no restriction on Eadulf assisting me?'

'We regard Eadulf as one of our own,' Brehon Barrán told her. 'Your names are inseparably linked. Cenn Faelad and I will withdraw from any connection to this matter except as witnesses. Abbot Colmán will act as your adviser on matters connected with Tara.'

'Very well,' agreed Fidelma. 'I presume that any witnesses have been detained in Tara?' When Brehon Barrán nodded, she added: 'We will want to examine the chamber where the murder took place.'

'Whenever you are ready.' Abbot Colmán spoke for the first time since they had entered Cenn Faelad's presence.

'I would like to ask some questions of all of you first.'

The Chief Brehon frowned slightly. 'Questions already? I thought this was just an informal discussion?'

DANCING WITH DEMONS

'I have no objection,' Cenn Faelad said immediately. 'The sooner a start is made, the sooner the matter is concluded. What question do you wish to ask, Fidelma?'

'On the night of Sechnussach's death, where were each of you?'

There was a brief silence.

Cenn Faelad decided to answer first.

'I was not in Tara but staying near the Hill of Uisnech.'

Eadulf tried not to show his surprise. Uisnech, the sacred hill, again. In this weather, Fidelma knew it to be two days' easy riding from Tara, but a good horseman such as Cenn Faelad could make it in a single day on a fast horse. She glanced at him, feeling guilty for having such suspicious thoughts without good reason.

'So when did you first hear of your brother's death?'

'It was when a messenger from Abbot Colmán arrived at Uisnech.'

Fidelma turned to the abbot. 'So you were here at Tara that night?'

The abbot gave an affirmative gesture. 'I was here in my chambers. A servant roused me, saying something had happened.'

'What time was that?'

'Before first light. It was light by the time I had dressed, hurried across to the royal enclosure and entered the High King's chamber. Irél, the captain of the guard, had already taken charge. He it was who sent for me as steward.'

'I assume, therefore, that you were not at Tara, Barrán?' Fidelma said. 'Otherwise, that duty would have fallen to you?'

The Chief Brehon smiled faintly. 'You are correct in your assumption. I was on my way to Emain Macha.'

'May I ask what business took you to the capital of the King of Ulaidh?'

'It has no relevance to this matter but it is no secret. I was to advise on a case involving a territorial dispute between the Dál Riada and Emain Macha. However, I did not reach Emain Macha as a messenger overtook me on the road and told me to hasten back to Tara. It was then that I heard that Sechnussach had been slain.'

Fidelma turned back to Abbot Colmán. 'So in the absence of the heir apparent and the Chief Brehon, you took responsibility at Tara, Abbot Colmán?'

'I did. As you know, I stand not only as spiritual adviser to the Great Assembly but also hold office as High King's *rechtaire*, his steward.'

'And, in taking charge, what did you do?'

51

'The High King's physician was sent for but that was merely a matter of procedure because we could see that he was dead. After all, his neck had been cut open so that the blood must have spurted like a great fountain.' He looked apologetically at Cenn Faelad, whose face was strained.

'I ordered a search of the adjoining rooms to ensure that the assassin acted alone, and then confirmed the identity of the assassin who had killed himself as soon as he had killed the King.'

'You confirmed his identity?' pressed Fidelma. 'So you knew him?'

'I had been told who it was by Irél. Irél had already recognised him. Dubh Duin was a member of the Great Assembly, and known in Tara. I had also seen him at the Assembly several times.'

'And then?'

'I ordered Irél to despatch messengers to alert Cenn Faelad and Brehon Barrán . . .'

'No one has mentioned the High King's wife and his daughters,' Eadulf pointed out. 'Were they not present?'

The abbot seemed suddenly defensive. 'They were not and I felt that it was more important to contact the heir apparent and Chief Brehon first.'

'Very well. What then?'

'Then I called a scribe to come and make such notes as I thought necessary to be placed in the *tech screpta*, the library. I asked the guards to give their statements . . .'

'Indeed. I will examine them later. It is more important to question a witness in person. The matter of the guards interests me. Was the High King's chamber not guarded that night?' asked Fidelma.

'The assassin eluded the two guards, Lugna and Cuan. They had been in the kitchen investigating a suspicious noise. Alerted by screams issuing from the King's chamber, they ran up the stairs and burst in just as the assassin turned his knife on himself.'

'Alerted by screams?' frowned Fidelma. 'What – from the High King?'

Abbot Colmán looked puzzled at the question. 'Who else would scream in these circumstances?'

'And were the guards able to explain how the assassin had managed to enter the royal enclosure, even gaining entrance to the High King's house and bedchamber while it was still dark? Was the building not locked from the inside?'

Abbot Colmán looked uncomfortable. 'In the centre of Tara, in the royal enclosure, it has always been thought unnecessary to bolt the doors, for two guards are always standing without.'

'And the door to the High King's bedchamber, was that not locked?' This time, Abbot Colmán reached into his leather purse and drew forth a bronze key. He held it out to her.

'We think it was, but the assassin carried a key.'

She took it and held it up. It was a well-crafted key and had a pattern on it.

'Where was this found?'

'In the assassin's *sparrán*.'

'Before you go further, Fidelma,' Cenn Faelad said softly, looking embarrassed, 'I know the key to be mine. It bears the same marks that are on my key.'

Fidelma looked curiously at him. 'You keep a key to the High King's bedchamber? When did you find your key was missing?'

'As heir apparent, I have a duplicate set of keys to all the royal apartments. But as for your second question,' he held out his hands helplessly. 'I didn't. I mean, it isn't.'

'I do not understand,' she replied impatiently.

Cenn Faelad drew forth another key and handed it to her. She took it and examined it. Then she held out both keys side by side and looked at them carefully. Now she understood.

'They have been cast from the same mould but also filed with exactly the same markings. That is unusual, but the explanation is simple. The intruder's key must have been copied from your key.'

Cenn Faelad nodded quickly. 'I agree. A locksmith has made both keys to bear the same personal markings. The keys of important buildings are given different markings so that their holders can be identified. In this case, the locksmith has ensured that both keys bear marks that identify them as mine.'

'How long have you had your key, Cenn Faelad?'

'Since I was elected *tánaiste* – that is, five years ago, and it has been in my possession ever since. But, look, that mark at the end of the key . . .'

'Like a deep score in the bronze?'

'That was made only three weeks ago. Yet the other key also has it.'

Fidelma compressed her lips thoughtfully. 'How was it done?' she asked. 'The mark, I mean.'

'I had been carrying out an inspection of all the locks with the *bollscari*, the head of the household staff, as he felt that some of them needed replacing. We tested the keys of the royal house. At the end of the inspection I was late for a sword practice with Irél, the commander of the guard, and I took the keys with me. I had laid them aside with my purse and belt. My sword was a new one and I was not sure of the balance. I made a swing to test it and the sword came down on this key. The blade nicked the bronze which, of course, was then dented.'

'And that was just three weeks ago? Did you leave the key with anyone during this time? Was it out of your possession at all?'

The young man shook his head. 'That is the frustrating part. I did not miss it at any time. To be honest, I never even check the keys unless there is a reason. They are kept in a box in my chamber in the royal house. The chamber is locked when I am not there.'

'Is the box also locked?'

'It was not felt there was a need.'

'Could any other person gain access to your chamber?'

'The *bollscari*, Brother Rogallach, is the person who keeps the only other key.'

'And you are there most of the time?'

'No. I have my own residence outside of Tara and am more often there.'

Fidelma sighed softly. 'We must return to this matter later. But it seems that our assassin was able to enter the High King's bedchamber because he had a key, one copied from your own within the last few weeks. Further, our assassin was able to get through the main gate of what should be the most fortified palace in all Éireann without challenge and walk directly into the High King's house without being seen.'

Brehon Barrán coloured a little at the note in her voice. He said, 'It seems that a guard on the main gate let him pass, through, without proper challenge. That guard has been held, pending your interrogation. He may have been in collusion with the assassin.'

'His name?' This was from Eadulf.

'Erc the Speckled.'

'You have said that the High King was alone in his bedchamber when he was murdered. This is a certainty?' Eadulf asked next.

'It is,' Brehon Barrán replied with a frown. 'Why, are you implying that—'

'What Eadulf meant,' Fidelma explained hurriedly, 'was that we have not been told where Sechnussach's wife, the lady Gormflaith, was that night. I think Abbot Colmán implied that she was not at the royal residence.'

'That is correct. The lady Gormflaith and her daughters had gone to Cluain Ioraird to spend the night in prayer for the repose of the soul of her mother,' Cenn Faelad told Fidelma.

'The abbey of Cluain Ioraird is on the road to Uisnech . . .' said Brehon Barrán.

'I accompanied Gormflaith to the abbey before riding on to Uisnech,' the young man said hastily.

'And presumably, once you heard the news of your brother's death, you returned to the abbey as it was on your way back here?'

'Of course,' replied Cenn Faelad, and he sighed. 'It was a logical thing to do. It was my sad task to inform the lady Gormflaith of her husband's death. It was decided that it would be best if she remained in the abbey until more was known about the assassin and his motives. But when it became clear that there was no immediate danger to her and her daughters, then they returned here.'

'So, at the moment,' Fidelma summed up, 'if there was no one else in the King's chamber, we may presume that the alarm was given by Sechnussach's death scream? Yet it seems unlikely. If a person's throat is cut open, there is little chance of emitting any sound, let alone a scream.'

Abbot Colmán was puzzled. 'Are you saying that someone else must have screamed?'

'What is known of Dubh Duin?' Fidelma went on, ignoring the question. 'What is known of his personality, of his family? I am aware that he was the chief of the Cinél Cairpre, but what else can you tell me about him?'

'Little else, except he was a member of the Great Assembly.'

'That was his right as chieftain of the Cinél Cairpre,' added Brehon Barrán.

'Is that the clan who dwell around the Plain of Nuada?' queried Eadulf.

Cenn Faelad smiled and shook his head. 'No. That is the Cairpre of Magh Nuada. The Cinél Cairpre Gabra dwell around the shores of Loch Gomhna, the lake of the calf. They are mainly hunters and farmers even though Dubh Duin was a direct descendant of my ancestor Niall of the Nine Hostages. He was proud of his lineage and boasted that he had some claims on the High Kingship. His ancestor Tuathal Maelgarb was the last successful claimant to the throne of Tara, but that was three or four generations ago. The only other thing I know is that Dubh Duin was not married.'

'Who is now chief of the Cinél Cairpre Gabra in his stead?' Fidelma asked.

'Ardgal,' supplied Brehon Barrán. 'A cousin of Dubh Duin.'

'Has any contact or embassy been sent to Ardgal and the Cinél Cairpre?' Cenn Faelad answered. 'Given the circumstances, it could not be otherwise. The slaughter of a High King by the chief of a clan is no insignificant event. When Aonghus of the Terrible Spear blinded the High King Cormac mac Art, he and his clan, the Déisi, were driven into exile. Half were given sanctuary in your own lands of Muman while the others fled across the sea to Britain and settled in the kingdom called Dyfed.'

Fidelma knew the story well and was impatient. 'I presume that is a confirmation that Ardgal has been contacted?'

'Of course. Irél and members of the Fianna, with the Brehon Sedna, were sent to the Cinél Cairpre. Ardgal, the *tánaiste*, was instructed to pick eight of the leading men of the clan, especially members of Dubh Duin's immediate family, and send them to Tara to present themselves as hostages for the good behaviour of the clan while the crime of their chief was investigated.'

'And did they?' asked Eadulf sceptically. As a Saxon he was, in many ways, still unused to the curious rituals of the law of the Éireannach.

'Naturally. Ardgal sent eight leading men of his clan as hostages. They have been here for several days at the Mound of the Hostages.'

Fidelma smiled at them all. 'That is all I need to know from you at this time. Tomorrow I propose to start with questions to the witnesses, such as they are. And, of course, I will wish to see where the assassination took place.'

'Abbot Colmán will see to all your needs,' Cenn Faelad agreed quietly. 'He has full authority to take you wherever you wish to go and also to force all and every one to answer your questions, should they seem reluctant.'

'That should not be necessary, seeing that I am a *dálaigh* qualified to the level of *anruth*,' Fidelma informed him somewhat tartly.

'Agreed, but these are not normal times,' Cenn Faelad sighed. 'And there is much suspicion here, especially against strangers.'

'We will do our best to find a resolution to this mystery so that we may return to normal times as soon as possible,' Fidelma said, not unkindly.

Cenn Faelad rose and they followed his example.

'And now we have had food for our thoughts,' he said, 'let us refresh ourselves with food for our bodies.'

Abbot Colmán opened a side door, revealing a small chamber where a table had been laid out ready.

'My servants have prepared a cold meal as I did not know what time our discussion might end and, of course, it was better that no servants were present to hear it.'

Eadulf glanced at the table in approval. There were plates of *sercoltorsan* or cold venison, and slices of *mairt-fheol* or beef. A dish of hardboiled goose eggs stood to one side, with dishes of *gruth-caisse* or curd cheese and hard cheese called *tanag*, and several kinds of bread. There were salads of *cneamh* or wild garlic with cress and wood sorrel, mixed with sloes as a condiment, and dishes of hazelnut, apples, whortleberries and honey. Drink was plentiful: jugs of cider, juice made from elderflower and apples, and even imported red wine. It was truly a feast.

The conversation as they ate studiously avoided the matter of Sechnussach's death but turned on the state of the kingdoms, the harvest and the threat of a new outbreak of the feared Yellow Plague that had devastated the country.

Finally, it was time for Fidelma and Eadulf to return to the guesthouse. Cenn Faelad held out his hand to Fidelma.

'God guide your work, lady. Let us hope for a quick resolution. It is dangerous for the five kingdoms to be without a High King confirmed in ancient ceremony. We have much work to do before we call the provincial kings to my inauguration. We will also need to call the Brehons of Ireland to appoint a new Chief Brehon as well.'

Fidelma was puzzled and glanced towards Brehon Barrán with an unspoken query.

Cenn Faelad saw the glance and explained. 'As we have said, Barrán is my cousin and I have persuaded him to stand as my *tánaiste*, for his will be a steady hand in helping to govern. Therefore, we need to find a new Chief Brehon to fill his place. That is why there is now urgency in resolving matters.'

'Then I will do my best to ensure that the result matches the urgency,' she promised. 'We will have to make an early start in the morning when it is light. I would like to see over Sechnussach's chambers.'

'There is not much to see there,' Cenn Faelad replied. 'Since the assassination took place, most things have been cleared from the apartments.'

'Nevertheless,' insisted Fidelma, 'it is good to see where the crime took place so that I can visualise the events.'

Abbot Colmán said: 'In that case I will come by the guesthouse after you have broken your fast and take you there. As Cenn Faelad said, you have only to ask, and I am at your service.'

'Then we will make a start after breakfast,' replied Fidelma solemnly.

CHAPTER SIX

E adulf woke just before first light.

He could hear Fidelma's regular breathing and knew that she was still asleep. At first he did not know why he had awoken and then he heard the noise of a pan being moved from the *ircha*, the kitchen area of the guesthouse. He looked out of the window and saw from the sky that it would soon be dawn. He wanted to turn over and go back to the warm comfort of the dream he was having but knew that, even if he could recapture the moment, within moments he would be roused sharply. With a sigh, he decided to make the best of it and crept out of bed.

If someone was already stirring in the kitchen, he could take the opportunity to wash before Fidelma and the others rose. He went to the door and opened it softly so as not to disturb her, and moved out into the corridor.

Having passed beyond the door he now heard the soft whispers of a conversation. He wondered who was awake apart from himself. Stepping quietly down the corridor, he then halted in embarrassment as he heard a female voice. He tried to place where he had heard it before and then he recalled that it was the plainfaced girl with the strange name – what was it? – Cnucha?

It was not her tone but what she said that halted him.

'She is a . . .' He did not understand the word that was used but had a feeling it was not a nice expression. Resentfully, the girl's voice continued: 'I don't see why *I* should do her work for her!'

'Because there is no one else to do it, my girl. That is why.'

He did not recognise the stern tones of the woman who answered her.

'She is always getting out of her duties recently, ever since . . . ever since – well, you know.'

'I have no time to argue, Cnucha. The meal for the guests must be prepared and the water heated for their wash. When Báine is not here, then it is up to you to fulfil these chores.'

'It occurs to me that Báine is hardly ever here when needed. She spends too much time with the High King's daughter, if you ask me.'

'She cannot help the fact that the lady Muirgel has taken a fancy to her company. And you are in enough trouble with Muirgel and Brehon Barrán without complaining about others.'

The girl sniffed. 'It was not my fault.'

'They caught you searching the High King's chambers the day after the assassination. Why were you doing that?'

'I had a right to be there,' the girl replied sulkily. 'One of my tasks was to attend the chambers and keep them clean.'

'The lady Muirgel did not think so.'

'She shouldn't have lost her temper and struck me! Bitch! Then Barrán came in and supported her, saying I had no business to be there.'

'And he was right. Sechnussach had been assassinated. The chambers should have been closed.'

'Brehon Barrán said as much, but . . .' Her voice trailed off.

Eadulf heard the other woman sigh impatiently.

'I don't know what possessed you. Whatever were you doing in the High King's chambers? Come on – the truth now. Surely not cleaning.'

Cnucha seemed to hesitate. Then: 'If you must know, I was looking for something, that is all. I probably lost it elsewhere. It was . . . personal. A bracelet.'

'I see. Well, I know jewellery can be of sentimental value, but—'

'It was also valuable,' the girl protested. 'It was a bracelet of silver Gaulish coins. I must have lost it when I was cleaning. I did not want to lose it.'

'Well, if it hasn't turned up during the last ten or more days, I think you will have to resign yourself to its loss. It seems an expensive sort of thing for someone like you to come by.' The voice was suspicious.

'It was a gift from . . . a friend.' The girl's voice was defiant.

'Well, wealthy friend or not, it still doesn't absolve you from work, Cnucha. And with Báine not here, I suggest you get started on your duties.'

'Then why doesn't Báine go to Muirgel and be her attendant, so that we may get another person to help us in our work?'

'All will be changed when this investigation is over and Cenn Faelad becomes High King. He will then choose his attendants as he considers fit.'

Eadulf heard the girl sniff.

'And will you be staying on then, Brónach? Will you be in charge?'

'Brother Rogallach is in charge. I am only the senior female servant.'

'I doubt whether Cenn Faelad will want Brother Rogallach to continue to be in charge of his household. Cenn Faelad is a real man and not so outwardly pious as Sechnussach was.'

'That is no way to talk about the late High King.' The voice was stern with disapproval.

'Why not? Anyway, I am comparing Sechnussach to Cenn Faelad. Sechnussach may have surrounded himself with pious religious, but he was no more than—'

'You should have a care what you say about Sechnussach, my girl!' Brónach hissed. 'Especially now you have a *dálaigh* in this guesthouse who is investigating his assassination.'

'Huh! Another so-called pious religieuse with her Saxon lover!' Cnucha sneered.

'Watch your tongue. They are married and well-respected. She is also sister to the King of Muman. Now, for the last time, get about your chores! When I see Báine, I will discuss this matter with her. She should let us have more notification if she has to attend to other duties.'

Eadulf heard a door closing and reasoned that the woman, Brónach, must have left by the side door. He paused for a moment and then decided to continue his mission to find water for washing. Cnucha was alone in the kitchen preparing oatmeal cakes for breakfast. She looked up with a start of surprise as he entered.

'I did not know you were up, Brother.'

Eadulf pretended to stifle a yawn as he saw the girl flush guiltily.

'I have only just risen. I am looking for water to wash. Was there someone else here before me? I thought I heard a voice.'

'Oh, it was only Brónach. She is in charge of us.'

'Ah. I don't think we have met her yet.'

Cnucha shrugged and went on kneading oatmeal. She gestured with her head towards the wash room. 'The water is heating ready for you.'

'Thank you.'

Her tone had been dismissive and so the opportunity to develop the conversation was thus lost. Eadulf, with a sigh, accepted it with good grace.

Abbot Colmán arrived, as promised, as they finished their morning meal and took them to the royal residence called *Tech Cormaic*. It was a large rectangular building of two storeys with several outhouses, standing inside the ramparts of the royal enclosure, well away from the defensive system that surrounded the buildings of the nobles who dwelt at Tara. The High King's house was built of a variety of woods, but chiefly of oak and yew. The *slinntech darach*, the overlapping boards of polished oak, which comprised the roof, shone in the morning sun.

The abbot led the way to the massive double doors of thick oak. A guard with a drawn sword resting against his shoulder saluted Abbot Colmán and stood to one side.

'It would appear that the assassin entered this way in the dead of night,' explained the abbot as he opened the doors.

'And these doors are never locked or bolted?' Eadulf enquired, seeking confirmation of what they had been told the previous night.

The abbot gestured at the ramparts that surrounded the royal enclosure. 'To get here, one has to come through many guarded gates, and the main gate to the royal enclosure is always bolted and guarded on the inside.'

'But the assassin did reach here,' Eadulf pointed out softly.

Abbot Colmán flushed but did not respond.

Fidelma made no comment either as they passed into the dimly lit hall beyond, for there was only one window providing light. This, called a *forless*, was placed above the door. Its glass panel was thick, opaque, and the light it emitted was little enough. The main light came from pungent-smelling oil lamps.

Again Eadulf pursed his lips thoughtfully. 'It was a lucky coincidence for the assassin that the guards were not where they should have been, on guard within this hall. They were not here because they had heard a suspicious noise in the kitchen – is that right?'

The abbot nodded.

Eadulf raised his eyebrows a fraction. 'Perhaps the assassin had more than luck on his side,' he muttered.

'We will question these guards when the time comes,' Fidelma said, smiling acknowledgement at Eadulf for picking up the point. 'Certainly it seems that the assassin had exceptional luck. Is there an entrance to the kitchen area from here?'

'The kitchen is a separate building at the rear. There is a door at the back of the hall and the meals, once cooked, are carried into the High King through it. It is usually locked during the night. The commander of the guard has a key.' Abbot Colmán hesitated and then pointed up the stairs. 'From here, the assassin would have gone up these stairs.'

'Are all the bedchambers above the stair?' Eadulf asked.

'Not all. The High King's apartments are there. There are rooms for his family and for his personal attendants. On this floor, the ground floor, there is a room for the commander of the Fianna, the High King's body-guard. When Cenn Faelad stays in the royal house, he has a chamber on this level also. There are rooms for some of the servants here as well. There is a private chamber for the High King's meetings with his advisers which also serves as a library, a small room for meals when there is no great feasting to preside over, and the remaining rooms are given to storage and bedchambers for the maids.'

'Very well,' acknowledged Fidelma, following the layout as the abbot indicated it. 'So we shall follow the steps of our assassin, through these main doors, across the hall, which is luckily empty of the guard, and up the stairs. Proceed.'

The abbot led the way up the broad wooden staircase and halted on the landing.

'To the left is the High King's apartment, through that door. The next door enters into the apartments reserved for his family when they stay here. Needless to say, they are residing elsewhere in the royal enclosure at the moment.'

'And those other doors?' Fidelma queried, indicating the ones in the corridor leading to the right off the landing.

'The far door is the chamber of the High King's *bollscari*, Brother Rogallach.'

'*Bollscari*? What exactly is the difference between the factotum and yourself?'

'I deal with administrative matters for the High King whereas the *bollscari* is in charge of all the domestic servants.'

'And these servants – who are they?'

'His personal attendants, three females and three males. I think you have met two of the females for they are attending you in the guesthouse.'

'What are their normal functions?'

'They are in charge of cleaning here, one of them is the cook, and so on.'

'So, only the servants and the commander of the Fianna were staying here that night?'

The abbot hesitated before replying. 'In the royal house . . . yes.'

Fidelma noticed the hesitation and immediately asked: 'You have thought of something?'

'Nothing of consequence, but perhaps a matter of clarification. You may know that Sechnussach and Gormflaith had three daughters. The youngest are Mumain and Bé Bhail. They were with their mother at Cluain Ioraird that night. I think we overlooked the fact that Muirgel, the eldest daughter, was in Tara.'

'If I am to conduct a proper investigation I must be in possession of all the facts,' Fidelma said sharply. 'You are now certain that Muirgel was in Tara that night?'

'I believe so.'

'You *believe* so?' she repeated with emphasis.

'Muirgel is a strong-willed young woman. She does not stay at the *Tech Cormaic* but I was told in the morning that one of the servants went to her house and she was there. Gormflaith and her daughters have a separate dwelling on the other side of the royal enclosure.'

Fidelma grimaced. 'We shall talk to Muirgel later. But are you saying that Gormflaith and her daughters do not live in the royal residence? So their apartment would not be in use anyway.'

'That is so.'

'Apart from Brother Rogallach, can you name the attendants who were here?'

'Certainly. There is the High King's personal cook, Torpach. There is his assistant, Maoláin, and the handyman, Duirnín. Then there are three female servants, the senior being Brónach. You already have met Báine. The other servant girl is Cnucha, a general maid. When the High King had personal or special guests, they also served the guests' hostel. Only the servants who were here at the time of the assassination have been retained, for usually there are many more attending all the royal enclosure. Chief Barrán decided to set them to work in the other residences. They were all roused by the noise of the discovery that night but saw nothing that would help you, of course.'

Fidelma noted the names carefully in her mind before asking: 'And these servants have their chambers . . . where exactly?'

'The senior members of the staff have chambers on this floor, along the corridor there. The others have chambers on the floor below.'

'Very well. Let us examine the High King's chambers as our first step.' The abbot moved to the first door that he had indicated to their left.

'As we have discussed, this door was usually locked from the inside when the High King retired for the night. There were only two keys – one in the possession of the High King and the other in the possession of Cenn Faelad.'

Abbot Colmán opened the door and ushered them in.

The room was spacious, as one might expect of the chamber of the High King. It contained two fairly large *seinester* or windows of opaque glass, one of which was directly behind the great *tolg* or bedframe. The walls were of red yew panels, and the one directly facing the end of the bed had a large ornate cross of native design hung on it. Fidelma was not sure what wood it was made of. Apart from the bed, the other furnishings were fairly simple – a *brothrach* or couch along one wall, a table by the bed and a few assorted boxes. The bedframe was devoid of any covering.

The abbot saw Fidelma's scrutiny and offered: 'The coverings, including the *dergud*, the mattress, were removed and disposed of. Likewise the *adart*, pillow, and *setigi*, blankets. In fact, all of Sechnussach's personal belongings have now been removed.'

Fidelma made no response, merely looking from the door to the bed. All the assassin had to do was take a few swift steps from the door . . . She raised her head and looked to the far side of the room. There were two doors in the opposite wall.

'Where do those lead?' she asked.

'One is the room that is used as the *fialtech*, the privy, and it is where the High King usually took his bath. It has an outside door and staircase. Water is heated on the lower floor and brought up to the bath by this stair. That door was bolted from the inside. Next to the privy room is the *erdam*, a side room where the High King kept his clothes and weapons. It has a window but there are no means of entering it, apart from the door in this chamber. The bedchamber can only be entered by the door we came in by, or by the door to the privy room. Irél checked all the rooms and bolts at the time. If the assassin had an accomplice, they could not have entered nor left by the outside door. The bolts were still in place.'

'Let's examine these other rooms,' Fidelma announced, and walked around the dark wooden bedframe to open the first door.

The small room beyond had another opaque glass window. The bottom of it came up to her chest height and she saw that it could be opened from the inside.

Abbot Colmán saw her examining its frame.

'It was designed to open from the inside so that the steam from the bath, the *dabach*, could be released from the room. Also, of course, the fumes from the . . .' He gestured at the covered receptacles in the corner.

Fidelma looked at the door and examined the bolts. There were two strong bolts as well as a lock.

'And Irél, the commander of the guard, was sure that these bolts were in place on the night of the assassination?'

'As I say, as soon as the body was discovered, Irél examined the chamber in case of anyone being in collusion with the assassin. The bolts were firmly in place so that no one could have escaped from the chamber through that route.'

'Similarly, this window was secured that night?'

'It was. Although, had it been open, it would have been a tight squeeze for anyone and it is a long drop to the ground below.'

She nodded absently and moved back into the bedchamber before leading the way into the second small chamber. In this side room there was, indeed, no separate outside door although there was another opaque glass window but again positioned at chest height and with no means of it being opened. Like the bedchamber, the walls were covered in red yew panels. Apart from a double line of wooden pegs and hooks along one wall, which was doubtless where Sechnussach hung his clothes, or weapons or even book satchels, all the rest of the furniture had been removed.

Fidelma stood examining the room for a moment and then shrugged.

'As you say, Colmán, there is only one means of entry and exit if the other door and windows were secured that night from the inside. They could not have been secured after anyone had passed from this chamber. But there is one thing that bothers me . . .'

Abbot Colmán waited.

Fidelma pointed to the lock on the bedchamber door. 'Why didn't Sechnussach leave the key in the lock? Had the key been in the lock then the assassin would not have been able to insert his own, or if he was able to push the other key out, he would have made enough noise to rouse the High King from his slumber before he struck.'

The abbot looked thoughtful. 'It didn't occur to me . . .' he began.

'As a matter of fact,' interrupted Eadulf, 'where was the High King's key found?'

'On the table by the bed.'

'Then perhaps there is no mystery there,' suggested Eadulf. 'It might have been his habit to lock the chamber door and remove the key to the bedside.'

Fidelma glanced round the room again before speaking.

'I have seen enough. Now I can, at least, visualise where and in what manner this crime was committed. I think we may now begin to examine the witnesses.'

CHAPTER SEVEN

The abbot had conducted her to the *tech screpta*, the small royal library house. She chose a chair in a corner and Eadulf borrowed some *ceraculum*, writing tablets of beechwood base covered in wax or *cera* from which their name derived. With a stylus he could then make notes on them which could be transcribed to parchment or vellum at a later stage. Thus prepared, with Abbot Colmán acting as their steward, Fidelma had asked to see the physician who had attended Sechnussach.

As she expected, the physician merely confirmed the facts of the High King's manner of death. However, it was important in her eyes that nothing, and especially no one, was overlooked in this matter. The physician, appropriately named Iceadh, for the name actually meant 'healer', was elderly with a curious habit of issuing his sentences in staccato fashion as though he had to get them out in one breath.

'His throat was cut. The jugular vein severed. Short stab in the heart. Either wound fatal. Sharp instrument found with assassin. A hunter's knife. Honed to sharpness. Could slice anything. No chance of saving his life. Died almost instantly.'

'So, in your expert opinion,' Fidelma smiled encouragingly, 'would you say that the High King was attacked while asleep in his bed?'

'Asleep? Assuredly. No time for a struggle. Doubt if he would have known anything. The assassin knew what he was doing.'

'And did you also examine the body of the assassin?' queried Eadulf.

The physician sniffed. 'Dubh Duin? Of course. He was also beyond help. Expert knife-thrust into the heart. Self-inflicted when caught by guards. Told he survived a few moments. Said something to one of the guards.'

Fidelma nodded and dismissed the man, calling for the warrior Lugna to come in.

The warrior was deferential and stood uncomfortably before her. He was a tall young man, red-headed, tough-looking and typical of the muscular members of the Fianna, the élite warriors of the High King.

'I am told that you were the senior guard at the royal house on the night of Sechnussach's assassination. Is that so?'

Lugna replied stiffly, 'Even as you have been told, lady.'

Fidelma frowned at the warrior's awkward manner, knowing that unless he relaxed it would be hard to obtain any useful information from him. She motioned to a seat before her. 'You may sit, Lugna.'

The young man glanced nervously at Abbot Colmán, who was standing at Fidelma's side. Then he clumsily sat down.

Fidelma glanced up at Abbot Colmán. 'It seems our young friend would feel more comfortable if you sat as well, Colmán,' she said gently. It was not protocol for a young warrior to be seated when an abbot was on his feet.

The abbot hesitated for a moment, then took a chair from nearby and sat down.

'Now that we are all seated,' resumed Fidelma, 'we can begin. All I am wanting from you, Lugna, is an account of the events of that night as you saw them. I am not here to apportion any blame. My aim is to learn the truth of those events.'

'The facts are known. I have told the abbot,' replied the warrior, still formal in manner and indicating Abbot Colmán with a slight nod of his head.

'But you have not told *me*,' she pointed out, her voice even and almost gentle. 'And I am the one who has been designated by the Great Assembly to investigate this matter. Now – I understand that you were in charge of the guards at the royal residence on that night. How long have you been in the service of the High King?'

Lugna raised his chin slightly. 'I have served in the Fianna for five years. I am a *toisech cóicat* of the first *catha*.'

Eadulf looked puzzled, as he was unacquainted with the military vocabulary. Fidelma quickly explained.

'In time of peace the High Kings maintain three *catha* or battalions of the Fianna. In wartime, the Fianna is usually raised to nine battalions. But the standing three battalions are professional warriors, just as my brother maintains the Nasc Niadh of Muman. The first battalion is always at the side of the High King and guarding the royal domains.' And turning back to Lugna she added: 'And you say you were the commander of a *cóicat*, that is a troop of fifty warriors?'

Lugna was still impassive. 'As I have said, lady.'

'So you are an experienced warrior, Lugna,' Fidelma observed. 'Where are you from?'

Lugna blinked a little in surprise at the question. 'I am of the Uí Mac Uais Breg of Brega, lady.'

'Who dwell north of here, beyond the River Bóinn?'

'As you say, lady.'

'What time did you come on watch?'

'My watch was from midnight until dawn.'

'Tell me what happened.'

'It was just before dawn. My comrade Cuan and I had made an inspection of the guards in the royal enclosure. This is done several times during the watch. We returned to the entrance of the royal house.'

Fidelma sat back thoughtfully. 'As I understand, your position was usually in the hallway?'

'It is. But while we were still outside, Cuan heard a noise in the kitchen at the back of the royal house and we went to investigate.'

'You did not enter and go in through the hallway?'

'The kitchen door is usually locked at night and we did not want to disturb the house if there was no need, so we went round the side of the house to the outbuildings.'

'Why did you think there was no need to rouse the household, if you heard a noise?'

Lugna coloured a little. 'Cuan was not exactly sure what he heard and I had not heard anything,' he admitted.

'So you went along the side of the building,' Fidelma said. 'Wasn't that ill-advised? You left the main door of the house unguarded to go round the back?'

Lugna did not meet her eye. 'We thought we should investigate.'

'Leaving the house unguarded?' she repeated with emphasis.

'I cannot deny that.'

'I gather the commander of the Fianna slept on the same floor not far away. You did not think of alerting him before you left?'

Lugna actually smiled with a bitter humour. 'Wake Irél for no good reason? I would not think of doing so in the circumstances.'

'And did you find an explanation for the noise?' she asked.

The soldier was obviously embarrassed. 'We did not.'

'And you returned – when?'

'We were in the kitchen when we heard a scream. The adjoining door between the kitchen area and the main house was, as I have said, locked. We had to run back along the side of the building again, in order to enter at the front doors and then come up the stairs.'

'So now we begin to build a picture of the events.' Fidelma paused a moment and then continued: 'Describe the circumstances of what happened at the moment you heard this scream.'

Lugna considered for a moment as if to gather his thoughts.

'The scream raised all those who were in the house. By the time we arrived at the High King's chamber, several people were stirring and calling out in alarm.'

'Was the bedchamber door locked?'

'It was not. We found the key on the table by the bed. But another key was also found in the assassin's purse later.'

'So, you entered Sechnussach's chamber?'

'I entered first. The assassin was slumped by the bed and he was already dying. He had clearly taken his own life with the same dagger with which he had cut the throat of our King. Cuan entered moments later, having paused to pick up a lantern. I saw by its light that the High King was beyond mortal help.'

'There was no one else in the chamber?'

'Not at that time. It was moments after Cuan and I entered that the servants began to crowd in. I told them to stay back and then our commander, Irél, entered and later Abbot Colmán.'

'Did you recognise the assassin?'

'Not at first. I think it was Irél who identified him and when I looked closer, I realised that he was right. It was Dubh Duin of the Cinél Cairpre.'

'You said that he was dying. Did he say anything before he died?'

'Matter of fact, he gasped something, but it was of little consequence.'

'I think I should be the judge of that,' Fidelma said.

'He simply admitted that he was to blame.'

Eadulf looked up from his note-taking. 'How did he phrase that exactly?' he asked.

The warrior shrugged. 'The word *cron* – blame. It was just a dying whisper. It was all I heard. Nothing else.'

Fidelma noticed that a thoughtful frown had settled on Eadulf's brow. She turned back to Lugna.

'There is one thing that troubles me,' she told him. 'This scream that everyone heard: you and your companion are standing in the kitchen, you hear the scream and run to the High King's chamber.'

'That is so.'

'The assassin had cut the High King's throat?'

'He had.'

'Surely the High King could not have screamed with his throat cut?'

'The same idea occurred to Irél and he ordered us to search the privy and the adjoining room, but there was no one else in the apartments. It must have been Sechnussach's dying breath.'

'As I see it, if Sechnussach had had the power to scream, he would also have had the power to struggle with his assailant. However, the physician is sure that *no* struggle took place and that the assassin struck while the High King lay asleep. *There would have been no time for him to scream.* So who was it who did so?'

Lugna thought for a moment or two but was clearly puzzled and said so.

'I do not know, lady. When I think of it, the scream was of a high pitch, and so you may be right that it is unlikely to have been the High King who uttered such a sound. Sechnussach was fond of singing, so I know the resonance of his voice – a deep baritone.'

When Lugna's comrade, Cuan, was called in to answer her questions, he said he could add no more to the story than Lugna had told them. He was a taciturn young man with dark hair, bony features and close-set eyes, and had a slight scar over his right eye.

'I gather that you were the one who heard the noise from the kitchen which caused you and Lugna to leave the door unguarded during the vital time when the assassin must have passed inside the High King's house?'

Cuan stirred uncomfortably. 'I heard something,' he replied. 'I told Lugna and he said we should investigate.'

'And he was your superior that night?' mused Fidelma.

'He is a commander of a troop of fifty. I am a mere warrior.'

Fidelma regarded his stubborn features for a while. Then she sighed. She knew that she was not being told the truth, but it was obvious that she could not push against an immovable force without some means of leverage. It was best to leave it for the moment. Of the two, perhaps Lugna would be the better person to apply pressure to, and find out why they had deserted their post at that crucial time.

After Abbot Colmán had escorted Cuan to the door of the library, she leaned towards Eadulf and said quietly: 'Already I feel there is far more here than simply an assassin who strikes and then kills himself. As we remarked before, this man seems to have had extraordinary luck. He is let into the royal enclosure by a guard, contrary to orders that only people with permission of the High King can be admitted after nightfall. Then he enters the High King's residence because the two men who are supposed to be guarding it have chosen that very moment to go out to the kitchen to investigate a noise. He can also enter the High King's chamber because he has a duplicate key which has been recently cut from the heir apparent's own key. Indeed, that is not luck, Eadulf. I think there is collusion somewhere.'

'Do you think the noise was deliberately made to lure the guards to the kitchen?' Eadulf asked.

'No. I think they are lying,' Fidelma replied bluntly. 'They claim to have heard this noise while at the front of the royal house. That is possible – yet it aroused no one else. No one in the rooms at the back heard anything. If it was some confederate of the assassin seeking to lure the guards away so that he could enter unopposed, it was not a good plan. The sound might have woken lots of other people.'

Eadulf reflected silently. 'When do you plan to challenge Lugna and Cuan then?'

'I need something to break through their story and get at the truth. I think they have agreed on this lie and I shall need more information in order to challenge them. Meanwhile, we will continue our investigations with the other witnesses.'

Abbot Colmán had returned. 'Whom shall I call in now?' he asked.

'I think we should see the other guard, the one that was at the main gate. Erc, I think his name is?'

The abbot nodded. 'He is being held in the cells. Shall I send for him to be brought here?'

Fidelma rose abruptly. 'We will go and see him where he is held. Perhaps his surroundings will help him concentrate on my questions.'

Erc the Speckled rose from his wooden bench in the dungeon in which he had been incarcerated and stood with a woebegone expression as Fidelma and Eadulf entered with Abbot Colmán. He gave the appearance of a man resigned to fate – and that fate was like an irresistible force that was going to destroy him.

Abbot Colmán announced Fidelma and her status with a solemn tone.

'Well, Erc the Speckled,' Fidelma gave the man a smile of encouragement as she seated herself on a stool, 'you appear to be in a sorry situation.'

The warrior sighed deeply. 'I am at fault, lady,' he said tonelessly. 'I
have no excuse.'

Fidelma pointed to the wooden bench and instructed the man to be
seated.

Erc sat down nervously.

'I am told that the facts are simple,' Fidelma began. 'On the night that
Sechnussach was murdered, you were on guard at the main gates of the
royal enclosure. Is that so?'

Erc nodded.

'Tell me about the events as you know them to be.'

'I have no defence, lady,' he repeated. 'I let the man who murdered the
High King into the royal enclosure at a time when entry should have been
forbidden.'

'That is not what I asked you,' replied Fidelma firmly.

'I do not understand, lady,' Erc said with a frown of bewilderment.

'At what time did you go on guard that night?' she prompted.

'About midnight,' the warrior replied slowly, realising what she wanted.
'The watches are changed then and I was to take the watch from midnight
until after dawn. The main gates are closed and bolted at that time and
my task was to stand as sentinel by the gates. On no account are the gates
to be opened – but for special people, there is a door set within the gate
which can give one person access at a time.'

'I understand. Now tell me, did anyone else come or go through the
gate while you were on watch? I mean, before the arrival of the assassin?'

Erc shook his head. 'No, lady.'

'So – only the assassin came to the main gate?'

'Yes. He arrived a short while before dawn. It was still dark but there
was a hint of light on the eastern hills.'

'What then?'

'I challenged him, of course. Then he walked into the light of the torches
so that I could see his features.'

'You knew him?'

Erc nodded. 'That is why I let him in. He was Dubh Duin of the Cinél
Cairpre.'

Fidelma frowned slightly. 'You let him into the royal enclosure simply because he was a chieftain that you knew? If I remember my protocol correctly, no one, not even a distant relation of a king, is allowed into a royal enclosure after the gates are shut and barred at night.' She turned to Abbot Colmán. 'This is a sorry state of affairs, that an assassin can come to the great complex of Tara, be admitted through gates that are usually bolted all through the hours of darkness. That he can then walk to the house of the High King himself, go through an unlocked door that has been left unguarded, make his way to the High King's bedchamber, enter with a key provided and kill him.'

Abbot Colmán shrugged uncomfortably. 'I admit that we must learn some lessons here. We must speak with Irél who is the *aire-echtra*, the commander of the Fianna. The only time that Dubh Duin has ever been admitted within these precincts has been when the Great Assembly was sitting.'

Erc's features were even more woebegone than ever. 'That's not true,' he said suddenly. 'During the previous two weeks, Dubh Duin had been admitted several times into the royal enclosure after midnight.'

Fidelma glanced swiftly at Abbot Colmán, but he seemed as surprised as she was.

'And who authorised his admittance?' she asked sharply.

'It was the lady Muirgel.'

'Muirgel? You mean the High King's eldest daughter?'

'The same, lady. She had the authority to pass him through the guards. How could I question the orders of the daughter of Sechnussach?'

Fidelma regarded the man thoughtfully for a moment. 'Let me get this correct in my mind,' she said. 'Are you saying that the lady Muirgel, daughter of Sechnussach, gave you orders to pass Dubh Duin into the royal enclosure after midnight, and on more than one occasion during the last two weeks?'

Erc nodded eagerly. 'Exactly so. And the last time, she said that if I was ever on watch and she was not there to greet Dubh Duin, he should be allowed to pass unhindered at her word. That is why I did not question him on that night.'

'Did you tell anyone this in your defence?' demanded Fidelma.

'No one asked me before I was brought here.'

Abbot Colmán added quickly: 'He has not really been questioned on the matter before. He was only asked if he allowed Dubh Duin through the gates and when he admitted that he had, he was brought here to await examination by a Brehon.'

Eadulf leaned forward to Erc. 'Did the lady Muirgel give you specific orders to permit entry to Dubh Duin on the night of the High King's assassination?'

'No,' said Erc, 'but I thought my instructions from her were clear. As I have said, having let him in on so many previous occasions on lady Muirgel's authority, I assumed he should be allowed to pass unhindered again. But I have already admitted that it is my responsibility,' he added with resignation. 'I was at fault that night. I should have demanded that the lady Muirgel be sent for, even though the hour was late.'

'Did Muirgel give you any reason for her actions on previous nights? Why would she give her authority to the admittance of this man?' asked Eadulf.

Erc smiled wanly. 'I am a simple warrior, Brother Saxon. Who am I to question the order of a daughter of the High King and one, after all, who is at the age of choice.'

'Yet had you questioned her, perhaps a High King's life might have been saved,' Eadulf snapped.

'Are you suggesting that Muirgel had something to do with her father's assassination?' Abbot Colmán burst out. 'For shame, Brother Eadulf . . . why, she is only seventeen years old!'

'Girls of a younger age than seventeen have been known to harbour patricidal thoughts,' Fidelma interposed quietly. 'I am sure you will agree that Muirgel must be questioned on this matter which is, to say the least, curious.'

'You are right, of course,' Abbot Colmán said heavily. 'Doubtless the girl will be able to present an explanation.'

'Doubtless,' commented Fidelma dryly before turning back to Erc. 'When you say that the chieftain was admitted to the royal enclosure several times after midnight during the previous two weeks, can you be exact?'

Erc pondered aloud. 'Exact? Oh, the exact number of times . . . I would say five times at least and perhaps more, well – no more than six times.'

'Is that unusual?' asked Eadulf.

'Unusual? In what way?'

'That a stranger to the palace be admitted to the royal enclosure after midnight? For example, how many other people were admitted to the royal enclosure after midnight during the same period?'

Erc hesitated, his brows drawn together, trying to remember. 'You mean outsiders to the royal household? Well, none who did not have a right to be there.'

'And of those who had a right to be there?' pressed Fidelma.

'No one came after the gates were shut at midnight.'

Fidelma raised an eyebrow in query. 'No one? Not even someone who had a right to be in the enclosure who was returning late?'

'No one,' asserted the warrior. Then he changed his mind. 'Except . . . except for the Bishop of Delbna Mór. I recall now that he came in late one night. Ah, it was on the night before the assassination. The commander of the Fianna himself accompanied him. Orders also came from the High King to admit him.'

Fidelma glanced at Abbot Colmán. 'The Bishop of Delbna Mór?' she echoed, and noticed that the abbot was looking perplexed.

'I did not know that the bishop had come to Tara,' he said. 'Usually I am informed of all the ecclesiastics who arrive here. Certainly, at such an unusual hour, I should have been told.'

'Who is this bishop and where is Delbna Mór?' asked Fidelma.

'The bishop is one Luachan. And Delbna Mór is to the west in the territory of Midhe. I am surprised that you have not heard of it, for it is associated with your brother's kingdom.'

Fidelma was puzzled and said so.

'I think it was a story that goes back many centuries. Something about a chieftain of your brother's kingdom having to flee to the north, settling in the land and giving it the name of Delbna Mór.'

Fidelma sniffed a little impatiently. 'I am more concerned with the immediate past than legend. So tell me more about this Bishop Luachan,' she invited.

Abbot Colmán made a slight motion with his shoulder. 'Little to tell. I know that I have heard nothing in criticism of the man. I have only seen him in the abbey at Cluain Ioraird at a council of the bishops of Midhe.'

'So he is not someone who comes to Tara regularly?' asked Eadulf.

'I would have said never, until Erc told us the contrary.'

Fidelma turned back to the warrior. 'You did not know the bishop?'

The man shook his head.

'But he was escorted by one of the High King's warriors and you had orders to admit him?'

'I did.'

'Did you say that the warrior who accompanied him was the commander of the Fianna?' asked Eadulf, who was becoming frustrated by the brevity of the man's answers.

'It was Irél,' he confirmed.

'And it was he who gave you orders to admit Bishop Luachan?'

Erc shook his head again and Eadulf exhaled in frustration, at which the warrior, realising that he was expected to answer more fully, added: 'Brother Rogallach came to the gate with orders from the High King himself. It was from him that I heard that the man's name was Bishop Luachan.'

'Brother Rogallach?' Eadulf paused thoughtfully. 'He is the *bollscari*?'

'He is in close attendance on the High King,' the abbot reminded them.

'And you say Bishop Luachan came with Irél after midnight on the night *before* the assassination? Do you know when he departed from Tara?' Fidelma asked.

Erc nodded and then, as he saw the gathering of her brows, went on hastily: 'He left just an hour or two later, before dawn, and still in the company of Irél, though the captain of the guard returned but an hour later when my watch was being relieved.'

'I wonder what could have brought him hither?' muttered the abbot.

'Whatever it was, it sounds as though he was summoned by the High King himself,' Fidelma pointed out.

'Why so?'

'Because he came escorted by the commander of the High King's warriors and Brother Rogallach was sent to the gate to ensure they were admitted to the royal enclosure.'

'Do you think that this has something to do with his subsequent assassination?' Abbot Colmán asked.

'That would be speculation. At this stage, more information has to be gathered,' Fidelma said quickly. 'It is only later that one can put it all in a proper perspective. So anything that happens that is unusual in the time leading up to the assassination is of interest.'

'No speculation without information,' grinned Eadulf, addressing himself to the abbot and paraphrasing one of Fidelma's axioms.

Fidelma rose to her feet.

'I think this is all I need from this man for the time being,' she told the abbot, indicating the woeful countenance of Erc. 'Erc is only guilty of a mistake caused by presumption. He is *not* guilty of any involvement in the assassination. Therefore, I would say it is up to his commander to discipline him for lack of attention while on watch and not for any other punishment.'

Erc glanced up from where he sat, a gleam of hope on his face.

'Do you say so truly, lady?' he asked.

'A mistake is still a grave offence when the life of a High King hangs in the balance, Erc the Speckled. I suspect you will be demoted from the guard of the royal enclosure.'

But it was clear that Erc had expected a far worse punishment for his transgression and he was looking more optimistic than he had at first appeared in his dungeon confinement.

Eadulf led the way up the narrow stone stairs from the cell to the door to the outside world. He paused for a moment, trying to focus his eyes against the bright sun, and became immediately aware of a figure a short distance away – a hunched figure seated on a low stone wall. He heard his name spoken in a rasping breathless voice. He was trying to remember where he had heard it before when he gave a gasp. It was the old woman they had encountered at the bridge. She was laughing at him now with a toothless, gaping mouth but there was no sound.

He blinked rapidly, trying to focus properly but when he did so there was no longer any figure seated there. A cold chill spread through his body, and he wheeled round towards his companions.

'Where to now, Fidelma?' Abbot Colmán was asking.

'We have to speak with Muirgel, and also I need to question Irél, the guard commander who came hither with this Bishop Luachan, as well as Brother Rogallach.'

'Did you see her?' Eadulf gulped, staring from Fidelma to the abbot.

'See who?' asked the abbot distractedly.

Eadulf ran across to the low wall and peered over it. No one was hiding there and he gazed round in all directions. The old woman had vanished.

'What's wrong, Eadulf?' asked Fidelma.

He hesitated. For some reason, she had not mentioned the encounter at the river to Abbot Colmán so he quickly decided that he should take her lead and speak with her later on the matter privately. He drew a breath and shrugged casually.

'For a moment I thought I saw someone I recognised. I was mistaken,' he said, walking back to rejoin them.

chapter eight

It was chance that dictated that they should next question Irél, the commander of the Fianna at the royal enclosure. They were returning to the library in the royal residence when they met a young warrior emerging from the main doors. He was about twenty-five years old, handsome, with red-brown hair and light blue eyes, cleanshaven jaw and a tall, well-muscled body. His accoutrements proclaimed him a warrior of some importance.

'Fidelma of Cashel?' He hailed her before Abbot Colmán identified him.

'I am she.'

'Then, lady, I believe you may wish to speak with me. I am Irél of the Fianna, at your service. I am the *caithmhileadh*.'

Although he was unacquainted with military ranks, Eadulf worked out that this meant that the man commanded a *cath* or battalion of the High King's bodyguard.

'Then, indeed, I do wish a few words,' replied Fidelma. 'This is—'

'Brother Eadulf,' interrupted Irél with a smile. 'You name is well-known here in association with the deeds of Fidelma of Cashel. You will not remember me but I commanded the High King's bodyguard earlier this year when he came down to Cashel to attend your wedding celebrations.'

It was true that neither Fidelma nor Eadulf could recall the warrior but they merely smiled and passed no comment.

'Come into the library and be seated,' Fidelma instructed.

Abbot Colmán cleared his throat and said, 'Lady, if you have no need for my attendance, there are some duties that I have to be about.'

Fidelma agreed that there was no need for him to remain and he hurried off while they followed Irél into the library.

'Alas,' Irél observed, as they seated themselves, 'I cannot help much about the night Sechnussach was murdered. I did not arrive until it was too late. The deed was done and the murderer had killed himself.'

'We were told that you identified him,' said Eadulf.

'I did so,' said the guard. 'Dubh Duin was a regular attendee at the Great Assembly. I saw him there several times. His territory lies to the north-west of Midhe and he was one of the most important chieftains of the kingdom.'

'I understand he was a distant relative of Sechnussach,' Fidelma said. 'Was he a close confidant of the High King?'

Irél chuckled derisively. 'On the contrary, I suspect there was some strong antagonism between them.'

'How so?'

'Just the manner, one towards the other, during the debates in the Great Assembly. My duties in the assembly are but to stand as guard there and so I have time to watch the arguments and debates and perhaps notice things which others, more involved in the discussions, might miss. Dubh Duin would support nothing that the High King suggested and always had some objection to it.'

'So there was no love lost between them. Very well. Let us go back to the night of the assassination. Lugna was the commander of the guard in the royal enclosure that night. Where were you?'

'My duty had ended when I handed over to Lugna at midnight. I had retired to my chamber in the royal house.'

'Then you are not married?' Eadulf stated.

'I am – I have three sons. Why do you ask?' queried the warrior with interest.

'A false assumption,' replied Eadulf. 'You say that you had retired to your chamber. I did not know that the families of the guards and attendants stayed in the royal house.'

'They don't. I have a farmstead close by the great river – that is where my family live. Being often on duty late at night, I stay here in Tara to save the journey in the middle of the night. Therefore I am provided with a chamber to sleep in.'

'And what brought you to Sechnussach's chamber that night?'

'The sound of a disturbance.'

'Can you be more specific?'

'At first, I think my sleep was disturbed by a cry. But I cannot be sure.

By the time I was fully awake, I heard several cries as if of a disturbance. I took my sword and threw on a cloak. Anyway, when I reached the chamber, Brother Rogallach was already there and some of the servants. And of course Lugna and Cuan.'

'Tell us what happened.'

'I pushed my way through, as the servants were crowded around the chamber door trying to look in. One of the guards had a lantern. I could see the High King lying on his back. Blood was everywhere. Lugna was trying to keep the servants out while Cuan was crouching by the side of a man slumped against the bed. Lugna looked at me and said – "Sechnussach is slain and this is the man who did it".' He paused and grimaced. 'I could tell that Sechnussach was dead. Not that he had bled much from the cutting of his throat. I've seen many men slain in battle with blood gushing like a fountain from such a wound and . . .' He paused and looked a little guilty. 'I beg your pardon, lady. Anyway, I asked whether Lugna had killed the assassin. He replied, sorrowfully, that the man had taken his own life as he and Cuan had entered the chamber. That was when I looked down and recognised Dubh Duin. I sent for Abbot Colmán, being steward.'

Fidelma leaned forward. 'Had the High King been alone in his chamber?' she asked.

Irél frowned. 'Alone? Well, there was the body of Dubh Duin.'

Fidelma smiled without humour. 'What I meant to say was, was there anyone else present? I want to find out who raised the alarm that alerted the guards, Lugna and his comrade. They tell me that they heard a scream. But *who* screamed?'

'I am a warrior, lady – and when I saw Sechnussach's wounds I asked myself the same question. I ordered a search of the adjacent rooms in case someone else was hiding there who had seen the murder, but there was no one. There are three rooms in the High King's apartment. All were empty. Only Sechnussach and his assassin were in the bedchamber.'

'No one else could have hidden in the other rooms? You are sure that the door of the privy that leads outside was firmly bolted on the inside?'

'Yes, I am certain. Dubh Duin was alone and did not have any accomplices. Lugna told me that when he and his comrade entered the bedchamber, Dubh Duin was in the act of collapsing to the ground, having stabbed himself. There was no one else. I had to conclude that the cry did come from the High King.'

Fidelma sighed softly. 'Then we will let the mystery remain for the time being. Let us move on to other matters. You have served in the Fianna for a long time, I presume?'

'Since the age of choice. I joined at seventeen.'

'You must be an accomplished warrior, to have risen to command a battalion, one of the three permanent battalions of the Fianna, in so short a time. And, indeed, the premier battalion to guard Tara.'

'It was Sechnussach who promoted me to the command,' replied Irél.

'So he placed great trust in you?'

'That would have been for him to say, lady. I served him faithfully, if that is what you mean.'

'Not exactly. What I mean is that Sechnussach entrusted you to carry out missions on his behalf that required your loyalty.'

Irél frowned, not understanding what she was getting at. Then he said, 'As his commander and *tréin-fher*, his appointed champion, that was my job – to carry out whatever task he entrusted to me.'

'And now Sechnussach is dead. The Great Assembly has appointed me to investigate his assassination and therefore has given me authority to question all who might help in that task.'

Irél nodded slowly. 'That is understood, lady. That is why, when I heard you wished to speak with me, I came seeking you.'

'Just so. So now I want you to tell me what task Sechnussach asked you to undertake in the matter of Bishop Luachan of Delbna Mór.'

Irél's face showed his surprise at the question. 'That was supposed to be a secret matter,' he said.

'*Supposed* to be,' she replied with emphasis. 'But now it is part of my investigation.'

Irél hesitated a moment and then shrugged. 'It happened several days before the assassination. Sechnussach called me to him and asked me to take a journey to Delbna Mór and seek out the bishop. I was to escort Bishop Luachan to Tara, bringing him surreptitiously to the High King's house by night. Sechnussach said he would ensure that his personal steward . . .'

'Brother Rogallach?'

'Yes, that Brother Rogallach would be waiting at the gates at midnight to escort us directly to the High King.'

'And so you went to Delbna Mór?'

'Even as Sechnussach requested.'

'Was Bishop Luachan surprised to see you?'

Irél shook his head. 'He apparently knew in advance why I had come and that I was to escort him to Tara.'

'And what was the reason for this visit?'

'I do not know.'

Fidelma frowned irritably. 'You do not know?' she repeated in a tone of disbelief.

'I tell you the truth, lady. Sechnussach never told me anything more than I have told you. Luachan came willingly with no word spoken on the journey about its cause nor intention. As I say, he seemed to know the reason already.'

'It is a long ride from Delbna Mór to Tara. Did he really say nothing?'

'He seemed content with his own thoughts, although several times he appeared to be very nervous.'

'Nervous? In what way?'

'He would shy at shadows. I suspected that he thought we might be ambushed along the way. When I asked him, he muttered something about thieves and robbers.'

'I see. Go on.'

'Well, everything went as planned. We reached Tara in safety and we found Brother Rogallach awaiting us at the gate with the guard to pass us through. He took us straight to the royal house. I was told to take the horses to the stable, see to their needs and refresh myself and prepare to leave again before daylight . . .'

'Having arrived at what hour?'

'Just after midnight. In fact, now I recall, it was the very night before the High King's assassination.'

'What then?'

'I did as I was told. I came back well before dawn. I found Brother Rogallach standing guard outside the High King's bedchamber and the bishop still closeted with the High King.'

'In his bedchamber?'

Irél heard the note of incredulity and said, 'I know – it was unusual for anyone to be received there.'

'So even Brother Rogallach was not privy to the meeting?'

'It would seem not. Whatever passed between Sechnussach and Bishop Luachan passed in secret. In fact, I asked Brother Rogallach at the time what it was about and he swore that he knew nothing.'

Eadulf rubbed his chin thoughtfully. 'A strange affair, to be sure,' he said to Fidelma.

'I waited with Brother Rogallach,' went on Irél. 'After a while, Sechnussach unlocked the door of his chamber . . .'

'What! He and Luachan were meeting behind a locked door!' Fidelma exclaimed.

'Yes. That, too, was unusual,' agreed the guard commander. 'He opened the door and saw me standing ready. He asked whether I was ready to escort Bishop Luachan back to Delbna Mór. Naturally, I replied in the affirmative. But Luachan said that it would not be necessary. If I could escort him to the other side of the great river on the road to Delbna Mór, he would be satisfied.'

'He was prepared to undertake the long journey without adequate rest?' Fidelma asked curiously.

'Bishop Luachan is a strong man. Anyway, he explained that he had a friend on the other side of the great river, not far from the ferry landing, with whom he would rest before commencing the journey back.'

'And on your journey to the place where you left him, was anything said about this strange meeting? No word, no gossip?'

'Nothing at all. The bishop was just as silent as he had been on our journey to Tara. Grim and taciturn is how I would describe his attitude. All I know is all that I have told you, lady. I can add nothing else.' He paused and suddenly became thoughtful.

'Except?' prompted Fidelma.

'It is probably nothing at all, but I think that he brought a special gift for Sechnussach.'

'A gift?'

'He had a saddlebag. I remember that when we left Delbna Mór he put something in it wrapped in linen cloth. When we arrived here, he took it out and carried it into the meeting with Sechnussach. When he left, he was not carrying it, so it follows that he must have left it with the High King. I noted that it seemed to be a heavy object.'

'Heavy?' Eadulf queried.

'You could tell that by the way he carried it.'

'What shape was it? Can you recall?'

Irél thought for a moment. 'The shape may have been distorted by the wrapping of the cloth, but I think it was circular. It was about a *troighid* in diameter but very thin, like a plate.'

Eadulf quickly calculated the Irish measurement to something like the average foot in length.

'So it was not too large, but it was heavy. It must have been made of metal or stone – probably metal.'

'Perhaps.'

'And you have no idea what it was?'

'None.'

'Thank you, Irél. You have been most explicit. I may want to speak with you again.'

The warrior rose and raised a hand to his forehead in half-salute before turning and leaving them alone in the study.

Eadulf sighed. 'That really does not help us much.'

Fidelma glanced at him. 'One nut does not help a squirrel pass through a winter,' she replied. 'But the squirrel, each day, continues gathering a nut here and another nut there until he has built a pile of nuts which are his store that will help him survive.'

Eadulf regarded her blankly.

'We are the nut gatherers,' she relented and explained. 'We gather the nuts until we have our store, and looking at the store we come to the solution. One thing I should explain to you is that Delbna Mór is not that far away from the territory of the Cinél Cairpre whose chieftain was Dubh Duin. Now let us go in search of Muirgel.'

But the girl was difficult to find. Returning to the High King's house, Fidelma asked the guard outside where she was but he expressed his lack of knowledge in a disinterested tone and suggested that one of the servants might know. The couple passed inside but found little sign of the servants or anyone else.

Undeterred, Fidelma started up the stairs towards the apartments above. Eadulf followed nervously.

'Is it the custom to wander around the High King's house unannounced in this fashion?' he whispered.

'I see no one to challenge us on the matter,' Fidelma replied determinedly.

At the top of the stairs she paused and then stepped towards the door of the apartment in which the High King's family stayed when in residence. She halted, knocked and listened. There was no response or movement from inside. She waited a moment more and then glanced at Eadulf before reaching to turn the handle.

The room that met their gaze was almost as bare as the High King's own chamber.

Fidelma and Eadulf gazed around in surprise.

'Well, it seems as though none of the High King's family reside here, and I would say that they have not done so for some time,' Fidelma observed. 'Abbot Colmán said that Gormflaith and her daughters had another residence within the royal enclosure but it is certainly strange that there is no sign of an occupant of this apartment.'

She went round the room, noticing the layer of dust on the empty shelves and boxes.

'Who are you?' cried a commanding voice suddenly. 'How dare you enter these chambers without permission?'

The pair swung round and saw the figure of a woman standing in the open doorway, regarding them with suspicion. She was not young, like Báine or Cnucha, but she still had a voluptuous beauty, a figure that was mature but eye-catching even with the drab clothing of a house servant. She had dark hair, a pale skin and bright eyes whose colour was indiscernible in the shadowy light of the room.

Fidelma studied her for a moment or two before replying: 'I am Fidelma of Cashel, the *dálaigh* investigating the manner of the death of Sechnussach. That is the right by which I dare enter these chambers, and with the approval of Cenn Faelad and the Chief Brehon.'

The woman blinked and her features altered a little in what seemed to be a look of apology.

'I am sorry, lady. I did not know you. Of course, I have been told that you have arrived at the royal enclosure and are investigating this matter.'

'And you are?'

'I am Brónach. I am in charge of the female servants. Is there anything that I may help you with?'

'Ah, Brónach. Of course. Well, this chamber does not appear to have been cleaned in some while. Why is that?'

The woman moved further into the light. Eadulf regarded her movement and poise with appreciation. As handsome as she was now, she had probably once been a great beauty.

'There is no need to clean it regularly, lady,' replied Brónach. 'It is not used. It would have been a different matter if it were occupied.'

'It is obvious that it is not occupied,' agreed Fidelma. 'But I thought these were the chambers of Sechnussach's wife and family.'

'Not for some time,' the woman replied, but there seemed a reluctant tone in her voice as she admitted the fact.

'For how long?'

The woman did not reply and when it was obvious that she was not going to, Fidelma said: 'I am looking for Muirgel, the High King's daughter. Where would I find her?'

'There is a house to the south-east corner of the royal enclosure. You will find her there. It cannot be missed as it has a white-painted lintel. It is called Tech Laoghaire.'

It was then Fidelma remembered that Abbot Colmán had made a passing reference to the fact that Muirgel lived in another house in the royal enclosure. She was annoyed with herself for forgetting.

'Has the family of the High King lived there for long?'

Once again Brónach shook her head. 'I am sorry, lady, I am merely a servant in this house and am not allowed to talk about the High King and his family without direct permission of the Brother Rogallach, the *bollscari*.'

'Even though you know I am a *dálaigh*?'

'Even so, lady,' the other returned tightly.

'I am told that you were here on the night of the assassination.'

'As you were told it, I will not deny it, but—'

'You can answer fully, Brónach,' came the voice of Abbot Colmán as he ascended the top stair and crossed the landing to join them. 'You have full permission to answer all the questions that the *dálaigh* asks of you.'

The woman shrugged as if she did not care one way or the other. Fidelma recogniséd that she was the ultimate loyal servant, never offering information without the approval of her superior.

'I was here on the night of the assassination,' she repeated, almost in a wooden fashion.

Fidelma nodded briefly at the abbot as if to indicate her thanks and then turned back to Brónach.

'Tell me about it.'

'Nothing to tell. I was asleep and then I was awakened by people shouting. I went to my door and—'

'Your room is where?' Fidelma interrupted.

'Just along the corridor here.'

'Did you hear a scream? Was that what awakened you?'

The woman shook her head. 'I heard no scream but people were shouting. I went to the door and saw Torpach and Maoláin in the corridor with the girl Báine. Brother Rogallach was coming from his room.'

'I presume that it was they who were shouting?'

'They were speaking loudly, it is true,' Brónach said. 'However, I think the shout had come from one of the guards who had already entered the High King's chamber. Someone said that Sechnussach had been killed. We all moved to his door to see whether it was true. Then Irél came running up the stairs.' She turned to the abbot. 'I think the abbot arrived then and took charge. That is all I know.'

'Very well,' Fidelma said. Then: 'One other thing. I presume you or the other servants cleaned the High King's chambers after . . . after his body was taken away?'

Brónach seemed to stiffen a little. 'We did nothing until we had full permission from the abbot here, and he was acting with the authority of the Chief Brehon.'

'Of course,' Fidelma said soothingly. 'I would not suggest that you did anything without permission. However, when you were tidying the room and cleaning up, did you notice a particular object? It would have been circular in shape and about a *troighid* in diameter. Also, it would have been made of heavy metal.'

Brónach glanced nervously at the abbot before shaking her head.

'I would not have removed anything without permission,' she stated.

'I did not suggest otherwise. I said, did you observe such an object?'

'I do not recall seeing any such object like that,' the woman replied quietly.

Abbot Colmán was frowning. 'Was it something of importance?' he asked.

'Probably not,' Fidelma said. 'Just something I wanted to have clear in my mind.' She turned back to Brónach. 'What items did you remove from the High King's chambers?'

'Only the clothes and linen from the bed.'

'The bedlinen?'

'Indeed. That needed to be taken to be laundered for there was blood on it.'

'Of course. But I understand there would have been too much blood for the bedlinen to simply be laundered.'

Brónach shook her head. 'Not so much blood that the bedlinen could not be used again. But Brother Rogallach, who is the head of the household, said it was unlucky for the sheets to be used again in the royal household.'

'So what happened to them?'

'After I washed them? Well, on Brother Rogallach's instructions, I took them to the market and sold them.'

'And there was not so much blood on them that they could not be re-used?' queried Fidelma thoughtfully.

'I have said as much.'

'And you are sure that there was nothing else, no object of a circular nature, anywhere in the apartment?'

'I have said as much,' repeated the woman stubbornly.

'Have you served here for many years?'

'I came here three years ago, lady. When my husband was killed.'

'Your husband?'

'He was Curnán, son of Aed, of the Fianna, lady. He was killed in an attack by the Dál Riada. Sechnussach offered me a place in his house as the chief of his female servants. I have been here since.'

Fidelma glanced around the empty room. 'That will be all, Brónach. Thank you.'

As the woman left them, Abbot Colmán said: 'I came looking for you as I heard you had finished questioning Irél.'

'We were looking for Muirgel, the daughter of Sechnussach.'

The abbot was apologetic. 'I thought I had mentioned that Sechnussach's family dwell in their own house just outside the royal enclosure.'

'You had, and I had forgotten,' Fidelma admitted.

'So,' Eadulf put in, 'do we understand that the High King's wife and daughters dwelled separately from him?'

'Separately, yes,' confirmed the abbot. 'They live in *Tech Laoghaire*, a short distance to the south.'

Eadulf was about to comment when he caught Fidelma's eye and said nothing.

'Then you lead the way, Abbot Colmán,' Fidelma said. 'Let us see if we can find the lady Muirgel.'

CHAPTER NINE

There were two things that Eadulf noticed about Muirgel, daughter of the late High King. The first was that she was a very attractive girl. She had fair skin with a hint of freckles, black hair and dark eyes. The *aimsir togú*, or 'age of choice' in the five kingdoms was fourteen years old, when girls became women. Muirgel was seventeen and therefore of marriageable age. Eadulf imagined that she would have many suitors. However, the second thing he noticed about her was her arrogance. It was there in the way she held her head, the disdainful curve of her lip.

She reclined in her chair among an array of cushions as they entered and regarded them with an expression that made it clear that she did not welcome their presence. The young servant girl who had opened the chamber door to them and conducted them to her mistress hesitated as if waiting for further instructions before being dismissed with a haughty wave of her employer's hand.

Muirgel looked at the elderly abbot with disdain. She did not even bother to look at Fidelma or Eadulf.

'Well, Abbot Colmán, why is it that you must disturb my peace this afternoon? I have a headache and would prefer to rest alone, and yet I am told you must bring a *dálaigh* to plague me with questions.' The girl's voice was a low, drawling tone that seemed to express total boredom.

There was something apologetic in the manner in which Abbot Colmán stepped forward and began to clear his throat. Eadulf saw the look of annoyance on Fidelma's face and she interrupted.

'Your servant is not trained well, Muirgel,' she snapped.

The girl stared at her in surprise at the unexpected interjection. 'What?' The word seemed reluctantly jerked from her.

'At the door, we told the girl who we were. Are you saying that she did not tell you?'

Muirgel swallowed and tried to regain her composure as she heard the sarcasm in Fidelma's voice.

'She told me,' she snapped back. 'And one would expect those in the company of Abbot Colmán to know some court etiquette. You are addressing the daughter of the High King . . .'

Fidelma made a slight cutting motion of her hand as if to silence her. 'I know well whom I address. Just as your servant should have given you my name and, knowing it, there should be no excuse not to know who I am and my reason for coming here!'

The girl blinked at the sharpness in her tone. 'She told me that a Sister Fidelma . . .'

'I am here as a *dálaigh* qualified to the role of *anruth*. I presume that you are acquainted with this rank?'

'Of course,' Muirgel answered through a tight mouth, sitting up on her couch in a straighter position.

'And then you know well that it is I, Fidelma of Cashel, who comes to question you over the death of your father,' went on Fidelma with a hard and remorseless tone. 'So let us have no more acting the *mórluachach*.'

It was a word that Eadulf had seldom heard before, but he guessed that it meant someone who pretended to be high and mighty, who put on airs and graces. He knew that one thing Fidelma detested was arrogance in others – and it was only when such false pride was displayed that she reminded people of her own royal birth as one of the princely family of the Eóghanacht of Muman who once contended for the High Kingship itself.

Muirgel had turned pale and Abbot Colmán, in contrast, was red with embarrassment. In the silence Fidelma added an old axiom: 'Nobility has no pride.' She glanced around the room and pointed to some chairs. 'Eadulf, as no one has offered, will you bring chairs that we may sit and discuss our business in comfort.'

Smiling to himself, Eadulf moved quickly to bring the chairs while Muirgel sat in a stunned silence. Her expression became malignant as she fixed her eyes on Fidelma. Unconcerned, Fidelma stretched back in a relaxed attitude and then turned to Abbot Colmán.

'You are not sitting, Colmán,' she reproved.

'I have not the need, lady,' the abbot muttered, still embarrassed, for it was protocol for him to wait to be invited to sit by Muirgel.

'No matter,' Fidelma replied, turning her attention to Muirgel.

The girl had now gathered herself together.

'I am told the Eóghanacht of Cashel are ill-mannered,' she hissed.

Fidelma was not put out. 'It is a sign of nobility to be courteous to guests whatever their rank,' she admonished.

'The Uí Néill are to be treated with respect for we are a great house,' the girl said petulantly.

'And is it not said that the doorstep of a great house is often slippery?' replied Fidelma. 'Respect is something that is earned and not given by right of birth. I knew your father, Sechnussach, and he earned my respect. That is why I have travelled from Cashel to discover the reasons for his death.'

The girl's chin jutted as if she would argue further but Fidelma moved on quickly.

'Where were you on the night of your father's assassination?'

Muirgel did not answer.

'Remember,' Fidelma warned her, 'rank bears no privileges against the interrogation of the *dálaigh* of the rank of *anruth*. You are bound by honour to answer my questions or be fined accordingly.'

The girl swallowed, then muttered, 'You have doubtless been told where I was, so there is no need to ask.'

'I have been told only that some believed that you were here in Tara.'

'Then that is where I was.'

Fidelma exhaled irritably. 'All we know is that you did not attend the abbey Cluain Ioraird with your mother and sisters Mumain and Bé Bhail. Why not? I am told that they had gone there to offer prayers on the death of your grandmother.'

'My grandmother died some time ago and I was not close to her.'

'It was a matter of respect, lady,' muttered Abbot Colmán, feeling he should say something.

'Are you telling me what I should do?' Muirgel turned flashing angry eyes on him.

Fidelma and Eadulf glanced at one another. Here was certainly an unpleasant and self-willed young girl. At another time, Fidelma would have intervened for her ill manners to the abbot but she wanted information.

'When and where did the news of your father's death reach you?'

'I spent the evening with a . . . some friends. Then I came here as the girl,' she gestured towards the door to indicated her departed servant, 'as the girl will tell you. In the morning, I had decided to go to my father's house and break my fast with him. But a servant arrived here as I was making ready and told me the news.'

Fidelma could not sense any emotion in the girl's matter-of-fact voice.

'Did you like your father?' The question was swift and unexpected.

Muirgel blinked. 'Of course,' she said, tossing her head.

'That is good to hear,' Fidelma replied. 'It does not always follow that a daughter likes a father. She can love her father but that is not what I asked.'

Muirgel did not respond to this, merely looked at her nails.

'So what were your feelings when you heard of his death?' Fidelma tried again.

'I wanted those involved to pay for this outrage. Naturally.'

'Those involved? You think there was more than the assassin who struck him down?'

Muirgel pouted again. It seemed a favourite habit. 'I have no knowledge of such things,' she said, and yawned. 'I was using an expression, that is all.'

'But you did know the assassin,' Fidelma pointed out. 'When did you first meet Dubh Duin?'

The girl's eyes widened at her knowledge and she said nothing for a moment, trying to read what lay behind Fidelma's question.

'Dubh Duin was a distant relation, a chief of the Cairpre,' she said finally.

'We all know who he was,' Fidelma said. 'Come on – when did you first get to know him?'

'I don't know.' Muirgel hesitated a moment more. 'He used to attend my father's Great Assembly. Perhaps it was then that I met him.'

'He came often to the Great Assembly?'

Muirgel indicated Abbot Colmán. 'The abbot here would be better able to answer you for he is adviser and steward to the Assembly.'

'I suppose what I really want to ask is what relationship you had with Dubh Duin during these last few weeks?'

The girl suddenly turned bright scarlet and half-rose from her couch.

'Relationship?' she screeched. 'What? How dare you! What are you implying?'

'I was not aware that I was implying anything.' Fidelma remained relaxed. 'I was merely asking a question that needs an answer. I want to know why you gave authority to the guards to pass Dubh Duin through the gates of the royal enclosure after midnight on more than one occasion in the days leading up to your father's assassination.'

There was total silence in the room. If a needle had fallen, Eadulf believed he would have been able to hear it in the stillness.

'Who said . . . ?' began the girl.

Fidelma made an impatient gesture. 'Come, Muirgel, you do not think that such a thing could go unrecorded or unnoticed? Isn't it time that you spoke honestly about this matter?'

For a moment or two the girl relapsed into silence. Then she spoke slowly, as if measuring her words.

'I did not know Dubh Duin other than having seen him among those attending the Great Assembly and perhaps once or twice at my father's feastings. It was not my desire to have further acquaintance with him. It is the truth that I speak.'

'Then why—?'

This time it was the girl who held up her hand for silence.

'On the occasions when I brought him into the royal enclosure after the gates had been secured at nightfall, it was not my desire to do so, nor was it for myself. I was *asked* to do so. My role in this matter was to use my authority to pass him through the guards at the gate, and then to escort him to the royal enclosure. That was all.'

Fidelma examined the girl impassively.

'All?' she queried sardonically. 'Surely not! You took it on yourself to let this man into the royal enclosure on several occasions after nightfall, to escort him in, and then you say it was not your will nor desire to do so? Come, lady, there is much more you need to tell us. You must have known what reason brought the man hither?'

'I swear it was not any reason of mine,' rapped out Muirgel, with a return of her old spirit. 'I had no liking for Dubh Duin.'

'Then, why? What reason did he have for coming here?'

'I do not know,' she replied stubbornly.

'For the sake of all that is holy, that is not good enough!' Fidelma snapped in frustration. 'If you were told to use your authority to pass this man – the man who assassinated your own father for goodness sake! – into the royal enclosure, *who told you to do so?*'

The girl fell silent, dropping her gaze to the floor.

Abbot Colmán coughed uncomfortably. 'Come, lady,' he said gently. 'You must tell us all you know. If it wasn't you that wished Dubh Duin to gain entrance into the royal enclosure, who told you to use your authority to allow that to happen? And why would you do so? What hold would they have over you, to make such a request and know that you would obey it?'

Muirgel was hanging her head, her shoulders were hunched and shaking, and Eadulf suddenly realised that she was crying.

'Come, Muirgel,' Fidelma insisted, unmoved. 'We have little time to play games. Who ordered you to admit Dubh Duin on these occasions – and why would you obey?'

The girl raised a tearstained face to Fidelma.

'It was my mother,' she said simply.

CHAPTER TEN

The only sound that followed the girl's statement was Abbot Colmán's sharp exhalation of breath and her continued sobbing.

Fidelma remained impassive.

'Are you saying that it was your mother, Gormflaith, Sechnussach's own wife, who used to meet with his assassin at nights in the royal enclosure?' she asked slowly.

Muirgal tried to gather herself together. Then, as if she realised that, having admitted thus much, she had to confirm her statement, she replied between sniffs, 'I have said as much.'

'And when you took Dubh Duin to your mother, where did she receive him at such an hour?'

'In this house, in her own chambers,' the girl said. 'Since the birth of my baby sister, Bé Bhail, three years ago, my mother has had her own residence here. What better than this house, which was built by the great High King Laoghaire? We all live here.'

'And you say that your only connection with Dubh Duin was to pass him through the gates to bring him to your mother?'

'It was.'

'The reason being so that no one would associate his coming with your mother?' Eadulf queried.

'Yes. No one was to know that it was my mother that Dubh Duin had come to see,' agreed Muirgel quietly, wiping her eyes.

'Why was that?' asked Eadulf.

The girl turned on him with a pitying look. 'Why do you think?' she countered.

'Is that speculation or are you stating that you knew positively that your mother was having an affair with Dubh Duin?' Fidelma asked.

Muirgel turned back to her and shrugged. 'I am old enough to make my own deductions. However, my role was simply to escort him to my mother's chamber and there I left them together. You must ask my mother, should you want to know the details of the matter.'

'Lady Muirgel, you continued as an intermediary, having guessed the purpose of Dubh Duin's visits to your mother's chambers. Surely you did not approve of this?' Abbot Colmán said nervously. 'How could she and you betray your father into cuckoldry?'

'It was no business of mine,' the girl said sulkily. 'My mother made that clear to me. You must have known that she and my father had been estranged these last three years and that he had taken a *dormun* for his needs.'

The old abbot winced slightly. 'I knew of no such thing,' he protested.

Fidelma looked from the abbot to the girl and back again.

'This is important information, Colmán,' she said quietly. 'If Sechnussach had taken a *dormun*, a second wife, then I should have been informed.'

'I had no knowledge of it,' the abbot insisted. 'I am sure the Brehon Barrán had no knowledge of it either. If anyone would know about such a thing, it would have been him.'

'You say that it is so?' Fidelma looked the girl in the eye.

'I do not know it for a fact,' she said reluctantly. 'No one admits to it, and no one has identified any particular woman. All I know is that when my mother was pregnant with my baby sister, she claimed that she had discovered that my father had taken another woman to share his bed. That was when she insisted on her own apartments.'

'You speak of a *dormun* as a second wife,' Eadulf said. 'I am not sure that I understand this. I thought the word meant a mistress or a concubine.'

It was Abbot Colmán who enlightened him.

'Under our old law system, men could take a second wife who had fewer rights than the *cétmuintir* or first wife. The second wife was called a *dormun*. The custom is dying out, although some of our powerful kings and nobles insist on continuing the practice.'

Eadulf had heard of polygamy among other peoples.

'Such practices are condemned by Rome,' he commented piously.

'Rome's judgements on this matter are offered as a counsel of perfection and not a rule,' the abbot stated. 'Second marriages are still accepted under our law system.'

'There is currently a controversy among the Brehons on this matter,' Fidelma informed them. 'It is often argued whether monogamy or polygamy is the more proper form of marriage. At the moment, the judgement is that those who wish to take a second wife do not trespass against the teaching of the New Faith. The *Bretha Crólige* points out that God's chosen people lived in a plurality of marriages – Solomon, David and Jacob had many wives – therefore it is not more difficult to condemn polygamy than it is to praise it. Even if Sechnussach had taken a second wife, he stands within the law.'

'Monogamy is a counsel of perfection,' muttered Abbot Colmán again.

'However, unless there is evidence that Sechnussach took a *dormun*, according to law, then this remains speculation,' added Fidelma.

'My mother believed it,' growled Muirgel.

'Then we will question your mother,' Fidelma assured her, rising from her chair. 'For the moment, that will be all, Muirgel. However, I will want to talk with you again. I advise you to say nothing of this matter for the time being.'

The girl simply stared indifferently as they left her.

Outside, Fidelma turned to Abbot Colmán and said, 'Surely there must have been some indication of what the girl has told us? An estrangement between Sechnussach and his wife – rumours of his taking a second wife? The royal enclosure of Tara is not so big that such matters would go unnoticed and unremarked.'

Abbot Colmán met her gaze with a serious expression.

'Of the estrangement, perhaps we should have guessed,' he said. 'We knew that since the birth of little Bé Bhail, the lady Gormflaith has kept to herself and only appeared at her husband's side on those occasions where it was deemed necessary. Sometimes, though, after the birth of a child, a woman can take curious fancies into her mind. Be despondent and depressed. We merely thought that Gormflaith might have been experiencing such feelings.'

Fidelma coloured slightly for she knew exactly what Colmán meant. It had been her own experience after the birth of her son, Alchú.

'But after three years ... ?' she pressed.

'Well, all I can say is that during these past three years, if Sechnussach did take a second wife, it was a secret so well-kept that no one knew of her existence.'

'Perhaps it was well-kept from his advisers or even his *tánaiste*,' Eadulf observed, 'but it could hardly have been a secret from the servants who attended him. Perhaps we should speak with them?'

Fidelma nodded approvingly. 'A good thought.'

'I think I am beginning to see the reason for the assassination of the High King,' Eadulf suddenly said with confidence.

'You are?'

'It is obvious that if Gormflaith had taken Dubh Duin as a lover, then the pair of them might have conspired to kill Sechnussach so that Gormflaith would be free.'

Fidelma pursed her lips. 'You think so?'

'Gormflaith would not be the first woman to conspire with a lover to murder her husband.'

Fidelma simply shook her head. 'Under the law, they had no need to recourse to that act. She could surely have divorced. However, we will see firstly what Gormflaith has to say.'

Enquiries revealed that Gormflaith and her second daughter Murgain were out riding but were thought to be returning within the hour. The three of them left the *Tech Laoghaire* and began to walk back across the royal enclosure towards the guests' hostel.

'Perhaps Brehon Barrán would be able to contribute to this mystery about a second wife?' Abbot Colmán suggested.

'Is the Brehon still in Tara?'

Abbot Colmán affirmed that he was, adding, 'He has his own residence just outside the royal enclosure. But I think he is working at the hall of the Great Assembly.'

Fidelma thought about it but then dismissed the idea.

'It would be better to see Gormflaith first, without rousing ideas that might prove false,' she decided.

At that moment they saw Caol and Gormán approaching them. The men looked worried.

'Lady.' Caol halted.

'What is the matter?' asked Fidelma, gazing from him to Gormán.

Caol looked anxiously at Abbot Colmán.

'Come, speak up. There are no secrets among us here,' urged Fidelma, not unkindly.

'We have seen Badb again.'

'The old woman?' Fidelma was surprised.

Gormán nodded rapidly. 'She appeared out of nowhere as we were walking by the guesthouse. She shook her fist at us and told us to beware and return from whence we came – even as she did at the river.'

'Lady,' said Caol, 'as you know, we of the Nasc Niadh are afraid of no mortal. She appeared and then she seemed to vanish again, and although we searched, being mindful of what you said before, we could not find her.'

'Lady, we may be afraid of nothing in this world, but if there is the Otherworld to contend with, then we need to be told. Is it mortals with whom we deal, or might we be dancing with demons?' added Gormán.

Abbot Colmán looked taken aback by what the two warriors had to say and was about to speak when Eadulf cleared his throat nervously and turned to Fidelma.

'I did not mention it before, but I too have seen the old woman again – as we were coming from the cells after speaking with Erc. I came out into the light and there she was, standing on the wall. She repeated this same warning and when I blinked again she had disappeared.'

Fidelma regarded him thoughtfully. 'I wondered why you behaved so strangely. You ran to the wall to look for her?'

'I did. And there was no sight of her. Is she mortal or demon? I have no liking for mysterious apparitions.'

Caol and Gormán muttered their agreement but Fidelma was having none of it.

'To all mysteries there is a rational explanation,' she announced.

'But,' Caol protested, glancing at the abbot for support, 'begging your pardon, there is nothing rational when dealing with that which is beyond mortal explanation.'

'I would offer my counsel if I understood what it was that you are talking about,' the Abbot said fretfully.

He listened attentively while Fidelma told him of the meeting at the river crossing. He then asked for a closer description of the woman who called herself Badb. Finally, he allowed himself a sad chuckle.

'Poor Mer,' he said. 'I suppose that she could alarm those not used to her and her odd ways.'

'Mer?' queried Fidelma.

'We call her Mer the Demented. She is old and crazy and always scavenging around Tara. She probably picked up the news that you had been sent for, to investigate the death of Sechnussach. Then she dressed it up in her own fashion. She clings to the Old Faith but there is no evil in her.

She is crazy – but God blesses the insane and foolish, so we are told. She does no harm.'

'No harm when she utters curses and warnings?' Eadulf grunted, feeling a complete fool.

'No harm, Brother Saxon,' the abbot insisted. 'Here, we overlook her eccentricities. Her husband was killed at the great battle of Carn Conaill and that is what unhinged her mind.'

'That took place a long time ago,' Caol grumbled. 'It was a battle in Connacht.'

'You know your history well, warrior,' affirmed the abbot. 'No one knows what Mer's real name was, for that is the name she has been called since then. She was a woman of Connacht. Her husband was a warrior in the army of Guaire, the King of Connacht. The story is that an argument rose between Guaire and Diarmait of Tara. When Diarmait moved an army against him, Guaire sent to ask for a truce. But the abbot of Cluain Mic Nois and all his clergy urged Diarmait on to slaughter Guaire's army. The clerics of Cluain Mic Nois came to the field of the battle to pray and call upon God to support the victory.'

'Why are you telling us this?' Eadulf wanted to know.

'Because, as I say, I think that is what deranged her and why she became Mer the Demented One. Her husband was killed and so she not only blamed Diarmait of Tara but all the priests of the New Faith. She came to Tara to haunt it, so it is said, and call down imprecations on it and its entire clergy in the name of the old gods and goddesses. No one knows where she dwells, but she has scavenged for food and been seen around the hills of Tara for many years.'

'A tragic lady, then?' Fidelma glanced to Caol and Gormán, who were looking embarrassed. 'Not a demon but merely a mortal woman who feels life has treated her badly. One to be pitied and not to be feared.'

'She is as God made her,' added Abbot Colmán. 'No worse nor better than many. She need not alarm you.'

'She knew Fidelma's name and why we were coming to Cashel,' Eadulf said defensively. 'That was alarming enough.'

'She is mortal,' the abbot replied. 'Understand, she is old and sick.'

'Well, there is one thing which I still do not understand,' Eadulf replied stubbornly.

'Which is?' asked Fidelma.

'How did the old woman recognise you? She was sitting by the river

PETER TREMAYNE

as we rode by and accosted you by name and title. How could she do that?'

For a moment Fidelma paused, thinking, and then: 'Maybe she saw me on my last visit here,' she suggested. 'Don't forget, many years ago I studied here at Brehon Morann's school.'

'Then this woman Mer must have a long memory for faces,' muttered Eadulf.

'Perhaps,' Fidelma said, dismissing the subject. 'But now we have other and more pressing matters to attend to.' She turned to the abbot. 'I have no wish to take up your time, Abbot Colmán. I am sure you have more important things to do in governing the royal household.'

The abbot took the hint and was almost eager to do so.

'Indeed, I do have tasks that need to be attended to,' he said. 'Let us meet up at the *etar-shod*, the middle-meal of the day, and you can tell me if you have been able to gather any further information.' Then he went off about his duties.

Eadulf cast a puzzled glance in Fidelma's direction. 'It seems to me that you almost wanted to be rid of him.'

'Discerning as ever, Eadulf,' she replied softly. 'I do want to see Gormflaith on her own. And it is not wise to constantly have a witness to all one's investigations.'

Fidelma and Eadulf, with Caol and Gormán following and still somewhat morose, continued their journey towards the guesthouse. A warrior emerged from a nearby building and Fidelma called his name.

'Lugna! The very person!'

The young warrior halted nervously. 'You want me, lady?'

'Indeed, I do. I would like you to come with us, if you will.' She nodded towards the *Tech Cormaic*. 'There is something I am not sure about.'

The warrior fell in step with them. 'I am only too happy to be of service. What can I help with?' he ventured after some silence.

'I think you are the only person who can help,' Fidelma assured him as they halted outside the oak doors. The warrior on guard regarded them with unconcealed curiosity.

Fidelma turned to Caol and Gormán and motioned them to follow her while telling Lugna to stay with Eadulf before the main doors.

After halting at the corner of the building and apparently giving instructions to them, she returned, leaving Gormán in view while Caol disappeared to the back of the building. She smiled brightly at a puzzled Lugna.

'It is just a little experiment,' she assured him. 'You see, I am puzzled by the noise you heard in the kitchen area and why it did not rouse the rest of the house.'

'I have told you all I know,' Lugna replied with suddenly set features.

'Of course you have. But, alas, I have to envision it for myself. What we will do is make the noise so that I can be sure of the detail. That's fair, isn't it?'

Lugna shrugged but he seemed worried.

'Eadulf, stand here and when I signal to you, wave to Gormán and then he will make a sign to Caol to go into the kitchen and make a noise. Then we can see exactly how much sound resonates through the house.'

She turned to the doors. 'Come, Lugna. I believe that you and your comrade were standing in the hallway at your guard post when you heard the noise. Then you came out and went round the side of the house to investigate as the back door was locked – isn't that right?'

Lugna was clearly unhappy. He seemed to be struggling with his conscience before finally mumbling, 'It is not right, lady. Forgive me. I have not told the truth.'

'I thought not,' Fidelma said. 'I think, Lugna, it is time you told us what *really* happened.'

'We were standing outside the doors here. As I said, we had not gone into the hall.'

'Go on.'

'You see, lady, it was a cold night. As I told you, I had just returned with Cuan from checking the guards. We came back to the doors and we would have taken up our position in the hall but it was so cold . . . there was hot *corma* in the kitchen and we felt a drink would help keep out the chill air before we settled to our watch.' His expression was guilt-ridden as he turned haunted eyes from one to another of them. 'Nothing had ever happened before. Year after year, watch after watch, nothing had ever disturbed the peace of the royal enclosure. It was too well-guarded. How were we to know that . . . that . . .'

Fidelma was in no mood to reassure this man who had tried to cover his own failure by lying.

'So you deserted your post to obtain a drink,' she said flatly. 'As a result, the High King is dead. You realise there must be consequences? Irél, your commander, must be informed.'

The young man hung his head unhappily. 'It has been hard to live with the knowledge, lady,' he muttered. 'I am glad that I have told you.'

'But you have not told me all, Lugna.'

She turned and waved to Gormán to return and soon he and Caol had rejoined them.

'So we can dispense with any noises in the kitchen. You and Cuan went there for a drink. What then?'

'I swear, lady, that all else happened as I said. The kitchen area is overlooked from the apartment of the High King. You have seen that stairs lead from nearby the kitchen up to the back door from which the servants take his bathing water and empty the privy . . . but the door is always shut and bolted from inside at night. There is no entrance that way. Anyway, we were taking our drink when we heard a scream – exactly as I said. Cuan ran straight up the stairs to the back door. That was locked. I knew that the ground-floor door into the back of the house was also locked, so I raced around the side of the house and went up the stairs as I said. It was a few moments afterwards when Cuan joined me.'

'Thank you, Lugna,' Fidelma said. 'Things begin to make more sense now. Tell me, you say that you have served in the Fianna for many years and you are a *toisech cóicat*, a commander of fifty warriors. Even accepting that the night was chill and the watch was boring, a warrior of your experience must have realised how serious it was to leave your post to take a drink?'

The young man was contrite. 'Yes, I do realise it and have no excuses. I wish I hadn't listened to—' He hesitated. 'I was the guard commander. Mine is the fault.'

Fidelma's eyes narrowed slightly. 'You wish you had not listened . . . to whom? I want the truth, Lugna.' Then, when he did not reply: 'Was it Cuan who suggested the drink?'

Lugna bit his lip and did not reply.

'Were you persuaded by your comrade Cuan to leave your post and go for the drink? Was it Cuan who knew where this drink was to be found?' Her voice was sharp.

Lugna bowed his head and nodded. 'It was.'

'Very well, Lugna.' Fidelma exhaled softly. 'You may return to your quarters – but do not speak of this to anyone, *especially* to Cuan. I am afraid this story must be told to Irél, the commander of the Fianna. Your only defence lies in the truth, and I want to be assured that you have told the truth.'

'That I have, lady, by the Holy Family. I swear that is the truth.'

Fidelma waved her hand in dismissal. When he had gone, she turned to Eadulf with a grim look.

'I begin to see that luck may not have played so great a part in this matter after all.'

Eadulf was in agreement. 'It seems that Cuan deliberately enticed Lugna away from his post at that particular time. But what of Erc? Surely it was luck that he let the assassin in the main gate.'

'He had been . . .' She paused for the right word. 'He had been *prepared* in such a way that he would not challenge Erc. The conspirators knew that Erc would be on duty that night, and because Dubh Duin had frequently been admitted into the royal enclosure after dark, they knew that he would not challenge him.'

'Conspirators?' echoed Eadulf.

'I see conspiracy in this, not a single assassin. I keep thinking about the key. Who stole it and had a copy made for the assassin?'

'Whatever the answer to that, we must find Cuan, as he is certainly an integral part of this plot.'

'Exactly so.' She turned and approached the solitary guard who remained outside the royal residence. 'Where is Irél, your commander?'

The man drew himself up respectfully. 'I think he may be at the stables, lady.'

Fidelma thanked him and gestured to Eadulf. Once again, the couple set off across the royal enclosure, with Caol and Gormán trailing behind.

Irél, the commander of the Fianna, was indeed at the stables. He turned as they approached.

'You want me again, lady?' He saluted as they came up.

'Do you know where your man Cuan is?'

Irél shook his head. 'You need to question him again?'

'I do. Can you make a search for him and hold him securely until I am sent for?'

Irél looked surprised. 'Hold him? Why is that necessary, lady?'

'Because a *dálaigh* says it is necessary,' she replied impatiently.

Irél flushed. 'It shall be as you order, of course.' His tone indicated his sense of pique.

Fidelma immediately regretted her curtness. 'I apologise. As commander you have a right to know. Both Lugna and Cuan have committed a grave disregard of their duty. I have spoken with Lugna and told him to confine himself to his quarters and await a hearing. After that, it will be up to you, as his commander, to decide how to discipline him. I have little knowledge of the law as it applies in the military service.'

Irél was clearly concerned. 'If it is as serious as that, then loss of rank and fines must follow. Can you give me details?'

'We will wait for full explanations until I sum up my findings. But it is essential that we find Cuan.'

'I will instigate a search for him at once, lady. It will be as you say.' Yet he still appeared hesitant.

'You have something that you wish to tell me, Irél?'

'Apart from a neglect of duty, is it that you suspect Cuan had some involvement with Dubh Duin?'

'Exactly that.'

'Then you should know that Cuan was originally of the Uí Beccon, a small clan who pay fealty to the Cinél Cairpre Gabra. Their territory is on the northern borders of Cinél Cairpre.'

Only Eadulf, who knew Fidelma's features well, could see the surprise on her face and knew how well she controlled it.

'No one told me this,' she said slowly.

Irél shrugged. 'The Fianna are recruited from many clans of Midhe and they all take oath to serve the High King. Once they take the oath, any service to their own clans must take second place to that of the High King. It makes no difference where a man comes from. But if you suspect Cuan, it might be wise to know that he was of the Uí Beccon.'

'Tell me of the Uí Beccon.'

'Little to tell. They are a small tributary clan in the far north of Midhe next to the lands of Cinél Cairpre. They keep themselves to themselves. I have never known them to create trouble.'

'And Cuan came to Tara to enlist in the ranks of the Fianna?'

'We do not take just anyone,' Irél replied. 'The men must be warriors of above average ability. Their training is hard. They must prove themselves in physical and mental stamina.'

'I am well aware of what is demanded from the warrior élite, Irél,' Fidelma said patiently. 'You may rest assured that I am interested in Cuan for matters other than his place of origin.'

Fidelma was about to leave the stable when she remembered her previous task.

'Do you know if the lady Gormflaith has returned from riding?'

Irél nodded immediately. 'I saw her and her daughter Murgain stable their horses a short time ago. Gormflaith has returned to her residence and her daughter has gone off to play with her friends.'

Fidelma thanked him and turned to Caol and Gormán. 'I am going to see Gormflaith. Perhaps you can make yourself useful to Irél and help him find Cuan.'

They acknowledged her diplomatic way of dismissing them without comment. Eadulf accompanied Fidelma back towards the residence of Gormflaith.

'I need to return to the guesthouse,' he said. 'I know you desire to see Gormflaith on your own, but should you not summon Abbot Colmán to attend? After all, she is the widow of the High King.'

Fidelma shook her head. 'The abbot does not need to oversee all our enquiries, and widow of the High King or not, I am a *dálaigh* who has been given the task to investigate this matter.'

'You think that this conspiracy will show that there is a link between the assassin Dubh Duin, Gormflaith and Cuan? It seems logical. Now we know that Cuan is from a clan that is in service to the Cinél Cairpre and that Dubh Duin was, therefore, his chieftain . . .'

'I think there is a conspiracy,' Fidelma interrupted, 'but, as I have said many times, it is no good speculating until . . .'

Eadulf groaned softly. 'I know, I know. No speculation before you have gathered all the facts. Even so . . .'

'Even so, Eadulf, the rule cannot be broken. I am thinking that there are more facts that we do not know than the ones we do know.'

Eadulf left her and returned to the guesthouse. It seemed deserted, for which he was grateful because he needed to visit the *fialtech* or privy that was at the back. Having dutifully washed himself – it had taken him many years to adjust to what he saw as the obsession of the people of the country in washing, with their morning ablutions and then a full bath every evening before the main meal – Eadulf was returning through the guest house when a noise caught his ear from the room in which the meals for the guests were prepared. It was suspiciously like someone sobbing.

He paused, pushed open the door and looked in.

It was the plain-looking girl, Cnucha, who sat at the table with her head buried in her arms, clearly weeping.

'Can I be of any help to you?' asked Eadulf gently.

Startled, the girl glanced up and Eadulf saw that one of her cheeks was red and starting to bruise. The girl's eyes were round with fear for a moment, her mouth an almost perfect 'o' shape.

'I'm sorry. I didn't mean to startle you,' he said contritely. 'What is wrong?'

The girl seemed to recover her wits and sniffed, wiping away her tears. 'Nothing.'

'Nothing?' smiled Eadulf, sitting down. 'Nothing does not create tears.'

The girl swiftly put her hand up to her cheek as if to hide it and then seemed to realise the futility of the gesture.

'There is nothing you can do,' she said in a dull voice. 'Thank you for asking.'

'Perhaps I should be the judge of that,' Eadulf said firmly. 'A trouble told is a trouble shared, and a trouble shared is . . .'

The girl gave him a quivering smile and said, 'My trouble is the lady Muirgel. She has taken a dislike to me and it seems she has persuaded the Brehon Barrán that she is in the right.'

'Why should she dislike you?' queried Eadulf, suddenly remembering the conversation he had overheard between Cnucha and the senior female servant, Brónach.

'The lady Muirgel does not have to give reasons.'

'Surely you will be supported by Brother Rogallach or Abbot Colmán if her behaviour is unreasonable?'

She was anxious again and shook her head. 'I cannot complain to them.'

'Why? Who are you afraid of?'

'I am not afraid. I know that nothing could be done.'

'Why?' he demanded.

There was a movement behind him and Cnucha sprang up with a guilty expression.

'You are forgetting yourself, Cnucha,' came the iron tone of Brónach. 'Brother Eadulf is a guest here and you should be attending to his wants, not sitting gossiping.'

Eadulf turned to the attractive woman, who was in charge of the female servants, and said lightly, 'It is all right, Brónach. I did not need anything. It was just that . . .' He turned back to Cnucha and suddenly saw her expression, as if silently imploring him to say no more. Eadulf shrugged. 'It was just that I wondered how long Cnucha here had worked in Tara and we fell to talking.'

Brónach looked critically at the younger girl. 'Well, she has many duties to fulfil, Brother Eadulf. And time is pressing. This place must be cleaned, for a start. Anyway, I was looking for Báine. Have you seen her, Cnucha?'

The young girl shook her head and with a sigh the older woman left.

Cnucha looked at him gratefully and mouthed a silent, 'Thank you.'

Eadulf went to the door to check. It was clear that Brónach had left the guesthouse altogether. He turned back to Cnucha.

'You need not take any abuse from Muirgel, even if you feel that you are in the wrong,' he counselled her. 'Why didn't you want Brónach to know about it? She might have been able to help as she is in charge.'

'I know Brónach was very friendly with the High King when he was alive and with his family, so I doubt whether she would stand up for me against Muirgel,' Cnucha said despondently. 'And saying anything to Báine is like saying it to Muirgel. They are as thick as thieves, those two. I have often seen them together. Even when her duties are over, Báine often goes to the house of the High King's – the late High King's – wife. I am sure she does not go there to see Gormflaith.'

'I have seen the way Muirgel treats her attendant,' Eadulf remarked. 'It is neither courteous nor proper. But what manner of relationship could she have with Báine?'

Cnucha grimaced sourly. 'Báine! That one! She is a strange person.' She rubbed a hand across her eyes. 'But now I must go, Brother Eadulf, lest either of them return and the work is not done.'

'I will take the blame,' replied Eadulf to reassure her.

'I am the one who has to live here,' replied the girl, unimpressed. 'You do not.'

Picking up a broom, she began to sweep and thus dismissed, Eadulf left.

Fidelma entered the residence of the wife and children of the High King at the *Tech Laoghaire* and a maid confirmed that Gormflaith was in her chambers. While the maid went off to see if Gormflaith would receive a visitor, Fidelma moved to the window that provided a view down the hill to the stables. She was about to turn away when she spotted the tall figure of Brehon Barrán strolling to the stables in the company of a young woman. They seemed to be engaged in earnest talk, the young woman leaning close to the elderly judge and touching his arm as if to make a point now and then.

It was only when Fidelma realised that the girl was Muirgel that she paused to take a second look. She wondered if Muirgel was telling him what she had revealed to Fidelma. They had halted and someone was bringing out a horse from the stable. Once again, the girl leaned close to the Brehon and touched his arm, though not in an imperious way; more of an intimate expression. Then she mounted and rode away with Barrán gazing after her for a few moments before turning and walking slowly back in the direction of the royal house from which they had obviously come.

At that moment the maid returned and announced that the lady Gormflaith would see Fidelma immediately.

CHAPTER ELEVEN

Eadulf had left the guesthouse and was walking towards the stable buildings when no less a person than Cenn Faelad emerged from them. The commander of his guard, Irél, was at his side and another warrior walked two paces behind, eyes watchful and hand on his sword. Cenn Faelad beckoned in friendly fashion to Eadulf to join him.

'How are things going with your investigations?' Cenn Faelad asked. It was the greeting of an equal, with no differentiation of rank or of nationality, and Eadulf felt slightly flattered, although he had heard that Cenn Faelad, in his role as *tánaiste*, the heir apparent, had earned popularity by being accessible to all his people.

'We are making some progress,' Eadulf replied. 'Fidelma is even now conducting an interview with—'

'With my brother's widow,' intervened Cenn Faelad with a grim smile. 'I saw the lady Fidelma going into her residence a moment ago. She is very thorough, that wife of yours.'

Eadulf smiled with pride. 'There is little that escapes her attention in these matters.'

'But I see that you do not attend all her interrogations?'

'In this instance it was thought more circumspect for me to stay away. Diplomacy . . .'

'We do not stand on ceremony here, Eadulf,' Cenn Faelad said immediately. 'Or should not. You have been in our country long enough to know that. After all, there is a saying here that we are all kings' sons.'

'Alas, Cenn Faelad, not all of us can prove it,' replied Eadulf wryly.

The High King elect's features broadened and he burst out laughing.

'That was well and truly said, my friend. Well done! You show a ready wit. But it is true, in our system we say that a people is stronger than a lord, for they have the final vote at the clan assemblies.'

Irél coughed pointedly at his side.

'My commander reminds me not to delay,' Cenn Faelad said. 'We are on our way to the marketplace below,' he motioned down the hill outside the walls of Tara. 'A foreign merchant ship has arrived and we wish to see what goods it brings. It is one of the privileges of my rank that I can see his goods first before he opens his stall in the market. Thus I can make first choice of anything new and interesting.'

Eadulf asked slyly: 'And does that fit in with your people being stronger than a lord?'

Again Cenn Faelad laughed.

'I can see that you have the same quality of humour as Fidelma,' he beamed. 'But I will answer – I said it was a privilege, not a right. Anyway, perhaps you'll walk with us and see? It will not take long and I doubt whether Fidelma will be brief in talking with my sister-in-law.'

Again, Eadulf stifled a feeling of being flattered.

'I would be delighted. Is it known where this merchant ship comes from?'

'It's from Gaul, I think. From the port of An Naoned.'

They fell in step and began to move towards the gates of the palace complex.

'Merchant ships from Gaul are large,' observed Eadulf. 'Do they anchor at some coastal port and bring their goods on overland or by smaller vessels?'

'Some ships can negotiate along the main river, which we call the Bóinn. There is an island in the river just north of here, beyond which it is dangerous to proceed. But a good local river man can pilot a fairly big vessel to the island there and that is where goods are offloaded at a place we call An Uaimh and then brought here overland. We have a good trade with Britain and Gaul.'

Eadulf noticed that Irél had now moved ahead and that both he and the guard behind were looking round cautiously.

Cenn Faelad observed his interest. 'I am told,' he said in a low voice, 'that it is wise for me to be closely guarded until we know the reason for the slaughter of my brother.'

'I presume that you have some theories?' Eadulf replied.

The young High King elect gave him a searching glance. Then he said quietly, 'I suppose that we all speculate.'

'As Sechnussach was your brother, your speculation would be interesting.'

'My brother was High King. In that office one is never universally loved. What is justice for one can be construed as injustice for another. Dubh Duin was a man of fixed ideas and he was known for these ideas in the Great Assembly. They were ideas that were not shared by my brother. But that should be no motive for assassination. The place to really change matters is in the assembly, not with the High King – for you can change a High King but the decision of the assembly can only be changed because it is the will of the majority of its members. As I said before, it is the assembly who constrains the High King.'

Eadulf nodded slowly. 'So you dismiss the motivation of a disagreement of ideas?'

'Not as such. Dubh Duin might have been consumed by madness. Killing is the ultimate madness, whether done in hot or cold blood.'

They had walked out of the gates and through respectful groups of people, beyond the dwellings that arose around the walls of Tara. Eadulf was aware of great crowds of people, horses, carts, tents pitched wherever there was space. Of course, Tara was the principal city of the five kingdoms of Éireann, its biggest centre, to which all manner of people would be attracted. Having dwelled in Cashel, which was less turbulent, and become used to quieter ways, he had forgotten the hustle and bustle of great towns.

Irél led the way through the maze of people who crowded around the tents and more permanent buildings into a great railed-off enclosure.

'This is where the foreign merchants are allowed to ply their trade,' Cenn Faelad explained.

Several stalls had been set up and Eadulf saw all manner of people. There were men in bright colours and styles of dress that he associated with the peoples of southern Gaul or Rome. He could see a few merchants who were unmistakably from the Saxon lands. Then he could hear the rolling accents of the Britons who had for centuries had a constant interchange with their neighbours in Éireann.

'Where is the new merchant, Irél?' asked Cenn Faelad.

'Over here.' The bodyguard pointed to one corner, where a large tent had been erected.

A tall man was standing at the entrance, clad in fairly rich clothes. He was swarthy but cleanshaven. At his side was a boy about fourteen years old. The boy had a metal collar around his neck, fastened at one side with a padlock.

Irél halted before the man and addressed him. 'Identify yourself, merchant. You are in the presence of the High King elect, lord of all the five kingdoms of this land.'

To Eadulf's surprise, it was the boy who began to address the tall man in a tongue that he could not identify. It was he who was obviously the merchant's translator.

The man smiled thinly, raised a hand to his forehead in salutation and bowed low. He uttered a few words.

'I am Verbas of Peqini, Majesty,' interpreted the boy in a hesitant but obvious accent of Éireann.

Cenn Faelad looked at the lad with a frown. 'And who are you?'

The boy grimaced. 'I am the property of my lord Verbas.'

Eadulf knew that slavery was uncommon among the people of Éireann but his own people had always practised slavery like the Romans. However, Cenn Faelad was disapproving.

'I was told that you were a merchant from Gaul,' he said through the boy.

Verbas of Peqini smiled. It was the insincere smile of a merchant.

'My ship has sailed here from the port of An Naoned in Armorica, Majesty, but I am from a land far to the east, plying my trade throughout the great lands of the world.'

'And this boy is your interpreter?'

'He is my voice, Majesty, in these far western lands.'

'Know then, Verbas of Peqini, that in this land we do not accept that one man may hold another in bondage.' When the boy seemed scared to translate this, Cenn Faelad sharply ordered him to do so. 'Only if such a person has stood before the law and forfeited his right to freedom by some crime, or has been taken hostage in war, does he lose the right to conduct his life freely and must work under the jurisdiction of the clan to regain such freedoms.'

Fury was gathering on the merchant's face and the false smile was rapidly disappearing as his slave translated haltingly.

'Keep translating, boy,' instructed Cenn Faelad. 'Tell your master this, that we will respect his customs as a visitor to our shores. But in turn he must respect our laws. Should you escape him, out of the confines of this foreign merchants' quarter, or from his ship, and seek sanctuary in our land, then that sanctuary will be granted and you will be free.'

The boy was staring at him, wide-eyed.

'Tell him,' insisted Cenn Faelad.

Verbas was also staring as the boy translated and it was a sullen, almost malignant stare. Through his slave, he replied slowly.

'Majesty, I am an honest merchant and visitor to your land. I do not know your customs. I will try not to cause you anger by keeping to mine. I come to trade and not impose myself. As soon as my business is conducted, I shall return to my ship with my property intact and leave your shores.'

The High King elected nodded absently. He turned to the boy, asking, 'How do you speak our tongue so well, eh? What is your name?'

'Assíd, lord.'

'Assíd? But that is a name of Éireann,' replied Cenn Faelad in astonishment. 'Where are you from and how came you in this state?'

'I do not remember where I am from, lord. I recall being on a boat with those I was later told were probably followers of the god Christ. Then there was fighting. I was taken from the ship and many of those on it were killed. I remember another ship. Then I was taken to a land where I was put in a cage. I think that was when this was placed on me.' He raised a hand to touch his iron collar. 'And I was given to this man, Verbas.'

Verbas interrupted sharply and was obviously asking Assíd what he was saying.

'Tell him,' Cenn Faelad instructed quickly, 'that I am asking about the goods you have.'

The boy did so and this seemed to appease the merchant.

'You remember nothing else before being on the ship?'

The boy shook his head.

'But was this the language you spoke? Are you of this country?'

'I seemed to know the language, lord,' the boy said hesitantly. 'There was a woman who was in Verbas's house. She was older than me and spoke it as her native tongue. I learned more from her. She said she had been a pilgrim on her way to the holy land of Christ when her ship was seized and she was sold to Verbas, our master.'

Cenn Faelad sighed deeply. 'It is a sad tale, Assíd. I will consult the Brehons and see what they advise. But it is true that if you are able to get away and seek sanctuary, it will be given you. But this man is becoming suspicious. Now show me the goods.'

Assíd muttered something to Verbas and he stood aside from the tent entrance and motioned them in.

Cenn Faelad entered, followed by Eadulf and Irél, and looked round. There were many amphorae in one corner and cloths of various bright colours, shimmering, were hanging up.

'There is red wine from Gaul,' Verbas said through Assíd.

Cenn Faelad barely glanced at the amphorae.

'If the wine tastes good, I'll get Brother Rogallach to select a few of the amphorae for the kitchens,' he observed. 'But first, let me look at these garments.'

'These are the finest of their kind from the East, lord,' Verbas said through the boy. 'You have a discerning eye, Majesty.'

Cenn Faelad let his hand slide lightly over the material. 'It is beautiful, is it not, Eadulf my friend?'

Eadulf joined him and examined the cloth. 'It is what you call *sidna* or *siriac*,' he said, feeling it.

'Indeed, it is silk, and good for cloaks or undershirts,' agreed Cenn Faelad. 'The other is *sróll*, satin. It is usually expensive.' He addressed the boy. 'I shall want to buy enough for some cloaks and other garments. Later this day, I will send my *bollscari* to make the purchases – sell them to no other. He will also come to taste some of the wine and purchase several amphorae. Sell that to no other.'

Surprisingly, the merchant did not look happy.

'I was hoping to make the deal quickly, Majesty, and be on my way back to my ship.'

'Tell him,' Cenn Faelad said to the boy Assíd, 'we cannot let you depart so quickly as your journey has brought you such a long way. As soon as my steward has conducted my purchases with you, you may open your stall to others, but not before. Then you must remain and feast with us before returning to your ship.'

Eadulf understood what Cenn Faelad was about. He was giving the opportunity for the boy to escape and seek sanctuary from his slave master.

'Assíd, I hope you understand what has been said here,' Cenn Faelad stated, looking with a smile directly at Verbas as if he were addressing him. 'Assure your master, Verbas, that he will get a fair price. And if you escape, you will be treated fairly too.'

The boy translated the necessary part of the sentence to the man, who raised a hand again to his forehead and bowed – but his features bore a sullen look.

Cenn Faelad turned to Irél. 'Let your man stay here and keep an eye on Verbas just in case he intends to remove himself back to his ship before I am ready.'

'It shall be done,' Irél said.

To Assíd, Cenn Faelad said: 'Explain to Verbas that I am leaving a warrior here for his own protection to make sure that others do not try to get his goods unfairly. Now,' the young man grinned at Eadulf, 'enough of these intrigues. I shall return to the royal enclosure.'

'In that case, with your indulgence,' Eadulf said, 'I'll look round the market for a while before I return.'

'As you will,' Cenn Faelad replied, turning away with Irél at his side.

Eadulf stood a moment, gazing after him. One thing worried him about Cenn Faelad. The heir apparent had shown himself capable of some duplicitous dealings and Eadulf was unsure whether to approve of his intentions or be suspicious of what this behaviour said about his character.

For a while Eadulf wandered through the noisy market, looking at the bright stalls and boisterous side-shows. All of a sudden, he came upon a smithy's forge. It was situated at the end of the market stalls but was clearly not a temporary affair. A burly man was beating metal on an anvil; with tongs in one hand and his hammer in the other, he was striking at it with ringing tones. Eadulf was about to pass on when he noticed some of the smith's work hanging up for passers-by to admire and purchase.

Among the items was a collection of keys.

An idea suddenly occurred to Eadulf.

'Are you the only blacksmith in Tara?' he asked the man.

The smith paused and put down his hammer.

'I am not, Brother Saxon,' he replied, showing his recognition of Eadulf's clothes and accent. 'But this is my forge. Why do you ask?'

'How many smiths would there be here?'

The man laughed uproariously. 'In the royal enclosure alone there may be half a dozen serving not only the nobles but the Fianna as well. Outside,' he waved his arm around, 'well, my friend, Tara is a large settlement.'

Eadulf nodded, slightly disappointed. Then: 'But you are nearest the main gates of the royal enclosure,' he observed.

'I'll not deny it and that, I grant, does help with my business. I get a

117

good trade. Now, why are you asking such questions? You don't want to set up as a smith, surely?'

Eadulf grinned and shook his head. 'If I wanted a key made, would I come to you?'

'A key, is it? I do make keys, but not often. Only the nobles want them. What sort of key do you want made?'

'I do not want a key made myself, but within the last few weeks someone from the royal enclosure did – and probably they did not want anyone to know.'

The smith looked surprised and then he frowned in recollection. After a moment's thought he asked: 'Would the man have been a member of the Fianna?'

A thrill of excitement went through Eadulf. 'You know of such a person?'

'A matter of fact, not so many weeks ago, a warrior from the Fianna did ask me to copy a key for him. He said it was a key to a lady's chamber – a lady who was jealously guarded by a husband . . .' He smiled and winked. 'You know how these things go, my friend, for you look like a man of the world.'

'Tell me, did the key have a nick on it, as if it had been struck by something sharp – and did the warrior ask you to copy even that mark?'

The smith suddenly looked apprehensive. 'You are not the husband, surely? I have done nothing wrong . . .'

'You have done nothing wrong,' Eadulf immediately reassured the man, 'and if you give me a description of the warrior, there is a *screpal* in it for you.' He produced the coin and held it up.

The smith scratched his head for a moment and said: 'He had dark hair, bony features and close-set eyes. Oh, and he had a scar over the right eye. I gave him the key and the copy of it and he paid and went away happy enough.'

Eadulf smiled broadly and handed the man the coin. He returned to the royal enclosure with a light step.

Fidelma had met Gormflaith only once before and that was less than a year ago when the latter had accompanied her husband Sechnussach, the High King, to the festivities of Fidelma's own wedding at Cashel. She was a handsome woman and no more than thirty-two or three. She must have married young, only a year or so after the age of choice, Fidelma thought, for her daughter, Muirgel, being sixteen, must have been born soon after. Gormflaith bore a striking resemblance to her daughter so that they could have been sisters. She had black hair, dark eyes and a pale skin, and the same arrogance about her features. She carried herself with that regal bearing that suited the meaning of her name – 'illustrious sovereignty'. At the same time, she wore an air of extreme melancholia. It was as if tears were glistening on her eyes which, Fidelma reasoned, was to be expected of someone whose husband or lover had met their death.

Unlike her daughter, Gormflaith rose and welcomed Fidelma as an equal, recognising her position as sister of the King of Muman, and acknowledging her with courtesy. She ordered refreshing drinks to be brought and bade her be seated.

'It is a sad business that brings you hither, Fidelma.'

'Sad indeed, lady. I presume that you know why I am here?'

'Cenn Faelad . . .' She paused. 'Cenn Faelad has told me that the Great Assembly had sent for you. A logical decision and one with which I agree. While I have great respect and friendship for Barrán, it is best if the people see that someone outside of the Uí Néill has investigated this matter. Have you made progress?'

'We can say that we are making steady progress,' replied Fidelma in a neutral way.

'That is good. How may I help you?'

Fidelma leaned forward confidentially. 'I hope you will bear with me, lady, when I ask you under which law you were married to Sechnussach?'

Gormflaith stared in surprise for a moment.

'Which law? Why, our marriage was under the *lánamnas comthinchuir* – the marriage of equals, of course.'

There were three main types of marriage in the five kingdoms: a marriage of equals, those of equal social and financial position; then there was the marriage where the man was of higher social and financial position, and the marriage where the woman was of higher social and financial position. Each type of marriage had particular rights and responsibilities.

Fidelma smiled gently. 'So you stood in equal position before the law?'

'I married Sechnussach before he was High King and when he was merely a noble of the Síl nÁedo of Brega. His being High King did not change our status under law.'

'Exactly so, lady,' agreed Fidelma. 'And, forgive me not knowing, what was your lineage?'

Gormflaith smiled thinly. 'I am a *banchormba*. My father was Airmetach Cáech, chieftain of Clan Cholmáin.'

'Clan Cholmáin, who dwell around the sacred Hill of Uisnech and by the shores of Loch Ainninne?'

'For someone from Muman, you are well-informed of the geography of Midhe, lady.'

'For eight years I studied at the college of Brehon Morann of Tara, not more than a short walk away from where we now sit,' pointed out Fidelma.

Gormflaith raised an eyebrow slightly. 'Ah, is it so? I must have forgotten, if I was ever told.'

'No matter. So, you and Sechnussach stood on equal terms?'.

'Even as I have said.'

'I am told that you and he were estranged?' The question came quickly and without preamble.

Gormflaith coloured a little and blinked, but that was all the emotion she showed.

'It seems that your enquiries are indeed making progress.'

'Do you confirm it?' Fidelma asked.

'Does it need confirmation?'

'It needs explanation.'

'Then it is easy to explain. Soon after Bé Bhail was born, perhaps there was a change in me or perhaps there was a change in Sechnussach. I cannot apportion blame as to who changed first. All I know is that we began to grow apart. He became arrogant towards me. Once he told me that he preferred a woman who made no demands on him and came and went like a maid when bidden to his bed. Our arguments grew strident and he struck me on three occasions. I demanded my own apartments and we no longer were man and wife. For the sake of the five kingdoms, we appeared together at feasting and other occasions when it was required.'

'Do I understand,' Fidelma asked softly, 'that there was no relationship between you other than your duty as wife of the High King?'

Gormflaith bowed her head. 'None.'

'And what was your relationship to Dubh Duin?'

The question was asked in the same soft voice so that for a moment it seemed that it had not registered with Gormflaith. Then her head came up sharply.

'What did you say?' she almost whispered.

'Dubh Duin,' repeated Fidelma. 'Your husband's assassin. What was the nature of your relationship with him?'

Several expressions crossed Gormflaith's features as she tried to form an answer.

'Perhaps,' Fidelma continued in her soft tone, 'it would save time if I tell you that we have questioned the guard who let him into the royal enclosure several times after midnight. He did so on the authority of your daughter, Muirgel. We have already spoken to her.'

Gormflaith's shoulders slumped noticeably. 'Then you must know that he was my lover,' she said simply.

Fidelma was nodding gently. 'You realise that there are implications to what you say, lady?'

'Implications?' Gormflaith was puzzled.

'It provides a motive as to why Dubh Duin killed your husband, and furthermore, it also casts suspicion on you as having some role in a conspiracy to kill him.'

Gormflaith stared at her for a moment and then, to Fidelma's surprise, she gave a wistful smile.

'I regret that Sechnussach's murder is not so easily solved, lady,' she replied.

'How so?'

'I believe you are suggesting that Dubh Duin killed my husband to release me from wedlock, so that he and I could go away and get married. Is that so?'

'It seems a logical thought,' agreed Fidelma.

'Logical for one not fully acquainted with the facts,' rebuked Gormflaith.

Fidelma looked carefully at her. 'It is my task to try to gather the facts.'

'The facts are that Dubh Duin was, indeed, my lover and that we planned to marry. That is why I do not believe that he assassinated Sechnussach.'

Fidelma started in surprise. 'But the evidence, the eyewitnesses to the killing . . . ?' she began.

'He had no reason to kill Sechnussach,' insisted Gormflaith.

'You have given me one, lady,' replied Fidelma. 'So explain why it is not valid.'

'Because there are the laws of *imscarad* – of divorce.'

Fidelma smiled tightly. She had already pointed this aspect out to Eadulf.

'Indeed there are,' she said. 'And, from what you say, being married in

PETER TREODAYNE

a union of equals and with claims that Sechnussach struck you and repudiated you for another, if you could convince a Brehon of this, then
you could simply have divorced him without loss of your wealth or honour.
But, lady, you did not and there is the reason why we come back to Dubh
Duin's motive.'

Gormflaith was already disagreeing. 'But I *did* begin the process of
imscarad, two weeks before Sechnussach was killed. I would have started
the proceedings earlier but my mother was ill, was dying, and she had a
naïve faith and pride in the fact that her daughter was wife of the High
King. I did not want her to feel shame that I had been treated so ill.'

There was a silence while Fidelma considered the implications of this.

'You can, of course, prove this? That you began the act of *imscarad*?'
she asked slowly.

'I would not say it otherwise.'

'And Duin Dubh was fully acquainted with this?'

'He was.'

Fidelma sat back, gazing thoughtfully at the woman and realising that,
if nothing else, Gormflaith believed the truth of what she was saying.

'So two weeks before Sechnussach was slain, you went to him and
proposed a divorce, as is custom.'

'I did. He agreed that it would be a divorce without contest, with no
fault on either side. I would therefore remain the owner of all I had brought
into the marriage and take away half of all the wealth that had accrued
during the period of the marriage which is right and proper according to
the laws of equal marriage.'

'And Sechnussach agreed to this?' pressed Fidelma.

'Not only agreed,' said Gormflaith, 'but I think he was pleased by it.'

'But was this merely a verbal agreement between you?'

'Not at all. As custom has it, we first discussed it and agreed. Then we
called the Brehon to transcribe it. While he was doing so, I went to the
abbey of Cluain Ioraird where my mother – indeed, all the chieftains of
Clann Cholmáin – are interred. I went there with my young daughters to
pray for her soul and to ask her forgiveness as she waited for me in the
Otherworld. The idea was, that by the time I returned, the Brehon would
have the document ready and could pronounce the divorce. Then Dubh
Duin and I would return to my father's lands in Clann Cholmáin.'

'If this were so,' Fidelma said quickly, 'why did Dubh Duin come to
Tara, knowing you were at Cluain Ioraird?'

Gormflaith blinked. 'That is the one thing I do not understand,' she acknowledged. 'There was no reason for him to be here at all until my return.'

'And you still claim that he did not kill your husband?'

'He had no reason to. The divorce was ready.'

'Why was this story not told to us immediately? In fact, we were informed that you had dutifully remained at Tara as the grieving widow with your children. That does not fit with the image of someone who was about to divorce,' Fidelma observed.

Gormflaith shrugged. 'You must think what you like, lady. I have told you the truth. And the fact is that when I returned and found Sechnussach dead, and my poor lover dead too, I did not think it politic to admit to what had happened.'

'But surely the Brehon who drew up the divorce settlement for you would know the real story?'

'He knew of my estrangement with Sechnussach and, of course, he knew that we had agreed a divorce as he had drawn up the agreement. In fact, he knew well my situation because it was he who had introduced me to Dubh Duin. He advised me that I should forget the matter for, as widow of the High King, I would inherit more than just the divorce settlement. Also, Sechnussach's name and reputation would then be untarnished in death. There was no need to besmirch his name as a cruel husband now that he was dead. So he was buried and I played the grieving widow, as you put it.'

'You surely realised that the truth must come out eventually?'

'The truth? I do not know the truth and I think that you are only guessing so that Dubh Duin becomes a scapegoat.'

Fidelma shook her head sadly. 'Then, lady, perhaps you had better let me start down the road to the truth. Let us begin by identifying this so-wise Brehon who gave you what appears to be such bad advice and to whom you entrusted the divorce proceedings.'

Gormflaith hesitated a moment.

'We must have that name, lady,' Fidelma advised her sharply, 'otherwise there is nothing said that does not refute our original thoughts of the motive for killing Sechnussach.'

Gormflaith bowed before the inevitable.

'Very well, Fidelma of Cashel. If you need to know the name – it was the Chief Brehon, Barrán.'

Fidelma stared at her in surprise. 'Well, that can be easily verified.'

'I have no objection to you doing so,' Gormflaith said confidently.

There was a silence and Fidelma said softly: 'I am confused. In spite of the evidence, the eyewitnesses, the fact that Dubh Duin took his own life and, in his dying breath, gasped a word to Lugna, apparently accepting the blame, you still maintain that you believe he was *not* the person who killed your husband?'

'I do.' Gormflaith met her gaze evenly. 'As I say, he had no reason to kill the King on my behalf. Once I was divorced then we would have married.'

'Then perhaps there was another motive?'

'Such as?' snapped Gormflaith. 'What other motive could there be?'

'There are many reasons why one man kills another but of those, if what you say is true, we can only speculate until we know more about the character of Dubh Duin.'

The other woman glowered at her.

'I am Gormflaith of the Clann Cholmáin and do not lie,' she said quietly and firmly.

'Even so, lady, with respect, I must confirm what you have said,' Fidelma replied suavely. 'And, as I say, so far we are lacking in any description of Dubh Duin's character.'

Gormflaith sniffed. 'Are you asking me for an opinion? If so, surely you will claim that I am biased in that regard since we were lovers?'

'That may be so, lady, but any opinion is better than none. Is that not so?'

'Then, leaving aside my personal emotions, I would say that Dubh Duin was a man of courage, not a coward who sneaks about in the night to murder people in their beds.'

'We'll accept that for the time being,' Fidelma assured her. 'Tell us more of his courage, his personality. How long had he been chieftain of the Cairpre Gabra – do you know?'

'Four or five years. I only met him when he was attending the Great Assembly here in Tara.'

'Have you met others of the Cinél Cairpre Gabra? Do you know how his people regarded him?'

'I know he was modest,' Gormflaith said. 'When he came to the Great Assembly only one companion attended him.'

'How would you assess him?'

'He was of strong physique and an attractive man in appearance . . .'

'Let us speak of personality.'

'I felt he possessed excellent judgement and he gave good counsel. He was very level-headed and congenial. He also had a good sense of humour. I suspect he was an idealist for he often spoke of how certain members of the New Faith were dragging the five kingdoms into new ways that rejected our culture and the values of our past. With the new fashion of committing all our histories and stories to the Latin form of writing, he would often deplore it when the scribes sought to change our history to blend it with the teachings of the New Faith. I've seen him argue that before the Assembly. He had a great deal of pride in his ancestry.'

'I understand he was an Uí Néill,' Fidelma said.

'As was Sechnussach. But Dubh Duin traced his descent back from Niall's son Cairpre while Sechnussach traced his back to Niall's son Conall and the line of Síl nÁedo Sláine.'

'Did Dubh Duin then resent Sechnussach being High King?' asked Fidelma. 'I mean, descending from that same family himself, did he think he should be High King?'

Gormflaith smiled sadly. 'The last High King of Dubh Duin's direct ancestry was some hundred years or so ago when Tuathal Máelgarb was chosen. I don't believe Dubh Duin was interested in kingship. Anyway, Sechnussach's brother had long been chosen as his *tánaiste*, his heir apparent.'

'You say that Dubh Duin was always level-headed. Was he never angry? Did you never see him, with that pride you speak of, angered – even if he curbed it or exercised control?'

'Never in my presence,' Gormflaith assured her.

'He was never impulsive?'

'Impulsive? I suppose he was, but that was due to his romantic nature. During the time we were falling in love, he would make impulsive gestures, give me gifts that a more circumspect person would not have done . . . certainly not while my husband was close by.'

'And you told no one of your affair except Muirgel?'

'No one except Muirgel and Brehon Barrán,' she confirmed.

'So your husband knew nothing of Dubh Duin?'

'Nothing. He knew nothing. Even when I went to him and demanded a divorce he agreed almost readily and did not even ask me why or, indeed, whether another had caught my attention. He was apparently content with whatever woman he was taking to his bed.'

Fidelma sighed deeply. 'Very well, lady. I may wish to question you again. What is your plan, now that both your husband and your prospective husband are dead?'

'Muirgel is of marrying age,' the woman said. 'I have a feeling that she is seeing someone with that prospect in mind, but she has not admitted it. So she will probably remain here in Tara. As for my other daughters, I shall take them back to my father's fortress by Loch Ainninne. There was nothing at Tara for me even when Sechnussach was alive and now ... now there is even less and nowhere to go except to my father's house. That is my plan.'

Fidelma rose to go, then hesitated and asked: 'One last thing. Do you know Cuan?'

Gormflaith frowned. 'Cuan?'

'A member of the Fianna. One of the guards at the royal residence.'

'Apart from the commander of the Fianna, I am not in the habit of interesting myself in the names of the members of his companies,' Gormflaith said, but not crossly. 'Why do you ask?'

'Did Dubh Duin ever mention the Uí Beccon to you?'

Gormflaith looked uncertain. 'You ask the most odd questions, Fidelma of Cashel. The Uí Beccon? Why should he mention those people?'

'You know of them?'

'I know most of the clans of Midhe as you doubtless know the clans of Muman. They are a small clan and unremarkable.'

'But you knew that they paid tribute to Dubh Duin's own clan?'

'I did not, but I suppose it is logical as they dwell in the same area of the kingdom. Why are you interested?'

'No matter,' Fidelma assured her. 'It was just a thought.'

'Well.' Gormflaith rose and took her hand, speaking with a sudden earnestness. 'I wish you luck in your enquiry, lady. I have not only to mourn Sechnussach for my daughters' sakes but also to mourn Dubh Duin for my own sake. Whatever you can do in order to bring the truth to light as to who was responsible for their deaths and why, I will support it. Find out though the seas rise to engulf us, or the sky falls to crush us: only the truth is sacred.'

CbAPTER TWELVE

Fidelma met Eadulf in the royal enclosure.

'You look pleased with yourself,' she greeted him. 'What have you been up to?'

Eadulf told her about his trip to the market and his meeting with the .blacksmith.

'So it was Cuan who had the key made,' Fidelma said with satisfaction. 'We must find him before he gets suspicious. What took you to this market?'

Eadulf explained about Cenn Faelad's invitation to accompany him, and his meeting with the arrogant merchant, Verbas of Peqini, and his young slave, Assíd.

'Poor lad,' Fidelma said at once. 'We hear several tales of pilgrim ships being attacked on their way to visit the Holy Land. People are sometimes taken as slaves by marauders. The boy is obviously one such victim. I approve of Cenn Faelad's motives.'

'It is not the motives that concern me but the duplicity,' Eadulf pointed out. 'Someone who is that devious needs to be watched carefully and their truths questioned.'

Fidelma smiled and patted his arm.

'We shall be extra-watchful. But I do hope that the young boy can find his freedom. As a foreign visitor, this Verbas cannot be admonished. Cenn Faelad is right in what he has said. The boy can demand sanctuary once he escapes.'

Eadulf nodded slightly and then asked: 'And what of your news?'

Fidelma quickly told him the result of her meeting with Gormflaith, announcing her intention of going straightway to verify matters with the Chief Brehon, Barrán.

'I saw him and Muirgel go to the stables but then he returned to the royal house.' She glanced awkwardly at Eadulf. 'It may be better for you not to attend this meeting either. It will be unseemly for me to berate Barrán for withholding pertinent information before a witness – yet berate him I must. He is, after all, the Chief Brehon of the Five Kingdoms and if Gormflaith speaks the truth, he should have known better than to withhold this information from me.'

Eadulf had no objection to being excluded. He had already assumed that it would be a contentious meeting.

'Perhaps I can make myself useful by going to the hall of the Great Assembly to see if there is anyone there who might have cause to know Dubh Duin. I was interested to hear Cenn Faelad refer to the views he expressed in the assembly. If he regularly attended as a representative of his people, there may be some who knew him well. We need to learn more about him, not merely information from someone who was enamoured by him.'

Fidelma approved his intention.

'You are right, Eadulf. You will make a *dálaigh* yet. That is certainly something we must pursue in this matter. We need to get a clearer understanding of the character of this assassin. It seems that poor Gormflaith is flying in the face of the witnesses when she doubts it was his hand that struck Sechnussach down.'

'Gormflaith is misleading herself to think otherwise, Fidelma.' Eadulf nodded sadly in agreement. 'It occurs to me that perhaps that is not the only thing she was misleading herself about.'

'You suspect that Dubh Duin was merely using her to get to Sechnussach?'

'There might have been no question of love on his part at all,' Eadulf pointed out. 'But your expression tells me that you do not agree.'

'It would make sense if he had not known that Gormflaith and Sechnussach lived apart, albeit in the same royal enclosure. But the path to Sechnussach clearly lay elsewhere, and not through an estranged wife.'

Eadulf looked disappointed. 'I suppose you are right,' he admitted reluctantly.

'It was a good point to consider, though,' she smiled encouragingly. 'Now, don't forget to keep a sharp lookout for Cuan. I just hope that he has not been warned as yet.'

Eadulf inclined his head in acknowledgement and went off about this task. He saw Gormán with the Fianna commander, Irél, by the stables and crossed to them.

'Any sign of Cuan yet?' he asked at once.

'No,' Irél said, 'but that is not unusual. He is not due on watch duty until later today so he may well have gone hunting or even walked down to the market. He is certainly not in the royal enclosure or at the *Tech Láechda*.'

Eadulf understood this, literally the 'house of heroes', as the name of the military barracks of the Fianna.

'Well, at least he has to return to take his watch,' Eadulf observed brightly. 'I was going to walk to the place where you have the Great Assembly to see if there is anyone there who might have known Dubh Duin. I need someone to enlighten me about what sort of man he was.'

'There is no one about at the place of the Great Assembly at this time,' Irél told him. 'What sort of information were you looking for, because I knew the chief of the Cinél Cairpre to some extent.'

Eadulf was surprised and said so.

'I thought I had mentioned it before,' Irél said. 'Part of the duty of the Fianna is to provide guards at the Great Assembly. I met Dubh Duin there many times. I do not say that I knew him well, but I did have a few conversations with him. He was a man of firm opinions.'

Eadulf grinned. 'Is that a way of saying that he had set ideas and would not bend with discussion?'

'Just that, Brother Saxon.' Irél chuckled. 'I suppose it is a quality that is necessary for a chieftain, especially one whose territory lies on the borderlands.'

'Borderlands?'

'There is Connacht to the west and Bréifne to the north, and neither have much respect for the Cinél Cairpre who, if truth be known, are too out of step with them.'

Eadulf cocked his head. 'In what way, out of step?'

'The Cinél Cairpre have always been . . . shall we say, traditionalists? They don't like change.'

'Do you speak of a change in religion?' asked Eadulf.

Irél examined Eadulf with a soft smile of amusement. 'You have been listening to gossip, my friend.'

'And is there no truth in gossip?'

Irél shrugged. 'There have been such stories, and Dubh Duin has been accused of being obsessive among those in the Great Assembly. Indeed, surely his actions have now proved it?'

'You use the word *fraoch* to describe him,' Eadulf said. 'I am not entirely fluent in the language. Is there another word with which you could help me to understand it?'

'Very well. He could be called a fanatic about the past customs and traditions of his people,' explained Irél.

'Fanatic to what degree?' asked Eadulf after a few moments' thought.

'To what degree?' Irél chuckled again. 'You may have heard stories about the *dibergach*, the brigands who have been creating some problems throughout the kingdom, claiming that they act in the name of the old gods and goddesses?'

'We did see the result of their handiwork on our journey to Tara,' Eadulf recalled. 'Some brothers of the religion were slain at a tiny chapel on the road that passes the Plain of Nuada. What has Dubh Duin to do with that?'

'He was once accused in the Great Assembly of defending the *dibergach*. My men and I once chased a small band of them into the territory of the Cinél Cairpre, which was Dubh Duin's clan.' He shook his head. 'There was nothing to link them with the clan. I do not think Dubh Duin would be as fanatic as that. He merely argued that the New Faith was denying rights to those who would follow in the traditions of their fathers. He suggested to the Great Assembly that the same rights and freedoms of worship should be given to those who did not want to accept a new and foreign God and Faith. I think the argument was that withdrawing the cause of the raids would end them. Of course, he distanced himself from those involved by saying that he was only the mouthpiece for those who asked him to plead their cause to the High King.'

Eadulf raised his eyebrows in surprise. 'And how was that plea received?'

'As I have said, not with any degree of enthusiasm, you can be sure,' Irél grunted. 'You can imagine the outcry from the abbots and the bishops in attendance. But it did get support from some of the chieftains of the north-western clans. In spite of the New Faith being preached here for two centuries, there are still many who prefer the old gods and goddesses.'

'Such as the old woman whom Abbot Colmán calls Mer?'

'Mer the Demented One?' Irél laughed heartily. 'You must not mind her, my Saxon friend. She is crazy. She likes to scare people. She often sits for hours by river fords waiting for travellers and then pronounces a curse on them, implying that she is one of the goddesses of death and battle. It is her little joke.'

Eadulf pulled a face. 'An effective joke,' he observed. 'So what happened in this Great Assembly? How was Dubh Duin answered?'

'Well, certain of the clerics would have answered him quite violently, if you'll pardon me for saying so, Brother Saxon. Many are just as fanatical about their beliefs as was Dubh Duin. However, Sechnussach was the person who came forward and bade them all to be calm. He told them that there, in this same Great Assembly at Tara, Laoghaire, son of Niall of the Nine Hostages, progenitor of all the Uí Néill, had asked those present to agree that henceforth the New Faith, as taught by such as Patrick, who was in attendance, be the one faith of all five kingdoms. He argued that so many of the leading chiefs, nobles and kings throughout the five kingdoms had now accepted the new teachings that the old gods and goddesses were being vanquished to the hills. They were becoming the *sídhe*, the people of the hills, the fairy folk who were not deities at all.' Irél sounded quite animated as he recited the speech.

'You sound as though you endorsed Sechnussach's views,' Eadulf said.

The other man nodded quickly. 'Sechnussach was a great king and I never heard a better speech in the assembly. Anyway, he reminded them that Laoghaire's Great Assembly agreed that henceforth the five kingdoms should follow the faith of Christ. He also reminded them that from the Great Assembly, Laoghaire chose eight people as a commission that would spend the next three years consulting with all the Brehons and clergy to gather, study and then set down all the laws of the five kingdoms. They would remove from those laws anything that was not compatible with the New Faith. That was the law system and Dubh Duin should respect it.'

Eadulf was interested. 'So there was a commission that set down the laws in Laoghaire's time?'

'Laoghaire chose Corc, the King of Muman, and Dara, the King of Ulaidh, to sit with him. Then he asked his Chief Brehon, Dubhtach maccu Lugir, and the Brehons Rossa and Fergus, to join them. Finally, he asked Patrick, Benignus and Cáirnech, the preachers of the New Faith, to complete the commission. Three years later, the great books of law were drawn up, written in the new alphabet that came from Rome. What did not clash with the word of God and with the conscience of those drawing up the laws was set forth. Sechnussach reminded the assembly that they had all endorsed the modified laws when they had accepted the New Faith.

And all this was two centuries ago. There were no footsteps backwards.'

'And did Dubh Duin accept that?'

'It was then the man showed his fanaticism, for he argued with Sechnussach that the historian, Tirechán, had written that Laoghaire refused the Christian baptism and when he was killed fighting a rebellion in Laigin, he was buried near *Tech Laoghaire*, his own royal house, in the traditional manner of a High King – that was, in the ramparts of Tara, upright and fully armed, facing towards his hereditary enemies – the kingdom of Laigin. Dubh Duin claimed that Laoghaire never betrayed the Old Faith to Patrick. The Great Assembly erupted in anger at the affront and Dubh Duin never afterwards attended it.'

Eadulf was staring at him in amazement.

'But why was Fidelma not immediately told of this?' he cried. 'Surely this argument with the High King constitutes a motive for Dubh Duin's assassination of him?'

'In the Great Assembly, everyone can speak what is on their mind without fear,' Irél told him. 'Tempers may rise there but must fall before delegates leave the hall. It is the custom, Brother Saxon.'

Eadulf was dubious. 'It is a matter that I will have to bring before Fidelma. If nothing else, it may help towards an understanding of Dubh Duin's character.'

Fidelma crossed back to *Tech Cormaic*, passing the impassive guard outside, and pushed into the hallway. As she did so, Báine, the attractive young maid, was crossing the hallway and Fidelma asked her if Brehon Barrán was still in the building.

'He is in the High King's library, lady,' the servant replied.

Fidelma thanked her and moved on. Outside the door she paused. She was feeling nervous. After all, Barrán was the Chief Brehon. She felt the same apprehension as she had when a young student, waiting outside the door of the Brehon Morann, the chief professor of the law school. 'I think this is one interview I could do without,' she muttered to herself. Then she remembered that Barrán might have purposefully withheld information which was of importance to her investigation. Anger filled her, and with it came courage. She opened the door and marched in.

Barrán, Chief Brehon of the five kingdoms, glanced up in surprise as Fidelma entered the room. He had been poring over a manuscript. The place was dimly lit with tallow candles and there was no other light. When the room was built as the High King's sanctuary, the architect had realised that light was harmful to the vellums and papyri. Thus, the library had been built without natural light – which did not help with the study of the manuscripts. However, even in the gloom Barrán could see a fiery glint in Fidelma's eyes and the set of her features showed that something was seriously amiss. He began to rise from his chair but she made a cutting motion of her hand that stayed him.

'Is it true that Sechnussach and Gormflaith were about to divorce?' she demanded without preamble.

There was a fraction of a second of surprise before the Brehon resumed his seat. Then his handsome features relaxed into a smile of resignation and he motioned Fidelma to be seated in a chair before the desk on which he was working while he stretched back in his own chair.

'It seems your investigation is progressing thoroughly,' he murmured.

'Is it true?' she demanded once again.

'I have heard of the intention,' he admitted easily.

Her eyes narrowed with anger. 'With all respect, Barrán, as Chief Brehon you should know that withholding evidence in an investigation like this merits fines and could even bring you before the assembly of Brehons so that your appointment could be repudiated by them.'

For a moment the Chief Brehon was silent but his expression retained its good humour.

'In what manner have I withheld evidence?' he asked, and when she leaned forward as if to reply, he held up his hand to silence her. 'The fact was that the divorce did not take place. If the intention was serious then Sechnussach's death ended that. So Gormflaith became widow to the High King and therefore full heir to his entitlements. If the gossip of an impending divorce were made public then it might have had adverse conse-quences for her and her children's status.'

'Even though it was she who was divorcing Sechnussach?' she snapped. 'Divorcing him to marry Dubh Duin?'

Barrán's eyes widened a little. 'She intended to marry Dubh Duin? Did Gormflaith tell you that?'

'Does Gormflaith not speak the truth?'

'I cannot tell you about the truth of her intentions. I can only tell you what I know.'

Fidelma smiled cynically. 'You speak as a lawyer, Barrán.'

'I am a lawyer,' he reminded her with dry humour.

'You did not know that it was her intention to marry Dubh Duin?'

'If she expressed such an intention then I have forgotten.'

'You did not introduce her to Dubh Duin?'

He hesitated, frowning. 'I believe I did. But there are many people who throng the court at Tara that I might introduce to various others. Dubh Duin was a representative of his people in the Great Assembly. Those involved with the Great Assembly knew him. So, at some gathering, I might well have presented him to Gormflaith.'

'The fact is that Gormflaith says she was planning to marry the man who assassinated Sechnussach. Do you confirm that the divorce was arranged?'

Barrán compressed his lips for a moment before replying. 'I cannot. Gormflaith talked of the . . . the possibility. That is all.'

'I am told that Sechnussach and Gormflaith were agreed and that you were writing out the settlement which would have been sealed on the day Gormflaith returned from Cluain Ioraird. Can I see that settlement?'

'It does not exist, Fidelma. Does Gormflaith say it does? She must be upset. I do not understand this.'

Fidelma let out a breath of irritation. 'So, you say that while Gormflaith talked about possibilities of divorce from Sechnussach, you have no knowledge of it as an actuality? Sechnussach and Gormflaith made no agreement nor did you draw up such an agreement?'

'That is what I have said, Fidelma.' Brehon Barrán's expression was sad. 'Do you think Gormflaith's head has been turned by these events?'

'Why would she confess to Dubh Duin being her lover and then make up the story about the divorce?'

'Self-protection?' Barrán suggested.

'But she did not have to confess anything in the first place. She could have denied it. It does not follow.'

'Unless it is to absolve her from any suspicion in the affair. But even if she is not involved, we now have a resolution to this matter for it gives Dubh Duin a motive in his killing. He was jealous . . .'

'No, no,' Fidelma said immediately. 'Her argument is that there was to be a divorce and that Dubh Duin knew all about it. She claims that he had no motive to get rid of Sechnussach. Gormflaith would have been free to marry him within a few days.'

'There – you see? She is trying to exonerate herself by bringing in the matter of divorce. No one can seriously argue that Dubh Duin did not kill

Sechnussach. She is saying that all the eye-witnesses are therefore liars?'
Barrán pursed his lips. 'Mind you, if it comes to that, and she is stating
that I had knowledge of a divorce, then she claims that I am a liar also.'

Fidelma was silent for a moment, before saying, 'Yet she is admitting
to matters that would bring discredit to her, whereas she could easily deny
them.'

'She could be trying to protect Dubh Duin.'

'She could, but why? Why protect her lover in death while admitting
that he was her lover? Why not just say that he was infatuated with her
and she did not know his intentions? As I said, it puts her in a bad light.
She could well have presented herself as a wronged woman, deceived by
a lover who used her to kill the High King. No, it will not do. There is
something wrong here.'

Brehon Barrán regarded her thoughtfully. 'The investigation is yours
but there are still several questions to be asked.'

'I agree. The one fact we do know is that Dubh Duin killed Sechnussach.
Whatever Gormflaith says, it remains a fact. The warrior Lugna says that
the man admitted his guilt with his dying breath. If she is so besotted with
him, even in death, that might explain her not wanting to admit the possibility that he used to her to get close to Sechnussach.'

'You suspect that? But why would he want to kill Sechnussach, if not
for her?'

'Others are involved, and Dubh Duin is merely a tool. Otherwise, there
are matters that make no sense. But we still do not know the motive. The
motive becomes more important, the longer I think about things. Who
uttered the scream that alerted the warrior Lugna to the High King's death,
thus causing Dubh Duin to take his own life? And why *should* Dubh Duin
take his own life?'

Fidelma rose suddenly and regarded the Chief Brehon with a serious
expression.

'Do you know if Sechnussach, during the years of estrangement with
Gormflaith, ever took a second wife?'

Brehon Barrán chuckled, then said, 'Sechnussach could never have
disguised the fact that he had a *dormun*, a second wife. It would have
required many legal clarifications. You can be sure that he did not. His
personal household would have had to know that, and only they knew that
Sechnussach and Gormflaith were estranged. Outside the royal enclosure,
no one else was aware of it.'

'And who made the decision to live separately?'

Barrán looked surprised. 'Gormflaith in the first place,' he said. 'I think that Sechnussach once contemplated divorce. He was considering the no-faults divorce. They would part on equitable terms without blame to one another. You have to have agreement on the part of both people for that.'

'So Sechnussach spoke of it but you are sure that, contrary to what Gormflaith says, nothing was agreed?'

'To be perfectly honest,' the Brehon admitted, 'Sechnussach mentioned that it was Gormflaith who had first broached the matter, now I recall. They discussed matters between them but no agreement was made nor was I instructed to draw one up.'

'Nevertheless, they discussed it after three years of estrangement. Gormflaith admits to her lover, but Sechnussach was a handsome and virile man. Did he really remain a celibate during those years?'

Brehon Barrán pursed his lips. 'I doubt it,' he said. 'But if so, the High King was discreet – and discretion must have been imposed on anyone who was tempted to share his bed.'

'Are you speculating or do you know this for a fact?'

'I speculate, of course.'

'And so you are not aware if Sechnussach had a mistress or even a series of mistresses?'

'Sechnussach was not a man who gave his affections lightly.'

'But he was still a man,' Fidelma replied.

'Then we must assume, as I have, that if he had a mistress then no one has been able to identify her and she has never come forward.'

Fidelma focused on the edge of the desk in some thought.

'We are not in the middle of the forest here, Barrán. Someone must have known something, if such things were happening. Or else they are simply covering up their knowledge.'

'It would follow that one or other of his household servants must have some knowledge,' agreed the Chief Brehon. 'And if you wish to approach the person who is most likely to have that knowledge, I would say that his personal attendant, his *bollscari*, would be the place to start.'

'We are talking about Brother Rogallach?'

Barrán inclined his head in assent.

'He is one of the few witnesses that I have yet to question,' said Fidelma. 'Are you saying that he was close to Sechnussach?'

'As close as a servant may be to the person they serve.'

'And therefore he would know of any secret liaisons, and trysts in the dead of night?'

'Sechnussach could not have functioned without him. But – and far be it from me to offer you advice – isn't the more important question: why would the assassin commit suicide without offering a defence?'

It was a question that had been uppermost in Fidelma's mind and not merely since she had spoken with Gormflaith.

'We will not know that until we find out why he killed Sechnussach. Don't worry, I have pondered the problem. Why would a chieftain who, according to one report, is about to marry his lover, kill Sechnussach, make no effort to escape, and kill himself? We know that of all forms of *fingal*, or kin-slaying, self-slaughter is the worst of crimes. At the moment, it makes no sense at all unless Gormflaith has been frugal with the truth. Perhaps, as you say, she is trying to protect herself. At some stage, Barrán, I am afraid it will be a challenge between Gormflaith's word and your word on this matter of the divorce agreement.'

'I hope that may be avoided, Fidelma. The word of truth from a Brehon is a sacred matter.' The Chief Brehon lifted his shoulder in a curious gesture of resignation. 'I knew your task would not be easy,' he confessed. 'Had things been easy, then the Great Assembly would not have sent to Cashel to ask you to come.'

Fidelma raised her gaze to his. 'If I am to continue this investigation, Barrán, I must be assured that nothing is being held back. Whatever your concerns for public knowledge and protecting the reputation of the High King and his lady, you should have let me know how matters stood between Sechnussach and Gormflaith in their estrangement.'

'You found it out quickly enough,' responded Barrán defensively. 'And it does not bring you closer to a solution.'

'That is beside the point. If I am to succeed, nothing should be held back. It is a principle of the law.'

'You are right, of course,' the Chief Brehon conceded, before raising his hand and letting it fall in a helpless gesture. 'Sometimes, in the higher strata of politics . . .' he used the word *ríaglaid* as an act of governing and rule '. . . sometimes the right to information must take second place to the art of diplomacy.'

'Well, it seems that you will not have to struggle with a conflict of decisions for much longer,' she remarked.

Brehon Barrán looked puzzled.

'Cenn Faelad,' she reminded him, 'mentioned that he was nominating you as his heir-apparent, in which case you will give up the role of Chief Brehon.'

'Cenn Faelad is kind,' Barrán said, and gave a brief smile. 'It will be a honour to serve my cousin in this new role.'

'You do not feel it strange that he, being young, has nominated you, being older than he is, as his heir?' mused Fidelma.

Brehon Barrán appeared slightly affronted. 'I have several good years of service in me yet, Fidelma. I hope to be advising the High King and the Great Assembly for many years to come. It is a wise young king who appoints one more elderly to act as adviser.'

Fidelma shrugged indifferently. 'I am a simple *dálaigh*, Barrán, whose job it is to discover the truth, and truth is often bitter but truth must always prevail if there is to be any hope for good government.'

Brehon Barrán was not perturbed at her implied censure.

'You have my word, Fidelma. You have now had only the truth so far as it is in my possession to give it to you.'

'So be it. And you can tell me no more about Dubh Duin who, Gormflaith says, you introduced to her?'

'As I say, I have no recollection of it.' Barrán shrugged. 'I introduce many people to each other. All I recall about Dubh Duin is that he was regarded as a capable man, a good chieftain and a strong advocate of the rights of his people while in the Great Assembly. I would say he was inclined to be conservative in all his dealings.' He then added: 'I suspect he was conservative in matters of the old religion as well.'

'Why do you suggest that? Are you saying that he did not embrace the New Faith?'

'I really don't know. He raised a heated debate in the Great Assembly once, asking that people should have as much right to follow the Old Faith as follow the New Faith. I know harsh words were exchanged with Sechnussach, but I was not there so cannot give you the details.'

Fidelma was not happy. 'Harsh words between Sechnussach and Dubh Duin? Is this another question of information that would help my investigation that has somehow been overlooked?' she said indignantly.

'You must ask Irél, who was attending the Great Assembly that day or, indeed, one of those nobles who were present at the debate. I am not the investigator of this matter.' Brehon Barrán made a motion of his hand as if in dismissal. 'For me, there was nothing to mark Dubh Duin out significantly from the rest of the nobles of Midhe.' He relaxed a little and grinned. 'They are all egocentric with pretensions of high-minded morals. Dubh Duin liked to claim that the new religion was persecuting those who followed the old religion and that he was merely standing up for the rights of those who did so.'

Fidelma turned to the door, pausing with her hand about to open it. 'It would be best if nothing else was concealed from me in the future, Barrán,' she remarked tightly before she made her exit.

Outside, with the door closed, she exhaled deeply in exasperation. She was angry that the Chief Brehon had tried to conceal facts, claiming, in his defence, that it was good for the people. She returned along the corridor to the hallway of the *Tech Cormaic*, where she found Eadulf waiting for her.

'There is no one at the hall of the Great Assembly at this time,' he explained, 'but I do have some information that might be useful. I had a word with Irél about Dubh Duin and an argument he had in the assembly.'

'An argument with Sechnussach over religion?' Fidelma said.

Eadulf's face fell. 'You already know about it?'

She reached forward and took his arm in companionable fashion. 'In truth, I have only just heard that it took place. I have no details. Come, let us go into the fresh air and then tell me all you know.'

CHAPTER THIRTEEN

When Eadulf had related his conversation with Irél, the commander of the Fianna, Fidelma merely commented: 'It is background information that helps to paint a picture of our assassin, but not much else. There is still much to discover.'

'What did Brehon Barrán have to say to you? Did Gormflaith tell the truth?'

'I am afraid that both Gormflaith and Barrán tell stories that are impossible to reconcile. Barrán said that so far as he knew, no divorce was arranged and he was never asked to draw up a settlement to be agreed by them.'

She was about to speak further when the dowdy young woman who had been serving in the guesthouse, Cnucha, came hurrying by. Fidelma called to her and the girl, seeing who it was, came over immediately, her hands demurely folded before her.

'May I help, lady?' she asked, eyes downcast.

'I am looking for Brother Rogallach. Would you know where he is?'

The girl indicated towards the back of the *Tech Cormaic*.

'At this hour you will find him in the kitchen, lady. The door at the back is open, so you may go through the house to the kitchen.'

Fidelma was about to thank the girl when the figure of Brónach appeared on the steps of the royal residence and glowered angrily at them.

'Cnucha! What are you loitering there for? I sent you to help Báine in the guesthouse. Be off with you!' The woman turned on her heel and went inside.

Cnucha, in an uncharacteristic show of temper, suddenly stuck out a tongue in her direction and then, realising that the others had seen her, she blushed and lowered her head.

'I am sorry, lady. Sometimes it is difficult to put up with all the insults that have to be endured when people think you have no feelings and no ability to fight back. I am sure Brónach is usually a good person. Recently, however, she has become increasingly irritable. I think it is because her lover may have left her.'

Fidelma was disapproving. 'It is not seemly to speak of such things, Cnucha.'

The girl tried to appear contrite. 'It just slipped out, lady. Brónach is a nice woman, very attractive, and it was sad when her husband was killed. I am surprised that she did not take another husband. Someone like her could have many suitors. I am sure she had a lover until a few weeks ago – not that she ever told us or that we knew – but she has been so miserable and snappy of late, and—'

The girl caught sight of Fidelma's frown and stopped dead. 'Sorry, it's just . . . sorry.' She moved off quickly on her errand.

Eadulf was smiling at Fidelma's expression. 'Well, if there was gossip or rumour to be had, which might help us, we know where to come to,' he joked.

Fidelma pulled a face at him, indicating mock offence. 'It is not gossip we look for, Eadulf, but evidence.'

Eadulf raised his eyes towards the sky for a moment and said piously: 'Much truth in gossip, as your old saying goes.'

'*Vir sapit qui pauca loquitor*,' she quoted back. 'That person is wise who talks little.' Then she thought of something. 'Or maybe it should be the reverse . . .' She began to walk towards the kitchen of the royal house with Eadulf, puzzled, trailing in her wake.

It was the custom of the large wooden houses in the five kingdoms to have the *ircha*, or kitchen, constructed as a separate building at the back. This was because of the heat of the cooking fires and the dangers of sparks of heated oil causing a conflagration. There were still instances of such domestic fires destroying buildings and even entire families.

As they entered the big room, with its stifling heat emanating from two ovens, its pungent odours of herbs and heating foods, they found two people busy preparing the dishes. Fidelma could not see Brother Rogallach although one of the men, who was cutting joints of pork on a thick wooden table, looked up and, laying aside his large-bladed knife, took a step towards them.

'Can I help you?' he asked deferentially. 'I am Torpach the cook.'

Fidelma explained who she was looking for.

'Ah, Brother Rogallach is in the *seallad*. He is doing an inventory of the goods there. You'll find him beyond that door.'

Eadulf recognised *seallad* as the word for a pantry where provisions were stored and was about to move off but Torpach halted them. 'Excuse me, lady, but you are the *dálaigh* come to investigate Sechnussach's death, aren't you?'

'I am,' she affirmed.

'He was a good man,' sighed Torpach. 'A good cook, too. He was often down in this kitchen, trying out recipes. He was down here even at dawn on the day before his death. I got here early that day to prepare some dishes and surprised him. He told me he couldn't sleep, poor man, and so came to get his own breakfast ready. Another lord would have roused his servants to do such a task. That was the last time I saw him. Why Dubh Duin wanted to kill him, I do not know.'

Fidelma smiled reassuringly at the cook's expression of woe.

'That is what I must discover, Torpach. Thank you for your concern. I hope to have the answers before long.'

The *seallad* was a separate building from the kitchen, a place without fire so that the heat of cooking would not ruin the foodstuffs that were stored there. Fidelma led the way out into what was a large yard. In one corner of the yard was a medium-sized kiln, an *aith*, which was used for the drying of corn or other grains to make bread. The large wooden store-house opposite to it had no windows, although its one door was slightly ajar. This was clearly the *seallad* or the pantry.

'Brother Rogallach?' called Fidelma as they approached. There was no answer.

With a shrug, she moved to the door and pushed it open. The interior of the pantry was in darkness. Eadulf stood at her shoulder.

'Brother Rogallach?' She raised her voice a little. 'Are you in there?'

They both heard it. As if in answer there came a soft moaning sound.

Fidelma stepped inside, trying to adjust her eyes to the gloom and clicked her tongue in frustration that she could not make out anything. It was Eadulf who noticed the extinguished candle on the ground almost at their feet. He had nearly trodden on it as he moved forward. He now bent down and picked it up.

'Can you light it?' asked Fidelma.

'Stay there, don't go inside,' Eadulf instructed firmly and hurried back to the kitchen where, without a word to the surprised cook and his assistant, he ignited the candle from one of the cooking fires. It was easier than spending time with flint and tinder trying to produce a flame. One hand cupped over the flickering flame of the tallow candle, he went as fast as he could back to the *seallad* where Fidelma was waiting impatiently on the threshold.

'Let me go first,' Eadulf insisted, and so she stood aside to let him pass within.

The single room of the pantry building was stacked with barrels and sacks in the centre, while all around the walls was wooden shelving on which were placed various items of foodstuffs. Eadulf stood looking round, seeing no sign of anyone.

There came another moan.

Raising his candle high he stepped in the direction of the sound and saw a sandalled foot sticking out from behind one of the barrels.

'Here!' he called to Fidelma. Behind the barrels was stretched the figure of a stocky religieux, face downwards, one arm under his body, the other stretched out. A little distance from the open hand was an empty candle-holder. Eadulf bent down and touched the pulse in the man's neck. It beat regularly and steadily, but the back of his head was covered in blood. Carefully, he turned the man on his side, away from the injury.

'Rogallach!' exclaimed Fidelma, standing above him and peering down at the semi-conscious moonfaced man. 'I thought I knew his name. I met him once before when I was here in Tara. Is he badly hurt?'

'He has taken a blow on the back of the head. I'll shift him out into the light where I can have a better look.'

Giving the candle to Fidelma, Eadulf put his forearms under the man's shoulders, then dragged him backward out of the pantry and into the light beyond. By this time, the moonfaced man was blinking and coming around.

'Lie still,' instructed Eadulf gently, as he began to examine him. Finally he sat back. 'You have a nasty gash on the back of the head, Brother. How did you come by it?'

The man stared up at him. 'Who are you?' he demanded, even though his voice was still weak.

'I am Eadulf.'

Fidelma bent across his shoulder. 'You remember me, Brother Rogallach? I am Fidelma of Cashel.'

The man's eyes flickered past Eadulf to her. 'Fidelma the *dálaigh?*' he asked hesitantly.

'The same.'

Brother Rogallach closed his eyes as if tired for the moment and then he tried to sit up but Eadulf pressed him back.

'Stay still for the moment, my friend. I do not know what damage might have been caused. Did you hit your head on something?'

'I was struck from behind.'

Eadulf glanced back to Fidelma and then to the man once more. 'Deliberately struck, do you mean?'

'I do. I had just opened the trap door which leads down to the *uaimha* where we store the meats and butter and other foodstuffs that require the cold to keep them . . .'

'Yes, I know what it is,' replied Eadulf, having but recently learned the word for the souterrain.

'I opened the trap door and turned to fasten it before descending to get some butter for the kitchen. I had my back to the entrance and was still holding my candle ready to descend when someone hit me.'

Fidelma looked concerned. 'You are certain it was a blow deliberately struck?'

The moonfaced Brother Rogallach looked at her indignantly. 'I have not abandoned my senses that I do not know when someone has attacked me,' he replied.

'We should take you to an apothecary to get that wound dressed,' Eadulf suggested.

Fidelma ignored him and addressed the rotund *bollscari* again.

'Do you have any idea of the passing of time? How long ago was this?'

Brother Rogallach said shakily, 'I have been in blackness. I do not know.'

At that moment Torpach, the cook, came out of the kitchen door and paused, seeing Rogallach stretched on the ground and the others bending over him.

'What is happening?' he demanded.

'Brother Rogallach has met with a mishap,' Fidelma replied. 'Do you know when he left the kitchen to go to the pantry?'

The man looked slightly bewildered. 'Only moments before you came into the kitchen asking for him, lady. Why, did he slip?'

'Moments?' Fidelma did not answer the question. 'Then if the blow was deliberately struck, the culprit might still be hiding in the souterrain. Stay with Brother Rogallach,' she instructed the cook.

Rising, she motioned Eadulf to follow her. She had left the candle alight on a shelf inside the door of the pantry. She picked it up but again Eadulf held out his hand and stayed her impetuous movement forward. He moved in front of her, leading the way forward towards the gaping black hole down which some stone steps led into the souterrain. The trap door had indeed been opened and secured so that it would not fall back, as Brother Rogallach said. Eadulf hesitated a moment and then, holding the candle up and slightly in front of him, he moved carefully down the steps.

A figure was sitting at the far end of the stone-lined vault, resting with its back against one of the wooden pillars that reinforced the roof, legs stretched out in front of it. The eyes were wide open, staring at him as he crouched in the low underground room. The lips were drawn back in a merciless smile.

'*Deus misereatur!*' exclaimed Eadulf, starting back.

He had no trouble recognising the malignant features of the crone who had identified herself as Badb, the spirit of death and battles. What he did not realise for several moments, as he felt that his blood had turned to ice, was the fact that she was dead. A long-bladed dagger had entered the centre of the old woman's frail chest, pinning her to the wooden post against which she was leaning.

CHAPTER FOURTEEN

Brother Rogallach had been taken to have his wound dressed by the old physician, Iceadh, and Abbot Colmán had been summoned. The abbot had confirmed their identification of the old woman.

'Poor Mer,' he sighed. 'I told you, Mer the Demented One was well-known as a scavenger around the kitchens of the houses of Tara, yet I have never heard of her deliberately breaking into pantries to steal food. She was mad, but she was harmless. Whoever did this terrible thing?'

'We do not know,' replied Fidelma. 'I have yet to question Brother Rogallach in depth. However, it would appear that he must have entered the pantry a moment after it happened. The murderer was still in the souterrain and when Rogallach was about to enter, he was knocked unconscious.'

Abbot Colmán looked sad. 'And it was the murderer who knocked him unconscious? Did he see him? Can he identify him?'

'Unfortunately, he did not. Whoever did it came up behind him.'

'Well, at least there is no need for you to question him further.'

Fidelma frowned, her query obvious on her features.

'Of one thing we may be sure,' Abbot Colmán said gravely. 'The old woman's death is unconnected with the assassination of the High King. So one of the other Brehons can undertake the investigation into her death and leave you clear to continue to pursue the matter of Sechnussach's assassination.'

'Can we be sure that there is no connection?' mused Eadulf. 'After all, the woman first appeared warning us that our presence here investigating the murder was unwelcome. It seems a coincidence that she should now be killed as well.'

'She was crazy,' the abbot assured him. 'Maybe she was stealing from the storehouse here and someone else, with the same intent, encountered her and panicked. There is obviously no other connection.'

'I suppose so,' Fidelma agreed. Eadulf thought she acquiesced perhaps a little too readily – but her expression discouraged him from saying anything. 'Anyway, we still have to question Brother Rogallach on the matters related to Sechnussach's assassination. That was why we had come to the kitchen in search of him.'

Abbot Colmán nodded. 'I had forgotten. Well, let me know when you want to speak to him. Meantime, I will take care of . . .' he waved his hand towards the pantry '. . . of this matter.'

They had been aware during this time that Torpach, the cook, was hovering nearby with an anxious expression, as if trying to judge the right time to interrupt their conversation. Abbot Colmán finally noticed him and turned with a frown.

'What is it, Torpach? Do you wish to say something?'

The cook nodded unhappily. 'Forgive me, Abbot . . . forgive me, lady . . .'

'Well, speak, man!' snapped Abbot Colmán, otherwise it would seem that Torpach would ask forgiveness of everyone.

'I could not help overhearing that Mer was killed with a knife. I wonder if I could see it?'

'See it?' The abbot was astonished. 'What for?'

Sister Fidelma smiled encouragement at the cook, who was obviously nervous about asking permission.

'Why do you want to see it, Torpach?'

'Well, lady, one of our kitchen knives is missing. To be truthful, it's a favourite knife of mine for cutting meat. I reported it to Brother Rogallach but it has not been found.'

'When did it go missing?'

'Some time ago. I discovered it was missing the day after the death of the High King.'

'At least we know which knife killed him. You saw it yourself,' the abbot said grimly. 'But you are welcome to look at the knife which killed Mer.'

He unwrapped it, for he had taken it as evidence.

'You'll see that it is a warrior's knife,' he went on. 'I doubt if you would use it in your kitchen.'

Torpach glanced at it and then nodded sadly.

'I am sorry to have bothered you,' he said. 'It was merely a thought as we have not found it. I was particularly fond of it.'

Fidelma looked sympathetic. 'I understand. A favourite tool is a favourite tool in any art or craft. Did you also see the knife that killed Sechnussach?'

'I did and it was not that one.'

'Then I hope you find your own one again.'

Abbot Colmán re-wrapped the knife and, with a nod to Fidelma, went back to the yard outside where Mer's body was being taken away.

After they left the kitchen, walking back towards the guesthouse, Fidelma was silent. Eadulf, conscious of her moods, said nothing. Then she halted abruptly and looked round, as if wondering where she was. One of the Fianna was passing by.

'Where will I find the physician?' she asked.

'Iceadh, is it?' asked the man.

'It is. Where is his apothecary?'

'You see the building with the blue-painted posts ahead of you?' The man pointed. 'Turn to your right and you will see a small building with a yellow sign, and there you will find the physician.'

Fidelma thanked him and began to hurry forward with Eadulf falling in step with her.

'Have you thought of something?' he asked.

'Not really. I want to question Brother Rogallach now.'

'I thought Abbot Colmán wanted to be informed?'

'It wastes too much time to go back and inform him. But I think that I need to put my questions while things are clear in my mind.'

The apothecary of Iceadh was easy to find.

The old physician himself opened to Fidelma's knock and let them into a room packed with shelves of jars and bottles and with drying herbs hanging from all the beams. Although it was daylight outside, it was as if they were entering a darkened cave. Several lamps were burning and their heated tallow smell, combined with the powerful odours of a myriad of plants, caused them to catch their breath. It reminded Fidelma of old Brother Conchobhar's apothecary at Cashel. In answer to her question, the old physician replied in his curious staccato manner.

'Brother Rogallach is resting a moment. Given him a restorative. Superficial wound. Cut will heal in a day or two. Cleaned it. Bandaged it.' He indicated a door into another chamber in the wooden building.

It was a small, simply furnished room with two wooden beds, a table and chairs. It was clearly where Iceadh treated his seriously ill patients. Brother Rogallach was sitting on the edge of one of the beds, holding his bandaged head in one hand while the other held an empty glass from which he had apparently been taking Iceadh's medication.

The physician went to him, took the glass and nodded in satisfaction.

'Good, good. You may return to your own chambers, Brother. Lie down a while. No work. Not until tomorrow. Might have a headache. No matter. Bad blow. You'll be all right.'

Fidelma glanced at the pale face of Rogallach.

'Can we speak with him a moment?' she asked.

The physician shrugged. 'If he wishes. I have things to clear up.' He went out and Fidelma pushed the door shut behind him before turning back to the patient.

'How are you feeling now, Brother Rogallach?'

'Better, lady. Has the person who attacked me been caught?'

'I am afraid not.'

'But Mer is dead?'

'Yes, I am afraid so. Did you know her?' Fidelma asked.

'Of course. Most people around Tara knew her.'

'Do you know why she would be in the food cellar?'

Brother Rogallach gave a guffaw, then winced and put a hand to his head.

'Mer would steal when she could not beg, and beg when she could not scavenge.'

'So you think she had broken in to steal food?'

'What other reason would there be?'

'That is what I am trying to discover. We also have to place someone else in the *seallad* – the person who killed her.'

Brother Rogallach looked indignant. 'I hope you don't mean—'

'What I mean is that I want to know who would be there and who would want to kill her?'

'If anyone who worked in the *ircha* saw her, they would chase her out, certainly, but not without throwing her some bread or a piece of cheese, and she would go away cursing but content. They would not kill her nor attempt to kill me. It must have been some stranger.'

'A stranger who infiltrated the royal enclosure in daylight?' mused Fidelma.

'If Dubh Duin could infiltrate the High King's house at night, then anything is possible,' replied Rogallach defensively.

'Your point is a good one,' agreed Fidelma. Then she added thoughtfully: 'We either have Mer encountering a stranger in the *uaimh* or someone whom she knew and who did not want her to reveal that they were there. Since we are here, tell us about Bishop Luachan's visit.'

Brother Rogallach looked startled. 'I swore an oath to Sechnussach not to speak of it.'

'Sechnussach is dead,' Fidelma reminded him. 'Maintaining your oath might be aiding his killer.'

Brother Rogallach examined her for a moment. Doubt and indecision were plain in his features. Then he shrugged.

'Since you know that Bishop Luachan was here, then you must know all I know.'

'Let us hear what happened, in your own words.'

'It was the evening before the assassination. Sechnussach called me to him and told me that Irél, the captain of the Fianna, would arrive at the main gate around midnight. He would be escorting Bishop Luachan of Delbna Mór. I was to meet them at the gate and escort them to *Tech Cormaic*. Then I was to tell Irél to care for the horses, refresh himself and be ready to depart before dawn. I was to bring Luachan to Sechnussach in his bedchamber. I did so, and was told to wait outside and let no one in.'

'Did the High King himself instruct you?'

Brother Rogallach nodded. 'And not only that, but I was surprised when he closed his chamber door and locked it.'

'So that was unusual?'

'It was. Bishop Luachan was not a confidant of the High King. He never usually came to Tara. I would have known.'

'You had no idea what business brought Luachan here?'

'None at all.'

'Was Luachan carrying anything?'

Brother Rogallach looked surprised. 'You know that?'

'Tell me.'

'He was carrying a heavy saddlebag.'

'Did you see the contents?'

Brother Rogallach shook his head, then winced and added: 'Whatever it contained, he did not carry it away with him. The saddlebag was light on his arm when he left.'

'So whatever the object or gift was, it was left in the possession of Sechnussach. Therefore, it should be in his chamber. But his chamber is empty. Who cleared it?'

'I did,' Rogallach said. 'I cleared it with Brónach, but I can tell you there was nothing there that could account for the gift.'

'It could not have been hidden somewhere?'

'After Sechnussach had dismissed me, when Bishop Luachan had departed, it was approaching dawn. I had seen Irél and Bishop Luachan to the gate and then returned to my own chamber. I was just entering it when I heard the door of the High King's apartments swing open. My room is at the far end of the corridor and I have a view of his door from there. I saw Sechnussach emerge and was about to call out to enquire if he needed me. But I noticed that he was carrying something heavy in his hands; I could not see what it was because it was wrapped in cloth. Something made me press back into my room for the manner in which he emerged was surreptitious. When I looked out, he had crossed the landing and disappeared down the stairs.'

'Carrying the object?'

Brother Rogallach nodded.

'You did not follow to see if you were needed?'

'I concluded that he would have come to find me if he needed me. I believe that whatever it was Bishop Luachan had given him, he went to place it elsewhere than in his chamber.'

'Did he have a special place for storing things? Treasures and the like?' enquired Eadulf.

Brother Rogallach shook his head. 'Not specifically. However, I did hear the door that led out to the kitchen open and concluded that he had gone outside.'

Eadulf leaned forward excitedly. 'You suspect that he may have gone to the pantry ... perhaps to the *uaimh*?'

'It is not beyond the realm of possibility,' agreed Brother Rogallach.

'But it is speculation,' Fidelma pointed out, turning her remark to Eadulf.

'You've absolutely no idea what it was that Bishop Luachan brought to the High King that night?' pressed Eadulf, ignoring her.

Brother Rogallach sighed. 'Only that it was a circular object. The only other person who would have such knowledge is Bishop Luachan himself.'

Eadulf was disappointed.

'Well,' Fidelma said, 'you need not worry further about it, Brother Rogallach. At least you are looking better.'

'Thanks to Iceadh's noxious potion, my head is not aching as much,' admitted Rogallach. He raised a hand to massage his brow a little and gave a rueful smile. Then he frowned. 'What made you come to the pantry, lady? It was certainly a lucky thing for me that you and Brother Eadulf did so.'

'We were actually looking for you,' Fidelma told him.

'Why me?' asked the *bollscari*.

'We have been questioning everyone who was there on the night that Sechnussach was slain,' explained Eadulf.

Brother Rogallach nodded in understanding. 'Of course. I was not thinking. I knew that you had arrived and were questioning witnesses. There is not much I can add to what you must know already. Like the others that night, I was roused by a noise . . .'

'A scream?' suggested Eadulf.

'Perhaps. It is hard to say. You know what it is like when a noise arouses you from your sleep. You don't really know what it was and you spend a few moments trying to identify it. When I had all my senses, I heard others waking and there was movement in the corridor. I left my bed and went to see what the commotion was.'

'And was everyone in Sechnussach's chamber by the time you arrived?'

Brother Rogallach looked thoughtful. 'We crowded around the door together. Irél has his chamber on the lower floor and he arrived and pushed through us. I can't remember the order in which everyone arrived. Oh, I just remembered. As I passed by the rooms of the other servants – the senior servants are on the same floor with me – I saw Torpach's door opening and he was just coming out. He asked me what was happening. I replied that I did not know and then I realised that people were at the door of the High King's chambers. I noticed that Brónach's door was still closed. I paused to tap on it to alert her in case she had not been roused. I called to her and receiving no answer, opened the door. She was not in her chamber and so I moved on, thinking she was already awake and in attendance.'

'And was she?' asked Fidelma.

'I am not sure. I had the feeling that she was not there when I arrived and that she only turned up later.'

'And you took charge?'

'As I pushed my way into the chamber, I think Irél was just behind me. In matters of this sort he has precedence, being the commander of the High King's bodyguard. So I stood to one side while he took charge to ensure that the assassin was dead and that a search of the apartment was made to make certain there were no accomplices.'

At Fidelma's request, Brother Rogallach sketched what had happened but it was substantially the same story as they had been told before.

Outside the apothecary of Iceadh, Fidelma glanced reprovingly at Eadulf.

'One of the secrets of being a good investigator is never to reveal what you know or suspect, and to avoid showing your reactions to what others might tell you. Nor is it wise to suggest ideas to witnesses.'

Eadulf was apologetic. 'I was thinking about Sechnussach hiding the object and it is just that sometimes, after so long a time trying to demolish a stone wall, when it starts to crumble a little, you cannot help giving a shout of joy.'

Fidelma was still disapproving. 'I cannot agree with your specific analogy, Eadulf. But I do see your point.'

'I think that this object, this circular thing, is linked with the assassination. Sechnussach obviously hid it in the *uaimh* below the pantry. Whoever killed Mer was looking for it. I think that when Torpach said he saw Sechnussach in the kitchen at an early hour, it was because the King had sneaked down there to hide it.'

'It would seem a logical speculation, but it is a speculation nevertheless.'

'It is a speculation that needs to be followed by a search for information.'

Fidelma acquiesced. 'I mean to go directly to the *uaimh* and see if I can find any trace of this circular object. While I do so, I want you to find Caol and Gormán and discover how the search for Cuan is progressing. We should have heard something by now.'

'But . . .'

She sighed impatiently. 'It is no good both of us going on the same errand.'

Eadulf knew when to compromise. He was leaving the *Tech Cormaic* when he almost collided with someone. It was the young girl, Báine.

'You seem to be in a hurry, Brother Eadulf,' she observed in admonition as she recovered her balance.

'I am sorry.' Seeing that the girl was unhurt, he asked: 'Since I have bumped into you, so to speak, could I ask a question?'

Báine waited with an expectant expression.

'What is your opinion of Brónach? I was wondering if she is well-liked.'

Báine laughed. 'Brónach? I think you have been talking to Cnucha. It's not that she is *dis*likeable – she has high standards, that is all, and her temper can be sharp. Don't get me wrong. It is hard to find oneself ordered about all day. Cnucha does not like her, that's for sure.'

'And you?'

'You do not enter service in a great house and expect to be treated as the wife of a lord. Anyway, I shall soon be leaving here . . .'

Eadulf was surprised and said so. 'I thought you had been here some years?'

'That I have. But it is time for me to leave. This period in my life seems to have ended with the death of the High King. I do not think I could serve another.'

'Where will you go?'

'Home.'

'Which is where?'

'You would not know it.'

'Try me.'

'A little place under the shelter of a mountain to the north-west. The mountain is called Sliabh na Caillaigh.'

'The Hag's Mountain?' asked Eadulf.

The girl smiled and nodded.

'It sounds a forbidding place.'

'A place of wisdom much favoured by the ancients,' replied Báine solemnly. 'There are sacred buildings set up by the ancients that still stand on the top of the hill. It is a beautiful place. A holy place.'

'So when will you leave?'

'None of us can leave until after the investigation that you are conducting. The Great Assembly has to meet and hear the conclusion of that investigation before anyone can depart.'

'Won't you have any regrets at leaving Tara? In leaving your friends – say Cnucha, for example? She seems a pleasant girl to have as a friend.'

Again the girl smiled. 'Cnucha? Everyone thinks she is such a timid *luchóc.*'

'A what?' Eadulf had not heard the expression before.

'A little mouse. She is a strange one. Be advised, her meekness is superficial. I once made a joke at her expense and she threw a jug of water at me. I swear, she could have killed me. No, she is not my choice of friend.'

'Oh. But you must have made some friends here?'

Báine shook her head.

'Not with Brónach?' teased Eadulf, making it into a joke but hoping to guide the girl back to information about the voluptuous senior maid.

'Certainly not. She prefers friends of the male variety anyway.'

'Indeed?' Eadulf arched an eyebrow. 'Oh yes, I heard that she had ended some kind of an affair recently.'

Báine stared at him for a moment. 'I do not know where you got *that* from,' she began, and then said suddenly. 'Ah, from Cnucha?'

'Is it not true, then?'

'Perhaps. You can see for yourself, Brónach is very attractive still and you can tell by the speculative gaze in her eyes when she meets men that she is not averse to *amours*. You must have noticed it yourself, Brother Eadulf. You are a handsome, red-blooded male.'

Eadulf actually found himself blushing but the young girl's remarks were not displeasing to his ego.

'Any idea who she was having an affair with?' he asked.

Báine shrugged. 'If it is gossip that you want, Cnucha did tell me that she thought it was someone with access to the royal enclosure.'

'Why did she say that?'

'I suppose because Brónach never leaves here, to our knowledge. Anyway, you don't need me gossiping about Brónach, surely?'

'You were saying that you are going to leave here. Won't you regret anything? Don't you get on well with Muirgel, for example?'

He asked the question slyly and, for a moment, Eadulf thought he detected a spark of fire in the girl's eyes and then it vanished quickly.

'What gave you that impression?'

'I thought you were often asked to attend her?'

'That is my task here. I am a servant. Muirgel is not the best of people to serve. You might have noticed that if you were ever in her company.'

Eadulf chuckled. 'It is the one thing I have noticed, Báine. So you will not mind leaving her service?'

For a moment, a longing look came over the features of the girl.

'There are many things I regret, Brother Eadulf. But that will not be one of them. I long for the open countryside where one is not stuck behind forbidden walls with warriors patrolling up and down. I long for the hill-tops where one can touch the stars and be in tune with nature. There will be no regrets when I pass through the gates of Tara and go on my way to the north-west to rejoin my people and comrades.'

'Feeling like that, I wonder you ever came to Tara to take service at all?' mused Eadulf.

The girl opened her mouth, closed it again and then smiled.

'We often do things we think are for good reasons at the time we do them. Do not the ancients say that it is at the end of the year that a fisherman can tell his profits?'

'*Tempus omnia revelat*,' intoned Eadulf unctuously, supplying a Latin equivalent.

'Just so,' Báine agreed with bowed head. Then she straightened and smiled. 'And time will reveal that I am dilatory in my work unless I return to the guesthouse to prepare the meals for you and the lady Fidelma.'

She turned and walked away, leaving Eadulf gazing thoughtfully after her.

'Brother Eadulf!'

He turned at the call and saw Gormán striding towards him.

'Gormán! I was just about to look for you or Caol. Is there any news of Cuan yet?'

The young warrior shook his head immediately. 'No word as yet. Personally, I think he has gone from the royal enclosure. There is nowhere left that he can hide, if hide he wants to. Where is the lady Fidelma?'

'Gone to search the souterrain beneath the pantry.'

'Alone?' Gormán asked disapprovingly. 'Is it wise, in view of what has just happened? We heard about it from Abbot Colmán.'

Eadulf did not take offence at the implied censure.

'Can you tell a fish to walk on land?' he replied moodily. 'She sent me to look for you or Caol and discover the news about Cuan.'

'Perhaps we should go and find her, now you have accomplished your mission, Brother.'

Together they turned their footsteps to the *Tech Cormaic* and walked around it to the kitchen area at the back.

Fidelma was just emerging from the pantry building and seeing Eadulf and Gormán, asked immediately: 'Any sign of Cuan?'

'None, lady,' replied Gormán.

'And your search?' asked Eadulf.

'Nothing,' she admitted. 'If the object that Sechnussach had was ever there, then whoever attacked Rogallach and killed Mer took it.'

At that moment, Irél came striding through the kitchen, obviously in search of them. He raised his hand in greeting.

'Bad news. I am afraid our search for Cuan has proved useless. But just now I spoke to one of our sentinels at the main gates and he reported seeing Cuan leave Tara.'

'When was that?' demanded Fidelma.

'Not long after Rogallach was discovered. He was seen riding westward. He will be way beyond the west bank of the Bóinn by now.'

Eadulf looked annoyed. 'So he has fled. He probably recovered the object. Where is he taking it – and what is it? And does it indeed point to the reason why Sechnussach was assassinated?'

Irél was looking bewildered. 'I am not following any of this.'

'No need for you to be concerned,' replied Fidelma quickly, with a warning glance at Eadulf. 'My companions and I will be leaving Tara for a few days.' She glanced at the sky. Darkness came early in winter and it was too late to set off now. 'We will have to start at first light tomorrow. Gormán, go and find Caol and tell him of my intention.'

'Do you intend to chase Cuan?' Irél asked. 'If so, I could send a *cóicat*, a company of fifty warriors after him, and bring him back without you having to stir from here.'

'Cuan is one thing that draws me away. There are other things that I must do,' she assured him.

'But if you are going after him, you do not know the country beyond the great river.'

'Are there no roads? No stars in the sky to tell directions?' She dismissed his protests. 'Do not concern yourself for us, Irél.' Sending him away, she turned back into the *Tech Cormaic*.

Brónach was in the hall as they entered.

'Is Brehon Barrán still here?' Fidelma asked her.

'No, lady. I think he left just after you spoke to him,' the housekeeper said. 'He was going to his homestead outside of Tara.'

'And Abbot Colmán?'

'He is in the library room with the *tánaiste*, Cenn Faelad, lady.'

'Then we will announce ourselves,' Fidelma said firmly, moving off to the room with Eadulf following.

Cenn Faelad was peering over some papers with Abbot Colmán as Fidelma and Eadulf entered after a cursory knock.

'Ah, we were just examining the protocols for the hearing before the Great Assembly,' Cenn Faelad said, glancing up. Then, seeing her expression, he asked: 'Have you some news for me?'

Fidelma's voice was flat: 'Not the news that you are wanting, I am afraid.'

Abbot Colmán had also straightened up from the papers that he had been showing to the *tánaiste*.

'We cannot delay the report to the Great Assembly indefinitely, Fidelma. They will want something soon.'

'Then they will get it.'

'But we should already be sending couriers to announce a date when the Great Assembly can convene to hear your findings.'

To Eadulf's surprise Fidelma did not argue but said: 'Tell the couriers to announce that the Great Assembly should be able to meet in about a week's time. That will give them time to alert all in the five kingdoms who will send delegations to hear the result.'

Even Cenn Faelad looked astonished. 'You will be able to give a full report in a week's time?' he asked.

'I would not have suggested it if I did not think I could do so,' replied Fidelma waspishly. 'But I have come to say that, for the time being, we must conduct our enquiries elsewhere for a while.'

'Elsewhere?'

'We plan to travel west to Delbna Mór and then on to the Cinél Cairpre to see what we can learn about the character of Dubh Duin.'

Cenn Faelad frowned. 'The journey to see Ardgal of the Cinél Cairpre ... that I can understand. But why Delbna Mór? There is nothing there but a few farmsteads and a religious community run by Bishop Luachan.'

'It is Bishop Luachan I wish to see.'

Cenn Faelad shook his head to express his bewilderment. 'How long do you intend to be away from Tara?'

'No more than a few days.'

'And you can tell me nothing as to how things are progressing?'

'I can only say that they are progressing in spite of the inability of some to volunteer information. Getting at the facts has been like drawing teeth, and that applies to some I would not have expected to be reticent.'

'Are you referring to Brehon Barrán?' smiled the young King confidently.

Fidelma raised an eyebrow in surprise. 'What makes you say that?'

'Barrán is a good man, a fine man and wise counsel. That is why I am nominating him as my *tánaiste*. But like all professional men he is jealous of his abilities and reputation. That was why he may be reticent in responding to your questions. He told me that he had neglected to keep you fully informed.'

'He told you?'

'Of course. He is an honest man. He warned me that you might be criticising him because of his choice to pursue a diplomatic frugality of information.'

'Is that how he sees it?'

'You heard him say that it was the Great Assembly that decided we should send for a Brehon or *dálaigh* who was unconnected with our Uí Néill family? As Chief Brehon, he felt the investigation of the High King's death should have been his. In honesty, I think he resented your coming to take charge of it.'

'That is a natural enough response, I suppose,' replied Fidelma, unperturbed.

'Indeed,' Abbot Colmán joined in. 'But I understand that you have both reached an understanding now.'

'I hope we have.'

'Irél has told me of the flight of Cuan, a member of the Fianna,' said Cenn Faelad. 'I advised him to report that matter to you. I hope it is not because of him that you leave? Irél could easily send warriors to overtake him and bring him back, no matter where he is hiding.'

'There are other things that must claim my attention.'

'So you are not concerned with Cuan?'

'I am very much concerned with Cuan. He was part of the conspiracy and he deliberately acted as a decoy, getting Lugna to desert his post that night. Furthermore, he took your key to a smith and had it copied.'

'So it was Cuan?' Cenn Faelad started in surprise. 'That is a serious charge.'

'Which is obviously why he fled,' confirmed Fidelma.

'Yet you stop Irél from the pursuit. Why?'

'As I have said, I have other matters to attend to. Cuan is heading west.

If my suspicions are correct, I think that we may well encounter him before too long.'

Cenn Faelad gave her a hard look. 'Do you know something that you are not telling me?'

She shook her head. 'If I knew anything of pertinence, I would tell you. But it is no use to theorise at this stage.'

'Who are you taking on your trip?'

'Eadulf, of course, and Caol and Gormán, the warriors who accompanied me from Cashel.'

'Only two warriors? Come, I can give you a *cóicat*, a company of fifty warriors, or a *céit*, a hundred warriors, to escort you.'

Fidelma, smiling, declined. 'It will not be necessary.'

'Then take Irél, at least, for he has the authority of the Fianna behind him.'

She shook her head decisively. 'As we started out, so we'll go on, Cenn Faelad. It is better. But an authority from you might be welcome. Will you provide me with a wand of office on your behalf, in order that I can act accordingly when we get to the territory of the Cinél Cairpre?'

'Willingly.' Cenn Faelad gestured to Abbot Colmán. The latter moved to a locked cupboard that he opened with a key, and withdrew a wooden box. The box was locked also and another key opened it. From it he took a small wand of white rowan wood on which was fixed, at one end, a small upraised golden hand – the symbol of the Uí Néill. He handed it to Cenn Faelad solemnly.

The *tánaiste* held it out to her.

'By this wand you derive authority from the High Kings of Tara and speak with my voice,' he intoned the ancient formula.

Fidelma took the symbol and bowed her head slightly, remembering that the last time she had received such an emblem was from her brother when she had gone to Gleann Geis – the valley of the shadow.* It seemed so long ago.

'I will not dishonour it,' she said quietly.

'And may it not dishonour you,' Cenn Faelad replied. Then, more brightly: 'When do you set out?'

'At first light in the morning. We might be able to reach Delbna Mór by evening tomorrow.'

Valley of the Shadow (1998)

'Have you good horses? If there is anything I can provide, you need only ask.'

'We have everything we want.'

'Then, success to the journey and may we see you back safely as soon as possible.'

'Tonight we shall have a special feasting,' Abbot Colmán added, 'to wish you well on the journey.'

CHAPTER FIFTEEN

The territory of Delbna Mór lay mainly along the east bank of the dark waters of the River Daoil, which fed through a tiny loch that was named Diseart after the hermitage that had been built there. The ecclesiastical centre was located in picturesque wooded territory. Apart from the wooden church among a group of similarly constructed buildings, there was little else to distinguish it from the various settlements that were scattered throughout the hilly countryside.

Fidelma and Eadulf, with Caol and Gormán behind them, rode up the track towards what appeared to be the main building beside the wooden church. As they did so, they became aware of groups of religious emerging from the buildings in twos and threes.

Caol coughed discreatly to attract Fidelma's attention.

'Don't worry,' she called quietly to him. 'I have noticed.'

Eadulf then realised that every one of the brethren was carrying a weapon of some description and their expressions were certainly not welcoming.

'They don't seem very friendly,' he muttered.

'Perhaps they are just very frightened,' replied Fidelma as they came to a halt at the main building.

A short, stocky man, red of face and breathless, came forward and stared at them. He was middle-aged and was not armed. However, he was quickly joined by a young man who took a position by his side and his hand nervously fingered a sword.

'What is your business here?' the stocky man demanded harshly. There was neither customary greeting nor invitation to dismount.

Fidelma regarded him in silence for a moment and remained seated on her horse. Then she glanced at his companion with the sword before returning her gaze to the speaker.

'*Salve*,' she greeted him in the Roman fashion, making the words of the new Christian greeting in Latin seem ironic. 'Peace on you, brother, and upon this community.'

The man frowned uncertainly. 'And to you – peace,' he muttered, as if irritated at being reminded of his manners. 'What do you seek here?'

Fidelma sighed deeply before addressing him. 'I assumed that we had come to a Christian community. What else could we be seeking but the customary hospitality?' she began.

'But you are not,' he argued. 'Although two of you are dressed as in the manner of religious, your companions are warriors. So I doubt if you are just wanderers preaching the Faith and seeking Christian hospitality and alms.'

He was clearly hostile and the rest of the brethren were regarding them in a sullen and watchful manner. The young man at the side of the speaker held his sword as if waiting for the word to leap forward to attack. Eadulf was aware that the other members of the religious, each grasping staves and other objects that could be used as weapons, were beginning to form a semi-circle at their backs, although not yet closing in. He hoped Fidelma would do nothing precipitous.

'You have sharp eyes. We have come from Tara seeking Bishop Luachan,' she replied, remaining calm.

'Luachan is not here,' was the uncompromising response.

'Then tell us where he is and we will bother you no further,' Fidelma said.

'All I can tell you is that he is not here,' replied the other doggedly.

'That is not helpful,' she observed quietly.

'I cannot be responsible for the effect of the information that I give you,' snapped the rotund man. 'I can only give you the information.'

Caol could not restrain himself.

'Do you know to whom you speak?' he roared. 'This is Fidelma of Cashel, the *dálaigh* requested by the Great Assembly of the five kingdoms to investigate the assassination of Sechnussach. Shame on you and on your manners!'

The rotund man's eyes narrowed a little and an expression of uncertainty crossed his face.

'Of Cashel? Are you the sister to King Colgú? Fidelma the *dálaigh*?'

'This is she,' replied Caol belligerently before Fidelma could answer. 'Therefore, I suggest—'

Fidelma held up a hand to still his outburst, then reached into her saddlebag and took out the wand of office, which Cenn Faelad had given her.

'Do you recognise this?'

The man's eyes goggled. 'I do,' he said.

'Know then that this is my authority. We come here meaning you no harm. There is no need for your men to finger their weapons so anxiously. We wish to speak with Bishop Luachan, that is all.'

The man held her gaze for a while and then glanced at Eadulf and then at Caol and Gormán. He turned to his companion and nodded a dismissal. The younger man reluctantly lowered his sword and waved to the others to disperse.

'Please,' the stocky man said, his voice moderating from belligerency to apology, indicating that they should dismount, 'forgive this poor welcome but we live in fractious times. Indeed, we live in fear of our lives. But, let me greet you properly. I am Brother Céin and I am steward to Bishop Luachan and, in his absence, am in charge of our poor community.'

Fidelma introduced her companions as they dismounted.

Brother Céin greeted each before continuing: 'Have you ridden directly from Tara? Let me take you into the hostel and offer you refreshment.'

Fidelma indicated her assent and fell in step with him, while the others followed; the young man with the sword announced that he would see to their horses and have them rubbed down, watered and fed.

'So, is it true that Luachan is not here?' she asked. 'And why are you and your brothers in fear of your lives?'

Brother Céin shrugged. 'It is true the bishop is not here,' he confirmed, 'and the why and wherefore are long in the telling. Come in and take refreshment first.'

The travellers were seated, drinks were brought and a meal served, as it was well past midday. It was only after they had been served that Fidelma returned to the subject.

'So, tell us what has happened to put you in such fear, Brother Céin,' she invited.

The steward's expression was sad.

'Three days ago, Bishop Luachan was summon to attend a farmer's wife who was said to be dying. The bishop had known the farmer and his wife for many years. Their farm is not far from here so he left on his mission of mercy. The man who brought this message presented himself as a passing traveller. When Bishop Luachan did not return by nightfall, the next morning, we sent one of the brethren to find out why he was delayed. Imagine his astonishment on encountering the farmer's wife in robust health and claiming never to have sent a message at all. A search was made but the bishop had vanished.'

'I see. There was no mistake? The bishop was not summoned elsewhere?'

'He was not. Ever since young Brother Diomasach was killed last week Bishop Luachan had been fearful, and that is why he persuaded us to view any strangers, particularly warriors, with suspicion. He advised that we find weapons and kept them to hand.'

'Who was Brother Diomasach?'

'He was the bishop's scribe who wrote a good hand and spoke several languages.'

'How was he killed?'

'He disappeared from the nearby fields one day and was found floating in the Daoil, the river yonder. It looked as though he had been beaten – tortured, even – before he had been killed. God grant him peace.'

'Did Bishop Luachan have any suspicion as to why Brother Diomasach was killed? Who did he fear, that he suggested that you be so wary?'

'There have been several raids on isolated members of the Faith.'

'*Dibergach?*' queried Eadulf, practising the new-found word he had learned.

Brother Céin shrugged. 'Brigands? Perhaps. But they say there is a vigorous movement arising in the west that seeks to bring back the old religion. We have heard that these particular *dibergach* take pleasure in raiding Christian churches and communities.'

Fidelma was thoughtful for a moment. 'So it was felt that Brother Diomasach was attacked because he was simply one of the Faith and had been found alone in the fields?'

Brother Céin looked uneasy.

'There is more?' pressed Fidelma, catching his expression.

'What brought you here in search of the bishop?' countered the steward instead.

'No secret to that. Bishop Luachan visited the High King and took him some sort of gift. That was the very night before the High King was assassinated. There is now no sign of the gift and no one claims to have seen it. I was curious. What was this important gift? Did it have any bearing on the assassination of the High King? As Delbna Mór lay on our route to the country of the Cinél Cairpre, whose former chieftain is known to have been the assassin, I thought I might discuss this mysterious gift with Bishop Luachan.'

Brother Céin's face grew longer and he sighed deeply.

'I do not pretend to know all the answers, lady. But I have some knowledge which may be of help.' He glanced at the sky through the window and nodded half to himself. 'There is daylight left. If you have refreshed yourselves sufficiently, I would show you something but it is a short walk from here.'

Fidelma looked at Eadulf for his reaction.

'Come,' urged Brother Céin. 'You can bring your warriors and their weapons with you.' He rose and took an oil lamp from a table. Eadulf and Fidelma exchanged a curious glance for, as the steward had said, it was still daylight outside. They followed as he left the refectory and led them through the wooden buildings. They turned in a south-easterly direction, not more than 400 metres along a thickly wooded pathway.

'Be watchful,' Céin exhorted Caol and Gormán as he halted at a point on the pathway and peered quickly around at the undergrowth. Then he moved along a single path through the undergrowth and halted in a small clearing. There, to their surprise, he started to lift back some loose branches, which revealed a dark opening into the ground. Fidelma and Eadulf saw at once that it was manmade and not a natural cave.

Brother Céin took the oil lamp and held it above the hole in the ground.

'The bishop found this several weeks ago by accident,' he said to Fidelma. 'Brother Diomasach and Bishop Luachan had spotted a strange cairn over there,' he pointed to a rise behind them. 'It was overgrown with creepers and almost invisible to the eye. In going to discover what it was, Bishop Luachan almost fell down into the entrance. It seemed that he only noticed the cairn because a stag had rubbed its antlers against it and torn away the growth that surrounded it. All these details I received from Bishop Luachan afterwards. Initially, only he and Brother Diomasach made and shared the discovery.'

'What is it, an *uaimh*?' muttered Eadulf, staring down the hole.

'One might think so, Brother Eadulf,' replied Céin. 'This one leads into a passage which runs along two levels and terminates in a beehive-shaped chamber. From this entrance you move north along it and you have to be careful as the floor of the passage drops to the second level.'

'Is it ancient?' asked Fidelma.

'It is difficult to estimate the true age. It was completely overgrown as well, according to the bishop. The roof of the first level of the passage consists of large flat lintels. There are similar large lintels on the second level of the passage. The floor is spread with clay that has been hardened over the centuries. The chamber at the end is constructed with dry stone walls with a corbel roof with caps of two flat lintels. It is about three metres in diameter. The interesting thing about the chamber is that there are no air vents, which would be necessary if used for food storage – an *uaimh*, as you say – or even for a place of refuge in extreme threatening times.'

Fidelma was thoughtful. 'I will take your word for all this. You have gone into interesting detail. But what does it signify? What are you telling us?'

'I know the details only because the ancient buildings and their construction fascinated Bishop Luachan. When he discovered this particular underground chamber he was especially thrilled, as there are no known dwellings here before our little community was built. It was because of the deserted nature of this place that we chose to establish our hermitage here. That means there was no memory of a community that would want such an adjunct as an *uaimh* built here. He argued that these were very ancient – both the cairn and the *uaimh*.'

'When did Bishop Luachan tell you about it?'

'Not until after we found the body of Brother Diomasach.'

Fidelma began to see why the stocky steward was showing them these remains.

'You mean that Bishop Luachan felt there was some connection between this discovery and Brother Diomasach's death?'

'He did. You see, it was in the chamber down there that Bishop Luachan and Brother Diomasach made another discovery.' He paused as if waiting expectantly for a question to be put but when no one spoke he went on: 'Have you ever heard of the *Roth Fáil*?'

Fidelma started abruptly and then quickly controlled herself. The reaction was not lost on Eadulf.

'There are many legends about it,' she said. 'Why do you ask?'

Her mind was already thinking of the circular object that Bishop

Luachan gave to Sechnussach. She tried not to race ahead of what the man was telling her.

Brother Céin seemed pleased by her initial reaction.

'Bishop Luachan found something circular in the chamber. He brought it in secret back to our little abbey. He examined it and then the very next morning he despatched Brother Diomasach with a message for the High King Sechnussach at Tara. When Brother Diomasach returned, he spent some time with Bishop Luachan but refused to tell any of the brethren why he had been sent to Tara or what had transpired there. Also, after he returned, within a day or so, an important warrior from Tara arrived here. Bishop Luachan told us that he would be gone only a few days, and rode off with him. It was observed that he carried this circular object wrapped in cloth in his saddlebag and allowed no one else to see it. When he returned, he was without the object.'

'So this find was obviously the gift that he gave to the High King,' Eadulf observed thoughtfully.

'Did he really offer no explanation at all about what he had discovered and why he had sent news of it to the High King?' asked Fidelma.

'Not at the time,' Brother Céin said. 'It was afterwards, after poor Brother Diomasach's death, that he took me into his confidence and told me that he had discovered in the chamber a circle of silver metal, intricately worked. It had the ancient symbol of the sun in the centre and was surrounded by twenty heads around the edge.'

'It was a relatively small disk by all accounts, and now you say it was made of silver?' Fidelma queried. 'The stories about the wheel of destiny – the *Roth Fáil*, if ever it existed – would not place it so small, and it would have to be a great wheel of gold. Is it not also referred to as the *Roth Gréine* – the great celestial wheel? So are you telling me that Bishop Luachan thought this small object was the *Roth Fáil*?'

'You leap to the wrong conclusion, Sister Fidelma,' Brother Céin reproached her. 'Bishop Luachan merely believed it was the key to the *Roth Fáil*, and without this key the *Roth Fáil* could not be deciphered. That was why he felt that he should give it to the High King.'

'If it were a key, where is the object it opens?' Eadulf wanted to know.

Brother Céin shrugged. 'That is the mystery – and a mystery that no Christian would seek the answer to, for we are taught that the *Roth Fáil* is an engine of destruction that will destroy the Christian world.' He paused.

'That is the belief, anyway,' he added firmly, as if embarrassed at expressing the idea.

'Well, let us deal with facts, not legends,' Eadulf said, practical as ever. 'Bishop Luachan was implying that Brother Diomasach was killed because of this find. But it had already been given to the High King . . .'

'Who has also been slain,' pointed out Brother Céin. 'And you tell me that the disk is now missing?'

Fidelma was thoughtful. 'As is Bishop Luachan,' she said. 'Did he tell you nothing else about this matter? Why would he believe that the disk had a connection with the legend?'

'All he told me was that an evil was loose in the world and that the disk was the key. It brought death in its wake. He had hoped that Sechnussach would order it to be melted down, for only he had the authority to do so. With the news of the death of Sechnussach, he said that we must constantly be on our guard. When we found poor Brother Diomasach slain, he said that our enemies were near and told me the story.'

'Did he identify those enemies?'

'No. He just said that they were people who wanted to destroy the Faith of Christ in this land.'

'He never mentioned names? Did he not speculate on their identity?'

'He did not say. But he felt they were close by. As I said, there are indications that many isolated communities have been attacked and these attacks are now increasing. He thought the attackers were growing in strength and that they were being helped by some of the clan chiefs.'

'Such as Dubh Duin of the Cinél Cairpre?' she queried.

'Dubh Duin was certainly mentioned. He seemed to cling to the old ways but Bishop Luachan felt that within his clan, he kept his views in check.'

Eadulf frowned. 'How would that be possible?'

'You know how things work among us, Brother Eadulf? The *derbhfine* chooses a chief from the bloodline but he must be worthy. He must promote the welfare of his people. He has to govern under the law and, should he not conform to the wishes and welfare of his people, should he become negligent or despotic, then he could easily be replaced. Only the most worthy can succeed and remain as chief.'

Eadulf knew the system but it was not what he meant.

'Do you mean that Dubh Duin held views about religion that were not support by the Cinél Cairpre? I have heard that they too clung to the old traditions.'

'I have not travelled in the country of the Cinél Cairpre for some years now,' Brother Céin said, 'but when I was there last, most of those I encountered were Christian, while only some of the older folk still adhered to the gods of Danú.'

'The Old Faith?' pressed Eadulf.

'The Old Faith,' confirmed the steward. 'It is often difficult for some to leave the old path for the new.'

Fidelma was silent. If chieftains like Dubh Duin or his successor Ardgal were involved in backing these raiding bands, and were connected with Sechnussach's assassination, then she was looking at what had already developed into a rebellion against the High King and perhaps the onset of a civil war. But it would be a civil war like no other, for its terms would be defined by which religion the people supported. It was a frightening thought.

'Yet with all his fears, Bishop Luachan went alone to answer the call of a sick farmer's wife,' Eadulf pointed out.

'Bishop Luachan is a kind man, a generous man and one who takes his calling as both priest and healer seriously,' replied Brother Céin.

Fidelma held out her hand for the oil lamp.

'You brought us here to examine this chamber. Having come thus far, I shall look at it.'

Brother Eadulf immediately shook his head.

'I shall go in – who knows what wild beasts may have found this entrance and decided it was a warm nest? Wolves and even bears, perhaps. This is the time for brown bears to hibernate.'

'We don't often see brown bears in this country now,' Fidelma told him. 'But there are certainly wolves about, though they hardly make their lairs in human habitations – even deserted ones.'

'Nevertheless, I'd prefer to go first,' insisted Eadulf.

Fidelma decided not to argue. 'Very well, you go first and I will follow.'

Eadulf moved down into the narrow passageway and began to crawl along, one hand holding the spluttering oil lamp before him. The floor was of sandy clay but it was quite dry and hard. The ceiling was low, the walls narrow – definitely not the place for anyone with claustrophobia. He remembered that Brother Céin had warned him that the passageway would drop to another level, and he thought this just in time, for he had been so busy looking up at the narrowing roof that he almost came to the drop before he noticed. He paused and called back a warning to Fidelma. He could hear her scrambling along behind him.

As he looked cautiously at the drop he suddenly noticed that a candle stub stood on a stone by it. Bishop Luachan had doubtless left it on his excursion into this peculiar *uaimh*. Eadulf lit it from his lamp so that Fidelma, following him, would be able to see the drop. Then he descended to the next level which was more easily negotiated than he had anticipated, since, albeit awkward, the drop was only a waist-high one. He turned along the new tunnel and found it sloping upwards slightly before emerging into the curious stone-walled chamber. As Brother Céin had said, it was a beehive shape, almost conical, and he was able to stand up in it quite easily. A moment later, Fidelma joined him.

The flickering light of the oil lamp caused a myriad of shadows to dance on the walls as they peered around. The walls were filled with strange carvings, lines of spiral patterns and odd symbols.

'This place is very ancient,' Fidelma observed, finding herself whispering.

'What would it be used for, if not as a storage place for some nearby dwelling?' asked Eadulf.

Fidelma had moved forward to a place where stones had been grouped to form a box-like area on the ground at one end. A large flat stone was discarded nearby and it took her only a moment to see that this was the lid. She had seen ancient graves formed much the same way, but this was too tiny to hold any human remains.

'I think that is where Bishop Luachan must have found the silver disk,' she said.

Holding the lamp high, Eadulf bent down to examine the receptacle.

'Are you saying that we are in some ancient pagan temple?' he asked, a little apprehensively. Eadulf had been converted to the New Faith when he was a youth, but emotionally still felt the power of the old gods and goddesses of his people.

'I think it was a sacred place. Perhaps not a place for people to worship. Have you noticed that some of these walls have carvings on them?'

Eadulf had certainly noticed the strange motifs that spread around the interior. The shadows were not simply cast by the lamp but came from deep grooves in the rocks, depicting curious faces and symbols.

'Do they mean anything?' he asked, suppressing a shudder.

'Probably to someone who can read the signs of the old religion.' Fidelma pointed to the flat stone lid. 'Do you see the carving on the top of this stone? I know what that represents: it is the sign of the old sun god, the symbol of knowledge and wisdom.'

Eadulf peered down. From a central point, it appeared as if three arms or legs emerged and each arm had a little tail which gave the symbol its momentum.

'Is this why Bishop Luachan felt that he had discovered the ancient wheel of fate which Brother Céin mentioned?'

'It is logical,' agreed Fidelma. 'I have seen this motif many times on old coins, and even on one of the ancient crowns of the High Kings.'

At that moment, they heard Brother Céin's voice echoing faintly from above, apparently anxious that they were so long in the chamber.

Fidelma gave a last look round. 'Well, we can learn no more here,' she said.

'Was there anything *to* learn?' Eadulf asked with a sigh.

Fidelma looked at him reprovingly. 'There is always something to learn, and everything is interrelated in life, Eadulf, you must know that. An investigation is like unpicking a tapestry, tracing a strand here, and one there; sometimes they are not joined and you have to come back to the start; sometimes they are joined and you can move onwards.'

'Do you really think there is some connection here?' he asked doubtfully. 'That this is where the motivation for Sechnussach's assassination originated?'

'Too early to say. We only know that Bishop Luachan made a find here. He took it to Sechnussach. The latter was assassinated and the item is now missing. Then Brother Diomasach, who helped make the find, was killed and now Bishop Luachan himself is missing.'

'So . . . ?'

'So before any conclusions can be drawn, we need to find more information.'

'But the only person who can give us that information is Bishop Luachan himself,' Eadulf pointed out.

Brother Céin was calling again.

'Let us hope that he is still living and that we may find him, then,' Fidelma replied briskly, before turning to the passageway and beginning to move back out of the chamber.

Eadulf glanced around a final time. The grotesque carvings seemed to unite, their distorted features staring down at him accusingly from his own pre-Christian past.

He shuddered and quickly followed Fidelma.

It was good to be back out in the light.

Brother Céin was waiting anxiously for them. 'Well?' he asked. 'Does the place tell you anything? Did it help at all?'

Fidelma grimaced. 'It only supports your story about Bishop Luachan and his discovery, but has revealed little else.'

The steward sighed a little forlornly. 'I was hoping that there would be something else to learn down there.'

'When the bishop disappeared, where was this farmstead that he was supposed to have been called to?'

'Not far north of here. It is a place called the meadows of Nionn, Cluain Nionn. You will pass through there if you are determined to continue your journey northward.'

'I see no reason not to. We will go on.'

Brother Céin glanced at the darkening sky and the lengthening shadows.

'Not tonight anyway. You may recommence your journey in the morning. Let us offer you the hospitality of our community.'

'Which we will accept with pleasure,' replied Fidelma.

With Brother Céin leading the way, they walked back to the wooden buildings that constituted the settlement.

Before the evening meal, the *prainn*, which was the principal meal of the day, Fidelma allowed herself be conducted by the steward to the community's *tech screpta* or library. It contained some forty books, all hung in rows in their leather book satchels. Brother Céin was enormously proud of the library.

'Bishop Luachan was intent on building up our little community as a repository of knowledge,' he announced. 'Alas, these are the first things that will be destroyed, should the *dibergach* attack us and we are not able to hold them off. We have one of the great collections of books in the five kingdoms.'

Fidelma, who had seen many greater libraries in her travels, did not disagree with him. Any centre where books were gathered was a special place in her eyes.

'It is well worth defending, Brother Céin,' she agreed. Then a memory stirred. 'I was told this place had a connection with my own kingdom. Do you know the story?'

Brother Céin nodded. 'But that was in ancient times. It is one of those legends handed down by the local people.'

'Tell me.'

'It is said that long ago, so long that the facts have become myths, there was a chieftain in the north of your brother's kingdom of Muman. He was called Lugaid mac Táil. He had five sons and a daughter. The daughter was married to an ambitious warrior called Trad mac Tassaig. The daughter was also ambitious for her husband and, moreover, she was a great Druidess, adept in the magic arts.

'One day she claimed that she had had a vision that unless her father, Lugaid, handed over his chieftainship and land to her husband, then a flock of demons would come and destroy it and all the family. In fear, Lugaid did as she asked and fled north with his five sons.

'They came to Loch Lugborta and here Lugaid lit a magic fire to seek guidance. The fire spread in five directions and in those directions his five sons went and set up their homes. Lugaid stayed in the place where he had kindled the fire and thus the lake was named after him – Loch Lugborta. But he decided that he should take the name Delbaeth, from the ancient form *dolb-aed* – enchanted fire. Today, after many centuries, the name has been distorted and it is now called Delbna Mór.'

'I have never heard this story before,' Fidelma said quietly.

'No reason why you should. It is simply a local story of how the name of the territory came into being.'

She paused awhile examining and praising the books, and then a bell began to sound for the evening meal. As they walked back towards the *praintech*, or dining hall, Brother Céin asked anxiously: 'Do you still intend to go north-west tomorrow?'

'I do.'

'To the lands of the Cinél Cairpre?'

'Yes.'

'That may be where our enemies are,' Brother Céin said.

'Irél and his Fianna already went there. He saw the new chief, Ardgal, and obtained hostages for the clan's good behaviour after Sechnussach's assassination. If they meant harm, they would not have succumbed to Irél's authority.'

'Even so, it would be remiss of me if I did not counsel you against this journey. If Bishop Luachan were here, he would warn you of the dangers that beset this countryside.'

Fidelma smiled briefly. 'I think you have already made the dangers clear.'

'Well, should you return to Tara ... *when* you return to Tara,' he corrected hastily, 'and speak to the new High King, tell him of our situation and warn him about the growing power of the *dibergach*. There is only one other community between here and the land of the Cinél Cairpre and that is the abbey at Baile Fobhair, which you will also pass on your journey. They and we are the only communities of religious in the area who have not been attacked so far, thanks be to God. But we live in daily expectation of it.'

'Why have you not already sent to the Fianna at Tara for warriors to protect you?'

Brother Céin shrugged. 'We did not begin to realise the seriousness of the situation until poor Bishop Luachan was taken from us. If they can do that, there is nothing that will stop them perpetrating more serious crimes.'

'Where is this abbey of which you speak?'

'Baile Fobhair?'

She nodded.

'You will ride along the north side of a great loch, Loch Léibhinn. That is where the abbey is situated. But let me warn you again . . .'

She paused, turned and looked into his anxious face.

'Don't worry, Brother Céin,' she interrupted. 'I fully intend to return in safety to Tara and this mystery shall be cleared up. That is a promise.'

CHAPTER SIXTEEN

It was approaching noon on the next day when Fidelma decided to call a halt in order to rest and water the horses. They had ridden north-west, passing the farmstead identified as Cluain Nionn. Here they had paused briefly while Fidelma questioned the farmer and his wife about the disappearance of Bishop Luachan. But, as Brother Céin had foretold, the couple knew nothing at all. So they had journeyed on, reaching the large lake that the rotund steward of Delbna Mór had told Fidelma was called Loch Léibhinn. For the most part, the countryside seemed deserted. They rode along its northern shore without seeing any sign of the abbey of Baile Fobhair of which she had been told. After a while, north of the lake, they reached more hilly country. Fidelma began to believe that they had missed the abbey and so suggested they rest and attend to their horses' needs. To save time she decided not to light a fire to prepare a meal, but for them to have some fruit and the bread that the religious of Delbna Mór had given them that morning. As events turned out, it was a wise decision.

They had stopped by a small pool that was fed from a stream that gushed from the hills. It was surrounded by three great stone slabs and shaded by an ash tree. A little distance from the pool were the burned-out ruins of a watermill. The fire had obviously occurred recently, for the stench of the burned timbers still hung in the air. The countryside was heavily wooded, with many brooks and streams. There were plenty of evergreens, interspersed with wych elm, whitebeam and even strawberry trees, and in spite of it being winter the forest looked impenetrable. Both the thick woods and the rising ground were also, in retrospect, a matter of good fortune for them.

They had barely settled to eat when the sound of someone coughing came from the direction of the ruined mill. It sounded as though the person was desperately trying to stifle the cough and thereby only making the sound worse. At once Caol and Gormán were on their feet with drawn swords.

'Who's there?' snapped Caol, moving cautiously towards the blackened ruins.

There was no answer.

With a quick gesture to Gormán to indicate some prearranged tactic, Caol advanced, sword ready to strike, while Gormán made a flanking movement to cover him.

Then, from the blackened timbers, a sooty spectre rose. It was a man in torn and dirty religious robes, his face and hair covered in soot. He raised a hand as if to fend off Caol's sword.

'Do not kill me! Let me go in peace! I have done you no hurt.'

The voice was a despairing wail. Caol regarded the vision in some astonishment.

'Come forward and identify yourself,' he instructed.

The dishevelled man took a step or two and then he caught sight of Fidelma and Eadulf. A look of hope transformed his features.

'Are you of the Faith?' he demanded eagerly. 'Do you acknowledge the Christ?'

'Of course,' Eadulf said irritably. 'Who are you?'

'I am Brother Manchán. I am . . . I was . . . one of the community here.' He gestured beyond the trees.

'Where is here, Brother Manchán?' asked Fidelma gently. 'We are strangers in this land.'

'Just beyond is the abbey of Baile Fobhair, the homestead of the spring. It was founded by the Blessed Feicín who, alas, died from the Yellow Plague a few years ago.'

'I have heard of that holy man,' Fidelma reflected after a pause for thought. 'I am sorry to hear that the plague took him.'

The dishevelled religious sighed deeply. 'Better to be taken by the Yellow Plague than witness what has happened to his little abbey. Burned and destroyed.'

'When did it happen?' Caol wanted to know. 'Who did it?'

'*Dibergach* – raiders. They came riding down with their godless battle standard a few days ago and began to slaughter the brethren. I managed to escape and hide in the forest until they had gone. I did not know what to do – whom to trust. Five of the brethren were slaughtered and I am the only survivor.'

'Delbna Mór is the next biggest abbey I know of. Why did you not go there?'

'Does Delbna Mór still stand?' queried the man, hopefully.

'It did when we left it this morning.'

'While I hid, I heard some of the raiders talking about it. I thought they were going to attack it.'

'Which way did these raiders go?'

Brother Manchán shook his head. 'I don't know where they went immediately afterwards. I only know they came back this morning.'

They stared at the man.

'They came back?' Eadulf asked. 'Where are they now?'

'They are resting just over the rise,' Brother Manchán replied. 'That's why I was hiding in the ruins of the mill.'

Eadulf looked at Fidelma. 'We'd better move and find cover somewhere.'

'In which direction did you say they were encamped?' Fidelma remained calm.

The man indicated with his hand.

Fidelma turned to Caol. 'Go to the top of the rise, carefully now, and see what the situation is.'

Caol nodded. When he returned, he had an agitated look on his face. He indicated over his shoulder to the woods.

'This man is right, lady. The ground rises steeply as you see, but suddenly drops into a small defile. There is another track that leads through it. I could see the ruins of what must have been the abbey at one end.'

'And these raiders?'

'Twenty riders. Warriors, heavily armed. They have an assortment of clothing and weapons. They looked as though they were making ready to depart. From what I saw, they had been watering their horses.'

Fidelma turned to the woebegone religieux. 'And these were definitely the same raiders who attacked your abbey earlier?' she asked.

The man nodded quickly.

'They were leading a couple of pack horses on which some bags were tied,' added Caol. 'Poking out of one of them was a golden crucifix, and I doubt that these are pious religious on their way to donate some goods to an abbey out of charity.'

'Twenty, you say?' mused Fidelma with a frown.

'Twenty it was, lady,' replied Caol.

Fidelma was silent for a moment more.

'We need to know which direction they take. Caol, will you go back to observe them?'

'Of course,' he replied immediately, adding with a smile, 'If I am discovered, I will contrive to blow my horn in warning to alert you. If you hear it, mount, ride hard and do not tarry.'

'If that is all you have to suggest, you had better try not to be discovered,' replied Fidelma grimly.

Caol grinned and slipped away.

'What do you have in mind?' Eadulf asked when he had gone.

'It depends which way they go. If towards Delbna Mór, then I think we should try to warn Brother Céin. Also, we should warn Irél and bring the Fianna to capture them. They are pressing close to Tara now and need to have their raiding curbed. Let's pack up and get ready to ride as soon as Caol gives us the word.'

In fact, it was not long at all before they heard movement through the undergrowth. Gormán sprang forward with drawn sword in a defensive position. Then came Caol's voice.

'It's me,' he called softly. 'They have mounted and headed off.'

'Which way?' demanded Fidelma.

'In the same direction as we are taking . . . towards the north-west.'

'Towards the country of the Cinél Cairpre?' Eadulf asked.

'It would be logical if they were men who held allegiance to Dubh Duin,' Caol suggested.

'In that case,' Fidelma made up her mind quickly, 'we must follow them and see if they are, indeed, of the Cinél Cairpre.'

'But I thought . . .' began Eadulf.

She turned to him. 'I do not like to split up but I fear that you must carry the news back. Take Brother Manchán behind you on your horse and leave him at Delbna Mór for Brother Céin to look after. Tell Brother Céin what we have found. Then ride straightway to Tara and tell Irél.'

'Why me?' Eadulf demanded a little petulantly at being asked to go back.

'Because, if these are *dibergach*, I will need Caol and Gormán with me. Can you remember the path back?'

'I remember,' asserted Eadulf, suppressing his irritation.

'I am counting on you, Eadulf. I need warriors with me so you are the logical choice to go back. Bring Irél and his warriors here and we will leave signs along the track to show you where we have gone.'

Hiding his disapproval of her plan but accepting the logic of it, Eadulf watched Fidelma and the others ride away with some anxiety. He wished that they had accepted Irél's initial offer to accompany them with his warriors, but it was pointless to lament the fact now. Hindsight was always a good philosopher. He turned to Brother Manchán.

'Well, Brother, we must be away then. The sooner we set out, the sooner we can reach Delbna Mór and I can continue with my task.'

The religieux nodded unhappily.

Eadulf swung up onto his horse and, using one of the stone slabs as a mounting block, Brother Manchán clambered on the horse behind him. Eadulf turned the animal along the forest in the direction they had originally come. He disliked cantering because he was not an accomplished horseman but he felt it best to keep a quick pace. He held on firmly as the horse loped along the forest path. The soot-begrimed religious was clinging tightly around his waist behind him. Now and then he felt the beast begin to flex its powerful muscles as if changing the pace into a gallop but Eadulf tugged firmly on the reins to check it. He had already decided that it was going to be an exhausting journey.

Both Caol and Gormán were competent trackers and Caol decided to send Gormán on a little way ahead. There were two tasks: one was to follow the tracks and the other, to ensure that they would not be led into any ambush.

Waiting until he was out of sight, Caol and Fidelma then followed. The track they were following swung around the wooded hills and then they came to the blackened ruins of what must have been the little abbey that had been built a generation or so ago by the Blessed Feicín who had established many Christian communities in the country.

No one had yet been able to bury the bodies of the religious who had been slaughtered there, and now that the raiders had moved on, the black, scavenging crows had descended. Fidelma averted her eyes and mumbled a prayer for the repose of their souls.

Caol was more philosophical.

'The scavengers of battlefields,' he said quietly. 'The children of the Mórrígán.'

Fidelma did not reply. She knew that after great battles, these black crows and ravens were almost a blessing when it came to cleansing the corpses left to rot when survivors were too weak to bury them. But knowing it and seeing it were different things. She wished they had time to bury the corpses of these poor pious men and prevent them from being desecrated by the scavengers, for she knew that later, after the sun went down, wolves and other animals would be attracted to the leavings of the crows.

They rode on, increasing their pace. Eventually, they came in sight of Gormán who was leaning from his horse intent on examining the trail before him. It split in two. He turned, saw them and gave them a wave to show that he was continuing along the right path. Then he moved on at a quicker pace to put a little extra distance between them and himself.

'Is the plan to follow these people into the land of the Cinél Cairpre?' asked Caol after a while.

Fidelma nodded. 'If that is where they are heading.'

'I'd feel better if Irél and the Fianna had been with us, lady,' Caol confessed. 'After all, two swords against – we do not know how many – are not good odds.'

'Don't worry, Caol. I shall not do anything that is rash or precipitate us into an impossible situation. We will keep well back from these raiders. If they lead us to Ardgal, the new chieftain of the Cinél Cairpre now that Dubh Duin is dead, then we might draw conclusions without any confrontation.'

'I hope so, lady, I hope so,' rejoined Caol softly.

They rode on without incident for some time before the trees began to thin and they came to the shallow river, gushing over a stony bed. Gormán was waiting for them, leaning forward in his saddle in a resting position.

'What is the matter?' Fidelma demanded as they rode up.

Gormán gestured to the river.

'The riverbed is stony and the path on the far side is almost paved in pebbles and rocks. I have made a search and cannot find the tracks of the raiders' horses on the far side. I have ridden along the bank in both directions but have seen nothing.'

Caol eased his sword a little in its scabbard and glanced around. 'A good place for an ambush. Any sign that they have stopped?'

Gormán shook his head. 'If they were of the number you say and with pack animals, there would be some sign. If they even left a couple of men behind in ambush, there would be some unease among those animals' – he pointed to where a small herd of deer were grazing serenely on a hill a little distance from the river. A great antlered stag was standing apart, head raised proudly in the air, watching them.

'We will proceed onwards,' Fidelma decided. 'We may pick up their tracks later.'

Gormán nodded, turned his horse and rode off rapidly through the shallow waters to place himself ahead of them again.

As Eadulf rode along he was worried about Fidelma. What if the strange raiders realised that they were being followed and laid an ambush for her? He had every faith in Caol and Gormán as warriors but they were only two against so many. And Fidelma was heading right into the country of the Cinél Cairpre, whose former chieftain had killed the High King. The thought almost made him push the horse into a gallop himself but he knew he was not a good enough equestrian to sustain such a pace through the forest.

The path suddenly swung round a group of boulders that rose in the middle of the forest and before he knew it, he was in the middle of a band of armed riders. He heard Brother Manchán give a shriek of alarm before they closed in with drawn swords. His horse shied nervously and came to a halt of its own volition.

The question that sprang to Eadulf's lips died before he could utter it. There were about a score of riders and he could see a couple of pack horses. With a feeling of growing fear, he realised that the riders were the very same group that Fidelma had set off to follow. They must somehow have doubled back on their tracks and now he was their helpless captive.

Gormán came trotting back along the track with a frown on his face.

'I fear that we have lost them, lady,' he called to Fidelma as he approached. 'There are no tracks ahead.'

'They must have turned back at the river,' Caol sighed. 'They will have used the stony course to confuse their tracks.'

Fidelma was thoughtful. 'Did they do so because they were simply being cautious or because they knew that they were being followed?'

Gormán shook his head. 'I think they are old campaigners used to hiding their tracks anyway. It was a perfect spot to do so. As you recall, it was stony on the far side and we could not pick up their tracks again. I don't think they even crossed the river and came this way at all.'

'How far ahead have you checked?' Fidelma asked.

'This track goes through some soft ground and approaches a hill that overlooks a small wheat plain. Even if I had missed the tracks, when I climbed the hill and scanned the plain before me, there were no signs of riders.'

'Should we turn back?' asked Caol. 'Make another attempt to pick up their tracks?'

'They could have gone north or south at the river,' Fidelma pointed out. 'You said that you have checked a reasonable distance in both directions so it would take a long time before we picked up their tracks again. Our original intention was to see Ardgal in the land of the Cinél Cairpre. I think we should ride on and find him.'

The two warriors did not protest and the party set off again. Fidelma looked confident, but secretly she was now very worried. She hoped that Eadulf would reach Delbna Mór safely and warn Brother Céin. If the *dibergach* were as vicious as they had been told, it was dangerous to be an unarmed religious in these lands.

One of the riders who had surrounded Eadulf nudged his horse nearer. He was a black-bearded man with coarse ruddy features showing under a metal war bonnet which was decorated in a bizarre fashion with the stuffed head of a raven, its black wings spread out along either side. He held his sword loosely across the pommel of his saddle and wore no armour but a leather jerkin over his black and dirty clothing.

'Well, well, what have we here? A Christian who wears the mark of Rome's slavery! And carrying a poor wreck of another Christian who looks as though he has crawled out of an oven. Perhaps he has just been ejected from the Christian hellfire of which I have heard tell.'

His comrades laughed in appreciation of the humour.

Eadulf knew that the man had noted his tonsure, the *corona spina*, the tonsure of Peter, which was cut differently to that of John, adopted by the religious of the five kingdoms.

He made no answer but stared at the man defiantly. He felt Brother Manchán shaking with fear, still clinging behind him on the horse.

The man with the raven-feathered helmet, obviously the leader of the raiders, prodded him with the tip of his sword. It was sharp and Eadulf felt it draw blood through his sleeve. He winced but set his mouth firmly, determined not to show fear before these raiders.

'You are the first Christian I have met who has not squealed,' the man grinned patronisingly. 'Usually your kind use your tongues too freely. I wager your companion will sing without my prompting. Come, tell me who you are or will you die without a name?'

'Please, please,' cried Brother Manchán, sobbing in desperation. 'Please, my lord, have mercy on me. I'll tell you anything.'

Eadulf felt a little disgusted at his companion's obvious fear. Even though he himself felt an apprehension approaching dread, Eadulf knew that you should never show fear to your enemy for, by so doing, you are lost.

'If you need to know my name, know then that I am Eadulf of Seaxmund's Ham in the land of the South Folk.' Eadulf used an angry tone to disguise the fear he felt and hoped that his captors did not notice the tremor in his voice.

'A Saxon?' The man's bearded features broke into a black-toothed smile.

The question had an obvious answer and Eadulf made no reply.

'What brings you to the kingdom of Midhe, stranger? Come to spout your pernicious doctrines to twist our minds away from the true gods of Éireann?'

'I am husband to Fidelma of Cashel who is investigating the assassination of Sechnussach at Tara.'

This caused some surprised reaction among the warrior band.

'Fidelma of Cashel, the Eóghanacht?' the leader commented with a sudden frown. 'We had heard that the Great Assembly had sent for her. You are some way from Tara. What are you doing in this forest, Saxon? Where did you get that pitiful thing that clings to you? Where is the woman from Cashel?'

Eadulf's mind raced as to how best he should answer.

'We are going to the abbey at Delbna Mór.'

This raised another laugh.

'If you are coming from Tara, you must have ridden past it. At least you had the sense to turn back, for it lies in that direction.' The leader jerked his head over his shoulder.

'Thank you,' Eadulf said, thankful for the man's misunderstanding. 'I realised that we must have passed it and I was directed back in this direction by this wandering religious.' The lie came naturally to his lips and he resolved to utter an act of contrition later. 'We'll be on our way then.'

This caused a greater merriment among the band.

Their leader shook his head and turned to Brother Manchán.

'You are a strange religious to go wandering in soot-encrusted and torn robes. Is this to show some subservience to your God?'

Eadulf felt Brother Manchán still shaking in his terror. He feared that the man would tell the truth of their encounter and alert them to the route Fidelma and her companions had taken.

'Come,' snapped the leader of the raiders. 'Your name?'

'Bro . . . Brother Manchán of Fobhair, my lord. Please . . .'

'Fobhair? Ah, so you are one of the nits that escaped from its nest when we tried to cleanse it. How remiss of us not to have noticed you.'

Eadulf felt Brother Manchán start, felt his grip loosen and his body fall from the back of his horse. He turned round in horror as Brother Manchán's body hit the ground. He was already dead. The helmeted leader was leaning down and wiping his sword point on the clothes of the body. Then the black-bearded man glanced up and smiled crookedly at Eadulf.

'Now we must insist that you accompany us, Saxon. My *ceannard* will find your company very entertaining and I would not like to deprive her of it.'

'*Ceannard*? Your commander?'

'You do not ask questions, Saxon. Dismount so that my men may search you.'

'I protest,' began Eadulf, halfway between helpless rage and fear. 'You have murdered this man, a religious. You have killed him in cold blood.'

But two of the raiders had already dismounted and were pulling him from his horse. They searched him none too gently while another took his saddlebag. Having made sure he had neither weapons nor anything else of interest, one of them tied his hands in front of him, then a gag was suddenly inserted roughly into his mouth and, before he could do anything else, a blindfold shut the vision from his eyes. He found himself being hoisted back onto his horse. He clung desperately onto the edge of the saddle insofar as he was able. Someone must have taken the reins for the beast began to move and he could hear the other riders around him. He desperately strove to maintain his balance as the pace increased to a canter. He felt an icy, clawing sensation in his stomach as he considered the fact that these *dibergach* had killed a religious in cold blood, killed without any compunction. Eadulf knew that his life was now not worth anything.

CHAPTER SEVENTEEN

'There is a farmstead up ahead, lady,' Gormán called, having ridden back down the trail to rejoin Fidelma and Caol. 'It would be an ideal place to water and rest the horses and eat something ourselves.'

They had crossed the plain and had been riding through some hilly and thickly wooded country for some hours now. If the truth were known, Fidelma felt a little tired and thirsty herself and so she agreed without protest.

'We must have reached the borders of the country of the Cinél Cairpre by now,' she warned. 'Best have a care if the raiders do come from here, for we may not find a welcome.'

They approached the farmstead cautiously. There was some movement there and they could see a man rounding up cattle in an adjacent field, which was a sure sign of the lateness of the day. In farming terms the day began just before dawn when the cows were milked; it was called *am buarach* or spancel time, when the cows were led out. The spancel was a stout rope of twisted hair, two lengths of a man's arm from wrist to elbow, with a loop at one end and a piece of wood providing a knob at the other. The knob was thrust into the loop to bind the hind legs of the cow, should it be fidgety. The farmer or the cowherd doing the milking always carried the *buarach*, or spancel, when bringing the cows home.

The man in the field stopped when he saw them and then began to hurry towards the farmstead, leaving his cows to their own devices.

Fidelma glanced towards Caol and Gormán, noticing them slide their hands to rest on their swordhilts.

'Easy,' she said. 'The man has a right to be cautious at the sight of strangers.'

They turned their horses through a gate in the stone fence and into the farmyard. The man was now standing before his door, the spancel held almost as a weapon in his hands.

'That's far enough!' he called sharply before they had reached him. 'Who are you and what do you want?'

'There is no call for alarm,' Fidelma said pleasantly. 'We are travellers looking for the fortress of the chieftain of the Cinél Cairpre. We also need to rest, water our horses and take refreshment for ourselves. The sun is setting and soon it will be dark.'

'I know the time well enough. Stay still, all of you. I must warn you that there are arrows aimed at you, and if you move you will die. I want the warriors to disarm and get down from their horses.'

They sat still for a moment, hardly believing what the man said, for he continued in a quiet and reasonable tone: 'You think I am joking? My boys have their hunting bows strung. Ciar, loose a shot at the post behind me!'

A second later, a hunting arrow sped over the man's head and embedded itself in the post.

'My boys are good shots, so take heed,' added the man without bothering to observe how the arrow had landed.

Fidelma said quietly: 'Do as he says.'

'Gently now,' snapped the farmer. 'Throw down your swords to the right and dismount to the left. You, woman, remain seated.'

Caol and Gormán took off their sword belts and let them drop as instructed before dismounting.

Immediately, a small boy ran from an outhouse, gathered the weapons in one hand and the reins in another, leading the horses away.

'Now, warriors, move to one side. Remain seated, woman, for there is an arrow still aimed at you. No tricks now.'

As if at a hidden signal, a young man emerged with some rope and expertly tied the hands of Caol and Gormán behind them.

'Now you may alight, woman,' instructed the farmer.

Fidelma did so. Once again the small boy ran out to lead her horse away. A second young man now emerged; he was holding a long bow nearly two metres high, with an arrow loosely strung but ready to draw at a moment's notice.

'Take the warriors to the shed and make sure they are well bound, Ciar,' the man commanded.

'We meant you no harm,' Fidelma protested, but the man gestured for her to be silent.

'You think I believe you? Strangers and warriors?' He turned as the small boy came back. 'Cuana, saddle your horse and ride for the chief. You'll be there before dark. Tell him that we have visitors. He'll know what to do.'

'I am on my way, Father,' cried the boy, who was surely no more than twelve years old.

The young man addressed as Ciar came back, still holding his bow.

'They are secured, Father,' he reported.

Then the farmer relaxed a little and tossed his spancel to the other young man.

'You tend to the cows now. We'll take her inside. We might as well be comfortable while we wait.'

'Keep a close eye on her,' replied the young man. 'These people are full of tricks.'

Fidelma frowned as the farmer prompted her forward to the building. 'Who do you think I am?'

The man gave a sardonic snort. 'Try no games with me, woman. I have seen enough of them – from you and your people. Our chieftain will be here soon and then you may try your tricks on him. Now, sit in that chair.'

Fidelma had no sooner sat down than Ciar laid aside his bow, seized her wrists and bound them with a length of rope. Having done so he smiled at his father, who nodded in approval.

'You can put aside your bow now, Ciar, but keep it handy. There may be others about. Anyway, the chief should not be long.'

Eadulf was being dragged up a steep hill, the cords cutting deeply into his wrists. Even if he had wanted to cry out in pain, the tight gag effectively stopped any sound from emerging. His eyes began to water with the agony and he hoped his captors did not think it was some sign of weakness as, jeering, they pulled and prodded at him with the shafts of their spears. Several times he fell but they continued to pull, dragging him up the rough earth, until he was able to lurch to his feet again.

Earlier, he could not estimate how long, they had ridden before a halt was called and they had dismounted. He had been roughly manhandled from his horse, and forced to climb these steep slopes.

It seemed an age before they reached the top of the hill. It was cold and the wind was sharp, but somehow it gave his bruised and battered body some comfort. Then someone removed his blindfold and the same hand removed his gag. He stood, trying to catch his breath, and glanced around. The lowering sun still lit the land with its wintry soft golden light. He realised that he was on a high hill and noticed some curious structures there – stone-built edifices of the type he had seen elsewhere in the country. People had told him that such buildings were very ancient, constructed by the gods in the time beyond memory. He shivered slightly.

Nearer to where he stood with his captors, there were some rough wooden buildings and cooking fires, around which some women sat. But there were no signs of any children, only adults.

He became aware of one of the women approaching him.

She was tall, and her raven-black hair tumbled down almost to her waist. A silver headband bearing a strange crescent design held the hair in place around her forehead. Her features were angular but striking; the dark eyes flashed with some inner fire. It was a face used to command. It was also a face that he felt he had seen before – but could not think where. Eadulf also saw that around her neck and stretching across her chest was a great semi-circular collar. Then he realised that it was a silver equivalent of the great necklet that Fidelma had shown him in Cashel. The one she had found in the room of the dead guest at Ferloga's inn; the one she had said was a symbol of the Druids, the priests of the old gods.

His captors thrust him forward to face the woman by the expedient of prodding him with the tip of their swords. They all seemed to treat the woman with reverence.

In spite of the ropes binding him, Eadulf drew himself up, staring at her with his chin thrust forward defensively.

The woman halted before him. She was nearly half a head taller than he was. She looked down at him, and her thin lips parted in a smile without warmth. Her dark eyes seemed to bore deeply into his.

'Well, a Christian prisoner. You are welcome, my friend, welcome to Sliabh na Caillaigh.'

'The Mountain of the Hag?' Eadulf was frowning. He seemed to have heard the name before.

'You are a Saxon by your accent,' she observed.

'I am Eadulf, of Seaxmund's Ham in the land of the South Folk,' he replied proudly. 'Who are you?'

The woman laughed without humour.

'That is not for strangers to know, Eadulf of Seaxmund's Ham in the land of the South Folk,' she replied, mimicking his accent.

The woman was accompanied by several warriors. One of her entourage a fair-haired man, seemed familiar to Eadulf and he struggled to think where he had seen the man before. He found it curious that there were several things here that seemed known to him: the ornament at the woman's neck, her features – and now the face of this warrior.

Then the leader of his captors moved forward and addressed the woman, but with bowed head.

'*Ceannard*, this man claims to be husband to Fidelma of Cashel. We have heard that there was a female and male religious accompanied by two southern warriors at Tara recently.'

'Is this true?' demanded the woman, staring at Eadulf with sudden interest.

Eadulf smiled. 'Perhaps that is not for *you* to know,' he replied, with an attempt to mimic her.

The black-bearded warrior at his side struck him with the flat of his sword and Eadulf staggered a pace, biting his lip to stop from uttering a sound at the pain.

The woman turned behind her and called to one of the warriors nearby. 'Come forth and see if you recognise this man.'

The warrior came forward to examine him.

'That is the man called Brother Eadulf,' he confirmed.

Eadulf immediately recognised Cuan, the short, dark warrior of the Fianna who had fled from Tara.

'He was in the company of Fidelma of Cashel who was sent for to investigate Sechnussach's death,' the man continued. 'They were accompanied by two warriors of the Nasc Niadh, the golden collar, in the service of the King of Muman. I saw them all at Tara.'

'They will be searching for me even now,' Eadulf defiantly, 'as they are searching for you, Cuan. I am told the Fianna dislike deserters and traitors and have ways of dealing with them.'

'Their search will be in vain,' snapped Cuan, 'and you will be dead before they find you.' He raised his sword threateningly but the woman stayed him with a sharp command.

'Do not harm him lest you incur my displeasure, Cuan. And do not underestimate this man's companion,' she rebuked. 'I have heard of Fidelma of Cashel. She is very clever and in other circumstances I would welcome her to my homestead. She is a defender of many of the old ways against these pernicious ideas that are being spread through these lands. She is also an advocate of the ancient laws and that makes a worthy enemy.'

Cuan was immediately obeisant.

'Where is she now?' demanded the woman of Eadulf.

As Eadulf set his jaw firmly, his black-bearded captor moved forward and said confidently, '*Ceannard*, I will send two of my men to find out.'

The woman smiled thinly at him. 'You mean that you don't know already?' she sneered.

'We came upon the Saxon on the track to Delbna Mór. He was travelling with a survivor from Fobhair. We killed the other man. They rode with no one else.'

This was greeted with a frown.

'You allowed someone from Fobhair to survive?' There was a threat in her voice.

The man's face paled considerably. 'But I killed him when I found him.'

'How many others didn't you find, who escaped from Fobhair? And he was travelling with this Saxon – travelling to Delbna Mór? Did you not work out what that means!'

The questions were asked in an icy tone.

The leader of the raiders looked confused.

'I will tell you, you son of a pig. It means that the Saxon had already passed through Fobhair and was returning to Delbna Mór. It may also mean that Fidelma of Cashel was with him and may even now be on her way to Tara to raise the Fianna.' She turned to Eadulf. 'Is that so, Saxon? *Were* you travelling with Fidelma of Cashel?'

Eadulf simply shrugged.

'I'll beat the truth out of him, *ceannard*,' swore the black-bearded warrior.

'Oaf! You will never beat anything out of a man like this. You have little judgement of men. You can rip this one apart but he is stubborn. If he does not want to tell you, he will not tell you.' The woman raised her voice. 'Ensure that all our lookouts are doubled from now on. You will answer to me later. Meanwhile, take the Saxon and put him with the old man. A Saxon Christian will be a suitable gift for the Great One when the time comes.'

The man turned meekly away with a hand raised to his forehead in acknowledgement. Then he gestured to two of the warriors, who seized Eadulf with rough hands. He was hauled and pushed once more towards a strange, grey stone building which looked like one half of a great scallop shell, lying flat on the ground. There were several other similar construc-tions in the vicinity, but this was by far the largest. As he was marched towards it, Eadulf noticed some more recent wooden constructions nearby – pens for horses and other animals. He estimated that there must be at least a hundred or more fighting men and their women encamped on the hill and they held a good defensive position.

He gave an inward sigh. What was he thinking about, assessing their defences when there was no one who was going to storm this place to rescue him? He had not reached Delbna Mór to warn Brother Céin, let alone Tara. He wondered whether Fidelma had realised yet that the raiders had doubled back. He had to face the fact that he was on his own.

The two warriors shoved him towards an entrance in the stone construc-tion, which was revealed when a wicker gateway was swung aside. It was a small, narrow passage that seemed to lead into the bowels of the earth like the entrance to a tomb.

One of the men pointed along it. 'Down there, Saxon!'

Eadulf hung back, warily examining the darkness.

'Where does it lead?' he demanded.

The man sniggered and then struck him viciously across the face. Eadulf saw the blow coming and leaned backwards to defuse the force but it stung nevertheless.

'You do not ask questions. Get down in there.'

Eadulf had no option but to obey. He bent his head and moved along into the passage in a crouching position. The wicker gate swung shut behind him. He paused, expecting to be shrouded in blackness, but there was a flickering light some distance ahead at what was, presumably, the end of the passage. Cautiously he began to crawl forward. The passage was cold but it was dry and the ground easy underfoot. He had the light to guide him and it was not long before he found himself in the interior of the manmade structure.

The first thing he saw was an elderly man squatting on the floor with an oil lamp on one side of him and a clay jug on the other.

The man looked up as Eadulf emerged into the cavern. Despite his white hair and haggard features, he had a striking presence. Even with the shadows, Eadulf saw that he had once been handsome; his eyes were still dark and his gaze penetrating. The eyes widened a little as he took in Eadulf's clothing and tonsure.

'And who might you be?' he asked, not moving.

'Eadulf of Seaxmund's Ham,' replied Eadulf, staring around the cave-like room in which he found himself. The light showed the interior of it to be covered in intricate carvings, which seemed vaguely familiar. He realised they were like the carvings he had seen in the man-made cave near the Abbey of Delbna Mór.

'I welcome you, Brother Saxon. You will overlook the fact that I cannot rise. I feel my ankle was broken or sprained when they captured me.'

At once, Eadulf was concerned and bent to the old man, examining his puffy and swollen ankle by the faint light. He touched it gently.

'You have some knowledge of the physician's art?' asked the old man.

'I studied at Tuam Brecain,' replied Eadulf, before asking the man to attempt some movement on the ankle.

He did so, wincing a little. Eadulf observed the movement with an expert eye.

'When did it happen?'

The old man shrugged. 'Difficult to be accurate when imprisoned without sight of the sky. Perhaps three or four days ago.'

'Well, it's not a break, thanks be to God. I think it is a sprain. You really need some cold compress on it. I will ask the guards.'

The old man laughed and caught him by the arm, shaking his head.

'I don't think you'll find any compassion among them, Brother. They are not Christians.'

Eadulf nodded glumly. 'That I have already discovered for myself.'

'What brings you hither, Brother . . . Brother Eadulf? The name has a familiar ring.'

'I am husband to Fidelma of Cashel.'

The old man looked at him sharply. 'Fidelma the *dálaigh*? Is it so? I had heard that the High King's Great Assembly had sent for her to attend at Tara and investigate the High King's death.'

'Just so,' agreed Eadulf.

'Then tell me how you came here?'

'It is a story that will be long in the telling.'

The old man was amused. 'So far as I can see, we are not pressed for time.'

Eadulf squatted down beside him. 'So, first things first. You know who I am. What is your name?'

'I am Luachan,' the man replied.

'Bishop Luachan of Delbna Mór?' gasped Eadulf.

The man frowned. 'I am. How do you know of me?'

'We have been searching for you.'

'How so?' The old man was amazed.

'We had a report of your visit to Sechnussach on the night before he was murdered and of the strange gift you took to him. Fidelma and I set out to speak with you at Delbna Mór, and from Brother Céin we heard that you had gone missing.'

The old man groaned. 'You were with Fidelma? Don't tell me that they have captured her, or killed her?'

'They captured only me. Fidelma was on her way to see the Cinél Cairpre with two of Cashel's best warriors while I was riding back to Delbna Mór to report that the abbey at Baile Fobhair had been attacked.'

Bishop Luachan's face was woebegone.

'Baile Fobhair attacked?' He gave a deep sigh. Then he brightened a little. 'But Fidelma is not captured? Then there is some hope for her. But tell me your story in detail.'

'Before I do so, tell me . . . who are these people? I know they are raiders and hold no allegiance to the Faith.'

'They are the cursed of the earth!' hissed Bishop Luachan with such vehemence that even Eadulf was surprised.

'I know they are not followers of the Christ,' he said.

'They are not even followers of the old religion,' snorted Luachan. 'They follow an aberration of the old gods that even the Druids of old had to rise up and destroy many years ago. Worse, these animals believe in sacrificing human life to this idol. I am afraid, my friend, that we are their next intended victims.'

Eadulf shuddered. 'How long do we have?' he asked, trying to sound nonchalant.

'Oh, a few days yet. I have heard them talking. It is their intention to perform the sacrifice at the time of the sun-standing, the *grien tairisem*.'

'Sun-standing? Oh, the solstice. Well, that gives us some time to plan an escape.'

Bishop Luachan smiled in the gloom. 'You are optimistic, my brother in Christ.'

Eadulf grinned wryly. '*Dum spiro, spero,*' he rejoined. The phrase translated as: while I breathe, I hope.

'A good enough philosophy.'

'Do you know where they plan to carry out their unholy ritual?'

'Not here, that is for certain.'

'Why not? From what I have seen, this seems to be some ancient pagan site.'

Bishop Luachan sniffed. 'This is an ancient site where those of the old religion gathered and performed their rituals. But this is not part of the evil they worship. The ancients built this very chamber we are in, in order to show them the time of the *geiseabhan* . . .'

'The sun facing south?' queried Eadulf, trying to translate the term that he had not heard before.

'The time of the equal night,' explained Luachan. 'The equinox. That is what this complex of buildings were constructed for, not for the solstice. So I think that when the time comes for their ritual, they will have to take us to another site which will show them the appropriate time.'

Eadulf looked round and shuddered. 'How can a dark man-built cave such as this show the time of anything?'

Brother Luachan smiled. 'As you came through the entrance and were made to come along the passage into this chamber, you might have noticed all the strange carvings. Above the entrance is a hole through which, on the day of the equinox, at the specific time, a beam of light from the sun comes and spreads along the passage to hit the very stone I am leaning against. It lights certain things, carvings, designs on the stone, and indicates the very time. The ancient astronomers were clever.'

'So it tells us the time of the equinox but not the time of the solstice?' Eadulf asked.

'There are some other constructions in the country which do,' the bishop replied. 'That is why I think they will move us before that time.'

'Then we will have to ensure that we are not here to be moved,' Eadulf said firmly.

'That will be difficult, since there is only the one way in and out of this prison – the narrow passage whose entrance is always guarded.'

'Tell me more about their superstition. You have said that it does not really have much to do with the old beliefs and ideas that were followed before the teachings of Christ came here. Is there something, some weakness about their superstition, that we can use against them?'

'You have an inventive mind, my friend', Bishop Luachan said with a sigh. 'However, there is nothing that will put fear into these people. It is told that in the days of a High King called Tigernmas, which name means Lord of Death, the worship of a great golden idol called Crom Cróich became widespread. The people turned from their old gods and goddesses – the Children of Danú. Tigernmas approved of the worship of the idol and it was placed in Magh Slécht, which means the pain of slaughter, in the sub-kingdom of Breifne. He ordered sacrifices to be offered to the idol from the chief scions of every clan, including the firstborn of every issue. Many worshipped the idol, pouring blood around it, and their worship was frenzied and evil. Some say that Tigernmas and his priests in their worship of Crom slaughtered a third of the population.'

'How long ago was this?'

Bishop Luachan shrugged. 'Time beyond measure. According to the old chroniclers, Tigernmas was son of Follach, son of Eithrial, of the race of Eremon, and he held the sovereignty of Éireann for fifty years. They claim he was the seventh ruler after Eremon. According to some, he encouraged the mining of gold and introduced the custom of using colours in dress to denote the clans. He won twenty-seven great battles against the descendants of Eber, but all the good he did was set at naught by the evil religion he introduced.

'It was recorded that Tigernmas so roused the anger of the Druids that they gathered the people and, on the eve of Samhain, while the King and his fellow worshippers were in their frenzy before the idol on Magh Slécht, they attacked and killed him and three-quarters of his followers. Some say that afterwards the five kingdoms were without a High King for seven years because the Druids feared his legitimate successors. Others say that a High King called Eochaidh succeeded him and ruled the five kingdoms justly.'

Eadulf pursed his lips thoughtfully. 'So there is nothing that is deep in their superstition? They merely worshipped a golden idol and sacrificed people to it – that is all?'

'All except the slaughter of the innocents,' replied Bishop Luachan.

'How can this shallow superstition have survived to this day?'

The old bishop was serious. 'Consider what has happened in these lands in recent generations, my friend. Countless centuries of belief have been overturned by the New Faith. All in all, it has been a peaceful process, for our true ancient beliefs were not so far from the concepts that were brought to us from the East. This was not so elsewhere, for I have heard that great wars have been fought and many slaughtered as other peoples refused to accept the truth of Christ. Even in the empire of Rome itself, wars were fought between the rival emperors, Constantine and Licinius, as to whether the new or the old gods should dominate.'

'What are you saying?'

'That it is to be wondered at how peaceful the change was among the peoples of the five kingdoms. However, there are many areas where some have clung to the old beliefs. We have done our best to change those beliefs or subvert them to the New Faith . . .'

'It was so in my own land,' Eadulf nodded. 'When Gregory of Rome sent Abbot Mellitus to convert the Angles and the Saxons, he told him that it would be easier to convert the people if they were allowed to retain the outward form of their religious traditions, while claiming them in the name of the Christian God.'

'It was so here,' agreed Luachan. 'Holy wells became baptisteries, temples became the new churches and the old festivals were renamed in honour of the Christ. It seemed to work well. Soon people were worshipping Christ and His saints at the holy wells and springs or in certain forest glades without any remembrance of the ancient gods and goddesses. Then, in recent times, there seemed to arise a resistance to the spread of the Faith.'

'How so?'

'It happened a generation or two ago when Gregory, the servant of the servants of God, asserted that the papal offices in Rome were the primacy of all the Christian Faith. In the five kingdoms, we cannot yet agree which of our great centres is the primacy of the island, let alone agree that we must obey Rome in all things. Many saw it as the rise of the old empire of Rome in new form, an infringement of our liberties.'

Eadulf pulled a face. He had been at the Council of Witebia when Oswy had decided to follow the rule of Rome. Even recently at Cashel there had been much debate about the claims of Ard Macha as the centre of the Faith in the five kingdoms, at which claims and counter claims were made.

'Are you saying that those adhering to the Old Religion saw dissension within those holding to the Faith and have used that as a means of overturning it?'

'Perhaps not that, but they have seen the movement of many of the

Faith to uphold the ways of Rome, as you obviously do, judging from your tonsure, my friend. They see Roman-inspired laws, the Penitentials, being used to subvert our ancient law system, and the Brehons set at naught, just as the Druids had been banished into obscurity. They see that the Christianity they had accepted is now being changed yet again into something entirely alien to their beliefs.'

Eadulf smiled thinly in the gloom. 'I presume from what you say that you do not follow the path of Rome?'

'I wear the tonsure of the Blessed John, not the *corona spina* that I observe you wear, my friend. That should say enough.'

'So, this pagan faith is but a backlash to the growing influence of Rome here?'

'I cannot make it clearer.'

'But why so extreme? Why not merely support those in the five kingdoms who reject the Penitentials and other matters? Or why not go back to the faith of the Druids? Why would they choose such an aberration as this idol you call Crom?'

'In times of uncertainty, fear is the unifying force,' averred the old bishop. 'Fear binds people together in a way that cannot be achieved by other means. Those who would convert the people back to the old ways need fear, need something that will drive everyone back to the paths of darkness.'

'Well,' Eadulf remarked bitterly, 'I do not intend to become a martyr just yet. We will find a way out of this prison.'

Fidelma had been meditating, practising the old form of the *dercad*. She did not believe in unnecessary action when it was bound to be futile. She was tightly bound and the farmer and his son were continually present with watchful eyes. As it had grown dark, oil lamps were lit by the old man who then took a lantern outside. She presumed it was to check on Caol and Gormán and hoped they had not been hurt. They must be shackled in the barn outside. The old man came back after a while, and as he refused to answer her questions about her companions, so she returned to her meditation.

After a passage of time, the sound of horses' hooves aroused her from her trance. There were a fair-sized number of riders – perhaps twenty or more – clattering into the farmyard.

The farmer sprang up. 'The chief!' he said in a thankful tone to his son.

A moment later, a muscular young man burst into the room, closely followed by the farmer's younger son and a couple of other men who carried swords in their hands.

'Your son reported that you might have raiders,' began the young man, as his eyes fell on Fidelma. He had a shock of black hair, thick with curls, a full beard and not unpleasant features.

'She and two warriors came to the farmstead,' the farmer said respectfully. 'You told me to beware of strange warriors, so I had them trussed up in the barn and kept the woman here.'

The young warrior turned to Fidelma. 'You appear to be a Christian?' he said wonderingly, as his eyes fell on the cross she wore around her neck.

Fidelma regarded him with a thin smile. 'So far, no one has bothered to ask me who I am. Perhaps there is no courtesy left in this part of the country?'

The young man looked startled for a moment. 'There is courtesy for those who are courteous,' he replied. 'Very well – who are you?'

'I am Fidelma of Cashel, a *dálaigh* entrusted with the investigation of the assassination of the High King Sechnussach, by the Great Assembly.'

The young man's eyes widened and he glanced at the farmer with an interrogatory look in his eyes.

'I asked no question of her,' the man replied defensively. 'People can be deceitful with their tongues. She was with two strange warriors.'

As the young man turned back to her, Fidelma said, before he could ask the question: 'My companions are Caol, commander of the Nasc Niadh, the bodyguard of my brother, Colgú of Cashel, and Gormán, one of his men.'

'Fidelma of Cashel? Can you prove it?' he asked.

'Does it need proof?'

'In this time and in this place, it does.'

'In my saddlebag you will find the hazel wand of office of the High King, given me by Cenn Faelad to assert my authority.'

The young man turned to the farmer's son. 'Find the saddlebag and bring it here.'

It was the work of moments and the ornate hazel wand was produced. The young man exhaled softly and shook his head.

'Undo her bonds,' he instructed the farmer. 'Accept my apologies, lady. These are troubled times. I am Ardgal, chief of the Cinél Cairpre.'

Muttering that he was not to blame, the farmer released Fidelma from her bonds. Ignoring him, for a moment or two, Fidelma sat rubbing her chafed wrists.

'I trust my companions will also be released now?' she asked.

Ardgal addressed the farmer. 'Make it so!' he snapped. Then, turning back to her: 'Believe me, I am sorry. But, lady, this land is beset with raiders, burning churches and destroying the homes of any who support the clergy.'

Fidelma looked grim. 'Of that I am aware, Ardgal. It is part of the reason that I have ridden from Tara with the intention of meeting with you.'

Ardgal was once more surprised. Then he waved a hand to indicate the room.

'This is not the ideal place for hospitality but it must suffice for the moment.' He looked at the farmer's sons. 'See what you can offer the lady to make amends for this treatment.'

Their faces flushed with embarrassment, the young men went to fulfil the task.

Ardgal drew up a stool and sat down to face Fidelma with a concerned look.

'Why are you seeking me?' he asked.

'That will surely be no surprise when it was your chief who assassinated Sechnussach,' she said.

Ardgal inclined his head contritely. 'We are not all the same, lady. Dubh Duin was my cousin and my chief, it is true. A few years ago, we perceived some strange madness possessing him. He had always spoken of the old ways. We are a liberal people, believing in each to his own. We did not mind that he stood firm for the Old Faith and forsook the path of Christ. But when he became an advocate against the New Faith, then his beliefs began splitting the loyalties of our clan. He became a fanatic. In fact, while Dubh Duin was at Tara this last time, attending the Great Assembly, the *derbhfine* of our clan met and it was decided that he should be ousted under process of the law, and that I be installed as chief in his place.'

'Why was this?' demanded Fidelma, accepting a mug of cider from the farmer's son, and sipping it gently for her throat was very dry.

The farmer had returned, still muttering justifications, with Caol and Gormán. Ardgal took charge, ordering that a meal be prepared for the visitors while his men encamped in the barns outside. Then he turned back to her and repeated, 'Why? Because of the behaviour that resulted in the deed he carried out.'

'Tell me about it.'

'It is a tale that can be short in the telling but long in the recitation of its consequences.'

'Tell it as you see fit.'

Ardgal shrugged. 'As I said, he had always preferred the Old Faith to the new. No harm in that, for there are many in this land who prefer to offer their prayers to the gods and goddesses who have served our people for thousands of years, rather than to what some consider as a strange god from the East. But Dubh Duin began to change from tolerance to fanaticism. He became obsessed with trying to force the Old Religion on everyone.'

'And you?'

Ardgal smiled briefly. 'I am of the New Faith, lady. So are most of my people. But there were others in the clan who supported Dubh Duin. Most of them have now fled to the hills and forests since the assassination of the High King. When Irél came demanding hostages, we were able to provide him with some of Dubh Duin's followers, and these are now incarcerated at Tara as surety for the clan's good behaviour. That way, the innocent will not suffer.'

'But there are these raiders, the *dibergach*, who have been active,' Fidelma pointed out.

Ardgal's expression was serious. 'Dubh Duin was not their leader. There are others more powerful and influential than he. And what they adhere to is a perverted form of the Old Religion. Our old gods and goddesses were not out for bloodlust. The Tuatha Dé Danaan were deities of light and goodness who defeated the sinister forces of evil before they ruled in this land. Of course, they had their human vices. They experienced all human passion but they loved life. These misguided fools have set up the Crom Cróich, an aberration.'

'And yet,' Fidelma put in, 'this aberration seems to be attracting the allegiance of many.'

Ardgal laughed shortly. 'Allegiance? It is attracting the *fear* of many. Only fear sustains this new movement.'

'Is this why the farmer feared us?' intervened Caol, having recovered from his bruised dignity, a warrior bested by two farmer's lads with hunting bows.

'Yes,' Ardgal said. 'The raiders have killed too many people here. Every abbey and church within this area is coming under attack from them.'

'Do they really expect to overturn the New Faith?' Caol asked.

'That is their intention.'

'Dubh Duin's slaughter of the High King was part of this?'

'I believe so.'

'Well, it has not worked,' Fidelma stated. Then she suddenly gave a groan and closed her eyes.

'What is it?' demanded Ardgal in alarm.

'The raiders – I had forgotten. We encountered them at Baile Fobhair and thought they were on their way into your country. We now believe they turned back. Where are they now?'

'We have a series of sentinels who would warn us of their approach, like this farmer when he mistakenly thought you were part of their group.'

'That certainly means that they have doubled back. We must return immediately to the abbey of Delbna Mór.'

'Why there?'

'Because they will attack it next.' Briefly, Fidelma told him about Eadulf and his mission to warn Brother Céin, the steward of the abbey, and try to bring help from Tara.

'Little use starting off now that darkness has fallen,' Ardgal demurred. 'The road is treacherous in the darkness and there are rivers and marshlands to cross. We must rest here and then move before sun-up.'

'He's right, lady,' Caol agreed practically. 'We can do little on a strange road in the darkness.'

Fidelma was reluctant but saw the logic of it.

'Do you have any knowledge of who the leader of the raiders is and where they might be based?' she asked the young chief.

'We think they are based somewhere in the northern hills, since people there talk of some of the fanatical Druids who claim that the Tuatha Dé Danaan have betrayed the people. They call on the populace to welcome back the idol Crom Cróich with all the bloodthirsty rituals that Tigernmas demanded.'

'Bloodthirsty rituals?'

'Human sacrifice, lady. Woe betide anyone who falls into their hands, for these fanatics will slaughter them.'

chapter eighteen

Ardgal and his men had set up a rapid pace, and had Fidelma not been an expert horsewoman, she would have been hard pressed to keep up with them. As it was, they saw the outline of the abbey of Delbna Mór well before midday. They were aware that their approach had been spotted, but Fidelma's figure had obviously been identified, since there was no hostile reaction as the brethren gathered to meet them before the main abbey buildings.

Brother Céin himself came out to greet them personally.

'Sister Fidelma!' exclaimed the steward, and then he recognised her companion. 'Ardgal? What brings you here?'

Fidelma dismounted quickly from her horse. 'Where is Eadulf?' she demanded without preamble. 'Has he gone on to Tara yet?'

Brother Céin looked astonished. 'Gone on . . . ? I haven't seen Brother Eadulf since he left with you for Ardgal's country. Is he not with you?'

Fidelma went cold. 'Has not Eadulf and a Brother Manchán from Baile Fobhair come here, reporting destruction and death at the abbey?'

'He has not.' Brother Céin looked shocked. 'You say that the abbey of Baile Fobhair has been attacked?'

Fidelma groaned inwardly. 'Eadulf should have arrived here yesterday afternoon with Brother Manchán. He was to warn you that the raiders were overheard discussing an attack on Delbna Mór, and pass on my instructions that you should defend yourselves as best you could while he rode on to Tara to bring Irél and some warriors to help.'

Brother Céin was shaking his head. 'There has been no sign of him, sister. Nor of this Brother Manchán. I know him. Perhaps Eadulf missed the road and . . . but, surely, Brother Manchán of Baile Fobhair would know the road here very well. They would not get lost unless . . .'

'Unless he encountered some of the raiders,' Ardgal said grimly. 'Let me send out two of my best trackers to see if they can pick up their route along the road.'

Fidelma tried to hide her fear as the chief turned to give instructions.

'I think that we should also send to Irél at Tara immediately,' she added quietly, determined to be practical instead of giving way to the anxiety that beset her mind.

'I have a good lad with a fresh horse who can reach Tara quickly,' suggested Brother Céin.

'Let him do so then,' agreed Fidelma.

'We can remain here in readiness and wait for the Fianna to arrive.' Ardgal had returned from giving orders to his men.

The steward was solemn-faced, clearly worried at their news.

'That is good, because the *dibergach* could attack at any time. We need to be ready to defend ourselves.'

Eadulf came awake with a start. Bishop Luachan was already sitting up and peering down the passage that led out to the wicker gate.

'What is it?' whispered Eadulf.

'The guards are talking to someone outside,' replied the old bishop.

Eadulf shuddered. 'Is it time? Do they intend . . . ?'

'No. It is several days yet to the equinox, my friend. They will not do anything before then.'

Suddenly there was a commotion at the entrance and a voice called: 'Eadulf of Seaxmund's Ham! Come forth – quickly!'

Eadulf started a little. The voice called in Saxon without accent. He glanced at the old bishop and explained: 'I am being summoned outside.'

'Come forth, Eadulf. I mean you no harm,' repeated the voice.

There was no alternative but to obey. Eadulf began to move towards the tunnel.

'God go with you, my son,' the old bishop blessed him.

Eadulf pasued, smiled back in thanks, and then made his way down the tunnel. Outside, dawn's light was flooding the sky and it was fairly cold. There were two guards waiting for him with a third man. Eadulf rose out of the passageway and stood up, studying the man. He was tall, with long blond hair, a beard, drooping moustaches and angular features. It was the warrior whose features had appeared familiar to him when he was being questioned by the woman called the *ceannard*.

'Come with me, Eadulf,' he said in faultless Saxon.

'Do I know you?' Eadulf asked, as the tall man turned and motioned him forward. 'You are Saxon by your speech.'

The man smiled but said nothing. Instead, he led the way to one of the tents pitched in the shelter of the ancient stone buildings and entered. There was no one else inside. The man motioned to a chair and then went to a cask, took two mugs and filled them with ale. He handed one to Eadulf before sitting down opposite him.

'You do know me, Eadulf of Seaxmund's Ham,' the Saxon said, with an amused expression on his features.

Eadulf shook his head with a frown. 'I can't recall . . .'

'I grant you that it was many years ago. We were scarcely more than boys gathered at the feet of a new teacher named Fursa; Fursa a man of Éireann who tried to convert us to the New Faith.'

Eadulf closed his eyes for a moment, casting his memory back to the lad of sixteen summers that he had been when he had left the old gods and goddesses of his people and converted to the New Faith. A time when the missionaries of Éireann had come converting the South Folk to follow the path of the Christ. He suddenly saw an image of youths sitting in a circle at the feet of the elderly teacher.

'You are Beorhtric of Aeschild's Ham,' he said suddenly.

The blond-haired warrior smiled broadly now. 'Your memory does not play you false, Eadulf. I am, indeed, Beorhtric from the land of the East Saxons.'

Eadulf regarded him with astonishment as the memory flooded back. 'But what are you doing here? Why are you dressed as a warrior, Brother? I thought you went to join Fursa's abbey at Burgh in the land of the North Folk.'

Beorhtric laughed in good humour and took a sip of his ale. 'I am no Brother of the Christian Faith. After you left to study here I wandered with Fursa for a while. Then I realised my mistake and returned to the kingdom of Sigehere. I saw the devastation left by the Yellow Plague. Our new god had not protected us from the evil and so I supported Sigehere when he returned to the Old Faith and called on Woden to drive out the evil. I was with Sigehere when he destroyed the new Christian churches and re-opened the old temples.'

Eadulf grimaced. 'I had heard that the East Saxons had returned to the old ways. I am sad to find that you are one of them.' He frowned. 'Yet I heard that Sigehere had, with the guidance of Bishop Jaruman, returned to the Faith of Christ.'

'Sigehere was a fool,' snapped Beorhtric. 'He was not swayed by argument but because Wulfhere of Mercia, who fancied himself as a Christian overlord, promised him his niece, Osyth, in marriage. They now have a Christian brat called Offa. Sigehere is a weak king. He runs with the hare and tries to hunt with the hounds. He allowed Wulfhere to drive out those who remained true to Woden.'

'Is that why you are here?'

Beorhtric smiled thinly. 'With all the Saxon kingdoms falling to this Christian teaching, I and some companions decided to take service with those who would pay for our swordhands. We found ourselves coming to this land and by chance we fell in with this band who are fighting for the restitution of their old gods against the Christians.'

'Do you really hope to change the tide of the New Faith?'

'The tide is with *us*, Eadulf,' Beorhtric said. 'Soon this army will spread through the country and the few generations that separate the people from their old gods will be but a curious moment in time, a pause in the march forward to a new golden age.'

'You cannot believe that?' Eadulf looked aghast at the Saxon.

'And you are too intelligent not to consider it, my friend. Remember your youth when you worshipped at the grove of Woden? Are we not all descended from Woden's seven sons? How can you turn your back on him whose divine blood is in all of us?'

Eadulf shivered slightly.

It was true that, having accepted the New Faith with his intellect when he was seventeen, Eadulf's emotions still felt the power of Tyr, Woden, Thunor and Freya. Every time he spoke against them, he felt their lurking presence, waiting to seize him and consign him to the flames of Hel. Deliberately he raised the mug of ale and took a swallow in order to disguise his emotions.

'What is the purpose of this conversation, Beorhtric?' he asked coldly. 'Are you trying to reconvert me to the old ways?'

Beorhtric smiled pleasantly and sat back. 'I hope that I have the power to do so, Eadulf. You were an hereditary *gerefa* of your people and it was your duty to maintain the faith and code of your ancestors. I have persuaded our leader to give me an opportunity to save your life.'

'An opportunity?' Eadulf raised an eyebrow. 'What will that entail?'

'You may join us, be received into my warband with the respect I would give to any *gerefa* of my people . . .'

'On what condition?'

'That you tell us what you know about the happenings in Tara and whether the Fianna is marching against us.'

'You mean to ask me to make an act of betrayal?'

Beorhtric shook his head. 'It is no betrayal. Tell us what we need to know and we will not harm you. That is simple enough.'

'It is a betrayal of my wife and her people, as well as all I hold dear.'

'Your wife, this Fidelma of Cashel, will not be harmed. Our leader has said that she has great respect for her. We will capture her and then, if she won't join us, you can take her with you and go where you want.'

Eadulf stifled the refusal that came to his mind because something else occurred to him. Perhaps he could find out more about these people, the strange woman who led them and the strength of her army, if he did not make an immediate rejection of the offer.

'You cannot expect me to abandon all I believe in just like that,' he countered. 'Tell me more of why you fight for this woman.'

'The *ceannard*?'

'Yes. What is her name?'

'She is just the leader, the Wise One. A priestess of the god Crom.'

'So she has no name?'

'None that dare be spoken.'

'And she believes in this old god?'

'She believes that the Christians are just a new empire spreading from Rome as they once spread before; she believes that they are destroying the old ways and customs just as the Romans tried once before to make everyone bow down to their ways and government.'

'And that is why she fights?'

'That is why.'

'But the message of Christ is peace,' pointed out Eadulf.

Beorhtric laughed as if he found the idea uproarious. 'Peace among those who fall under the Roman heel? The real rulers of Rome recognise no peace. While they conquer, they preach that the conquered should have poverty of spirit. They are thus able to oppress them, for when men are of poor spirit then the proud and haughty can easily rule them. Oh yes, Eadulf, I know something of the religion you still uphold. "Blessed are the poor in spirit, for theirs is the kingdom of heaven". That's what is taught, eh?

'And what else do they teach?' he went on, goading Eadulf. '"Him that takes away your cloak, do not forbid him to take your coat also. Give to every man that asks something from you and of him that takes away your goods do not make protest". And if physical violence is used against you, why, "if you are struck on the one cheek, turn the other so they can strike you again"!'

Beorhtric burst out laughing. 'This is the religion that slave-masters teach to slaves, the better that they might enslave them.'

Eadulf stirred uneasily, for Beorhtric had certainly homed in on what he had always seen as the weakness of the new philosophy.

He and Fidelma had spent much time discussing such matters and they had always felt that resistance to wrong and the practice of moral right and self-reliance was the better course. But it was surely contrary to the teachings of the poverty of spirit that was claimed to be a virtue?

'And does this Crom uphold such virtues?' he demanded. 'I heard that this idol was some aberration of the Old Faith of Éireann whose priests demanded human sacrifices to appease their appetites.'

Beorhtric made a dismissive gesture as if it was of no consequence. 'Crom? That is for the people of this land. I have never foresworn Woden. And if Woden is using Crom to overthrow the New Faith, then so be it. Crom only demands the sacrifices of his enemies. He demands, moreover, that people stand up against the Christians who would oppress them by stealth. He commands us to drive the tide of Roman cunning back into the sea as the old Romans were driven back before.'

Eadulf shook his head sadly at the light of fanaticism in Beorhtric's face.

'And this is the reason for what is happening here?'

'It is a great cause. It is the freedom of people from the new oppression. Sadly, our Saxon brethren have been fooled into accepting these insidious ideas. Here we might win and then be able to bring our army back to our homelands to reconvert our people to the true ways and mend the harm that has been done.'

'To return to what?' demanded Eadulf. 'Was life so good when we sacrificed to the gods, when we left people with no hope but the utter void that follows death?'

'We had the choice,' Beorhtric said fiercely, 'to die with weapon in hand and the name of Woden on our lips so that we might live again in the Hall of Heroes.'

'And how many could hope for such a death, a futile death at that?'

For a moment, Beorhtric's eyes blazed. Then he said slowly: 'You are playing for time with me, Eadulf. I give you a final chance. Join us now. Tell us where Fidelma of Cashel is. Tell us what is happening at Tara and who is coming against us. If you do, you will live and the world will be yours. Refuse, and you will die a death at the next festival to Crom, a death in flames and so horrible that even you will cry out to Crom for mercy with your last breath.'

Eadulf had sat back. He glanced down at the mug that he still held in his hand. Now, with a quick movement, he threw its contents over the face of the Saxon warrior.

With an oath, Beorhtric sprang up and drew his sword in one swift motion. The blade was raised. Another moment and it would have sliced into Eadulf.

'Hold!' snapped a voice.

For a moment everything seemed frozen in time and space. Then slowly Beorhtric lowered his sword and sheathed it. Eadulf, transfixed in his seat in the chair, relaxed and began to breathe again.

The woman known as the *ceannard* had entered the tent. She looked at Eadulf with a curious smile.

'I was right about you, Eadulf of Seaxmund's Ham. For a Christian you display a remarkable courage. I did not think that they would break you and cause you to betray your beliefs or Fidelma of Cashel.' She glanced at the Saxon warrior. 'You see, Beorhtric? I know men. I knew he would not accept your offer to join us. No matter. My daughter will soon send us word about what is happening in Tara. Now take him back and ensure that he is confined properly. No harm must come to him before the time is right and we present him to Crom Cróich.'

Sullenly, Beorhtric moved forward and yanked Eadulf roughly from the chair.

The woman smiled almost encouragingly at Eadulf. 'It is good, my Saxon friend,' she said softly. 'If you were a coward, you would not make a fitting sacrifice to Crom.'

Then Beorhtric was hauling him out of the tent back to the stone prison to rejoin Bishop Luachan.

Ardgal found Fidelma pacing in the refectory of the abbey. He paused nervously at the door.

'Bad news, lady,' he blurted out.

Fidelma stood, the coldness clutching her heart. 'Eadulf has been found?' she asked hoarsely.

'No, lady. But my men have found the body of Brother Manchán. He had been run through with a sword. There were the tracks of many horses . . .'

'But no sign of Eadulf?'

'No sign of anyone else but the slain brother.'

'What did your trackers tell you?'

'They saw traces of a heavy-laden horse.'

'Eadulf and Brother Manchán were riding one horse.'

Ardgal nodded and continued: 'They think a number of riders were lying in wait for them and surrounded them. That was where Brother Manchán was killed. Then the horses moved off. There was no longer any sign of one horse being heavier than the others.'

'So they took Eadulf captive?' she asked hopefully.

'There is nothing to suggest otherwise, lady.'

'Which way did they go?'

'My trackers say they went north into the hill country. They followed the trail as far as they could without endangering themselves – up to within sight of Sliabh na Callaigh.'

'The Hag's Mountain? What is that?'

'It is the highest hill in these parts, lady. And one which the old pagans declared as sacred. There are buildings of great antiquity on it and some travellers have said that there have been campfires and bands of riders seen there recently. It accords with what we have heard before – that this is probably where the *dibergach* are encamped.'

'Then this is where we shall go to confront them,' Fidelma said decisively. 'We must follow and rescue Eadulf.'

'Lady, I have only twenty warriors,' protested Ardgal. 'The raiders might have ten times that number.'

Fidelma stamped her foot angrily. 'Might?' she sneered. 'Eadulf is a prisoner of these evil people. Should I allow a "might" to stop me?'

'Be reasonable, lady. Let us wait for the arrival of Irél and his Fianna.'

'By then it could be too late. Give me the help of your local tracker and I'll go alone with Caol and Gormán.'

Ardgal sighed. 'If you are determined, then I must go with you,' he said reluctantly. 'But my men must be allowed the same choice of whether to go or stay. It is suicide for a few men to attack the Hag's Mountain.'

'The choice is yours and theirs. But I will not delay long. Eadulf is in danger.'

'What did they want of you, my son?' asked Bishop Luachan, when Eadulf had rejoined him.

'They wanted me to betray my wife, my son and my religion.'

'And the alternative?'

'Death in some weird ritual.'

'Ah, as I have said. Some sacrifice at the equinox. At least we have a few days of life left.'

'A few days?' Eadulf snorted, still angered by Beorhtric. 'A bit more than that, if I have anything to do with it. I intend to seize the first opportunity for us to escape.'

'From this place?'

'No place is the perfect prison,' pronounced Eadulf optimistically. 'Though I have to say that this comes near to it.'

'There is only one way out of here,' Bishop Luachan pointed out again, 'and that is the way we came in. Along the tunnel and out of the entrance.'

'Which means that we need some way of distracting the guards, to get them away from the entrance . . .'

'Moving aside the wicker gate and running off down the hill.' The old man was cynical. 'How can we distract the guards from inside the tunnel in order for them to leave the entrance unguarded? You should think again.'

Eadulf pursed his lips. 'It is not the first time that I have been incarcerated with apparently no means to escape,' he said. He was thinking of the watery grave to which Uaman the Leper had once sought to consign him.[*]

'Then we must pray for divine intervention to rescue you again,' the old man said sarcastically. 'Meanwhile, I am going to try to sleep.'

Ardgal and his men were gathered round Fidelma in the refectory of the community of Delbna Mór.

'My men have all agreed to follow me, if I can assure them that the attack on the Hag's Mountain will not simply be a futile exercise that has no chance of success.'

Fidelma looked at them all with a smile of gratitude.

---

[*]See *The Leper's Bell* (2004)

'I do not believe in futility, Ardgal. I have an idea by which we may surprise them and rescue Eadulf.'

Ardgal continued to look serious. 'Very well. My men will listen to your idea and then I shall ask if they approve it. If they do not, that is their decision.'

Fidelma turned to meet their expectant gaze. 'My plan calls for hunters, not warriors. It was the farmer who took me prisoner who has inspired this idea . . .'

There was a noise at the door of the refectory and one of Ardgal's sentinels came breathlessly in.

'Warriors!' he called urgently. 'Warriors coming along the road from the east!'

For a moment there was pandemonium as the warriors began to draw their weapons. But Ardgal raised his voice above it.

'Are they *dibergach*?' he demanded.

The sentinel was hesitant. 'They ride with discipline and they have a banner at their head. There must be a hundred of them.'

Fidelma's eyes widened. A look of relief and hope spread on her features.

'The Fianna?' she gasped. 'If so, then this is an unexpected blessing. But we must be prepared in case it is a trap. Ardgal, disperse your men to cover. Brother Céin, come with me to greet whoever they may be.'

Within moments, her orders had been carried out and Fidelma and the steward of Delbna Mór took a stand by the gates, almost in the manner that Fidelma and her companions had first been greeted at Delbna Mór. But now there were only the two of them while everyone had taken defensive positions out of sight.

They heard the sound of many horses. It grew louder, and seconds later, the head of the column came into view. Two outriders swept into the courtyard and examined it swiftly. Then a familiar figure rode in at the head of the column.

'Irél!' called Fidelma as the young man halted his mount before them.

The commander of the Fianna was smiling at her. 'Fidelma! Is all well with you, lady?'

He swung down and Fidelma moved forward to greet him.

'It is a long story. How came you here?'

'Soon after you had departed from Tara, Cenn Faelad became worried, having heard tales of the raiders. He asked me to follow with a company of my men. We were resting at the church on the thorn island not a great distance away, when a merchant rode by and he told us that he had seen an abbey burning to the north-west. From what he said, I believed it to be Baile Fobhair.'

'It was,' confirmed Fidelma.

'Well, we set off straight away. Delbna Mór lies on our route. Then we met a young rider from here who said the abbey was expecting to be attacked.'

'The abbey at Baile Fobhair is burned and everyone slain,' Fidelma said sadly. 'And, indeed, we were expecting an attack here. But I think things are altered – and you may have arrived at an opportune moment.'

Irél looked at her in bafflement. 'I do not follow.'

'As I said, it is a story that is long in the telling. First, you may tell your men to dismount and rest. I have some twenty warriors led by Ardgal here with me. They took up positions thinking you were raiders.'

With Irél issuing orders to his men, Fidelma turned and called Ardgal to come forward and as soon as all were settled, she told Irél the story.

Irél turned to Ardgal. 'And your scouts actually saw this encampment on the Hill of the Hag?'

The chieftain nodded. 'They are men who know the country well. There is a camp there which they estimate contains about one hundred and fifty warriors, no more than two hundred. They have women with them but there seems no sign of children.'

'But they were unable to locate Brother Eadulf?'

Ardgal gave a negative gesture with his hand.

Irél sighed. 'It is one of the best defensive places in the area. I explored it once a few years ago. It will be a hard place to make a surprise attack on.'

'With conventional methods, yes,' Fidelma commented.

Irél frowned. 'You have an idea, lady?'

'I was about to explain it to Ardgal's men when you arrived.'

'That is true.' Ardgal smiled briefly. 'We were going to put the idea to a vote. You said something about it being a job for hunters, not warriors.'

'That is true. The element of surprise rests on our enemies' sentinels being stalked and silenced as a hunter will stalk game in the forest – silently, quickly, and striking without mercy.'

'Do you realise what you are saying, lady?' Irél stared at Fidelma. 'You are a woman, a woman of the religious but you are suggesting . . .'

'The women of the Eóghanacht were warriors from the dawn of time,' Fidelma replied sharply. 'My namesake Fidelma Noíchrothach, Fidelma the Nine Times Beautiful, was such a warrior champion. Indeed, aren't you forgetting that Creidne was female champion of the Fianna? Come, let us have no more comments arising from male ego. Let us address ourselves to how we may resolve the problem as efficiently as possible.'

'And that is?' demanded Ardgal, amused at the crestfallen features of the illustrious commander of the Fianna.

'Your men must approach the Hag's Hill in the manner of hunters. The attack must take place in the last moments of darkness before dawn. It is the time when most people are in a deep sleep and do not react so quickly. The attackers must rely on their long bows as if they are hunting game. Long bows and knives. They must pick off the sentinels, silently and accurately, one by one, as they find a path up to the hill. Now we have the Fianna to back us. So once that path is made, the Fianna will come silently up the hill; once on the hilltop they will have the eastern light to help them and may attack openly. As they do so, I with Caol and Gormán will attempt to discover where Eadulf is held and release him.'

'It sounds a simple plan in the telling,' muttered Irél begrudgingly.

'It should be simple in the execution.'

Ardgal was thoughtful. 'I will put it to my men. I think it is a plan that will appeal to them. Our people are hunters and farmers and not warriors. The prospect of overturning warriors with hunters' bows will amuse them.'

Irél snorted disdainfully. 'It is not exactly an honourable way of battle.'

'Is any battle honourable?' snapped Fidelma.

'The plan has its merits,' admitted Irél, flushing. 'As such, I accept it. I do not have to put it to my men, for we are of the Fianna.'

Fidelma repressed a smile at the arrogance of his tone.

'Excellent. If all is well, we will depart from here as soon as possible.'

Eadulf had finally fallen asleep. He had spent hours walking around the inside of their prison while Bishop Luachan lay snoring. It was true what the old man had said. There was only one way into this strange mausoleum and one way out of it. And as there was only room for one man crawling out at a time, there was no hope at all of surprising the two warriors who stood sentinel outside, let alone making an escape, even if the wicker gate was not in the way.

He had sat down and started turning over various plans in his mind, but had to discard each one before he had advanced far into it. It was while he was doing so that he had finally fallen into a sleep of troubled exhaustion.

It was dark and the chill of early morning made Fidelma feel cold and uncomfortable. She was thankful for the knowledge of Ardgal's men, for it appeared that Sliabh na Callaigh encompassed a row of several hills running east to west. Ardgal had told her that the extreme western peak and its close neighbour, the highest peak of all, were where the ancient pagan buildings were situated. His trackers believed that it was around this highest hill that the *dibergach* camp was to be found.

They had approached from the south towards the western side, passing a small lake through woodlands of densely branched trees. They had left their horses tethered in the woods then began to climb upwards. After a short distance, Ardgal had bade her wait with Caol and Gormán while he and his men advanced up the hill to deal with the sentinels. Behind them, the ranks of the Fianna had already halted and stood ready to make their ascent when instructed.

They waited in total silence.

It seemed strange. No sound came to them through the night air, and Fidelma was wondering if her plan was working at all when there came a rustle among the undergrowth and almost before they had time to react, one of Ardgal's men appeared in the shadows.

'We have dealt with all the sentinels on this side, lady,' he whispered. 'The Fianna can move up, but as quietly as possible.'

Irél was already motioning his men forward. Like a silent stream they ascended the hill with Fidelma, Caol and Gormán trailing in their wake.

They paused to regroup at the tree-line that gave access onto the bald peak. Fidelma could see the outline of stone buildings, of campfires, tents and some wooden structures. Then the Fianna were racing forwards; the timing was perfect. The sun was still below the eastern hills, but a thin shaft of light was creeping over the hill. The Fianna were on the sleeping *dibergach* before they knew it.

Pandemonium was suddenly let loose as the sword-wielding warriors clashed with their foes. Ardgal's men were still using their long bows to great effect as some of the sentinels from other sides of the hill began to run forward to engage the Fianna. Screams and roars of pain began to rise from all around.

Eadulf came awake with a start, blinking his eyes. The chamber was in darkness but someone was shaking him fiercely.

'Brother Eadulf, something is happening outside.' It was the voice of Bishop Luachan and he started to shake him again.

'All right! All right!' protested Eadulf. 'I am awake. What is it?' He heard the shouts and cries from outside.

'The camp must be under attack,' said the old bishop.

Immediately, Eadulf was on his knees.

'Quickly, this may be our only opportunity,' he said. 'Let's get down the tunnel and see what is happening. Perhaps the fighting will distract the guards. Follow me and keep close.'

Without waiting for an answer, he was already crawling swiftly on his hands and knees towards the faint grey light of dawn. Outside, through the wicker gate against which he now pressed his face, Eadulf could see only one guard, who seemed to be standing nervously, sword in hand. Eadulf could hear a terrible commotion but saw nothing. The encampment was definitely under attack – but sadly, there was no getting past the guard.

ChAPTER NINETEEN

Out of the corner of her eye, Fidelma saw Ardgal directing his archers against a group of men who looked strangely foreign, more like Saxon warriors than Irish. There were several hand-to-hand combats going on. Together, she and Caol dodged between the fighting groups, making their way towards the wooden buildings and tents. Gormán, on Caol's shouted instruction, was heading for some stone buildings.

Suddenly, a warrior rushed at them, brandishing his sword. Caol had not become commander of the Nasc Niadh, the élite bodyguard of the kings of Cashel, for nothing. He expertly parried the blows and slid his blade quickly under the ribs of the man, who slumped to the ground with a cry of pain and lay moaning in a spreading circle of blood.

Then Caol cried: 'Look out!'

Instinctively, Fidelma dodged aside, feeling the wind against her skin as a blade swung past her. She pivoted on her heel to find herself inches from the distorted face of a woman. The rage and hatred on those awesome features was so intense that she flinched. The sword was upraised again, and she grabbed for the woman's sword wrist and pulled with her full weight. As she did so, Fidelma registered the curious garb of her assailant and the strange symbols that she wore about her neck.

Although she had locked the woman's sword arm in the tight grasp of her two hands, she realised that the woman's left arm was free and that there was a sharp bladed-knife in her hand. Fidelma could not swing round and protect herself. She braced herself for the sharp impact, but it never came.

Instead, she felt the woman's body stiffen against her own and then it became a dead weight. She let go of the wrist and her attacker fell to the ground.

Behind the corpse stood Caol, sword in hand.

Fidelma glanced at him, one look of thanks before the intensity of the continuing combat claimed their attention.

Peering up through the wicker gate that blocked the entrance to the tunnel, Eadulf was still thinking desperately for a way of distracting the guard.

He heard a cry from somewhere and then the guard began to move away from the gate. Even as he saw the legs of the man take a step forward, he saw them buckle as the man fell, measuring his length on the ground outside. He did not question the why or wherefore, but thrust at the wicker gate with all his strength. Surprisingly, it jerked aside with ease and then Eadulf was scrambling out.

The guard lay on the ground, two hunting arrows embedded in his body.

Eadulf turned to help the old bishop out of the passage. They paused but a moment, looking at the noisy conflict that surrounded them. Then Eadulf pointed.

'Let us go down the hill, to the shelter of those trees until we know who is fighting whom.'

Bishop Luachan nodded. With Eadulf's help he limped painfully on his sprained ankle, stumbling a little. As they lurched down the hill, sliding and tripping on the increasingly steep slope, Eadulf began to feel exhilaration that they had made their escape without being observed.

Then, without warning, there came a cry from his elderly companion. At the same time, the old bishop shoved him in the back and Eadulf staggered forward and fell to his knees. Something hissed through the air behind him and he heard a thud as it fell. He was on his feet in a second and peering round. Bishop Luachan was also on his knees with the momentum of the push that he had given Eadulf. A short distance away was the Saxon warrior Beorhtric, and from his stance he had just thrown something at Eadulf, doubtless a knife. Bishop Luachan's action had prevented it from landing in his back.

Eadulf looked quickly round but could not see where it had fallen. He had no weapon with which to defend himself and the tall Saxon warrior had now unsheathed his battle-axe with a grim smile on his features.

'Move, Luachan! Go!' Eadulf shouted to the old man, who was clambering to his feet.

'Yes – hobble off, old one. I will catch up with you later,' sneered Beorhtric in the same language before reverting to his native Saxon. 'But you, Eadulf of Seaxmund's Ham, I shall deal with you *now*.'

Eadulf glanced desperately back up the hill. In the fiery dawn light, he could see the tents and buildings ablaze. Whoever was attacking them had surprised their sentinels and overwhelmed the camp. Beorhtric's comrades were being pressed back, leaving their dead strewn behind them. He saw some even dropping their weapons and holding up their hands in surrender.

'Give it up, Beorhtric! Your people are beaten!' he called, backing away slightly, still looking for some weapon with which to defend himself against the advancing Saxon, who was now making short swinging motions with his axe.

Instead, Beorhtric's features formed into an evil grin. 'Then I will have more pleasure in despatching you to Hel first,' he snarled.

It was all over in seconds.

With a great shout of hate, Beorhtric raised his battle-axe and rushed upon Eadulf, who jumped backwards, missed his footing and fell defence-less before the descending blade. He raised an arm in a futile effort to ward off the blow. But the blow never came. It seemed that Beorhtric had halted, frozen for a moment, with an expression of surprise on his face. He staggered, still holding himself erect and still with the weapon in his hands.

Eadulf rolled out of the way and, as he did so, he noticed something protruding from the Saxon warrior's chest; blood was soaking his tunic.

Then, with some effort, Beorhtric raised his battleaxe once more and gave a hoarse shout of *'Woden!'* before he fell sideways and lifeless on the ground.

A short distance away, Gormán, a long hunter's bow in his hand, stood ready to release a second arrow. Seeing it was unnecessary, he loosened the string, advanced down the hill and stood grinning at Eadulf.

'You should choose your friends more carefully, Brother Eadulf,' he rebuked. He reached forward and helped Eadulf up. The latter glanced down at the dead Saxon warrior before turning to Gormán with a shaky smile of relief and gratitude.

'What has happened?' he asked.

'Well,' Gormán said, 'it would seem that we have defeated these *dibergach.*'

'How did you learn about this place?' Eadulf wanted to know. Then: 'Are Fidelma and Caol with you?'

Gormán made an affirmative gesture. 'Who's this?' he asked, for old Bishop Luachan, panting with the exertion, was now limping slowly over to join them. Eadulf introduced him.

'Excellent,' Gormán smiled. 'They feared you were dead at Delbna Mór.'

'Is my community safe? The raiders did not harm it?' the old man immediately asked.

'It is untouched,' replied the warrior.

'Who is with you?' asked Eadulf wonderingly, as he observed the warriors now rounding up the survivors of the *dibergach*.

'Irél and members of the Fianna have joined Ardgal and some members of the Cinél Cairpre. We made the attack together. It was Fidelma's plan. Come, we'd better find her and Caol.'

There was a quiet over the Hag's Hill now, a curious quiet broken only by cries of pain from those wounded and dying. Dawn had broken over the hills, throwing a threatening red light across the scene. It was almost symbolic as it lit the carnage, but, of course, all it presaged was the bad weather to come. However, the sight that it lit was a bloody one.

Of the attacking force, only six had been killed and seven wounded. Of the raiders, some thirty had been killed and more than forty wounded. The others had surrendered, including most of the women.

After their simple but heartfelt reunion, Eadulf and Fidelma joined Irél in examining the dead. Eadulf realised that he had seen no sign of Cuan among the dead or survivors, and quickly told Fidelma of the man's presence among the *dibergach*.

For a second time they meticulously examined the bodies of the dead, as well as the wounded and the prisoners, but there was no trace of the warrior from Tara.

'A pity,' said Fidelma. 'He must have escaped during the attack.'

They had halted by the body of the tall, black-haired woman whom everyone had called the *ceannard*, the leader.

'Who was she?' asked Fidelma. This woman had nearly taken her life.

'She was apparently a priestess of their cult, but I heard no one call her by her real name,' Eadulf said. 'They addressed her as *ceannard* or leader.'

'I'll have the prisoners questioned,' offered Irél, who had joined them. 'Perhaps one of them will know who she is and can be persuaded to tell us.' He glanced down at the body. 'Strange,' he muttered.

Fidelma looked at him with interest. 'What is strange?'

'For a moment I thought there was something familiar about her face.'

'Now you mention it,' muttered Eadulf, 'I remember thinking the same thing when she was questioning me.'

Irél sighed: 'All faces in death become distorted and perhaps it is because we look on her in death that we see familiarity in it.'

Fidelma made no comment but regarded the dead priestess for a few moments more before turning down the hill to join Caol and Gormán who were standing talking with Bishop Luachan and Ardgal.

A warrior had approached Irél and was talking to him with some animation. The commander of the Fianna called Fidelma back.

'You were asking about Cuan, lady. One of my men recognised him. He and another man escaped. They were riding eastward. A third man was wounded as he tried to go with them. He has given us some interesting information . . . after some persuasion.' Irél smiled without humour.

Fidelma frowned with disapproval but did not comment.

'What information?' Eadulf asked.

'They had already grown tired of riding with these raiders and were planning to leave for Alba, to the kingdom of the Dál Riada on the seaboard of the Gael. The man said that when Cuan joined them he had a heavy plate – that was how he described it – a plate of silver in his saddlebag. He gave it to the woman – the *ceannard* – but when the attack started and he decide to leave with his companions, they stole it back and Cuan took it with him.'

'So they are now heading for the coast?' There was a tone of excitement in Fidelma's voice.

'For the Bóinn River,' confirmed Irél. 'Cuan told them he knew of a ship currently anchored there whose owner, he felt, was the sort who would take them across the Sruth na Maoile for a small consideration.'

'Sruth na Maoile – where's that?' asked Eadulf.

'The strait of water that separates the two Dál Riadas, the one in Éireann and the one in Alba. Apparently, the owner of this ship has no liking for us. He is the one whom Cenn Faelad rebuked in the market a few days ago.'

Eadulf's eyes widened. 'Verbas of Peqini?'

'The same,' confirmed Irél.

It was at noon the next day that Fidelma and Eadulf were part of a group of five riders trotting along the track which approached the banks of the great River Bóinn. They had entered the wooded plain where the Bóinn, flowing from the southern hills northward, encountered the powerful Dubh Abhainn, flowing from the west from the great Loch Rath Mór, the lake of the big fortress. The two rivers joined forces to swing eastwards to the sea north of Tara. The settlement at their juncture was curiously called An Uaimh, the cave. The river here was deep enough for some vessels to move up from the coast to anchor. So the settlement, at this confluence of the rivers, was an excellent spot for traders and merchants to meet. It was also the principal town of the Clann Colmáin, according to Ardgal.

Ardgal had agreed to join Fidelma and Eadulf on the journey back to Tara although Fidelma had made it clear that she must first find the ship of Verbas of Peqini and question Cuan. Bishop Luachan had promised to follow them to Tara as soon as his ankle was attended to. He could not add a great deal more to the facts that they had already garnered about his visit to Sechnussach on the night before the assassination. Bishop Luachan had been adamant that the silver disk that he had discovered with Brother Diomsach would be the key to the discovering of the real *Roth Fáil*, the wheel of destiny, which was so eagerly sought by the *dibergach* and their strange female priestess. He confirmed that the day before Sechnussach's murder, he had placed the silver disk in the hands of the High King. Ardgal could only give evidence of Dubh Duin's character but he was keen to exonerate his clan from being wholehearted supporters of their late chief. However, in any presentation to the Great Assembly, both would be needed as witnesses to what had happened on the Hag's Mountain.

The settlement of An Uaimh was fairly quiet as the five rode in, but they noticed with some satisfaction that there were three large ocean-going ships tied up against the wooden quays. An enquiry made to one man, lounging against bales of sheep's wool destined for transport beyond the seas, brought forth the information that the tall masted black vessel was from Gaul and that it was indeed the ship of the merchant named Verbas of Peqini.

When they started to move towards it, the man called them back.

'If you want to trade with the stranger, he is over at the *bruden* yonder.' He indicated one of the quayside inns.

Fidelma turned to Gormán. 'Take our horses to that other inn,' she instructed, pointing to a building at the opposite end of the quayside. 'Make sure they are watered, rubbed down and rested. Then come and join us.'

'Why not take them with us, lady?' asked Gormán. 'After all, we are going to an inn, aren't we?'

Fidelma smiled wryly. 'That's a sailors' inn. The one back there has stables; this one doesn't.'

Caol did not hide his grin at his comrade's irritation. 'A logical observation,' he said smugly.

As they began to walk away, a cry of pain rang out behind them, loud and clear. Caol, who was leading, halted and caused those behind him to do so as well. He glanced uneasily towards Fidelma and unsheathed his sword.

'That's a child's cry,' Fidelma observed grimly.

The cry came again and before anyone could move, the door of the sailors' inn opened and a small boy darted out; he ran unseeingly towards them, fear on his face. At the last moment, he saw them, tried to avoid them but collided with Brother Eadulf. For a few seconds, the boy struggled and then, seeing the silver crucifix around Eadulf's neck, he stared up with a sudden hope in his eyes. He did not seem to recognise him as Cenn Faelad's companion at the market in Tara.

'Help me!' he cried. 'Please. If you are a priest of the Christian god, protect me.'

Eadulf said gently: 'Of course, boy. There is nothing to fear. I promise.'

The lad almost collapsed in Eadulf's arms.

Just then, the door of the inn burst open again and a tall man of dark appearance lurched out. He was holding a small length of leather in his hand and stared moodily round. Spotting the boy, he began to move forward with an unsteady gait and a grin of triumph. He had clearly been drinking.

Caol halted the man with his sword-point and demanded to know what he was doing.

Eadulf recognised the man immediately.

'It's the merchant,' he said quietly to Fidelma. 'Verbas of Peqini.'

Fidelma regarded the man in disapproval.

Verbas of Peqini looked at the group, and lowered his hand with the flagellate. Swaying, he tried to encompass them in an oily smile and said something in a strange tongue. Meanwhile, Eadulf had been examining the boy's face and arms.

'This child has been badly beaten, Fidelma,' he said.

Verbas seemed to guess what he was saying. He looked at Fidelma and shrugged, then said something more in his own language.

'The child is his slave,' Eadulf volunteered. 'He acts as this man's translator.'

Fidelma had already noticed the metal slave ring around the boy's neck. Her frown deepened.

'What language do you speak?' she asked Verbas, resorting to Latin. 'Do you speak this language?'

The man nodded slowly. 'I speak a little,' he answered, to Eadulf's surprise. When Eadulf had first met Verbas at the market in Tara, it had not occurred to him that he would speak Latin. But, of course, the Roman Empire had spread its tongue throughout the known world as a language of trade and commerce, and not only the language of the conquering legions. Any merchant worth his salt would need to know Latin in order to conduct his business.

'What is happening here? Why are you maltreating that child?' demanded Fidelma.

Verbas frowned. 'Who are you, lady, who asks this? I am not used to women questioning me.'

'I am Fidelma of Cashel, a lawyer and sister to a king,' she said, trying to find the right words to translate her authority.

The man's eyes widened a little. 'You have authority in this land?'

'I have.'

'Then know, lady, this boy is my slave. He has just tried to escape from me: I am legally entitled to capture and chastise him. His life is mine to do with as I will. I have bought it.'

Assíd had now recognised Eadulf and spoke to him. 'Lord, it was said if I managed to escape I would find sanctuary in this land. I escaped and ask sanctuary. The great lord at Tara promised.'

'So he did,' agreed Eadulf in a kindly fashion.

Fidelma, hearing the boy speak, turned to him. 'You speak our language well, child. What is your name?'

'I am Assíd, lady.'

'Assíd? It is an ancient name in our land, from one of the ancestors of those they call the hounds of the sea, a tribe that live in Connacht. Are you of this land?'

'I do not know, lady. I only know that I want to find sanctuary here.'

Eadulf quickly explained what Cenn Faelad had promised, should the boy escape.

She nodded thoughtfully. Meanwhile Verbas, who had not understood this exchange since it was in the language of Éireann, was looking uncomfortable.

'The child is my property, bought fairly,' he repeated in Latin. 'I have a right to punish him for trying to escape me. I now intend to take him back to my ship.'

He moved forward a step but Fidelma snapped: 'You have no rights on this soil save the rights accorded to you under our laws. And under these laws, children have protection and their honour price is the same as that of a bishop until they are of age, which is seventeen years. It is not our custom to enslave anyone unless they have committed a heinous crime, and even then they are not incarcerated but allowed freedom to work for the restitution of their full right to freedom. Further, it seems that this is one of our own and entitled to our protection. The child comes with us.'

Verbas was staring at her sullenly.

Caol had been watching the two men who had left the inn after Verbas. It was obvious that they were crewmen and they started to move forward as if they would help him. Caol made a gesture with his sword, that they should stay back.

'This is an outrage, lady! I shall appeal to your king,' stormed Verbas.

Fidelma smiled faintly. 'Do so,' she replied. 'In the meantime, this child is under our protection and we shall decide his fate under our laws. He has demanded sanctuary. We have granted him that wish. We will consider his entitlement under the law. You may come and argue your case at Tara.'

If looks could kill then Verbas would have slain Fidelma on the spot. He had suddenly sobered up, and his alcohol-dimmed eyes were sharp and vicious.

'I will return to my ship and find out where I might bring a lawyer of your nation to come and argue my case before your king,' he said coldly. 'I did not come to this country to be robbed of my property.'

'We have different ideas of what constitutes property, my friend,' replied Fidelma firmly. 'But since we speak of why you came to our land, Verbas of Peqini, did you come here to forment rebellion against its king?'

The merchant snarled, 'You speak in riddles, woman.'

'I'll speak more plainly then. You are giving passage, I am told, to rebels who have lately been in arms against the legitimate authority of this land. You are sailing with them to Alba, is that not so?'

The answer was clearly written on the man's features.

'There are two ways of proceeding, Verbas of Pequini. The first way is for you to hand over Cuan and his companion, the men you are seeking to transport, so that they may be taken back to Tara for trial. The second way is for my warriors to come on board your ship and take them by force. If the latter, then you will be deemed as guilty as the man Cuan, and your ship may be confiscated in payment of the fines and compensation that will fall due.'

Verbas bit his lip and stood hesitating a moment. Then he shrugged.

'Whatever trouble the men have put themselves in, it is not my business. They came to me and offered money for a passage. In good faith, I accepted it. But if they are fugitives from your justice, I will . . .'

There was a call from along the quayside and they turned to see Gormán struggling with someone. Ardgal ran back to help him. Together, they succeeded in restraining and binding the man's hands before marching back with him to join the group. Gormán was grinning cheerfully. He was also carrying a saddlebag over his arm.

'Our friend Cuan,' he said, gesturing at the subdued and downcast warrior. 'He must have seen you talking with Verbas on the quayside from the ship and decided not to wait around for the result. So he slipped ashore . . . right into my waiting arms. However, his companion seems to have escaped. Luckily, Cuan decided to keep hold of *this*.'

He held out the bag to Fidelma, who immediately looked inside. She was smiling broadly.

'Excellent. I have some questions to ask you, Cuan. You will accompany us back to Tara to answer them.'

Eadulf was staring at the bracelet of silver coins around Cuan's left wrist and an idea suddenly occurred to him. He lifted the wrist to examine the bracelet.

'These appear to be Gaulish coins,' he observed. 'Rather an expensive piece of jewellery, isn't it?'

Cuan scowled at him. 'They are mine,' he grunted.

'Then I will have to ask some questions of my own, Cuan,' Eadulf said quietly and added no more, even though Fidelma was looking quizzically at him.

Verbas of Peqini coughed irritably. 'If that is all, I shall return to my ship and seek advice as to this robbery of my property.'

'You may do so,' Fidelma said nonchalantly.

'I shall remember you, Fidelma of Cashel,' the man added heavily.

'And I hope I will be able to forget you very quickly, Verbas of Peqini,' she replied evenly.

They watched as the merchant turned and rejoined his two equally sullen crewmen before moving along the quayside to board their ship.

Fidelma smiled encouragement at the boy, who was staring at them, still unable to believe that the threat had truly been lifted.

'Are you hurt?' she asked.

'Not much, lady,' he replied with a faint smile. 'Nothing that may not heal.'

'We will have an apothecary examine you as soon as we reach Tara,' she assured him. 'But perhaps we can find a blacksmith first to remove that loathsome metal collar from around your neck.'

There was still plenty of daylight left when, fed and rested, the party mounted their horses and moved downriver, along the west bank of the Bóinn to a place which Ardgal identified as the church of the cairn, where a ferry, a large flat-bottomed raft, plied its trade transporting horses, wagons and people across the broad river. From the landing on the east bank it was only a short ride to the great complex of the palace of Tara.

chapter twenty

Their welcome back was not as warm as Fidelma and Eadulf had expected. When news of their return had reached the Chief Brehon, Barrán, he lost no time in sending for them and was pacing his chamber when they entered.

'Well, what news?' he asked without preamble. 'Have you solved this riddle?'

Fidelma smiled faintly at his obvious anxiety.

'The reason why Dubh Duin killed Sechnussach?' she said as she seated herself without waiting to be asked.

Brehon Barrán looked taken aback. 'What other riddle is there?' he demanded.

'There are many riddles in life, Barrán. There is a boy named Assíd who presents a riddle.'

'I don't follow,' said the Chief Brehon.

'It seems that Assíd was captured and held prisoner by sea-raiders some years ago. He was probably travelling with a group of pilgrims to the Holy Land. His name and tongue indicate that his parents might have been from some Connacht religious group. Such things happen. From my own land there is the story of the Blessed Cathal who studied at Lios Mór. He went on a pilgrimage to the Holy Land some years ago and on the return voyage, his ship was wrecked in the Gulf of Taranto. Now I hear he is considered as a great miracle-worker in that area and renamed Cataldo . . .'

Brehon Barrán made a cutting motion with his hand.

'I fail to see how this story, interesting though it is, relates to the death of the High King!'

'Everything in life relates, one thing to another,' replied Fidelma philosophically. 'This poor mite sought asylum here, the land he came from, from a harsh slave-master who had bought him.'

'You helped the boy escape?' The Chief Brehon said irritably. 'That cannot be. We cannot interfere in the customs of others.'

'The boy escaped by himself,' interposed Eadulf. 'Cenn Faelad had warned his master, Verbas of Pequini, that if the lad escaped and sought sanctuary, he would be granted it.'

'Cenn Faelad wears his heart on his sleeve,' Brehon Barrán muttered. 'I should have been consulted before the law of sanctuary was invoked.'

Fidelma raised an eyebrow. 'Are you saying that the interpretation of the law is wrong in this respect?'

'I would have advised both Cenn Faelad and you, Eadulf, to let well alone,' Barrán said heavily. 'Other peoples have different customs and it does not do well to interfere. Since you have taken action, it is now something that has to be decided by a Brehon. I presume the merchant you mentioned, Verbas of Peqini, will lodge a complaint?'

'He might, but I doubt it,' Fidelma replied with satisfaction. 'And there is no way we can hand one of our own people back into slavery.'

'I would not be so worried over a small boy when you have the matter of the High King's death to consider,' snapped Brehon Barrán.

'Are we not a Christian land?' Fidelma snapped back. 'Is it not said that Christ exhorted us to look after one another, saying: "Inasmuch as you have done it unto one of the least of these, my brethren, you have done it unto Me". Or am I mistaken? I thought the words were written in the Holy Scriptures.'

'Are you seeking to lecture me, Fidelma of Cashel?' Brehon Barrán's face was red.

'Far be it for me to lecture the Chief Brehon on law. Perhaps my own interpretation is at fault. I was merely quoting from the religious writings that we now accept.'

Barrán snorted and then suddenly shrugged as if dismissing the entire matter.

'Well, the boy must remain confined here in the safekeeping of Brother Rogallach until the matter is decided. I have no time to consider the case at the moment so I will give it to the care of my deputy, the Brehon Sedna. The important thing is this question of a report on the causes of the death of Sechnussach. Abbot Colmán told me that before you left Tara, you had said that you would make your report within a week. We cannot allow the matter to drift on for ever! Cenn Faelad needs to be installed formally in office before the five kingdoms fall apart in argument and conflict. The kings and nobles have already begun to arrive for the Great Assembly.'

'I agree that the sooner the matter is resolved, the better for the five kingdoms,' Fidelma conceded. 'However, justice cannot be rushed. As to the exact date I can appear before the Great Assembly, I have a few more enquiries to make. When I have satisfied myself, I will let you and Cenn Faelad know.'

Brehon Barrán sighed impatiently. 'You have spent much time here, Fidelma of Cashel, and you have been allowed a great deal of licence. But time is pressing. Justice *must* be rushed, lest a greater injustice fall upon the people. If you feel that you are unable to resolve the matter, stand aside. We will pronounce it unresolved but state the known facts – that Sechnussach was slain by Dubh Duin who then took his own life; the motive remains unknown.'

Fidelma flushed angrily. 'I have *not* said I am unable to resolve the matter, and will *not* lend my name to any obfuscation of the truth! Understand me, Barrán. I mean to get to the bottom of this murder and demand to be allowed to do so. If you prevent me, I shall speak before the Great Assembly and tell them the reasons why I refuse to be bullied into an arbitrary resolution.'

Brehon Barrán looked for a moment as though he was going to lose his temper. Then he forced a smile to spread across his features as he replied.

'You possess too much of that Eóghanacht temper to be a religious, Fidelma of Cashel. Leave it and devote yourself entirely to the law. You will serve it better.' Then, seeing her eyes harden, he added: 'Very well. You may have one extra day but beyond that, no more time can be allowed. A kingdom without a strong figurehead is no kingdom at all but a place that descends into anarchy and warfare as each group struggles for power. Cenn Faelad must be acknowledged within the next few days.'

Fidelma sniffed angrily. 'I am fully aware of the circumstances. I will return to you as soon as I can.' With that she turned on her heel and, accompanied by a worried-looking Eadulf, left his chambers.

Outside, Eadulf was nervous.

'Dubh Duin assassinated the High King because of his link with the pagan raiders. The evidence is there. Should we not simply accept what

Brehon Barrán has advised – report just that fact? It will surely satisfy the Great Assembly.'

Fidelma shook her head firmly. 'But it will not satisfy *me*, Eadulf. There is evidence that Dubh Duin was connected with this return to the old religion and that can be presented. But I personally believe there is something more to this. I have all the strands in my hands but cannot, as yet, tie them together to make a complete tapestry. But I think I can, given time. Yes, I think I can.'

Night was falling as they walked slowly back to the guesthouse.

It was Brother Rogallach who welcomed them and offered to fill their baths in preparation for the evening ablutions before the main meal of the day. He was apologetic that the female servants had been needed to help at some feast Cenn Faelad was giving that evening for those kings and nobles attending the Great Assembly, who had arrived in their absence. He was, he told them with a smile, fully recovered from his injury and able to attend to their needs. Fidelma allowed Eadulf to bathe first. After the experience of Eadulf's capture and her desperate attempt to rescue him from the Hag's Mountain, she had come to realise just how much she really did care for the Saxon, and to be aware of how ill she had often treated him. She sat for a time, tapping her fingers on the tabletop in an unconscious rhythm, torn between feelings of guilt about Eadulf and irritation with herself, for she knew she was missing some vital clue about the death of Sechnussach.

'Something ails you, lady?' asked Brother Rogallach as he re-entered the room, having left Eadulf to his bath.

Fidelma grinned apologetically. 'I am sorry, I was distracted for a moment. I was trying to solve a riddle.'

The *bollscari* looked eager. 'I am good at riddles.'

'I doubt if you could solve this one,' she replied gravely.

'Try me.'

'Very well, then.' Fidelma chuckled. 'I was wondering what the formula was for a happy marriage.'

Brother Rogallach pulled a face. 'Oh. As you say, it is not a question I give much thought to. I have decided to follow the ways of celibacy which many in our Faith now argue is the best way to be.'

'Quite so,' smiled Fidelma, still grave.

'However . . .'

She looked up as Brother Rogallach paused thoughtfully. 'However?' she prompted.

Brother Rogallach actually blushed. 'Nothing, lady. At least, nothing that is appropriate to your question.'

'Tell me,' pressed Fidelma, intrigued.

'It was a favourite saying of the late High King. I believe it was an epigram from the poet Marcus Martialis.'

'And it was?'

Brother Rogallach looked embarrassed. '*Sit non doctissima conjux.*'

Fidelma snorted. 'May my wife not be very learned? That is not a good attitude towards my sex, Rogallach.'

Brother Rogallach smiled nervously. 'I have to say that Sechnussach utterd it many times recently, after ...' He stopped suddenly. 'I will set about heating more water now, lady.'

He left Fidelma sitting thoughtfully at the table.

'May my wife not be very learned,' she muttered. Then she leaned back and sank into a meditative silence.

CHAPTER TWENTY-ONE

'I think I am beginning to see a light in this matter,' announced Fidelma.

Eadulf pushed away his plate. They were finishing their first meal of the day in the guesthouse.

'So late?' he teased. 'I thought that you usually saw a light almost immediately when you were faced with a conundrum.'

Fidelma pouted at him but in good humour.

'You pay a pretty compliment, Eadulf, but it is unjustified. However, it is true that this matter has been more complicated than many we have encountered. At first, it seemed so easy – we knew the name of the killer and there were witnesses. The killer had committed suicide at the scene. Everything was clear. There were few questions to be asked, for the Great Assembly only needed confirmation of the facts and to learn whether Dubh Duin had had any help. Or so it was thought.'

'Except that the Great Assembly chose to send for you to enquire into the matter,' Eadulf pointed out. 'They did not count on your ability to unravel even the tightest knot.'

Fidelma was without when it came to her abilities.

'I would hope that it would not have been beyond the ability of any competent *dálaigh* to uncover the facts,' she said.

'Uncovering the facts and then piecing them together to make sense are two different arts.'

Fidelma chuckled softly. 'I swear, Eadulf, you are a salve for my ego. However, I am aware of my shortcomings and there are many things I should have done before reaching this point in the investigation. Anyway, it is not too late. Let us go to the *Tech Cormaic* to do something I should have done a long time ago.'

She left the guesthouse followed by Eadulf and walked to the royal house. The guard outside saluted them respectfully.

However Brónach, the chief of the female servants, greeted them with a suspicious look as they entered.

'Can I help you, lady?' she asked, addressing Fidelma.

'You cannot,' Fidelma assured her bluntly. 'We have no need of your services for the time being, thank you.'

For a moment it seemed to Eadulf that the woman would argue against being so peremptorily dismissed. But instead, she just tightened her lips and turned away.

Unperturbed, Fidelma climbed the stairway to the High King's chambers. Eadulf followed, wondering whether she was wise to be so antagonistic to the servant. But he knew that Fidelma never did anything without a purpose.

The royal apartments were unlocked as, indeed, they had been left empty. Cenn Faelad would only move into them after he had been formally inaugurated – and that would not be before Fidelma had delivered her findings to the Great Assembly.

She motioned Eadulf to close the door behind them and went to the side of the bed. It was now merely the bare bedframe made of yew. Everything else had been stripped. Eadulf stood with his back against the door watching her as she bent down and then looked around the room.

Eventually she straightened and walked over to the small *erdam*, the side room, in which, she had been told, the High King stored his clothes.

She opened the door and said to Eadulf, 'I'm going to need your help.'

'Why? What are we to do?' he asked, joining her.

'I made only a cursory examination of this room before, but now we must look for another exit to this room.'

'Another exit? I thought none could exist?'

'I am convinced that there was a witness in this side room when Dubh Duin cut the throat of Sechnussach.'

Eadulf frowned but he nodded. 'The mysterious scream in spite of the cut throat?'

'Exactly so.' She was pleased that he had caught the point. 'Now,' she glanced about, 'at least we know that there is only one wall in which any concealed door might be – unless it be a trapdoor leading down or up, and I would be surprised if that was possible.'

Eadulf regarded the wall on which there was a rack of pegs for hanging clothes fixed to the red yew panelling. His keen eyes ran over the wood and their joints and an idea came to him. He went to the rack and began to tug and twist at each peg in turn while Fidelma watched him curiously.

'When I was in Rome I saw a device which opened a secret door,' he explained to her, as he tackled the pegs. It was the middle one, turned to the side and pushed, which clicked a mechanism. One of the wall panels gave a little, and swung inwards.

'Well done!' Fidelma smiled triumphantly, moving forward to push the panel open. 'It looks like a narrow space and it leads downwards. We'll need a lamp.'

'I saw one in the bedchamber.' Eadulf went to fetch it, then had to spend some time igniting it with the flint and tinderbox he always carried in his *marsupium* at his belt. Fidelma was hardly able to restrain her impatience but with the lamp alight, she insisted on going first. They stepped through into a recess between the wall of this chamber and the wall of the adjoining one. Fidelma had paused to ensure there was no similar doorway immediately opposite. There was none; the small landing led onto a narrow and steep set of steps that led down to the lower floor. At the bottom, on the left-hand side, was a catch and hinges that showed the means of exit from the hidden passage.

Fidelma paused and said to Eadulf, who was directly behind her, for there was scarcely room to turn back: 'Let's see where this emerges.'

She reached forward to the mechanism that lay in a recess, and as she did so, her hand touched something cold and sharp. Holding the lamp closer, she reached in and withdrew the object.

'Well, well. I was not looking for this, but it confirms what I suspect.' She turned and showed the object to Eadulf.

It was a knife of the sort used in kitchens to cut meat. It had a thin, sharp blade which was now stained and a little rusty.

'Blood?' asked Eadulf laconically.

'Remember that Torpach the cook was moaning about a missing knife?' Fidelma said.

'But we already have the assassin's knife.'

Fidelma smiled softly. 'So we do, so we do,' she said as she carefully put the knife in her *marsupium* and then turned again to the recess. She fumbled and clicked the lever that obviously undid the mechanism.

The panel swung inward a fraction.

Fidelma had to move back up the step to allow it to swing inwards, so narrow was the space.

They emerged into a large but darkened room. Only the light from the lamp illuminated it. There were boxes stacked on one side and shelves containing all manner of linen and household items.

'A storeroom?' suggested Eadulf.

Fidelma nodded and turned back to the panel. 'I presume that this must operate two ways?'

There were a series of pegs to one side, a few with garments hanging on them. Eadulf checked them one by one. It was the same system as in the room above. The central peg turned and then clicked a mechanism. The secret door could, indeed, have been operated from either position – in the side room of the High King's chamber or here, from this storeroom.

Fidelma sighed softly. 'Well, there is not much else to learn here.' She gave a final glance round and moved towards the main door.

Opening it, they emerged into the main corridor of the lower part of the *Tech Cormaic.* As they did so, they heard a gasp. Brónach, her arms full of linen, was walking down the corridor.

'I thought you were above the stair!' gasped the woman. 'What are you doing in there?'

Fidelma ignored the question and asked one of her own. 'What is this room used for?' she demanded.

'Used for?' echoed Brónach. 'Why, you must have seen for yourself. It is used as storage – for bedlinen and old clothes and the like.'

'I see. Who usually has access to it?'

The head of the female servants gestured with her hand. 'Why, lady, the door is unlocked. Anyone can enter or exit freely of their own will.'

'Anyone? So is one particular person in charge of it?'

'I am the senior female servant. It is we, not the men, who are in charge of the household chores, therefore we control the linen.'

'Are you saying that you, Báine and Cnucha use this room more than anyone else?'

'Just so.'

'And it serves no other purpose than storing the bedlinen and old clothes?'

'What other purpose could a storeroom serve?'

'An interesting question,' replied Fidelma dryly. 'Tell me again, Brónach, where is your room?'

The woman scowled. 'On the floor above this one.'

'I see. I thought some of the maids slept on this level?'

'They do. Down the corridor.'

'And who are *they*?'

'Báine and Cnucha, of course.'

'They are both young,' observed Fidelma as if the thought had just occurred to her.

'Too young,' confirmed the woman. 'They have no conception of what it means to attend to the needs of a High King.'

'Yet they have worked here for some time?'

'If two or three years are long.' Brónach sniffed deprecatingly. 'I myself have been in service to this house for nine years. Apart from me, Báine has been here longest but she has ideas above her station. She claims to be the daughter of an *ollamh*, a learned man with an honour price of twenty *seds*. If this is so, why is she in service, and no more in rank than a *saer-fuidhir* – a servant? Her mind has been turned by— I mean, the lady Muirgel seems to have befriended her. That is not good. It gives food to her ideas of grandeur. She thinks that we, her fellows in service, are not good enough for her.'

'And Cnucha?' asked Fidelma.

'She is a poor thing, scuttling about, hardly dares say boo to a goose. She will not rise to be a trusted servant. The girl has been here three years, but she still has to be chased and told what she should do.'

Fidelma glanced along the corridor. 'And their rooms are at the end, along here?'

'They are.'

Fidelma nodded thoughtfully and thanked the woman before moving off towards the hall with Eadulf following.

'It doesn't help us, does it?' he asked softly.

'What . . . ?' She seemed distracted for a moment. 'Oh, you mean because anyone could have entered the storeroom and used the secret door if they knew how?'

'Just so. But there is one thing I have learned.'

'Which is?'

'That if there was a conspiracy to kill Sechnussach, the conspiracy could not have been so close to him, because they would have surely known about the secret passage and stair to his chamber. That would have been a perfect route to kill him and none the wiser.'

Fidelma paused in mid-stride and regarded him thoughtfully for a moment.

'Could it be that the passage is a secret that Sechnussach did not share with others?'

'Surely such a thing could not be completely hidden from the house-hold?'

'Had Brónach known, I think she would have guessed why we were no longer on the floor above and commented on it,' pointed out Fidelma. 'Nevertheless, it is worth pursuing. Let's go and find Brother Rogallach. If anyone knows about it, he would.'

They found Brother Rogallach in the library room checking an inventory. He looked up and smiled a greeting as they entered.

'Do I know about the history of the building of *Tech Cormaic*?' he replied to the question. 'Well, I am in charge of running the household and there is nothing that I do not know about it. I was *bollscari*, the house steward, to Sechnussach's father Blathmac and to his brother Diarmait when they were joint High Kings. I rode with them in the royal procession when they came to Tara over twelve years ago. It was an epoch in our history. They were just and kindly kings who, alas, fell victim to the dreadful Yellow Plague. Their deaths, for me, ended a golden age that is now sung of in ancient sagas.'

There was no doubt that Brother Rogallach was proud of his role.

'But what of the house, rather than the household?' pressed Eadulf.

Brother Rogallach shrugged as if dismissing the subject. 'As its name suggests, the great King Cormac, the son of Art, first built it. A magnificent structure.'

'You are know all the rooms?'

'Of course.'

'Are there any odd rooms?'

'Odd rooms?' He was puzzled.

'Secret rooms, passages, stairways, anything of that sort?' asked Fidelma.

Brother Rogallach chuckled. 'What need of secret rooms and passages in the house of the noble High Kings, lady?'

'So you've never encountered a secret passage?'

'Never. And I would know,' he added confidently.

'Of course you would,' smiled Fidelma. 'Thank you for your time.'

Outside, Eadulf turned a doleful expression to Fidelma. 'If Rogallach did not know . . .'

A look of satisfaction on her face, Fidelma began to say: 'I think I know how—'

'Lady!'

They turned together as Irél, the commander of the Fianna, approached and greeted them enthusiastically.

'I arrived back this morning. The prisoners we took from the raiders' encampment will be here soon. The wounded are being attended to at Ceananas and at Delbna Mór. A most satisfactory conclusion to this attempted rebellion. I thought I would report back to Cenn Faelad.'

The commander of the Fianna seemed pleased with himself.

'So peace has returned to Midhe?' Eadulf said.

Irél answered affirmatively. Then: 'I saw Ardgal, as I was entering Tara. He told me that you had caught up with Cuan, trying to escape to Alba. I look forward to my next meeting with him. He is the first deserter from the Fianna in many a year.'

Fidelma shook her head. 'That meeting will have to be deferred until after I have presented certain facts to the Great Assembly,' she said.

'About Sechnussach's death? So Cuan was involved?'

'I can say that much, at least.'

'Then I can wait,' Irél assured her. 'You have questioned him as you wanted?'

'I have.'

Irél paused and then added: 'There was a merchant from An Uaimh that I met on the way here. He gave me news about that foreigner, Verbas of Peqini.'

Fidelma was interested. 'What about him?'

'Apparently, he has sailed. The merchant consulted a local Brehon about his rights to get back his slave and the Brehon was so outraged to hear that Verbas felt he could own a child that he boxed his ears and told him the sooner he left our country, the better.'

Fidelma chuckled. 'Excellent. So he has left these shores. Let us hope that he decides to stay away from them in the future.'

'Oh, and Bishop Luachan and Brother Céin have arrived by wagon. His ankle is improving but, rather than wait, he felt his place should be here in Tara at this time.' Irél raised a hand, half in salute, as he turned away to continue on his way.

'What now?' asked Eadulf.

'Now I think that we can go to Cenn Faelad and Brehon Barrán. I have had enough of Tara and its intrigues. It is time we returned to the peace of Cashel and to our little Alchú. At this rate, our poor child will not know us. We barely spend any time at all with him.'

Eadulf grimaced but wisely said nothing.

They found the heir-elect with his Chief Brehon in the house of Abbot Colmán in the royal enclosure; the abbot had apparently been discussing some documents with them.

Cenn Faelad seemed relieved to see them.

'You have come at an appropriate moment. We have been discussing this matter of your report. All the members, or their representatives, of the Great Assembly are now in Tara. Brehon Barrán insists that we must bring matters to a conclusion by the end of today. We have run out of time.'

Behind him Brehon Barrán stood with a stern face.

'I warned you yesterday, Fidelma, that I could give you only a day more. By sundown tonight, that extra day is ended. I can do no more.'

Abbot Colmán was looking unhappy. Fidelma kept her gaze on Cenn Faelad.

'I will not protest,' she said demurely. 'In fact, I was seeking you out to say that it would be agreeable to me if you called the Great Assembly together tomorrow at an appropriate hour. I will then present my report and seek their pardon for taking so long in this matter.'

Cenn Faelad exchanged a glance of surprise with the others before turning back to her.

'So you have come to the end of your investigation?'

'I think I can present facts that will lead the Great Assembly to form a satisfactory conclusion as to the matter,' she replied pointedly.

'And what is that?' demanded Brehon Barrán.

Cenn Faelad looked surprised at this intervention, but before he could speak, Fidelma said disapprovingly: 'As Chief Brehon, you should know better than to ask the outcome of a report before it is presented for approval to the Great Assembly.'

Barrán flushed. 'It was but a natural curiosity,' he muttered. 'But it is good. As soon as the Great Assembly has met we can proceed with the inauguration of the High King and resume the business of governing the five kingdoms once again. We have been too long without power.'

Fidelma still regarded him in disapproval. 'Without power? Do we not boast that in this land, power resides with the people? Is it not an ancient saying – what makes a people stronger than a king? The answer being, because the people ordain the king, the king does not ordain the people.'

Cenn Faelad laughed jovially. 'The saying is true and you are right in law, as always, Fidelma. Barrán was using an expression, that's all. Nevertheless, he has been nervous that the lack of a strong centre could cause the individual parts of the five kingdoms to crumble and dissolve. So your news is good. I will issue the call for the Great Assembly to be convoked tomorrow.'

On the way back to the guesthouse, Eadulf was still perplexed.

'On the surface, the motivation seems straightforward,' he said. 'Dubh Duin was part of the fanatical pagan movement – but surely he must have known the law of succession, that the death of the High King would not advance his cause unless the successor was a supporter of that cause?'

Fidelma smiled appreciatively. 'You are perceptive, Eadulf.'

Eadulf frowned. 'I don't see . . .'

'Well, to be honest, neither did I see the real solution until Brother Rogallach repeated a favourite saying of Sechnussach last night.'

'A favourite saying . . . ?'

'*Sit non doctissima conjux.*' And at her husband's blank look, she took him by the arm. 'Come, I'll explain it all to you in preparation for what we must do tomorrow,' she said confidently.

ChAPTER TWENTY-TWO

It was noon when the nobles of the *Airlechas*, the Great Assembly, began to gather in the *Forradh* or royal seat to the east of the High King's residence rather than at the Rath of Great Assembly to the north of the royal enclosure. The *Airlechas* consisted of three groups: the first was the nobles representing the five kingdoms; if the kings were unable to attend, then their heir apparent came in their stead. Indeed, Fidelma had already seen the arrival of her cousin, Finguine mac Cathail, her brother's heir or *tánaiste*. The second group consisted of the leading Brehons, or judges, of the five kingdoms; and the third group were the leading churchmen, among whom was Abbot Ségdae of Imleach, the senior churchman of the southern kingdoms, and his rival, Ségéne, the abbot and bishop of Ard Macha, who claimed ecclesiastical seniority over the northern kingdoms.

The *Forradh* seemed packed with the great and the good and they sat in noisy rows in the large wooden hall.

Fidelma and Eadulf had taken their seats in the well of the hall. Two chairs had been placed there for them, behind which Caol and Gormán stood. When Fidelma emerged to accompany Eadulf to the *Forradh*, his eyes widened at the metamorphosis that had taken place. She had discarded the simple and practical garb that she usually wore as a member of the religious and had put on clothes that proclaimed her as the daughter, and the sister, of a King of Muman.

She had chosen a gown of deep blue satin with intricate gold thread patterning. It fitted snugly into the waist but then flowed out into a full skirt, which came to her ankles. The sleeves were of a style called *lamfhoss*, tight on the upper arms but spilling out just below the elbow and around the wrists in imitation of the lower part of the dress. Over this was a sleeveless tunic, called an *inar*, that covered the top of the dress but ended at the waist. From her shoulders hung a short *lummon*, a cape of contrasting, red-coloured satin edged with badger's fur. The cape was fastened on the left shoulder by a round brooch of silver and semi-precious stones. On her feet were specially decorated sandals, sewn with pieces of multi-coloured glass, and called *mael-assa*.

Around her wrists were bracelets of complementary-coloured glass, and at her neck was a simple golden torc, indicating not only her royal position but that she was of the élite Nasc Niadh of Muman. Around her fiery red hair was a band of silver with three semi-precious stones at the front – two emeralds from the country of the Corco Duibhne and a fiery red stone which Eadulf could not place – these reflected the stones used in the silver brooch that held her cape. This headband served to keep in place a piece of silk that covered her hair but left her face bare. It was called a *conniul* and indicated her married status, for it was the custom of married women and also of the female religious to cover their heads to show their status. Had not Paul instructed the Corinthians that a woman who did not have her hair covered when she prayed might as well have her hair cut off?

Eadulf had not seen Fidelma dressed in such finery since their official wedding day.

'Perhaps I should have borrowed warrior's clothing from Gormán,' he greeted her with dry humour.

'Don't be silly,' she retorted. 'We go to stand before the High King elect of the five kingdoms; and the kings and nobles of the five kingdoms gathered in the Great Assembly. In such a formal meeting there is a protocol in dress that is prescribed by law.'

'I should have known that the Brehons even have rules on dress. But it makes me seem a poor peasant by comparison,' he replied dolefully, glancing down at himself. He had put on his best clothes, but his simple garments were rough and homespun by contrast with hers.

'Just remember that you are Eadulf of Seaxmund's Ham,' Fidelma admonished firmly. 'And my husband.'

He had difficulty remembering it when they entered the hall of the Great Assembly. If there was one thing he had learned about the noble and wealthy classes of the people of Éireann, it was that they loved to dress up in bright colours and jewellery – and both males as well as females would add to it by putting on cosmetics – berry juice to brighten the lips or darken the eyebrows or enhance the blush of the cheek. He disapproved of it and was pleased to see that Fidelma had used red berry juice on her lips sparingly and added only a thin line to highlight her eyebrows. As he glanced round at the gathering, he realised that his fears were correct. It was not Fidelma who stood out in her choice of clothing but his plain and simple garments that drew the eye.

Around the hall, members of the Fianna stood sentinel and Irél himself commanded a detachment of warriors who formed up behind a row of empty benches at one side of the hall. These had been reserved for the witnesses that Fidelma, through Brehon Barrán, had instructed to attend the hearing; they were now awaiting the summons to enter.

Usually, at the Great Assembly meetings the positions of honour went to the High King and his Chief Brehon. As Cenn Faelad entered with Brehon Barrán and made towards these seats, the dour-faced Congal Cendfota of the Dál Fiatach of Ulaidh sprang up, raising his voice in objection. He shouted to make himself overheard above the hubbub. This caused even greater pandemonium. Finally, Cenn Faelad brought the place to order.

'We will only proceed when there is quiet among us,' he bellowed.

The noise died into a muttering and a shuffling of feet.

'Now, Congal Cendfota, why do you object to Brehon Barrán and I taking our seats to conduct the affairs of this Great Assembly?' demanded Cenn Faelad.

The burly northern noble still stood in his place.

'This Great Assembly made a decision at its last meeting – that there were potential conflicts in the Uí Néill about the investigation of the matter of Sechnussach's assassination. He was an Uí Néill and his assassin was an Uí Néill. The person that gains from his assassination is an Uí Néill. The Chief Brehon, overseeing such an investigation, is an Uí Néill. So it was decided that the Chief Brehon should not conduct the investigation. It was also decided that you, Cenn Faelad, while *tánaiste* to your brother, Sechnussach, should not be inaugurated until the investigation was concluded.'

Cenn Faelad grimaced impatiently. 'And this is exactly why we now meet, Congal Cendfota! As this Great Assembly instructed, Fidelma of Cashel – an Eóghanacht – came to investigate and is about to make her report. What is your objection?'

Congal Cendfota waited until the muttering subsided again. He pointed to the chairs of office in which Cenn Faelad and Brehon Barrán were about to be seated.

'Until that report and its conclusions are confirmed by this Assembly, I contend that neither you nor Brehon Barrán can have a say in conducting this meeting. It would be unseemly and implies a foregone conclusion.'

There were many who voiced their agreement with this argument and, indeed, Fidelma looked across at Eadulf and nodded approvingly.

'It seems a logical point of procedure,' she whispered, 'although slightly pedantic.'

Cenn Faelad held a whispered exchange with Barrán.

'Very well,' he said. 'We will sit in the Great Assembly only as observers. But who will conduct the proceedings?'

'Fianamail of Laigin,' proposed one of the Laigin churchmen.

This immediately brought protest from one of the Ulaidh nobles.

'If Fianamail of Laigin presides over this Great Assembly on behalf of the High King, then it would be tantamount to approving Laigin as next in line to the High Kingship!'

'Then I propose Diarmait, chieftain of Uisnech!' cried another voice.

'He is just another Uí Néill,' called a chieftain from Connacht.

Again, a hubbub broke out.

Then Ségéne of Ard Macha rose and walked across the chamber to where Ségdae of Imleach was seated. Ségdae rose to greet him and both men held a hurried conversation. They turned to face the Great Assembly.

'My brother in Christ and I have a proposal,' Abbot Ségéne announced, silencing the noise of speculation. 'The matter of delivering the report should be a relatively simple affair. We believe that the steward and spiritual adviser to this Great Assembly, Abbot Colmán, should control the proceedings, acting with the advice of Sedna, the deputy Chief Brehon. Neither is an Uí Néill and both have the authority of their office. Let anyone who has any objection to this, state that objection.'

There was a silence and then a murmuring of approval arose.

Cenn Faelad, with some relief, said: 'Then it seems we are agreed. We will sit here as observers. Come forward, Colmán, come forward, Sedna, so that we may proceed.'

Abbot Colmán and Brehon Sedna came forward to take their seats and an expectant hush fell on the assembly.

Abbot Colmán glanced at his companion and then turned to face the Great Assembly.

'There is little need to preamble these proceedings. For reasons we are all aware of, the Great Assembly decided that the matter of the assassination of our High King, Sechnussach, by Dubh Duin, chieftain of the Cinél Cairpre, should be investigated by an unbiased *dálaigh* – Fidelma of the Eóghanacht, Fidelma of Cashel. She was asked to investigate the motives and discover whether anyone other than Dubh Duin was involved in this matter.' He paused and looked to where Fidelma was seated. 'Fidelma of Cashel, are you prepared to present the results of such an investigation?'

Fidelma rose and cleared her throat. 'I am. In corroboration of my report, I have called on certain witnesses to stand ready to confirm or deny my contentions. I would ask the leniency of this Great Assembly to bring them into this hall to sit among us so that they respond to the arguments that I shall place before you.'

Abbot Colmán turned to Brehon Sedna and they held a hurried and whispered exchange. It was Brehon Sedna who spoke next.

'There is a legal objection to your request, Fidelma of Cashel.' He spoke in sharp, incisive tones. 'It must be made clear that this is not a court in which the guilty can be prosecuted. If it is found that anyone else has acted in collusion with the assassin, then this Great Assembly cannot make judgement. The procedure as laid down in the *Cóic Conara Fugill*, the Five Paths of Judgement, must be followed. Today is simply a hearing of your report . . .'

Fidelma inclined her head towards him. 'I would like to plead a precedent for bringing the witnesses here . . .'

'A precedent?' snapped Brehon Sedna. 'Surely the assassination of the High King has no precedent?'

Fidelma smiled softly. 'I would respectfully refer the learned Brehon to the scribes who record that the High King Muirchertach, son of Erc, was drowned in a vat full of wine at his house at Cleiteach on Ucht Cleitig by the banks of the Bóinn. It is true this took place many generations ago. Indeed, so we are told, it happened in the very year of the death of the Blessed Ailbe of Imleach, who brought the Christian teaching to our poor kingdom of Muman.'

Brehon Sedna flushed, turning to one of the scribes whose task it was to record the decisions of the Great Assembly and was learned in its protocols and history. He beckoned the man forward and there was a whispered exchange between them. Brehon Sedna turned with a surprised look to Fidelma.

'May I congratulate you on your knowledge,' he said. 'I am reminded that a woman named Sín was considered the culprit in the death of the High King Muirchertach which happened as you have said.'

Fidelma was not triumphant at making the point.

'You will find that, according to the records, it was a strange death. His house was set on fire and the High King climbed into a vat of wine to escape the flames. The ridgepole of the house, having been burned away, fell on the High King's head, knocking him unconscious, so that he fell back into the vat and drowned. This Great Assembly held a hearing and witnesses were brought to sit before it to hear the report presented by the Brehon appointed to investigate. That is the precedent that I argue.'

Brehon Sedna turned back to the scribe who nodded rapidly in agreement with her summary.

'We will accept the precedent and allow your witnesses to sit in the Great Assembly to hear your report.'

There was a silence while Irél led in Gormflaith and her daughter Muirgel, which caused a great deal of outspoken surprise among the Assembly. They were shown to empty benches guarded by members of the Fianna. Then came the warriors Lugna, Erc and Cuan, the latter closely guarded. All the servants of the High King's household, Brother Rogallach, Torpach, Brónach, Báine, Cnucha, Maoláin and Duirnín followed. Bishop Luachan, still limping, and his steward Brother Céin came next. Finally, Iceadh the apothecary entered and took his place. Brehon Sedna waited until they were all seated before addressing Fidelma.

'This procedure now brings forward a second point of law. Abbot Colmán must surely take his place with the witnesses and be excluded from sitting here.'

Abbot Colmán looked at his companion in surprise at the contention but Fidelma raised her hands to still the murmuring that broke out.

'Not so, Brehon Sedna. The abbot is not a witness to the events as I shall state them. He merely took charge of the royal household until the return of Cenn Faelad and Brehon Barrán. There was no reason for him to be excluded from conducting this meaning.'

Brehon Sedna looked as relieved as the abbot.

'Then if this procedure is acceptable to the Great Assembly . . . ?'

Everyone signified their agreement perhaps somewhat impatiently and several called out that the report be proceeded with.

'So, having clarified procedure, you may continue,' Brehon Sedna summed up, addressing Fidelma.

Fidelma paused, as if gathering her thoughts. Then she began her speech.

'All murder is heinous. The assassination of a High King is especially so. One fact has been absolutely clear from the start. Dubh Duin, the chieftain of the Cinél Cairpre, entered the bedchamber of the High King, cut his throat and then turned his knife on himself when he realised that there was no escape from capture. There is no disputing this fact.

'We initially had two main questions to ask. One: did Dubh Duin act alone? And two: what was his motive?'

She let her gaze sweep the Assembly as if seeking an answer there. It was a piece of drama that Eadulf had witnessed several times before when Fidelma was arguing before the *airechtaí* or courts.

'You may be assured that Dubh Duin did not act alone,' she went on confidently. 'This was no spur-of-the-moment killing, nor was it a matter of one person acting alone for reasons of personal hate. Indeed, there was a conspiracy to kill Sechnussach.'

A wave of outrage swept the hall and she allowed it to swell and ebb before she spoke again.

'As for the motive, at this stage I will firstly tell you what Dubh Duin's own motive was. I fear it was not the same motive of all those in the conspiracy. Dubh Duin was a traditionalist. He believed in the old ways and customs. Moreover, he believed in the Old Faith. Those in this Great Assembly already know how he argued here for the recognition of the rights of those who still held to their veneration of the old gods and goddesses. Some may recall his dispute on the matter with Sechnussach?'

There were many who were nodding, recalling the debate. Only Gormflaith among the witnesses seemed to shake her head in disbelief.

'Dubh Duin was fully committed to the Old Faith as we are to the New Faith,' Fidelma continued. 'Ardgal, now chief of the Cinél Cairpre, will testify to this. There is no need for me to tell you that scarcely two centuries have passed since the great teachers Patrick, Ailbe, Brigit, Brendan, Ciaran and the others, brought the word of Christ to this land. There are still areas which that word has not reached or where it is not accepted. Even within a day's ride of Tara, there are still many who gather at Uisnech, which the ancients regarded as the navel of the world, the centre of the five kingdoms, to practise the old rites.

'Further, there is no need for me to tell you that there is a movement abroad intent on overthrowing the new teachings and returning this land to the old ways.'

Abbot Colmán bent forward quickly. 'And are you claiming that Dubh Duin was part of this?'

'I am.'

'It can't be true!' cried Gormflaith, her strident tone startling everyone.

Fidelma looked at her sadly. 'I am afraid it can be, and it is,' she replied, before turning back to the Assembly. 'We know that there are pagan raiders, the *dibergach*, who have been attacking the abbeys and churches. They started by attacking small, isolated churches and communities, but those attacks are increasing. Many members of the religious have been killed.'

A member of the Great Assembly stood up and signalled that he wished to ask a question.

'I am sworn to the New Faith and have no advocacy for the old. But I must point out that the faith of our ancient fathers did not advocate violence and death as a way of life. Our fathers believed in the peace and oneness of this world. This was the teaching of our Druids. Why would they be raiding and killing in the name of the old gods and goddesses? It seems illogical.'

Fidelma acknowledged the man's statement, for it was hardly a question.

'There has been one sect among our forefathers which *did* advocate death and sacrifice,' she said. 'It was an aberration quickly dealt with by the Druids. It is claimed that during the days of Tigernmas, the twenty-sixth High King, dementia overtook him and he set up a great idol on Magh Slecht, the Plain of Slaughter, and demanded that people sacrifice to it. So much bloodshed was caused that finally the Druids rose up and destroyed both the idol and Tigernmas. The idol was called Crom Cróich.'

'So what are you saying?' demanded Brehon Sedna. 'That this idol worship has been reborn?'

'The sect that has arisen to attempt to overthrow the New Faith is dedicated to the worship of Crom Cróich,' she confirmed.

'How do you come to this conclusion?'

'We have witnesses to that fact, and Irél and Ardgal have led their warriors in the overthrow of these fanatics who were encamped at a place called the Hag's Mountain not even a day's ride from here. You need no longer fear them. But how does it fit in with the assassination of the High King? I will tell you. Firstly, when coming to Tara, while we were crossing the Plain of Nuada, we came on a destroyed church and members of the religious that had been slaughtered. But one was just alive. Brother Eadulf bent and heard his last word. Brother Eadulf thought he whispered something about blame.

'And when Dubh Duin lay dying by the High King's bed he too whispered something. Lugna, who caught the last words, also thought he said something about blame.'

'What is unusual about that?' Abbot Colmán wanted to know.

'Both Eadulf and Lugna misheard the word. The word was not *cron*, blame, but *Crom* – Crom Cróich. The religious was identifying the attackers just as Dubh Duin was calling on the idol that he thought was a god. This much we can now prove. We should have been alerted by this fact earlier.'

'Accepting this then, you say that Dubh Duin believed that Sechnussach's death would help him in his quest to bring back this evil worship. But how?' Brehon Sedna asked. 'I do not understand it.'

'Because he had been led to believe that the successor would return the five kingdoms to such worship,' Fidelma answered simply.

At once Cenn Faelad leaped to his feet, his face angry. 'This is a lie! As the holy cross is my banner and witness, I would not do such a thing!'

Fidelma held up a hand to quench the tumult that had broken out. 'I did not say it was you, Cenn Faelad,' she rebuked mildly.

'You said Sechnussach's successor.' Cenn Faelad was not mollified. 'I am the *tánaiste*, the heir apparent. Who else would you mean?'

'Your succession was not going to last long,' she replied starkly. 'The plot, in essence, was simple but its mechanics were complicated. Indeed, in all the cases that I have been involved in, this one has shocked me by the depth of intrigue and the convolution of its workings.'

Taken aback, Cenn Faelad sat down abruptly.

'This case has many layers of culpability,' Fidelma said. 'I will beg the forgiveness of this Great Assembly for taking them on a long journey through these layers of intrigue. The simplest layer was Dubh Duin, who was part of this sect devoted to bringing back the worship of Crom. Very well. Dubh Duin had tried to get some recognition for the Old Faith in this Great Assembly. When that failed, he turned to other methods. He was supported by the bands of brigands raiding the Christian centres. They were fanatics. But it was like the pricking of pins on a great bear. It did not even harm the body. So there had to be another way.

'Dubh Duin did not dream up the plot himself. Who persuaded him that the way forward lay in the assassination of Sechnussach? Someone in the royal household? There was one fanatic already who served in the royal enclosure . . .'

'Cuan!' declared Lugna loudly. 'Because he acted as the decoy that took me from my post at the doorway of the royal house that night.'

Surprisingly, Fidelma shook her head.

'Not Cuan. He did not have the intelligence to think out this complicated plot. He was subverted later, and was ambivalent about religious beliefs anyway.'

'So how was he subverted? By what means?' demanded Brehon Sedna.

'By means of sexual favours,' Fidelma said. 'His recruitment to the scheme was later on in the advancement of the plot after it had been thought out.'

Gormflaith suddenly stood up. 'I wish to make a statement to the Great Assembly,' she said.

Faces turned expectantly towards her.

Brehon Sedna glanced at Fidelma.

'I have no objection,' she said.

'You will doubtless hear from Fidelma that Dubh Duin was my lover,' declared Gormflaith. 'I shall not deny it . . .'

Once more they had to wait until the tumult died down.

'. . . But I deny that I was part of this so-called plot. I am a Christian. Dubh Duin never ever spoke to me, either of his faith or his lack of it. We did not discuss religion. Nor did Dubh Duin kill my husband to gain favour with me. I can present evidence that Sechnussach and I were estranged for three years from the royal servants, but I also *can* present a witness that I had agreed a divorce with Sechnussach and it was to be sealed on the day after I was due to return from Cluain Ioraird. But by then . . .' She shrugged. 'That witness is Brehon Barrán.'

Fidelma saw that Brehon Barrán was shaking his head, and she turned back to Gormflaith with a sad smile.

'I am afraid that the Chief Brehon will not be your witness to this matter of the divorce agreement,' she said softly.

'Dubh Duin had no reason to kill Sechnussach on my account,' Gormflaith repeated stubbornly. 'We were going to be married and leave Tara.'

In the shocked silence that followed, as Gormflaith reseated herself, Fidelma spoke clearly.

'Regretfully, lady, Dubh Duin had no intention of marrying you. You were merely a means by which he could reach Sechnussach. As your lover, he could gain access to the royal enclosure almost at will, as the warrior Erc will state. Dubh Duin's purpose was always the slaughter of Sechnussach. You were misled, lady, an innocent victim of the conspiracy.'

Abbot Colmán cleared his throat. 'But it has been pointed out that even with Sechnussach dead, Cenn Faelad would have succeeded. Cenn Faelad is known for his Christian piety and largesse to the Church. As he has already stated, he would not tolerate a return to idolatry and he has said so before this Assembly.'

'And as *I* have said, he would not have lasted long in office even had he made it to his inauguration,' replied Fidelma. 'It was not Cenn Faelad who conspired with Dubh Duin. Indeed, as I have also said, it was the chief conspirator who suggested this plot to Dubh Duin. After Sechnussach was assassinated, Cenn Faelad would also be eliminated. That would lead to this chief conspirator taking control and returning the country to the Old Faith.'

Brehon Sedna frowned. 'So Dubh Duin was guided by another?'

'Exactly. One person introduced Dubh Duin to Gormflaith, knowing Gormflaith's emotional situation,' Fidelma explained. 'Sechnussach and she had already parted. The reasons why are not pertinent but they are known to me. Gormflaith was alone, unhappy and vulnerable. At the time of the birth of her last daughter, probably during her confinement, Sechnussach had taken a mistress. Dubh Duin was handsome and personable. He was told that he could make himself even more personable to Gormflaith and did so with inevitable results.

'But the chief conspirator was not concerned with Gormflaith's emotional happiness. While he had told Dubh Duin that such a relationship was a means of reaching Sechnussach, this chief conspirator had another reason. He wanted to deflect suspicion from himself and another conspirator so that no blame would fall on them . . .'

'*Another* conspirator?' repeated Brehon Sedna with a helpless sigh. 'How many conspirators were there in this plot?'

'It is a very complicated plot,' admitted Fidelma. 'I apologise to the Great Assembly. It is like peeling away the skins of an onion. The person who involved Dubh Duin had a motive, which was purely power. His ambition was to be High King. But he was, in turn, motivated by a woman who also wanted power. She would share power with him if he were successful. Together, they worked on Dubh Duin, knowing his fanaticism for the old religion. He would, therefore, be the means of clearing the way to their taking power.

'Dubh Duin knew that there were some in Tara who would help him – people who still worshipped the old gods and goddesses. People so placed that they could even steal the key of the High King's chambers and make a copy in readiness for the attack.'

'We have heard many assertions so far, Fidelma,' Abbot Colmán said, becoming impatient. 'Perhaps you had better start stating facts and naming names of these conspirators.'

Fidelma pouted in annoyance. 'The assertions I have made, Abbot Colmán, are *facts*. The trouble is, as I have said repeatedly, this is a many-layered plot. I will try to make it all simple.

'Knowing of Dubh Duin's fanaticism, the chief conspirator and his lover introduced him into a plot where he was to assassinate the High King but in such a way that if he were caught, it would bring suspicion only on Dubh Duin and his lover, Gormflaith. What the chief conspirator and his lover had not realised was that Dubh Duin had his own band of followers in Tara, and when he struck it was, I think, at the wrong moment – and this has led to a loose skein with which this tangled ball can be unravelled. I will start this process of unravelling.

'Why did Dubh Duin strike when he did? It has long been a legend among those of the Old Faith that when the "wheel of destiny", crafted by the sun god of our forefathers, was found, it would be the instrument that would destroy the New Faith. It was thought that it would point the way to where the great Cauldron of Murias, the secret of all life, was hidden and with this sacred object in their hands, those of the Old Faith would be triumphant and drive out Christianity.

'There was at Tara an old woman called Mer the Demented. Many of you treated her as a joke. But she boasted about the finding of the wheel of destiny even before I reached Tara.

'Then I heard of Bishop Luachan's visit to Sechnussach on the night before his death. Bishop Luachan sits before you. He will tell you that he and Brother Diomsach discovered a circular object in a hidden manmade cave dedicated to the Old Faith. Bishop Luachan is learned in such things, and he believes the circular object he found to be an integral part of the wheel of destiny. Knowing the legend, Bishop Luachan posted Brother Diomsach to Tara to tell Sechnussach. Irél was sent from Tara to escort

Bishop Luachan and the object here. The object was handed to Sechnussach the night before his death. Bishop Luachan then returned to Delbna Mór.'

She paused and Abbot Colmán, who was leaning forward, trying to follow her story, cleared his throat.

'What has happened to this wheel of destiny?' he asked.

Fidelma smiled briefly. 'As soon as Bishop Luachan left, Sechnussach realised the weight of responsibility upon him and knew that he should not hide it in his chambers, but somewhere safer. In the early hours, he went down to the kitchen of the royal residence and hid it in the *uaimh* or souterrain where foodstuffs are kept. He was seen taking it from his chamber by Brother Rogallach, who thought little about it. Torpach the cook came upon Sechnussach in the kitchens early in the morning and the High King explained that he could not sleep and so had come to make a meal. That was a lie. Sechnussach had taken the object to the souterrain to hide it.

'I think it was Mer who discovered where it was hidden and she went to the souterrain to find it. Cuan followed and, for whatever reason, he killed her and took the precious object. Before he could escape, Brother Rogallach entered and Cuan knocked him unconscious from behind. Rogallach did not see him. Cuan then fled to the territory to join those at Hag's Mountain. He realised that there was little future with them and so escaped as we attacked their camp. He took the object and fled but we eventually caught up with him.'

'So the wheel is still hidden somewhere?' said Brehon Sedna.

'It is not,' Fidelma said with a quick gesture to Eadulf. The latter took a piece of sackcloth from his feet and removed something from it. There was a gasp around the Great Assembly as he held up a circular object, its bright silver reflecting the lights of the great hall. There was a solar motif in the centre and the edge of the object was engraved with many heads forming the outside circle. He placed it on the floor before Abbot Colmán.

Fidelma had been watching the faces of the witnesses as he did so.

'Just for the members of this assembly, Bishop Luachan, can you confirm that this was the object that you presented to Sechnussach?'

The elderly bishop indicated it was.

'Bishop Luachan's visit to the High King in the dead of night was discovered by one of Dubh Duin's fanatical conspirators. That was why the decision was made to strike at Sechnussach the next night. And that was also when things began to go wrong, for there was no synchronisation with the person who had put these events in motion in the first place. That person, whom I have called the chief conspirator, had wanted Gormflaith to be *in* Tara when Sechnussach died; and he had wanted his lover – who was his co-conspirator – to be *away* from Tara. But Dubh Duin and his religious faction was not interested in these conspirators' plans. They were true fanatics.

'The plan, as I said, went wrong because someone was with Sechnussach when Dubh Duin entered his chamber; someone whose scream alerted the servants and guards and led to Dubh Duin turning the knife on himself.'

'An interesting story,' snapped Brehon Sedna. 'But we want names.'

'And names you shall have.' Fidelma turned to the witnesses.

'Dubh Duin was to be the assassin, as you know. Mer the Demented played some part, perhaps identifying the fact that Sechnussach had possession of what to them was a sacred wheel. Cuan's role was to take a key to the High King's chamber and get a smith to copy it. Then, on the night of the murder, he was to distract his fellow warrior, Lugna, to remove him from his guardpost at the doors of the royal house. That left one other conspirator who worked in the royal house and who passed the key of Sechnussach's chamber to the assassin for him to enter. It was this same female servant who, as I have said, used her sexual favours to ensure Cuan's role in the plot. She was one of the central figures in this conspiracy.'

'Who is it?' demanded Brehon Sedna.

Fidelma was grim. 'Mer the Demented unintentionally told me her name before we even came to Tara. She referred to "the white one". There is only one servant who bears the name – for what does Báine mean but "the white one"?'

Báine was sitting back with a sneer of derision making her pretty features ugly.

'Very clever,' she hissed, 'but cleverness will not save you and your kind when the sacred wheel leads us back to the Great Cauldron of Murias which has been touched by the hands of The Dagda himself. You will tremble and sacrifice before Crom.'

Another cacophony of sound burst out in the Great Assembly chamber and it took several minutes before Abbot Colmán and Brehon Sedna could restore order.

'So it was Báine who stole the key and gave it to Cuan to make a copy?' asked Abbot Colmán. 'It was she who persuaded Cuan to betray his warrior's code.'

'Yes. And Báine was the daughter of the priestess of Crom whose body now lies in a grave on Hag's Mountain,' added Fidelma. 'It took Eadulf, Irél and I a while to recall where we had seen the features of the woman called the *ceannard* before. Báine is clearly the daughter of her mother.'

Báine sat back, her arms folded defiantly, and stuck her chin in the air as if she was no longer part of the proceedings.

Cuan stood up and said nervously: 'If I confirm all this, lord, may I plead for clemency? She bewitched me, I swear it.'

Brehon Sedna scowled at him. 'It is neither the place nor time to hear such pleas,' he declared. Then, returning his gaze to Fidelma, he added: 'Apart from Dubh Duin, Báine, Cuan and Mer, you have claimed – if I understand correctly – that there was a chief conspirator, someone motivated by power and not by religious fanaticism?'

'I did. The person who thought they would succeed to the High Kingship – and I did not mean Cenn Faelad.'

'And you will name him?'

'He has named himself. He was the one who introduced Dubh Duin to Gormflaith, engaged himself in supporting Gormflaith's relationship with him, and, knowing how he could win the support of Cenn Faelad to nominate him as *tánaiste*, promised Dubh Duin that when he took over as High King, after deposing Cenn Faelad sometime in the future, he would bring about the changes to recognise the Old Faith once more. Whether he would have done so, once firmly in power, I do not know. I doubt it. But promises are cheap. The Old Faith was his route to the High Kingship.'

All eyes in the Council had turned on the urbane figure of Brehon Barrán who had been sitting without any reaction to Fidelma's recital.

Brehon Sedna looked troubled. 'You deny this charge, of course, Brehon Barrán?' he asked, albeit without conviction.

Brehon Barrán looked across to Fidelma. 'I have seen this *dálaigh* presenting her cases several times before. I do not doubt that she can produce evidence in support of her claims.'

'I would be the last person to remind you, Barrán, that the law-texts state how guilt may be judged other than by direct evidence,' Fidelma said. 'The law acknowledges that indirect or circumstantial evidence can be applied, provided it is strong. I think that Báine and Cuan will be persuaded to speak against you.'

'To save themselves,' Barrán sneered. 'I suppose you feel that you have a strong case?'

'Oh, I *know* I have a strong case, Barrán,' replied Fidelma. She gestured at Báine. 'I am sure that Báine will be persuaded to come forward as a witness to the conspiracy, especially when she understands that you had no intention of fulfilling your promises to Dubh Duin to recognise the old religion. You fully intended to betray him.'

'Your saying so does not make it so,' Brehon Barrán replied.

'Then *my* saying so does!' came Báine's sharp tone. 'I know the promises you made to us. I was with Dubh Duin when you made them. But it seems that it was all a plot just to prepare your path to power. You will be the first to suffer the wrath of Crom when we arise . . . Already the warriors of my mother's people are raiding and destroy your churches, and soon they will sweep into Tara and destroy . . . My mother's . . .'

She suddenly dissolved into tears. Whatever else she was going to say was lost in her grief-stricken realisation of her mother's death on Hag's Mountain.

In the tumult that broke out in the Great Assembly, Irél had motioned to several of his warriors who, according to Fidelma's prearranged instructions, had moved into various positions around the conspirators.

When order was restored, Fidelma stared across at Brehon Barrán, who now looked less confident.

'I suggest that this crime is so heinous that it has to be retried before a court. I am sure that the members of this Great Assembly will agree,' she said.

'We can accommodate you on that,' Cenn Faelad replied with satisfaction. 'Is it the wish of this assembly that Barrán and Báine be tried as soon as arrangements can be made? And, at the same time, the lesser conspirator Cuan should be tried with them?'

The Great Assembly vocally signified its agreement.

It was Gormflaith who now rose and demanded to be heard again.

'You are all forgetting one thing,' she said.

A silence descended and Brehon Sedna turned a disapproving look on her.

'What do we forget, lady?' he asked coldly.

'I accept that I have been a dupe, a fool, that Brehon Barrán did, indeed, manoeuvre me into the company of Dubh Duin who purposefully made himself attractive to me. Lonely women can be misled by kind and gentle

words from honey-tongued suitors. It is true that all along I confided in
Barrán, who promised to draw up the agreement for my divorce from
Sechnussach and now denies it was so. I see now how he was putting the
blame on me. But there is something the lady Fidelma said that we have
all overlooked.'

When she looked at Fidelma, the latter smiled encouragement and
motioned for her to continue.

'Fidelma said that Brehon Barrán was working with someone else, his
lover, someone who wanted to share the power with him and was as ambitious for it as he was. So when Báine charges Barrán, let us remember
the full extent of the part she played. She obviously led Barrán on. She
was his lover.'

But Fidelma was already answering her. 'Lady Gormflaith, I would
have spared you this with the best will in the world. However, you are
right in your reminder to the Great Assembly that there was someone else
working with the Chief Brehon. But it was not Báine, a lowly servant in
the royal house, who was Barrán's lover and co-conspirator – someone
eager to share power with him as High King.'

'Then name the woman, if you know it,' instructed Brehon Sedna.

'I am afraid that there was one other person who helped bring Dubh
Duin into your life, Gormflaith. One other person who gave their authority
to ask the guards to pass Dubh Duin into the royal enclosure at night, and
finally gave instruction to the guard Erc to allow Dubh Duin free access
at night so that he could pass in when the time came for the assassination . . .'

Muirgel, with a scream, had leaped up and seemed for a moment to be
trying to escape but Irél had seized her.

Gormflaith gazed ashen-faced at her eldest daughter.

'It's not true!' shouted Brehon Barrán, springing up, and found the hand
of one of the Fianna on his shoulder restraining him.

'Of course it's true,' jeered Báine from her seat. 'Muirgel was in this
plot from the start. Again, I will bear witness to it.'

'But in a plot to . . . to kill her own father!' Brehon Sedna was horrified.

'Ambition destroys the feelings of its possessor,' muttered Abbot
Colmán, using an old saying.

Muirgel stood, held by Irél, scowling at them; her blazing eyes seemed
to be cursing them silently.

'She thought to use us all,' Báine said in disgust. 'We were together as conspirators, each with our own ambitions. She was too arrogant to see that we were using her and her clownish lover, Barrán. Clownish, aye, for how could a young girl like Muirgel love him, a decrepit old man? She was using him, just as she used everyone else. She was ambitious for power – power was her only god.'

Fidelma let her gaze wander from the snarling young woman to the suddenly deflated old man who had once been Chief Brehon of the five kingdoms, renowned throughout the land. Now he seemed a feeble, emotional wreck of a man. He sat forward, his head in his hands as he realised how he, in turn, had been manipulated.

'Ambition is a mounting demon who first corrupts and then rots the heart and the mind.' Fidelma spoke out strongly, addressing all present. 'It invites the shallow residue of humanity to dance with it and, if the dance be successful, it has but one reward – a transient power and fame before sinking into the oblivion of the grave.'

Eadulf regarded her in surprise. She smiled back.

'They are lines from a pagan poet,' she explained softly.

Abbot Colmán and Brehon Sedna were now calling for order among the astonished and voluble Great Assembly.

'The Chief Brehon Barrán is, of course, suspended from his office and his nomination as *tánaiste* to the High King is withdrawn. He, together with Muirgel, daughter of Sechnussach, and Báine and Cuan, will be held for the conspiracy in the assassination of Sechnussach,' Brehon Sedna announced solemnly.

Abbot Colmán nodded his agreement with the announcement.

'It is good to come to an end of this affair,' he said. 'My only regret is that Dubh Duin killed himself so that we cannot try him for the murder of the High King.'

'But Dubh Duin did *not* murder the High King.'

The sentence clearly spoken by Fidelma caused a silence more complete than any that had gone before. It seemed that all present held their breath.

Brehon Sedna stared at her in disbelief. 'Are you joking with us, Fidelma?'

'It is no joke.'

'What of the witnesses – what of the fact that, when caught in the act, Dubh Duin took his own life? Be reasonable.'

'Nevertheless, the truth remains that Dubh Duin did not murder Sechnussach,' she said again, more firmly still.

'You will have to explain yourself.'

'It is simple to do so. When Dubh Duin took his knife and cut Sechnussach's throat, the High King was already dead.'

CḃAPTER TWENTY-TḃREE

This new announcement was greeted with a stunned silence, as if everyone present had suddenly been transformed into statues of stone. Even the conspirators, about to be led away, looked shocked.

It was Abbot Colmán who finally broke the spell that had descended on the hall.

'I think you had better explain, Fidelma,' he said at last, trying to sound stern but sounding merely bewildered.

Fidelma turned to Iceadh the physician. 'I would like to present my first witnesses for this statement. Stand up, Iceadh.'

The old physician did so, peering round nervously at the assembly.

'When I first asked you to describe to me the wounds inflicted on Sechnussach's body, what exactly did you tell me?'

Iceadh sniffed impatiently. 'My account was no different from the one I gave everyone else. Sechnussach's throat was cut. The jugular vein severed. Short stab to the heart. Either could have been fatal. Sharp instrument found with assassin. A hunter's knife. Honed to sharpness that would slice anything. Sechnussach died instantly.'

'Precisely,' agreed Fidelma. 'And the one thing that we have been overlooking was the short stab to the heart that, as you say, could be just as fatal as the cutting of the throat.'

Iceadh frowned and shook his head fiercely. 'I did not overlook it,' he said grumpily. 'I reported it as I saw it.'

'And I am glad you did so,' confirmed Fidelma, with a pacifying smile. 'But everyone else overlooked it. You see,' she went on, turning to the Great Assembly, 'Sechnussach had already been stabbed in the heart and killed before Dubh Duin entered the chamber and cut his throat.'

Brehon Sedna was leaning back and smiling sceptically as a ripple of sound ran round the Great Assembly.

'Now that is a theory that you will be hard-pressed to prove, Fidelma,' he remarked, almost patronisingly.

Fidelma flushed a moment and then returned his smile with her most dangerous icy look.

'I *never* make claims that I cannot substantiate, Brehon Sedna. I now intend to prove it,' she said sharply. She turned again to the physician. 'Now, Iceadh, I know little of your profession but I have often watched my old mentor, Brother Conchobhair, at his work in Cashel.'

'Brother Conchobhair is known to me,' Iceadh acknowledged, 'for I have read his treatise on the treatment of *galar poil* – the epilepsy which it is thought that Paul of Tarsus suffered after his vision.'

'Would you have any objection if Brother Eadulf asked you a few questions? Most of you will know that Brother Eadulf studied for a while at the great medical school of Tuam Brecain.'

'I will answer any question worthy of an answer,' replied Iceadh coldly.

Eadulf stood up and smiled briefly at the physician.

'I have but few questions, but hope you will find all of them worthy of answers, Iceadh. Let me begin by pointing out the obvious so that all members of the Great Assembly can follow our logic. Arriving here two weeks after the assassination, we were not able to inspect the body of Sechnussach, who had already been buried according to custom. That being so, we must rely on your eyes and observations.'

'My observations are as sharp now as when I first examined the body,' Iceadh replied fussily. 'It is not often that one is called to examine the murdered body of one's High King. I see the body very clearly in my mind's eye.'

'And that is good, for you have given us a weighty piece of evidence. As indicated by Fidelma, you pointed to the wound to the heart, which you said was as fatal as the cutting of the throat.'

'That is true,' Iceadh conceded, 'but in what order the wound came, whether it was made before the cutting of the jugular or after it, I cannot say.'

'I think, as we examine this, you will be able to do so,' Eadulf assured him, to more gasps from the members of the Great Assembly. 'I make no claims to be a surgeon, but at the medical school where I studied, I attended many lectures and demonstrations of surgery.'

'Tuam Brecain is one of our greatest medical schools,' Iceadh admitted. 'I grant that the teaching there is of the best.'

'I have never seen a man have his throat cut,' went on Eadulf, 'and, *Deo volente*, I hope I never will. However, the skilled masters at Tuam Brecain taught by showing what happens when the throat of an animal is cut, how the blood spurts forth like a great spring, powerful and strong.'

Iceadh smiled as if patiently trying to humour him. 'Just so. Just so,' he murmured.

'Stay there a moment, Iceadh. For I would like to ask a question of Brónach,' Eadulf said.

The woman looked startled and then rose to face Eadulf. 'Must I answer this stranger?' she demanded belligerently of Brehon Sedna.

The Brehon frowned in annoyance. 'If you do not answer him, then you will answer to *me*,' he snapped. 'Eadulf is no stranger to us and has our entire confidence.'

Brónach flushed.

'As a servant in the royal household, part of your duties was the washing of all the bedlinen. Is that not so?' Eadulf did not seemed put out by her antagonism.

'And still is,' replied the woman tersely.

'I recall that you told Fidelma and me that you took all the bedlinen and clothes from the High King's chamber after his assassination for washing. Is that correct?'

'If you remember, why ask me?'

'So that you may confirm this to the Great Assembly and show that I am not putting words into your mouth,' explained Eadulf patiently.

Brehon Sedna leaned forward. 'I tell you again, Brónach, you will answer Eadulf's questions promptly and without prevarication.'

'It is so,' snapped the woman.

'Excellent,' smiled Eadulf. 'And there was, of course, blood on the linen?'

'Of course.'

Eadulf glanced at her. 'Do you recall telling us that there was so little blood that you were able to wash the sheets so that they could be used again, but Brother Rogallach told you to sell them as it would be unlucky for the royal household to keep them?'

'I do.' The woman looked wary now, trying to see if Eadulf was leading her into some dangerous admission.

'Did you find it strange that there was so little blood?'

'No – why should I?'

'Because I have seen what happens when a sheep's throat is cut. There is so much blood that I would say that the entire bed would be soaked in it. Anyway, I have finished. You may be re-seated, Brónach. Indeed, the matter of the lack of blood was perplexing. When we arrived here, Abbot Colmán mentioned that blood must have spurted like a fountain from the wound. It was only later that I discovered he had not actually examined the wounds. But if the throat was cut, the presumption was a valid one.'

Eadulf turned to indicate Irél. 'It was the commander of the Fianna who first alerted us to the fact that there was little blood and its significance. He had seen many such neck wounds in battle and so commented at the lack of blood that flowed from Sechnussach's wound.'

Iceadh, the physician, was now looking thoughtful.

'It is true, now I think on it, that there was remarkably little blood that came from the area of the jugular; as you point out, one would expect fountains to have issued.' He paused and his eyes widened. 'The main area of blood was around the heart area. The High King lay on his back and most blood was pooled there. You have made a good observation,' he said approvingly to Eadulf.

Brehon Sedna leaned forward to interrupt. 'So what you are saying is that you think the wound into the heart was the fatal one and the throat was cut afterwards?'

'Just so, just so,' replied Iceadh. 'I would agree with that contention. Mind you, there would have to be a short delay between the wounds – otherwise there would have been no negligible effect in the bloodflow. But, as I say, either one was fatal. Dubh Duin could have stabbed Sechnussach in the chest and then, not realising it was fatal, he could have also cut Sechnussach's throat some time later. I do not see how the order of the wounds can prove . . .'

Eadulf held up his hand to stop the old physician.

'One more question, Iceadh. You observed the wounds. Were you able to ascertain any difference between the knives that inflicted the wounds?'

'Knives? There was only one knife. It was found in the assassin's own heart.'

'Ah, so I don't suppose you compared the type of wounds inflicted?' asked Eadulf. 'The measurements, for example?'

'I observed only that the wound in the High King's chest was one simple thrust, a sharp incision. The one in Dubh Duin's chest was a jagged wound but this was probably due to the fact that he was in a hurry, having, as I am told, been discovered at that point.'

'Is there any possibility that the two wounds were caused by two different knives?'

Iceadh stared at him. 'It is not *impossible*. But only one knife was found and one assassin.'

Eadulf reached forward to take the knife that Fidelma had handed him from her *marsupium*. He passed it to Iceadh.

'Had that knife been found next to the High King's body, would you say that it could have been used in his fatal stabbing?'

Iceadh gazed at the knife. 'Had it been found next to the body, yes I would have to say that it could have been the knife. But it was *not* found there.'

Eadulf smiled broadly at the other's caveats.

'At this stage,' he said, 'you do not have to make any other comment than confirm the possibility.'

'Where was the knife found?' demanded Brehon Sedna.

'If you will be patient a moment or two longer,' Eadulf replied, 'Fidelma will come to that point. In the meantime, I would like to ask a question of Torpach, the cook.'

Torpach rose, looking puzzled. 'What can I say about this, Brother Saxon?' he muttered nervously.

'Take the knife from Iceadh and tell us if you recognise it.'

The cook did so, examined it and then swallowed quickly. 'It is the knife that went missing from my kitchen. A favourite knife. I think I mentioned it to you when poor Mer the Demented was found killed. But she was stabbed with a warrior's knife. You said so.'

'Indeed, she was – by the knife of Cuan, who confesses the deed and to the wounding of Brother Rogallach. But are you sure that this knife that you now hold is your own knife?'

'I use it for slaughtering meat for the High King's table. I have used it for many years. I know its marks on the handle. Oh yes, I know this knife very well.'

'And when did you find it missing? I think you mentioned that to us.'

'It was the day after the High King's assassination, for there was a pig to be slaughtered. When I found it missing, I went to Brother Rogallach and told him. I even wondered whether the assassin had stolen it to use

265

in his murder. Brother Rogallach assured me that it was not the same knife, for that knife had been found. Where was my knife discovered?'

Fidelma now stood up and allowed Eadulf to resume his seat. She looked quickly around the Great Assembly, noting that most of those present were visibly struggling to follow the arguments, before allowing her gaze to rest on Brehon Sedna.

'Thank you for your indulgence,' she told them all. 'We will not be long now. The witnesses can resume their seats.'

Brehon Sedna addressed her. 'You must tell us where the knife was found, Sister Fidelma. You have implied that it was used to kill the High King before Dubh Duin entered his bedchamber and cut his throat. It is a fascinating argument, but it must be backed by fact.'

'I am coming to the facts,' Fidelma replied calmly. 'The knife was found in a secret passageway which leads from the High King's chambers to a linen storeroom on the lower floor of the *Tech Cormaic*. The real killer left it there as they fled from the chamber when Dubh Duin entered. You see, Dubh Duin cut the throat of a man who was already dead.'

Brother Rogallach was expostulating. 'I know of no such passageway, even though I have served here for many years!'

'It can easily be shown to you after these proceedings,' Eadulf promised.

'We are now drawing to the final conclusion,' Fidelma said. 'Let me explain. From the very beginning, one thing became obvious to me. There was another person in the High King's chambers when Dubh Duin entered to kill him. How do I know this? Because the guards were alerted by a scream from those chambers. They assumed it was Sechnussach's death scream – but even had the High King not been dead already, how can a man with a severed throat scream? So who was responsible? The answer is: the person who was caught unawares by Dubh Duin. They fled through the secret passage, hiding the knife that they had plunged into the High King's heart when he slept.'

'I do not suppose we can identify this mysterious killer?' Brehon Sedna asked.

Fidelma smiled quietly at his cynicism. 'Certainly. It was the maid, Cnucha.'

Cnucha, who had been sitting quietly through all the proceedings, made no movement at all, other than to raise her head and smile faintly. Her expression seemed to say 'prove it'.

The ripple of reaction in the chamber died away after a moment or two. 'And will you tell us how you came to this conclusion and what motive Cnucha had?' Brehon Sedna carried on.

'Following the birth of her last child, Bé Bhail, three years ago, the lady Gormflaith noticed an estrangement between herself and her husband. I have already mentioned this. As many of you know, it was soon afterwards that she set up her own household in the royal enclosure. She was sure, as she told her daughter Muirgel, that Sechnussach had taken a mistress or even a secret second wife. Why did Sechnussach reject Gormflaith? Who knows the deeper workings of a man's mind. All he told her, as she repeated it to me, was that he preferred a girl – *a girl* was the word – who made no demands but, when called for, came to his bed like a maid. It is an interesting expression and one that revealed much about his mind. Gormflaith was a strong character, an intelligent person, and we can speculate that Sechnussach was not happy in his relationship.'

She looked to where Gormflaith was sitting. She could not see her expression, for the widow of the High King sat with bowed head.

'If Gormflaith suspected that her husband had taken a mistress, but she didn't know who it was, then I had to consider the possibilities. In the circumstances there seemed three candidates. It finally became clear in my mind who I was looking for when Brother Rogallach repeated a favourite saying of Sechnussach. *Sit non doctissima conjux* – may my wife not be very learned. He wanted a mistress who simply obeyed him and who would make no demands. Alas, there are such arrogant men in this world.'

Brehon Sedna was frowning. 'But what you are now describing, Fidelma, is not the kind of person who would stab her sleeping lover in the heart and kill him.'

'With respect, Brehon Sedna, I disagree,' Fidelma said. 'Cnucha is a plain-looking girl, quiet and overlooked by many. Her fellow maids thought of her as being timid as a mouse. Eadulf overheard her speaking to Brónach about Sechnussach early on, and it was very obvious that she had no high opinion of the High King's attitudes. That was interesting. How did she know his attitudes?

'In reality, Cnucha was far from being a quiet mouse. That was shown on two occasions, when she showed a flash of temper towards Brónach and then confessed that she got angry when people thought they could insult her because she seemed so meek and mild. Báine even told Eadulf that Cnucha had thrown a jug at her once in a fit of temper. So, a passion was simmering there behind that quiet exterior.'

Brehon Sedna was having none of it. 'These are merely circumstantial arguments, Fidelma. We need proof that places Cnucha in the High King's bedchamber that night with the knife in her hand and then all these arguments might back your case.'

Fidelma turned to the girl. 'I have a question to put to Cnucha.'

The girl slowly stood up. The pale eyes that stared at Fidelma were like ice; the face was a mask.

'Do you recall a conversation with Brónach in the guesthouse in which you were discussing a time, just after Sechnussach's death, when the lady Muirgel caught you searching his chambers?'

'I cannot recall all conversations that passed between us.'

'This one was interesting. Muirgel had struck you. You told Brónach that you had been searching for something that you had lost. Muirgel and Barrán actually thought you were spying on their conspiracy.'

A slight look of uncertainty came into the girl's eyes. She made no reply.

'Why were you searching there?'

'I had lost something, that is all,' Cnucha said hesitantly. 'A personal possession. I noticed that I had lost it after I had been cleaning the chamber.'

'Brónach cleaned the High King's chambers after his death. I think you had lost this possession beforehand. You told Brónach what it was, didn't you? It was valuable, wasn't it?'

The girl mumbled, 'It was valuable to me.'

'Because a special person gave it to you? Come, Cnucha. We no longer have time to play games.'

'It was a bracelet. That's all.'

'A bracelet worth a lot of money,' added Eadulf.

'It was a bracelet made up of silver Gaulish coins,' Cnucha replied defensively.

Fidelma reached forward and held up the silver bracelet that she had taken from Cuan.

'Where would you have dropped it? In the secret passageway, perhaps?' she asked softly.

The girl's eyes started as they looked at the bracelet.

'Of course not! I was careful when—' She suddenly realised what she was saying and then, without warning, she rushed towards Fidelma with outstretched hands. 'It's mine! Give it to me! Give it to me! It's the only thing he ever gave me . . . it's mine!'

Two members of the Fianna caught her flaying arms before she reached Fidelma and held her tightly.

'So,' sighed Brehon Sedna, 'you seem to have proved your point. You found the bracelet with the knife in this passageway?'

Fidelma surprised him by shaking her head.

'Cuan will confirm the details. He stands confessed of Mer's death and the wounding of Brother Rogallach, so has nothing to gain by lying now. When he and Lugna entered Sechnussach's chamber, he saw the bracelet by the bed. Cnucha had discarded it, probably during that last night of lovemaking, before she killed her lover. While Lugna was distracted, Cuan picked it up, saw it was valuable and stole it. Cnucha had told Eadulf it was a bracelet of Gaulish coins. Eadulf is blessed with a good memory for detail and when he noticed that Cuan was wearing such a bracelet, he told me his suspicion. It was easy to get Cuan to confess how he had really come by it.'

Brehon Sedna sat back. 'You have argued that Cnucha was the mistress of Sechnussach, and Cnucha's actions here have now betrayed her. But what was her motive in killing the High King, her lover?'

'A motive as old as the mountains, Brehon Sedna,' replied Fidelma. 'Love and hate can be two sides of the same coin. Perhaps Cnucha would like to explain?'

But the girl had relapsed into silence.

After waiting a moment, Fidelma turned back to the Brehon.

'While Sechnussach saw Cnucha as merely a girl to have his way with, a timid thing whom he could summon to his bed at will and who would make no demands on him, like some pet dog to come at his beck and call, Cnucha truly loved him. Perhaps Sechnussach made her promises. He certainly gave her this valuable bracelet of Gaulish coins. Maybe one of those promises was that he would marry her, if only he was able to.

'Then Cnucha probably learned, how does not matter, that Gormflaith was divorcing Sechnussach. She went to him, fully expecting him to say that he would marry her. He—'

'Laughed at me!' came Cnucha's cold voice. 'Laughed at the very idea of marriage to me . . . a mere servant. I could go to bed with him but I could not appear in public with him. That was when I took the knife from the kitchen and, after he had had his way with me, as he lay sleeping, I stabbed him in the heart. The pig will betray no one else again.'

After the tumult that greeted this declaration had died down and everyone was leaving the chamber, Eadulf turned to Fidelma and said privately, 'I have to say, she was the last person I would have suspected. So quiet, so outwardly shy. You would hardly notice her in company. I felt sorry for her – I still do. It's hard to think that she could rise to such passion that would make her into a killer.'

'You should remember the old Roman saying – *altissima quarque fiumina minimo sono labi,*' replied Fidelma philosophically.

'The deepest rivers flow with the least sound,' translated Eadulf.

'However, you are right,' she continued. 'In a way, you must feel sorry for her. Sechnussach abused her. Yet I admired Sechnussach as High King. Indeed, I helped him come to the throne some years ago. We all have our faults, but his was a grievous fault in his attitude to women.'

'What will happen to her?'

'To Cnucha?'

Eadulf nodded.

'She will be charged with *duinethaide* – secret killing. For she sought to hide her guilt.'

'And if found guilty, as she will be?'

'She or her family will have to pay Sechnussach's honour price. That is twenty-one *cumals.*'

'And if they can't?'

'At best, she will be consigned into service more or less as she is now, serving as a maid until the debt is paid or until she dies.'

'At worst?'

'At worst, and it rarely happens, she could be put into a boat with one paddle, food and water for a day and set adrift on an offshore wind. But I think a good defence will point out the circumstances of her case and how she was driven to her action. I will speak to Brehon Sedna and ensure she is well represented. The honour price could be greatly reduced in the circumstances, but she will have to pay or serve until such time she has paid off the debt.'

epilogue

'*Si finis bonus est, totum bonum erit*,' sighed Eadulf as they sat together a few days later with Cenn Faelad's newly appointed Chief Brehon in the library of *Tech Cormaic*.

Brehon Sedna smiled indulgently. 'If the end is good, everything will be good,' he repeated, translating the Latin saying. 'Yet it was truly a complicated matter and one that might well have led to bloodshed and war, or even brought about the devastation of the five kingdoms. You both are owed much. You have but to ask.'

'All we wish is to return to our child and the peace of Cashel,' replied Fidelma gravely.

'We cannot tempt you to remain in Tara? There is much work here for a keen and alert legal mind.'

Fidelma glanced at Eadulf and they both uttered the negative in such positive unison that Brehon Sedna burst out laughing.

'Is it really so bad here?' he protested.

Fidelma gave him an answering smile. 'It is just that it is so much better in Cashel because . . .' she was about to say, 'because it is my home,' but, glancing again at Eadulf, she altered it to 'because our son is there.'

'I understand,' Brehon Sedna replied solemnly. 'I have children of my own.'

'Which reminds me,' Eadulf said. 'What of the boy, Assíd?'

'Yes – what will happen to him?' Fidelma added. 'I will argue his case, if need be, before we return to Cashel.'

'Ah, poor child. He has had an evil star to guide him. As you know, Verbas of Peqini has sailed from our shores without contesting what he claimed to be the theft of his property. While one could say that this matter of slavery was his culture, that it was the custom of his people, and therefore it is hard to lay our moral blame on him when his people did not share our morality, he was, nevertheless, a rather vain and cruel man. As for the law, it was quite clear that you and Fidelma were entirely correct in granting the boy sanctuary when he fled into your arms.'

'We did not doubt it,' agreed Fidelma. 'So what will be his fate?'

'I have discussed it with both Bishop Luachan and Brother Rogallach, and they have come up with an excellent suggestion. Do you know of Abbot Tírechán?'

Fidelma answered at once. 'Tírechán of Ard Breacan? He who wrote lives of both the Blessed Patrick and of Brigid of Cill Dara? That is an excellent idea.'

'I do not know of him,' protested Eadulf. 'What is an excellent idea?'

'He is abbot and bishop of a community not far to the north of here,' explained Brehon Sedna. 'The place is called the Height of Breacan after a blessed teacher who established a community of Christ there. When Brecain died, Ultán succeeded him as abbot.'

'Not Ultán . . . ?' began Eadulf, remembering their investigation of the murder of Abbot Ultán of Cill Ria.*

'There are many who are called Ultán,' Fidelma reminded him. 'It just means a man from Ulaidh.'

'During the scourge of the Yellow Plague in this land,' went on Brehon Sedna, 'there were many young ones left without father, mother or even any kith or kin to care for them. It was one of the great horrors of that deadly pestilence. Ultán and members of his community went out and gathered these poor mites together, the crying, hungry babies and wandering children. They brought them to their community and cared for them, educated them and thus they were able to survive.'

'Abbot Ultán died ten years ago,' added Fidelma, 'so Tírechán succeeded him as abbot and bishop there. He continues this great work of caring for orphans.'

Brehon Sedna nodded in agreement.

'Both Bishop Luachan and Brother Rogallach suggested that the boy, Assíd, would find a home there until he reached the age of choice and decided what he should do in life. The boy is intelligent and speaks three languages and also reads and writes them. While he has no clear memories of his origins, those he does have seem to confirm what you already deduced – that he was on a pilgrim ship from one of the five kingdoms,

*A Prayer for the Damned (2006)

perhaps Connacht, judging by his name, and perhaps he is the son of religious. So what better place for him? I have put the idea to him and he is willing.'

'An excellent resolution to the matter,' Fidelma said decidedly.

'The boy would like to see you both to also thank you for your intervention at the river. So before you depart for Cashel, you will find him staying with Brother Rogallach.'

'That reminds me of another thing,' Eadulf suddenly said. 'That ancient relic, the silver disc. It was the source of much trouble, and if your legends are correct, it could well be used again by those who want to overthrow the Faith.'

'We have talked much about it, the High King's advisers. Cenn Faelad has agreed that what does not exist cannot be used as a weapon. The High King's smith has already melted it down and the proceeds will help rebuild the ruined abbeys and churches.'

'Another good resolution,' approved Eadulf.

However, Brehon Sedna was watching Fidelma's expression. 'You do not entirely agree?' he asked.

'Part of my mind agrees,' she replied slowly. 'Yet I cannot help thinking, it was made in good faith by our ancestors long before the coming of the word of Christ. It was a sacred and dear object to them. By melting it down, we are in danger of cutting ourselves off from our forefathers. Is that a good thing?'

'But it could have been used as a weapon in the future to destroy our faith and forment bloodshed,' repeated Brehon Sedna. 'It surely is better to prevent such an eventuality. Such objects can provoke an evil fanaticism.'

'That does not arise from the object itself – that arises from the interpretations people place on it,' countered Fidelma. 'Part of me is worried that we are creating a deep abyss between our new world and those of our ancestors in the old world. Once that chasm has been made, we will never be able to re-cross it and know their thoughts, their fears and their hopes.'

Brehon Sedna was not convinced. 'Perhaps we are too busy trying to deal with our own thoughts, fears and hopes,' he pointed out.

'Just as a child is,' agreed Fidelma. 'But a child has parents to advise him. And through the parents' experience, knowledge and example, the child is guided. I fear we may soon be stumbling forth in the world, never knowing what knowledge and example our parents would have bequeathed to us.'

She stopped and then smiled fondly at Eadulf. 'Speaking of the examples of parents, I would like to start back on the road to Cashel as soon as possible.'

> "Tremayne writes so authentically about this remote time period that readers will feel they are there in every way...a delight!"
>
> —*Library Journal* (starred review)

The year is A.D. 670 and Fidelma of Cashel and her companion, Brother Eadulf, have found themselves trapped in the middle of a murder investigation involving some of the most powerful religious leaders around, soon realizing that this is proving to be one of the most sinister and deadly puzzles they have ever faced.

> "The action is tense and gripping... a compelling, enjoyable adventure."
>
> —*The Philadelphia Inquirer* on *The Monk Who Vanished*

"Tremayne has created a great character in Fidelma and brilliantly conjures the world she inhabits.... This is masterly storytelling from an author who breathes fascinating life into the world he is writing about." —*The Belfast Telegraph*

More titles in the Sister Fidelma series

The Leper's Bell
Master of Souls
A Prayer for the Damned
Dancing with Demons
Hemlock at Vespers (story collection)
Whispers of the Damned (story collection)

CPSIA information can be obtained at www.ICGtesting.com
Printed in the USA
LVOW07s1225111114

413102LV00001B/1/P